A
Precious Cargo

"In Jojo Boudreaux, Linda Sands has created an original, an unforgettable, fearless, take-no-prisoners cross-country female trucker you do not want to mess with. After reading *Precious Cargo*, I guarantee you'll never look at a truck stop or a trucker the same way ever again."

—Charles Salzberg, author of the
Henry Swann Mystery Series

"*Precious Cargo* is a riveting tale of 'highway robbery' where the victims are the dispossessed, the criminals modern day slavers, and the heroine a trucker with a suicidal sense for justice."

—Leonardo Wild, author of the
Paradigm Shift Thrillers

Acclaim for *Grand Theft Cargo*

"This is eighteen wheels of mystery firing on all cylinders. Get behind the wheel and enjoy the ride."

—Eric Beetner, author of *Rumrunners*

"Linda Sands knows how to tell one hell of a story...replete with clever dialogue and colorful characters, and a plot that speeds along like a Freightliner. Strap yourself in before you start to read this one."

—Baron R. Birtcher, award-winning
author of *Rain Dogs*

"Fresh, meaty and thrilling, *Grand Theft Cargo* grabs you by the short hairs and refuses to let go. Linda Sands is a power-house of a writer and one we'll be hearing from for a long time to come."

—Karin Gillespie, author
of *Love Literary Style*

PRECIOUS
CARGO

Kerry —

LINDA SANDS

Thanks for coming to A.N.I.

PRECIOUS

CARGO

THE CARGO SERIES

[signature]

DOWN & OUT
BOOKS

Down & Out Books
3959 Van Dyke Rd, Ste. 265
Lutz, FL 33558
www.DownAndOutBooks.com

Cover design by JT Lindroos

ISBN: 1-946502-57-X
ISBN-13: 978-1-946502-57-5

For the millions of people fighting slavery of their bodies, minds and souls, may you find honest love, true peace and the strength to forgive.

For those who enslaved you...
a special place in hell awaits.

CHAPTER 1

Someone once told me, if you do what you love, you'll never work a day in your life. As a long-haul trucker who spends three hundred and fifty days a year exploring the contiguous states of America, I'd say I was on permanent vacation.

Last month, I shared this wisdom with my co-driver and boyfriend, Gator Natoli.

He said, "It's not the same, you're still working."

"But it doesn't *feel* like work," I said stretching and cracking my back. "That's the beauty of it."

"Wait," he said. "Let me get this straight. You have to go where someone tells you to go, be there when they tell you to be there, wait for as long as they tell you to wait, submit their paperwork in their designated manner, deal with their rules and regulations, even telling you how many hours you can work, when and where to sleep and then, maybe then, you'll get paid—after the government takes their share, of course—and that's a vacation to you?"

"Well, when you put it that way…"

I flipped my long, brown hair over my shoulder and stared out the window. We'd stopped Sabrina, our custom Kenworth T-800, at a truck stop diner outside of Austin, en route to Los Angeles. I'd been craving hash browns, and not for the reasons some women crave things, I just liked potatoes. The crispier the better. Add cheese and I might kiss you.

The waitress had been sweet, one of those bless her heart sorts who talked about her grandkids so much I figured she was probably raising them, wondered if that was why she was still working at her age, and with that bum knee. I wanted to give her a much bigger tip, but Gator said it might insult her.

I was sitting at the kitchenette thinking about that, one's pride verses a pair of orthotic shoes when Gator opened the rear door of the sleeper.

"You okay?" he asked.

"Yeah, sure. Why?"

"Looking a little spacey," he said, bending down to kiss my cheek, whiskers tickling, hand cool on the nape of my neck. Before I got the wrong idea, he slid the fuel receipt across the table, patted me on the back, then headed to the driver's seat.

Not that there wasn't time for the wrong idea. I leaned forward to catch Gator's face in the small mirror we'd installed on the dash. He smiled back at me and winked. Yep, there was always time for the wrong idea.

I blew my man a kiss, then waved him off and scooted down the bench seat to my portable office, where I scanned the receipt and added it to our books. As the truck began rolling, I opened the laptop to check out the day's news from trucker pals and less reliable sources.

I'd barely updated my Facebook status when the truck pulled hard to the right, lurching to an abrupt stop, knocking my bottle of water off the table and sending it rolling across the floor.

"Hey!" I yelled over the hissing brakes.

"Sorry. Some crazy girl ran in front of the truck!"

Closing the laptop, I went up front where Gator was motioning for the girl to get out of the way. We were hardly out of the truck stop lot, half on the shoulder, the road empty in both directions.

The girl kept waving her arms like she was flagging down a rescue plane.

Gator's grip tightened on the wheel as she ran to the driver's side.

"Can you help me?" she called. "Please?"

Even if I hadn't been able to hear her, the look on her face was enough. I tapped Gator's arm. "Pull over."

Gator maneuvered us off the road, set the brakes and gave me his best *I hope you know what you're doing* look.

I motioned for the girl to go to the back door of the sleeper, then rushed to unlock it. She barreled in, headed straight for the window over the sink and pulled aside the small curtain.

I could smell fear on her and something else. It reminded me of my grandmother's cellar on rainy days.

She was pretty with dark shiny hair and almond eyes. Her face was heart-shaped, with perfectly proportioned childlike features, the kind of face a camera would love. Sporting a modern canvas messenger bag over her navy miniskirt and white top, she might have stepped off the pages of a teen magazine's "Back to School" ad. The only thing that threw me was the cork platform wedgie sandals and purple-painted toenails.

"It's my boyfriend," she said. "My *ex*-boyfriend. He...."

She looked at me, then at Gator in the driver's seat, then back again.

"It's okay," I said. "He's okay."

The girl nodded, like we had an unwritten agreement, something only people with estrogen understood.

"What happened?" I asked, looking at her closer. "Did he hit you?" I was ready to beat the shit out of a guy I'd never seen, ready to right centuries of wrongs.

She shook her head and turned from the window, apparently satisfied that the boyfriend hadn't followed her. Her shoulders dropped an inch. "No. It's not that, it's...well, he wanted me to do something I didn't want to do."

I looked over the girl's shoulder at Gator and mouthed, *See?*

"How can we help?" I asked. "Do you need to call someone or should we report—"

She grabbed my arm. "No. I mean, no thanks." She met my eyes and drilled into me. I squirmed. She ran her fingers down my sleeve and leaned in, my conspirator. "Could you, maybe, have him drive me somewhere? It's not far. I'd be...really grateful."

3

Oh. She was good.

My eyes never left hers as I called, "Gator? Start driving."

"Where to?" he asked.

The girl mouthed *Thank you,* then called out to Gator, "Just go straight until you hit Primrose."

Gator reached back and drew the curtain between the cab and our living quarters, before he pulled the truck back onto the road.

"Have a seat," I said, moving to the kitchenette, as the truck picked up speed.

She slid in, put her bag on the bench beside her, tucking it in close.

"Skipping school?" I said, tipping my chin toward her bag.

She shrugged, pulling a lock of hair over her shoulder and twirling it.

"What's your name?" I asked.

"Candy," she said, in the way you give the answer you've been supplied.

I'd seen enough shit in Bunkie and other small towns of Louisiana to know when someone was living deep in a lie. Question was, did this involve me? And, did I want it to? I looked toward the drawn curtain, thought about Gator, the handsome, gentle man I'd fallen in love with, and then was quickly reminded of Boone, the first man I'd driven with. The man I'd thought I'd be with forever. So, no. That was the short, clean answer. This was not my deal. We'd drop the girl off and that was that.

Candy stared at our flat screen TV, the decked-out kitchen, the polished wood floors. "This is nice," she said. "Real nice. You fix it up yourself?"

"Not really," I said. "It pretty much came like this."

"Wow. Most trucks don't even have—I mean, I *thought* most trucks just had cubbies and a small bunk."

I smiled. "You'd be surprised what you can buy these days."

She looked away. "'Yeah, I guess."

4

Before I could ask her about the boyfriend or school or why she seemed so fucking sad—I mean seriously, she was young and beautiful with her whole life ahead of her—Gator pulled the drape and said, "Coming up on Primrose."

Candy stood, slinging her bag across her chest. "Take a right and you can stop anywhere after the tennis courts." She bent to see out the windshield, confirming the location, then went to the back door where I'd let her in.

Gator hit the brakes and we glided to a shushing stop. I expected this was the first time a semi like ours had traveled these streets.

Candy grabbed the doorknob. "Tell him he should be able to turn around in the cul-de-sac at the end of the street. It's wide enough and pretty slow this time of day. When you come back out, take a right and in two miles you'll see signs to get back on the highway."

"Okay," I said, wondering why I suddenly felt like the student.

"Hey," she called, stepping out onto the platform. "Thanks."

And she was gone, jogging off to an upscale suburban neighborhood, The Estates of Something or Other. Her ponytail swinging shoulder to shoulder as her messenger bag—a bit too light for a serious schoolgirl—smacked her thigh.

"We good?" Gator asked, as I came up front, tucked the curtains back, letting in the light.

"Yeah," I said, pausing to kiss his cheek. "We're good."

I went back to my laptop and tried to not think about Candy and her little life glitch that we'd been a part of. Because maybe that was all it was—a fight with a boyfriend, a moment that would be forgotten soon enough—written off as a bump in the road for a good student from a decent enough family, with a dad that played golf on the weekends and a mother who took banana bread to sick people. Just a glitch.

My father, Manny Boudreaux, taught me that people come into your life and you can choose to make it matter—for them or for you—but never both at the same time. In other words, somebody's gonna be on the giving side and somebody's gonna be on the taking side. I don't know a soul in this world who would disagree with that statement, and if they do, they're either big fucking liars or rich-ass preachers. Which may be the same thing.

I replied to a few emails, checked the weather for our route, then read for a while, catching up on other truck drivers via blog posts and comments on the trucking forums. Every so often I'd read something funny and repeat it for Gator. He was beginning to understand who was who—the rookie who used to be a rodeo cowboy, the lesbian couple with the truck cat, and the old timer who collected donations at every truck show so he could get dental implants—though I think his wife might be behind that movement.

The world of trucking is more than shifting gears and delivering loads. It's about the people, the community. We're the subculture that keeps the world going. Without truckers on the road, life would cease to exist as you know it in less than three weeks.

That's some serious fucking power right there. You'd think we'd get paid better or at least get thanked daily by a total stranger. Yeah, not so much.

I logged off and went up front.

"How are you doing?" I asked, buckling into the passenger seat.

Gator lowered the radio. He'd recently begun listening to strange public radio stations that featured true stories and quirky scientific finds and other nerdy stuff. It was better than the country stations he used to tune in, so I wasn't complaining—not out loud anyway.

"I'm good."

"Good."

We sat in awkward silence, neither one of us ready to break it. I closed my eyes, concentrating on the whirr of tires on pavement, the high-pitched whine from the engine, the solid rumble like a tiger's chuff. Custom seats supported my back and legs. There was no bounce or shudder like regular truck seats. Instead it felt like two large hands were holding me, patting me, a momma saying, *there, there, child.* And for a few seconds, I let myself be happy.

"What?" Gator said.

I opened my eyes and looked at him. "I didn't say anything."

"I know, but you looked...I don't know." He shook his head, glanced in the side mirror and changed lanes, preparing to exit and take us west.

I closed my eyes again, but the feeling was gone. And worse than that, I sensed Gator staring at me.

He cleared his throat, then said, "Would you have done what she did?"

I figured he was talking about Candy, but it wasn't up to me to make conversation easy on him.

"Who?" I asked.

"That girl," he said. "Would you have climbed inside a total stranger's truck and asked them to help you?"

"Given the same circumstances?" I asked.

"Yes."

I shrugged. "Probably not. But then again, I know jujitsu, *and* I carry a knife." I flicked my right wrist and produced a blade, scalpel thin, spun it twice, then stowed it away without a trace.

"Impressive," Gator said, grinning. "Would it be crude of me to say that was a chub-worthy move?"

"Crude, perhaps," I said, smiling and glancing at his crotch. "But I'll take the compliment."

I waited until we'd merged with traffic and settled into the slow lane, cruise control on, before I spoke again. "I did think it was weird that she and the boyfriend were even at the truck stop. I mean, there were other gas stations along that road and most of the food places were across the street. You know?"

Gator nodded. "I know."

"So either the boyfriend is a driver—"

"Or, he works at the truck stop," Gator added. "Don't forget that."

I ran my thumbnail over my bottom lip.

"Uh oh, look out. She's thinking," Gator said.

"Shut up."

We could have gone on like that for hours. But my phone rang—an obscenely loud Zydeco version of *Don't Mess with my Toot Toot*. I let it play long enough that we got to sing the refrain. It made Gator laugh every time.

"Hey, Père."

Gator whispered, *Toot Toot*, as my father answered on his end of the phone, "Hey, Shâ."

I'd missed his voice, the honey and whiskey purr, the way he could curl up a word on his tongue and unleash it like a chameleon after a fly.

There was a song in the mouth of every Cajun, and none knew how to sing it as well as Manny Boudreaux. I'd put him through a lot in the last year and a half. I owed him my life. Without his support I might never have recuperated from the crash—physically or mentally—even though I was a tough ass Boudreaux through and through.

I clicked on the speaker and set my phone in the cup holder, figuring this way I wouldn't have to try to regurgitate the conversation to Gator later on.

I said, "How's everything in Bunkie? Pilar treating you right?"

"You know she is. I got me a fine woman."

"That you do," Gator said.

I rolled my eyes and shook my head, surprised that my man still fell into that weird accent whenever he talked to my father.

What? he mouthed.

Toot Toot, I mouthed back.

Père told us he was concerned about heating all the rooms in the plantation house, now that winter had settled in and they had begun hosting hunters on overnights.

"Overnights? And that's a good idea, why?" I asked.

"Men under the same roof are easier to gather up in the morning and get in the field. Men at night under the same roof are bound to buy more *product*, seeing their counterparts buying the same product."

"Product?" Gator asked.

Père chuckled. "Pilar and I set up a small shop in the den. Simply some necessary items a hunter might have left at home."

"Uh huh," I said. "This *product* would not be bottles of Grand Père's Rumdelicious, now would it?"

There was a pause on the other end. Père coughed. "I gotta go, Shâ, Pilar be calling me."

Uh huh. "All right. Listen you go down to see Ivory Joe in town. He'll know where you can get some safe electric heaters that look like fireplaces. If he has any questions, tell him to call me. Hell, tell him to call me anyway. Been a coon's age since I heard from him."

He said he'd do that and we should have a nice day, then added a bit of Cajun lingo just to fuck with Gator.

I clicked off the call and hit the touchscreen to check emails.

Gator said, "Okay, so I know *podna* is for partner, but what did he mean by *tahyo*? And what was that other thing he said, a *boog*?"

I laughed. "He told me to take care of you, because you're more like a little boy—a little bug—than a big, hungry dog."

Gator stared at me long enough that the truck drifted over the lane line. "He did not," he said, pulling on the wheel, getting us back on track.

"Okay. He didn't," I said, going back to my phone and the word game I was playing with a faceless man in Missouri. I counted to five.

9

Gator said, "I'll show you a hungry dog. You just wait till we park this thing. I'm telling you."

"Uh-huh," I said. It was almost like we were married.

CHAPTER 2

By the time we crossed the California border, Gator managed to convince me to take two weeks off and enjoy our first real vacation—one without the truck anywhere near us.

"Come on, it's spring, almost summer in some places. We worked through Christmas and missed New Year's Eve all together." He grinned. "Full sized beds, Jojo. Deep Jacuzzi bathtubs. Wine with every meal. Biking through Northern California vineyards."

I met his eyes, smiled into their blueness, then leaned over meeting him halfway and kissed him, a soft graze of lips with a promise under the surface.

"You had me at Jacuzzi." I kissed him again. "Wait. Biking?"

Gator ran me through the details. He'd done such a good job with the planning, said he'd already cleared it with our dispatcher, Charlene. I didn't have the heart to object. Plus, I could tell he needed this—wanted this. For both of us. After months of rehab following my accident and then the crazy cargo theft ordeal we'd just been through, I was more than willing to give someone else the reins for a while. Not that any of that had been my fault. Not at all. Though, I'll admit, I did appreciate the chance to play superhero—rescuing my father from kidnappers, shutting down a ring of drug thieves and exposing a cancer drug monopoly—all while solving my ex's murder.

Superhero wasn't that much of a stretch for Gator, a former Texas State Trooper turned PI, a guy with enough military background that he could spout the words, *unable to confirm or deny* with *uber* credibility. But he didn't need any of that background to be appealing. He had money. Not that I'm a gold dig-ger or anything, but my father always said it's better to be rich and unhappy than broke ass and pathetic.

Gator's family had done the whole oil thing at the right time, then kindly died off slowly leaving their fortune to a man who deserved it, but couldn't care less. Now that was sexy.

We pulled off the 101 and found the address for the delivery outside West Hollywood. According to the GPS, the warehouse was equidistant from two hills: Hollywood and Beverly. I'd never been to either. I put off asking Gator if we had enough time to scratch some items off my photo op list: me shooting the moon next to the Hollywood letters and me looking serious by the sign for Beverly Hills: the place without cemeteries or hos-pitals, because no one's born in Beverly Hills and no one dies in Beverly Hills.

I wriggled out of my jacket, suddenly warm, then checked the Qualcomm for jobs. Nothing offered sounded doable or that we couldn't afford to pass on. Maybe Gator was right about that vacation.

I grabbed my phone and dialed our carrier, DeSalena Trans-port.

Through the side-view mirror, I watched Gator deal with the receiver. He ran his hand through his hair the way he did when he was thinking about something, or bored, or thinking about being bored. I liked the width of his strong back, how he filled out his jeans in all the right places. I would have done some more mulling on that subject, but Charlene answered the phone.

"Hey, girl! I was just thinking about you," she said.

"Is that right?" I said, smoothing my shirt, pulling down the mirror behind the sun shield to check my face. I ran a finger under my eye, cleaning up old, smudged mascara. I never wore much makeup, and sometimes went for days forgetting to wash off what little I did have on. I called it an occupational hazard. Gator called it lazy.

"We wanted to let you know we're at the final drop."

"Your man told me about the vacation plans," she said. "Didn't think you had it in you. I mean when Boone was alive—"

I snapped the sun shield up. "Don't go there, Char."

"Hey, Jojo. I didn't mean any disrespect. It's just—"

"People can change," I said.

Charlene scoffed. "People can make people change."

She said something about contacting her when we wanted to get back to work and to let her know where we'd be, so she could watch out for us. I wasn't really listening. I hadn't had a mother in a very long time and I didn't need one now, especially someone like Charlene who was all about the greater good—herself.

I hung up telling her thanks and have a good day, reducing the conversation to telemarketer mode.

Gator hopped off the dock, saying something to the receiver that made him laugh. He waved his clipboard at the guy as he walked back to the truck, and when he climbed into the front grinning, I couldn't help but grin right back at him.

"You sure seem happy," I said. "What was all that about?"

Gator closed the door and squeezed past the driver's seat, planting a kiss on my head, then moved into the sleeper unit. "Funny guy, that Freddy. Asked me if I knew what you call a lot lizard with a mattress strapped to her back."

I twisted around in my seat and raised a brow.

Gator grinned. "An owner-operator."

It was worth a chuckle, and I threw in the *ba dum bum* with a fake cymbal crash finish, as Gator went to our kitchenette fridge for a soda.

He took a long drink, then said, "By the way, I got the okay to leave Sabrina here. We can park her down by the fence where we came in. I also got a number for a car rental place that has a bunch of new inventory. Freddy knows because they shipped it."

"Well, aren't you the man?" I said, partly happy that he had handled so many things at once, and partly peeved that I wasn't in control. I knew it was my issue, and I was working on it. It was the one thing that kept me from being perfect.

Gator said, "Yes, I am," then burped. "So, are you thinking luxury or sport?"

"You have to ask?" I said. "Darlin' puh-lease."

There was only one thing I liked better than fast cars, and he was standing in front of me.

The guy from the rental car place raised a few concerns when we told him where we wanted to be picked up.

"It's okay," I said. "We're professionals."

I told him to look for the big black shiny truck with the extended sleeper and a shitload of chrome, or the guy who looked like a displaced cowboy fit to ride a Clydesdale.

When the silver sedan bearing the agency sign rolled into the lot, the guy stuck his head out of the window and stared at our rig, shaking his head. "You weren't kidding. That is the biggest one I've ever seen."

Gator smiled. "That's what she said."

Before I could berate him on the childishness of his comeback, or correct him on its improper use, he ushered me into the backseat of the sedan, leaned over and kissed me, turning me into a giggly schoolgirl stealing kisses while Daddy drove. Well, almost.

At the rental agency, the rep dangled the keys to a new Mustang GT and strongly suggested we take their insurance plan. Gator started to object, due to his extensive knowledge of insurance company fraud and his general they're-all-out-to-screw-us-over mentality. I shortened the transaction and saved the agent an earful by nudging Gator over and signing on the dotted line, making a mental note to remind Gator what happened to the last car we'd driven.

We tossed our bags in the trunk, flipped a quarter to see who got to drive first, then I drove off the lot and headed north as

Gator played navigator and DJ.

It could take time to get into the rhythm of a non-working life. Whatever that was. I figured it was going to be harder than being home in Louisiana where I knew what to expect—afternoons visiting friends, nights at the local hangouts and mornings doing all the chores that needed tending to. This vacation was going to be different. This voyage into an *ordinary life* was something I hadn't lived in a long time—maybe never.

But, I'd give it a chance. I was learning that this was part of sharing your life. You did things to please your partner. Plus, Gator did say full-sized beds, Jacuzzi tubs and wine. How bad could Napa Valley be?

After three days of vineyards and bicycles, followed by three more days of slow motion living, wandering quiet country roads in the early mornings, window shopping at overpriced stores, sitting through foreign films in mostly empty movie theaters, doing the things young unemployed Americans do—though we weren't unemployed and Gator wasn't that young—I was ready to shoot myself, or go back to work.

I eased my man into the transition, understanding that giving up full body massages and a real, adult-sized bed was a big deal for him. I told him that the wine tour had been great. I'd also loved the biking and the mountain hikes, even the French films, but enough was enough. I missed shitty meals, tiny showers and smelly rest stops. I missed nights filled with the fresh air of the Rockies, followed by heat-wave days in the desert. It wasn't that I didn't want to be with him, or spend lazy mornings in bed, it was that I wanted that bed to be moving.

"Baby, thank you. This has been a wonderful vacation, and we'll do it more often, I promise. But, right now? I need three things: you, eighteen wheels and asphalt."

It took a good deal of convincing, partly because it was five in the morning and I'd had to shake Gator awake to tell him how I felt—I swear the guy slept like a hibernating bear—and partly because Gator liked the way I *convinced* him. I went slow so he could follow along, starting with his lips, then moving to that sweet, soft spot below his left ear, where I repeated in a breathless whisper, "You, eighteen wheels and asphalt."

By round two, Gator was ready to concede, saying, "It's a good thing you put me *first* on that list."

Down in the lobby, bags packed and bellies full of crappy hotel coffee, cold cereal and bananas, we flipped another coin to see who would drive the final leg in the Mustang back to the rental place in West Hollywood.

"Heads," I called and heads it was.

"Let's take the scenic route," I said, tapping the GPS touch screen and enlarging an area labeled Topanga Canyon.

"Why not?" Gator said, reclining his seat and tipping his hat over his eyes.

I was about to explain how *scenic* usually meant good sights and that one might want to A, have a camera ready and B, stay awake for the trip, but Gator was already dozing. If he wasn't so cute I might have punched his arm two or eight times, but as it was the same sexual escapades that had made him sleepy had put me in a damn good mood.

I rolled down my window and braced my elbow on the ledge. This drive was going to be a piece of cake. We just had to get around the country part of LA and back into the citified money-hungry part. I'd get to see my Beverly Hills sign, pose for a few pictures on Rodeo Drive and we'd be back in the rig and on the highway before dark. Sometimes I could see the future so clearly I surprised myself.

CHAPTER 3

A little later I had to remind myself that sometimes cakes fall. Sometimes ingredients go bad, the pan isn't the right kind or someone slams the oven door and ruins a sweet dessert.

In my case, the bad ingredient was a curving country road. The wrong pan was an old man in a red 1968 VW Beetle and the slamming came in the form of a large Hereford bull.

It felt like a scene from one of those crazy YouTube videos that go viral. The Volkswagen was trashed, its front end crunched, steam rising from a hissing radiator. At least one tire was flat, and the front bumper dented with what looked like hoof prints was strewn across the road.

The driver was half out of his seat, crouching behind the door as if he was deciding what to do—keep yelling at the bull or climb back inside and weather the storm——when I pulled to a stop, far enough away to safely park the Mustang.

The old man stared in my direction. His hair stuck out from his head mad-scientist style. He dabbed at a bloody nose with a blue bandana. The bull snorted and shook his head flinging bits of glass from a broken headlamp. With one horn dangling off the side of his head he looked more like an inebriated Viking than a hormone-driven bovine.

I took a picture through the windshield. It was getting to be a habit. If I didn't stop myself, I'd become one of those Twittering, Facebooking, vlogging people who shared every bit of minutia that made up their day. All that blah-blah-blah-look-at-the-crazy-day-I'm-having whorish behavior that pissed off a lot of conventional, boring, politically correct judgmental folks.

I already seemed to have the capability to piss people off. I couldn't think of a good reason to add to my numbers. Unless there was a contest or something.

In the passenger seat, Gator was snoring. The man could sleep through anything. I turned up the radio and made sure I wasn't wearing anything red before I climbed out of the GT.

The old man shouted, "Get back! He's evil! He's the devil, look at him!"

The bull was indeed an impressive sight, especially as riled up as he was. With his sights set on the grill of the VW, he paid no attention to me. Massive hooves pawed the ground, kicking up dust as he raised his head calling for a mate, or something. I tried not to look, but there was no avoiding it—huge testicles swung between his back legs as he reared up and mounted the hood of the car.

"Sweet Jesus!" The old man yelled.

We took cover behind the VW as the man kept on about Baby Jesus, Grown-up Jesus and something about his damn wife needing eggs at this hour and who did she think she was, anyway? I hardly heard him. I was fascinated by the bull. In an embarrassing showing for the male species, it was over as quickly as it began. The beast uttered a single self-satisfied grunt, hopped off the hood, then turned and walked into the fields, everything swinging.

We walked around to the front of the classic car. The bull had left his calling card on the hood—a splat of semen and two distinct hoof prints about two inches deep. Paint flecks floated to the ground as the last of the air wheezed from the damaged front tire. The old man began to cry.

I put my arm around this stranger's shoulder and felt his pain.

"Now that is bullshit," the old man said, shaking his head.

Gator joined us, stretching and yawning. "What the hell happened here?"

"I'll tell you later," I said. "Help me with this."

We put the VW's bumper in the trunk of the GT and gave the old man a ride home. He was still shaking and muttering when we pulled up in front of his house. I helped him out of the back and Gator walked him to the door, handing him his bumper and wishing him luck before jogging back to the car. The man stood there a moment, as if he wasn't sure what to do next.

As he went inside we could hear his wife yelling, asking for the eggs he didn't have.

I looked at Gator who shrugged. He was getting good at that.

At the rental agency, the squirrelly little man behind the counter took the keys, then came outside to check for a full gas tank and make notes where minuscule scratches had surfaced on door panels and bumpers. I rolled my eyes at Gator while miming the hand-stroking universal symbol for jerking off behind Squirrelly's back as he bent over searching for more paint damage.

Gator laughed, then wiped the smile from his face when the dude looked his way.

We got Squirrelly to drop us back at the warehouse and Gator put an end to the guy's questions with a twenty-dollar tip.

Parked behind the wire fencing right where we'd left her, Sabrina loomed big and black, her chrome a bit dusty and a stain where someone's dog had pissed on the front wheel. She was still the most beautiful thing I'd ever seen.

Gator pointed to the wheel. "They say truckers are like dogs. They piss on tires, chase cars, live in a box and occasionally get to bury the bone." He almost got through the whole thing with a straight face.

"Come on funny man," I said. "Your day job's calling." I handed him the key to the back door of the sleeper and followed him up the steps, feeling a thrill as he turned the lock. *Home.*

Even with the doors sealed up and the windows locked down, she smelled good inside, all one hundred and fifty-six inches of her—like cherry pie and new boots. I'd straightened, cleaned and polished everything before our vacation. It was like stepping into a truck showroom, except everything on display was ours.

I stowed our gear in customized cabinets, glad we'd taken out the gas fireplace and added a cedar-lined closet instead. Ambiance was nice, but storage space was better and candles were a buck at the dollar store.

Gator must have been tired of playing passenger, the way he made a beeline for the driver's seat. He flicked some switches and played with some dials, but I knew he was just killing time before he could start her up and head for the truck wash. He had a thing about the outside looking as pretty as the inside. If I thought about that for a bit, it might end up sounding like a nice compliment that he'd chosen to spend his days with me. Then again, I might be reading way too much into that.

"You still good with the side trip?" I called up to him.

"If that's what you want, Jojo," he said. "You know I can suffer through anything—once."

"It might not be as bad as you think," I said.

He laughed. "Now you sound like a guy convincing his girl to do some...experimenting."

"Experimenting?" I said, closing the closet door and heading for the kitchenette.

"You know like in the bedroom."

"Why Gator Natoli, are you projecting your personal desires into this conversation?" I asked, popping open the lid to the coffee maker, filling the carafe with water.

He chuckled. "No, baby. Need I remind you that you're the one who wants to drop her pants at the Hollywood sign?"

I started the coffee maker, then went up front and leaned

over Gator's shoulder, hugging him from behind. I said, "I'm making a statement. I don't agree with the way Hollywood portrays women. The way they demand certain body shapes, ages and types—it's just not real."

"Baby, it's the movies. It's not supposed to be real. It's supposed to be an escape from reality. A place people go to forget their *real* shitty life."

I sighed and snuggled my chin into the space between his neck and shoulder. "Yeah. But what if you don't have a shitty life?"

"Then that means you're doing something right," Gator said, running his hand through my hair, scratching the back of my head until I moaned. I pressed my lips to his neck, felt the bristle of his unshaven chin against my tongue as I made my way to his mouth.

A minute later he said, "So, are we getting on the road or...I mean, I'm pretty sure there's a bed back there." He tipped his head toward the sleeper, then wriggled his brow like a lecherous Groucho Marx until I laughed.

"And that bed will still be there after Beverly Hills," I said.

"Apparently so will this," Gator said, gesturing to the stretched fabric in the front of his jeans.

I was about to make a smart remark when the blinking red of the GPS unit caught my eye. "Shit. Looks like we may have a problem."

According to the current traffic conditions, delays were an hour plus to our destination. Los Angeles had a morning commute that ran straight into dinnertime.

Gator reached for his seatbelt. "Guess we'll have to do a bit of rerouting to get your photo bucket list checked off. You okay with that?'

It was my turn to shrug. Bucket lists don't usually come with time constraints. Unless you're dying. And shit, weren't we all?

I brought two mugs of coffee to the cab and buckled in, then clicked on the Qualcomm and sent a message to Charlene that we were back in business.

Immediately the board lit up with jobs. I read a few of them to Gator and when I got to the high priority load of electronics going from Santa Barbara to Oklahoma City, the profit margin was something we couldn't pass up.

"Flagstaff?" Gator offered.

"Barstow," I replied, shaking my head.

"Albuquerque?" he said, one upping the offer.

I hesitated enough so he'd know it was going to cost him then said, "Deal."

And so, I put my dreams of mooning the world from the Hollywood sign behind me—literally—and concentrated on finding a roadside stand or a small grocery store where I could pick up something halfway decent to add to my one pot meal.

"Sorry, babe," Gator said. "Looks like that's the best I can do." He pointed to the spot on the GPS in the near distance. I enlarged the screen and read: Big Wheels Petro Stop.

"Oh, hell no. Last one of those we stopped in was disgusting." I shook my head. "Let me check something." I hit the updated map search on my phone and came up with an alternative truck stop. Unfortunately, it was twenty miles out of the way and happened to be a lesbian dance club—not a convenience store for truckers—though some might disagree.

"How can they call it The Truckstop?" I whined, "There's no trucks!"

But, according to the long list of reviews, The Truckstop put on a pretty sexy bar show featuring scantily-clad dancing girls dousing themselves with cups of water while *Pour Some Sugar On Me* played at deafening decibels. Or so I imagined. The video was small and the sound on my phone left something to be desired. Gator asked me to send the link to his email where he could check it out later. "You know for research purposes."

We found the Big Wheels place easy enough. It was about what I'd expected.

While Gator fueled up, I went inside and made my usual

rounds: checking out the arcade area, then the restroom and finally making my way through the rows of product for sale. It was easy to forget where you were—geographically—when you were inside a truck stop. They all looked the same, offered the same stuff, even the weather-related items because a truck driver might see all four seasons of weather in one day.

I picked up some canned veggies, a chunk of local cheese that didn't smell half bad and a bar of lavender soap. I paid the woman behind the counter who could have been the poster child for why kids should stay in school.

I don't know why I was so hung up on the delusion that was the state of California. Growing up in Louisiana, we thought California *was* Los Angeles, that everyone that lived there was thin and pretty and healthy and tan. We thought they all worked in TV or films, drove nice cars and lived on the beach in Malibu. The idea that other areas with other eccentricities could exist in the state wasn't something we dwelled on. We just wanted to fly into LAX, walk around and bump into celebrities, get invited to crazy parties, date people we'd later see on a big screen and wonder why they'd seemed so much shorter in person.

In reality, the area around Los Angeles might as well be three separate states—three separate countries for that matter. If you gathered people from the farthest reaches of the state of California and put them in one room they would all look different, speak differently and have extremely different ideas about their native state. It might be the most diverse state in the USA, and one that made me the most homesick.

I could see how people could stake their dreams on California. How the same types of people running toward stardom, toward notoriety, might choose beaches, sun and easy living over the harshness of gritty, cool, impersonal New York. Even the name sounded like whispered promises, *Cali*-fornia. A place where homeless people didn't even *need* houses.

It was that image of America—that glorified image of

underdog success, of striking it rich, when they—the anonymous *they*—said you'd fail that made people chase impossible dreams to begin with. Who were we going to blame for that? I'll bet even Neanderthals had one guy who thought he could survive living in a tree instead of a cave, eating fruit instead of giant deer. But, as I've learned in the past, success doesn't always take the shape of your dreams.

While Gator finished re-fueling and completing the pre-trip inspection, I let myself in the sleeper's back door, then busied myself in the kitchen trying to come up with a creative dish that was both healthy and tasty. The added plus that it would only dirty one pan—a disposable aluminum one—because if there was one thing I hated, it was scrubbing pans.

I'd learned a few things about spices and flavors when I dated a New York City chef. He was well known in the celebrity circuit, had even cooked for presidents. I told Gator once how the guy's secret recipes were copyrighted and protected by some kind of culinary law. He laughed.

"It's true!"

"C'mon Jojo, you can't copyright a recipe. Anybody can put the same ingredients together and put it on a plate. Next thing you're going to tell me is that his hands are insured."

"How did you know?"

He stared at me.

I said, "Well, they're really nice hands."

"Oh for God's sake."

Gator never missed an opportunity to tease me about my past relationships, seeing as every time something strange came up, I'd either done something like it already, or slept with someone who had.

"Don't tell me," he'd say. "It's another case of the magic dick."

I tried telling him there was no such thing as a *magic dick*, that no matter how near it came to me I didn't just *absorb* the traits of the man behind the dick. It wasn't that simple. It took time and usually some conversations outside of the bedroom before it happened.

"I was only kidding when I said that, Jojo."

"Well, I kind of liked the idea."

He sighed. "You would."

"A lot of women would," I said.

"Not just women," Gator said.

"Yeah, someone's probably working on that screenplay as we speak."

Gator mumbled something about how he bet I knew someone in *that* industry too.

I didn't want him to be right, so I shut up. You could say that I knew a little about a lot. Or you could say that I'd had a lot of past relationships.

CHAPTER 4

Gator ran out his eleven hours in the chair, while I did the boring, yet necessary truck driver stuff like filing receipts, paying bills and organizing paper work—all the things Gator hated to do. I glanced out the window occasionally as we drove across Arizona, but it all looked the same. Desert and more desert, with a bit of Flagstaff thrown in.

I needed to sleep as I'd be taking over the drive once we crossed into New Mexico, but first I had to finish helping my father with the family hunting business.

Manny and his fiery Brazilian girlfriend, Pilar, were in the process of converting the Boudreaux family plantation in Bunkie, Louisiana into one of the South's finest waterfowl and wildlife hunting lodges. Père assured me my inheritance would not only be safe, but would be worth a heck of a lot more this way. I reminded him that nothing was worth much if it was riddled with buckshot.

He'd kissed me on the cheek, saying, "That's my Shâ, always looking on the dark side."

I would have corrected him, would have explained that I wasn't being pessimistic. I was being realistic. I wasn't being negative. I was being wary. It was different. And after all, he was older, wiser, and should know better. I would have said those things, but it would have been to his retreating back not to his grinning mouth and twinkling eyes. I wouldn't have been able to. I hated to admit his optimism was contagious.

I finished placing the orders for cards and flyers, updated the wording on the magazine ads for coon, duck and boar hunts and was about to shut it down when I thought to send reminders to the local stores in Bunkie to make sure they had enough ammo in stock for our heavy-handed shooters.

The last ding and chime went off and I slid the laptop onto the shelf and pulled out the bed, changing my office/kitchen into a bedroom. I found my eye mask and stripped down to pink underwear. A quick trip up front to the toilet/shower earned a whistle from the driver's seat and the obligatory single finger salute in return. Maybe mounting that stretch-armed mirror on the dash hadn't been such a great idea.

If I fell right to sleep, I'd log in six good hours before I had to relieve Gator. That would have been plenty of rest for me if I hadn't been thinking of the big bed we'd shared in Napa Valley, the way Gator had tucked me in every night. Thoughts like that led to less rest and more dreams—dreams that included sexy faceless men with roving hands and lips. I woke up feeling a little guilty, a lot sweaty and rumpled and very happy that I was not a sleep talker.

I showered and dressed, made some fresh coffee, then went up to the cab with my commuter cup. Gator was singing softly, one of his stay alert tricks and I leaned in for a kiss.

"Everything all right?" I asked.

"It's been quiet." He said. "Except for you moaning back there."

"What?" I might have blushed if I'd been that sort of girl.

He laughed. "Just kidding." He pointed to a flagged spot on the GPS monitor.

"Coming up on a rest area."

"How are we doing on fuel?"

"Not bad."

I leaned in to judge for myself. My man was good at many things. Math wasn't one of them.

"You mind driving to a truck stop instead?" I asked, enlarging the GPS screen, checking the distance.

"It's on the way," I added, pointing to the nearest gas pump icon. "That way we can avoid stopping right away after the delivery. Oklahoma City is a shithole."

Gator grinned. "Oh, Jojo, it's not all bad. It happens to be the home of the shopping cart, the parking meter and the twist tie machine."

"Really?" I said. "No, I did not know that. Wait. There's a twist tie *machine*?" I laughed. "Jesus. We should seriously send you on one of those useless trivia shows."

Gator said, "Like *Jeopardy*?"

"No, more like, '*I might look like a dumb redneck, but I know shit*.'"

He snorted and shook his head. "Do I even want to know what channel *that's* on?"

"Oh look," I said. "I know something The Great Natoli doesn't. Aren't I special?"

"Yes. Yes, you are," he said. "Special *ed*."

I leaned over to smack his arm but he dodged me. I'd get him later. I was nothing if not persistent.

We pulled into the crowded lot at the truck stop in Gallup, New Mexico and waited our turn at the pumps. It was surprisingly busy for nine o'clock on a Tuesday night.

I did my own version of recon, checking out the other rigs, looking for familiar faces or new ones as Gator inched us forward, finally rolling to a stop, lining us up perfectly for fueling.

He wriggled into his coat, zipped up and handed me the fuel card. "There you go, darlin'. I'm going inside to see a man about a snake." He winked. He could do that. It hardly looked cheesy on him.

We both climbed down into the chilly spring night of New Mexico. Just because it had *Mexico* in its name did not automatically mean *warm days on a beach with barely dressed, brown-skinned cabana boys bearing fruity rum coconut-flavored beverages*. I tugged on a hat and gloves, then locked the door behind me, engaging the alarm system. It was as much habit as necessary procedure. A professional thief could pop a lock, climb up and drive away, stealing an entire rig in under thirty seconds. I knew that from personal experience.

Wind whipped around the fuel pumps, sending signs swinging and paper towels fluttering. An electronic advertisement on the front of the pump reminded me to buy oil and something called gas-ease. I wasn't sure if that was for me or my truck. Starting on the driver's side, I inserted the nozzles in both tanks, checking the fit and being careful not to bump the hose as I walked back around to pay. Inserting the Comdata card, I punched in our unit number and sent up the same prayer I did every time I used a satellite pump system. *Please please, don't let one of these hoses escape from the tank and spew flammable, expensive liquid all over my rig, or me or anyone for that matter. Amen.*

My breath clouded the air as if I was smoking a fat cigar, which given the circumstances would have been stupid. I rested my hand on the diesel gas hose, feeling the fuel course through at forty gallons per minute beneath my gloved fingers. Surrounded by rows of idling engines, with the occasional snippet of talk radio escaping from a nearby rig and the sounds of drivers greeting each other—asking where they're going or where they've been, commenting about newly painted cabs and trailers, offering opinions on wind, weather, traffic and luck, good and bad—I got a warm almost cozy feeling.

This was my world. It was hard to believe I'd ever thought of giving this up. These were my people and though I knew it was strange to most folks, we were here and we were staying. Like it or not. You might not want to drive beside us, get pinned between us or even sit at a table near us in a restaurant, but guess what, you fucking need every single one of us.

The numbers were still clicking away on the pump when Gator approached holding a double espresso that he offered with a little bow and a head tilt. If he'd been a beagle I would have said, "Aw, isn't he cute?" As it was, I still kind of wanted to say it.

"Hot and strong," Gator said. "Just like you like your—"

"—men." I finished for him.

He smiled as I downed the espresso and handed him the empty cup.

He tossed it toward the open trash bin as the wind kicked up. The cup hovered over the rim for a second before dropping in with a thunk.

"Gallup, the other windy city," I said.

"Gallup," Gator said, "Where business is still done with a handshake and hard work."

"What the fuck?" I said, giving him my *are-you-serious* look. It was well-practiced. Better than my *I-know-you-farted-so-don't pretend-you-didn't* glare.

He reached into his back pocket and produced a colorful brochure. "Says so right there in my bathroom reading. Page two, under the picture of Sky City."

"Huh," I said. Because sometimes, that's all I've got.

"Yep," he said. "Could be worse though, imagine if it said, the place where business is done with a .45 and a bullwhip."

"Some people might like that," I mumbled as Gator climbed up the back steps to the sleeper entrance. I disengaged the alarm with the button on the keychain and he blew me a kiss complete with finger guns before locking himself in.

Couldn't it always be worse? I thought. If you told someone you just lost your car keys and they say, "It could be worse, you could have been driving and ended up dead in that pile-up on Route 100." Well, yeah. Why didn't people ever say, "It could be better?" Or, "It will be better?"

It could be better suggested that you could have lost your keys which meant you had to call your semi-estranged father who had the extra set, who not only came to pick you up, but also bought you lunch and gave you gas money. Now, that would make losing your keys a pretty fucking cool thing, right?

I made a mental note to start a "Make it Better" Campaign on social media. One in which all of us would be called to fix somebody's shit just one time by making it better and vowing to A, not say it could be worse and B, never, ever one up their bad experience with your own tale of woe.

I leaned against the side of the truck. It was almost my favorite part of the night, the quiet, dark and lonely part that most people slept through. Not me. I wanted to be driving. I wanted to be the only one on the road except for a couple of trucks to run with and keep me company, and maybe a really good DJ on the radio who could keep me awake sharing the old songs I knew and some new ones I'd grow to love just as much.

The numbers on the diesel pump clicked higher and higher. I couldn't watch. I opened the Gallup brochure, angled it into the light and had almost finished reading the recreational section— all the while wondering why *every* rural town thought they had the best camping, best hunting and best fishing around—when a skinny black girl approached, clomping up to me in boots a few sizes too big. Her hands were shoved deep in shallow pockets, shoulders hitched up to her ears.

If I'd had a few beers in me, I would have made a joke about Gallup being aptly named, how even the girls in this town looked like horses. But I hadn't had a drink in days and this chick looked so out of it, I'd probably have to explain the fucking joke to her.

"Wanna party?" she asked, fidgeting in her corduroy coat, then looking around. The coat was too short in the arms and so faded in parts the red had turned pink.

"Uh. No thanks," I said, checking the pump, wishing I hadn't chosen to fill both tanks.

She leaned in. I smelled cheeseburger, but just the grease and charred part, none of the good cheesy parts. "You sure?" she asked. "I could give you something extra…"

I had no doubt that she would. That something extra being a raging case of chlamydia or the gift that never stops giving: herpes.

I shook my head and went back to the brochure.

The girl wasn't going anywhere. She attempted a chuckle, a sound that turned into a raspy, sick cough. When I looked at her she pushed clumps of orange processed hair out of her face, then made a production out of licking her lips, but her tongue got stuck behind her teeth.

She finally controlled her mouth enough to ask, "This your truck?"

"Yep." I nodded. Oh, she was a bright one. Bet her momma was real proud.

She leaned in again, losing her balance, catching herself on the side of the truck. I fought the urge to polish out her handprint. She said in her horsey voice, "You could pretend we was having a date, but I could come inside and do something else."

"No. I don't think so," I said, willing the tanks to fill faster, trying to not think of the *something else* she had in mind.

She lowered her voice. I heard the hitch before she said, "Please?"

The pumps clicked off signaling full. "Really, I'm sorry, but I've got to go. My husband's inside." I gave the nozzle a couple of taps on the fill spout then hung it up with a clunk. The husband part just slipped out, but I thought it sounded more legit than partner, or even boyfriend. Maybe that was why people still wanted to get married, even if they'd been living as common law partners, raising kids, sharing all the work and taxes and most of the good things life had given one or the other.

She wiped a finger under her nose. A scab had opened on her cheek, blood dripped in a crooked line, mixing with tears that might have been real. Or it could have been from the drugs. I wasn't about to find out. She was a train wreck. I could hear the whistle blowing.

She followed me as I hung up the other nozzle, screwed the fuel cap on and waited for the receipt to print, pulling myself up taller than I felt. I wasn't a small girl. Never had been. But being cruel to someone in need, maybe even judging them, that could

32

shrink a person.

She took a half step back, then looked over her shoulder. A man in a long dark coat wearing a red beanie passed behind the trailer. He hesitated, tipped his chin in our direction then continued on. The girl turned back. Her eyes were squeezed tight and a pale sheen of sweat had broken out on her brow, though it was barely forty degrees.

She mumbled something I couldn't understand, then pulled her lips down around her big teeth and said, "Sometimes, I clean."

"You...clean?" I said, shoving the receipt in my pocket.

She nodded.

I thought she was going to say that she was off drugs, or maybe *clean* was a euphemism for something else. I couldn't imagine what kind of sex act would simulate someone cleaning, though I'll admit I was a bit rushed and cold and honestly wasn't thinking in that creative mindset.

She leaned in. "Not everyone likes to do the dirty work, but everyone wants to have a nice place, you know?" she said, suddenly shy when it came to selling her abilities as a housekeeper instead of a prostitute.

I looked at her closer. *Yep.* She really *cleans* trucks, like dusting and wiping down surfaces and all that normal stuff. I was turning this over in my head, the idea of her doing a maid's job for truckers, then giving the money to a pimp, lying about the services performed, saying she'd turned a trick—or three.

I started toward the driver's door, wondering if she charged per task, and how much it would be to scrub a shower stall verses mop a floor. I imagined her handing out a brochure like the one Gator had found in the truck stop, only hers would list cleaning prices, options and her availability, because she'd have to work you in between blow jobs.

When I looked back at the girl she was wringing her hands, her expectant eyes on me, a bit of the wildness gone.

"Really," I said. "I can't. Maybe another time." I reached

into my pocket for the truck key, felt a few crumpled bills and paused, thinking *what would it hurt?* But in the end, I took out the key, jammed it in the lock, then climbed into the truck without looking back.

I won't say I didn't think about the horse-faced hooker-maid on the rest of the drive to Oklahoma City, or about the red beanie-wearing man who was probably going to beat the shit out of her, or withhold her fix or maybe leave her behind. I will say that I figured out not every broken thing out there was my problem. It wasn't up to me to fix everything.

CHAPTER 5

Tornado City. Truckers don't call it that for nothing. Oklahoma City is one windy motherfucking place.

I used to think storm chasing would be cool, but then I realized most of the people who did that were either geeks or comic convention-loving couch potatoes and I just wasn't going to fit in. If you asked people who'd known me for a while they might say I already lived like a storm chaser, always prepared for disaster, choosing to drive right into the bad shit, then hanging around for even worse shit to happen. I might even be a shit magnet, the way it always came right at me. I didn't have to do much chasing at all.

I tried to not think about the whistling wind outside, the storm warnings on the radio. I lowered the volume and listened for Gator's soft snores. He'd been asleep for hours but only snored when he rolled onto his back. Sometimes I'd hit a nice big pothole just to get him to roll over. Not tonight. I was feeling magnanimous. I changed the station to classic rock and turned up the volume just in time for *Dust in the Wind*.

"Perfect," I said to myself, tightening my grip on the wheel and aiming the nose of the Kenworth straight down the highway. I glanced at the fuel gauge. I'd been pushing it, using up fuel we could have saved. Gator wasn't going to like that. But, it was for a good reason—trying to get across the county, out of the warning range of the storm and into a more developed area. Preferably one with street lights. I didn't mind a good storm, but I wanted to able to see it.

The squeak and rattle of the trailer meant it too was battling the shear. I knew I could keep her on the road, I just had to get those images of spinning cows out of my head. Too many movies. Too many videos of tornado disasters. Your mind could seriously fuck with you.

While training for my CDL, I had to sit through a lecture on wind elements and aerodynamics. They showed weather reports and aftermaths of disasters. They showed demolished towns and pieces of houses embedded in trees, boats on top of buildings. But it got the most real when they showed a video of an obese truck driver stepping into a wind tunnel simulator. As they discussed mass and form and the different strengths and types of wind and air currents, we laughed, seeing her hair pulled up and away, her chubby face rippling, her pants flattened to her skin, the whole of her jiggling. But when her feet left the ground and her body spun around, when she was slammed into the padded walls, then dropped like a kid's toy in the lull of the wind, we stopped laughing, because sometimes the weight of all the cheeseburgers in the world wasn't enough.

The GPS showed that we were coming up on Oklahoma City. According to the jumbled lines on the display, a whole bunch of highways meant a whole bunch of choices. You could go north, south, west, east, southwest or northeast and each one of those choices led to a whole new road. It was like the board game with chutes and ladders. If you took the longest chute you'd end up sliding through Oklahoma and Texas right into Mexico.

There wasn't a long-haul trucker in the nation that hadn't passed through Oklahoma City in one direction or another at some point of their career. I remembered meeting an old timer in Nebraska when I was driving with Boone. The guy told us he'd driven through a bizarre snowstorm in Oklahoma City where the snow was falling between thunderclaps. It seemed to me like that was impossible, but then again nature did a lot of weird shit and the guy didn't seem the sort to make things up.

I checked my watch. If I kept this pace I'd arrive at the

delivery point thirty minutes ahead of schedule which might short Gator some time in the sack, but it should please the customer, and what was more important?

The phone screen was still blank. No service. I'd lost it about fifteen miles back, partly a battery issue and partly a poor cell tower reception issue. I played with the dial on the satellite radio looking for local weather and traffic. When I came back with nothing closer than forty miles out, I remembered the CB. We rarely used the thing, but Gator had insisted we have one, for those *just in case* moments. When I'd told him there really wasn't that sort of moment in this day and age—one in which anyone would *need* a CB radio—he shook his head and said, "We'll see about that."

A quick glance over my shoulder confirmed a sleeping partner. I reached down and faked a cough to hide the sound of the click as I turned on the clunky device he'd shoved under the dash. Not that a mere click would wake Gator. That guy could sleep through fireworks and howling cats in heat. Even if something had stirred the man, he wouldn't hear a thing with those noise-canceling earphones on. He said he liked to listen to audio books before bed, reminded him of being a boy and the special night-time ritual with his mother. I'd said that was a wimp-ass thing to admit and he might not want to ever tell anyone that ever again. Secretly, I loved that about Gator, that he needed a story to help him sleep, that he was comforted by thoughts of his mother, but mostly, that he'd been so open and honest with me.

I remembered when he found the CB radio at a garage sale in Houston. I told him, "There is no way I'm going to have a mic dangling from my header, or some ugly black box mounted to my windshield and *hell to the no* will I let you give yourself some lame ass call name like Bandit."

He'd agreed, kissing my neck and calling me darlin', but not sweetheart. Never sweetheart. And the way it made him happy, made me happy. So now, we not only had gorgeous hardwood flooring and travertine, but we also had a thirty-year-old scratched-up CB radio in our two hundred-thousand dollar custom rig.

I adjusted the volume and twisted the dial until I heard a voice. The first words—after the static—weren't exactly the sort of thing I'd want to repeat or even admit I'd heard, and I had heard a lot of crap in my day. It wasn't even the words so much as the creepy as fuck sound of the voice that spoke them. I quickly moved off that channel and spun the dial until I hit on a soft-spoken Southerner reciting Psalms.

If anyone understood potential trouble, it was someone who knew The Book of Psalms.

I keyed the mic and said in my nicest voice, "Sabrina here, looking for weather and traffic: location OK City. Come back." I had no idea how to say the real CB jargon, but I figured I had given it enough of a shot that no one would be offended. I likened it to attempting to speak French in Paris. As long as you showed that you were trying, and said the *mercis* and *s'il vous plaits* close enough, they pretty much forgave your American attitude and crude apparel. At least, that was what I was told by Jasper, a sexy European tour guide I once dated. He also recommended that Americans make it easier on themselves and claim to be Canadian.

The guy on the other end of the CB spoke, jarring me out of a Jasper-induced reverie. I shook off images better suited for bodice-ripper book covers and focused on his words, which sounded like, "Accident, delay, and back-up."

"Are you saying the highway's jammed all the way in?" I squinted at the dark road unfurling in front of me. As far as I could see traffic was slow but moving.

"That's affirmative."

He spouted some exit numbers and alternate routes that were also backed up, then cursed the hour he'd been sitting in the jam and assured me I'd make much better time if I found myself a handy get-off ramp. It took me a second to understand he meant an exit ramp. I was glad I hadn't jumped the gun and gone off on some tirade about sexual deviants. I checked the address for the drop, then my current position on the GPS and figured the next exit was my best bet.

"Appreciate your help," I said.

He chuckled. "My pleasure, little lady. Keep the shiny side up and the rubber side down."

I said, "Ten-four," then hung up the mic and clicked off the machine before I could slip any deeper into trucker old timer's disease. I signaled for the exit, moved into the lane and thought about learning CB lingo, how there must be an app for that.

The GPS voice let me know I was veering off course.

"Oh shut it," I said, hitting the mute button until it had a chance to recalibrate. I used to think the male Australian accent was hot, but now he was a whiny bitch and if I could have, I'd have left him and his damn shrimp on the bar-bee.

I grabbed my phone and hit the memo app. "Note to self: change out GPS voice, download CB app."

Lately, I'd been forgetting things. Not important things, or things that made you think you were going crazy or anything, but things that just pissed you off, like the name of that actor or the title of that song or where you'd seen those shoes before. Gator had insisted I get myself checked out and knowing me well enough, he also insisted on coming along. The doctor ran some tests, asked me a bunch of questions and a few hours later gave me a clean bill of health, clearing me to drive and do anything else, though he suggested running with the bulls in Spain or deep sea diving in the Cook Islands be put on the back burner— just for a little while. He said that with all the stress of the last year it was normal to have a few things slip my mind.

I didn't like his answer but there wasn't much I could do except take my supplements and keep playing internet word games.

I turned off the exit and headed toward the other side of town. I had never been to Oklahoma City before but I was sure

I'd find the address. There were warehouses all over the world and they shared a few qualities: big, cold and usually gray, similar to today's weather.

If you asked someone who lived in Oklahoma City they'd say that August is bad, but April and May are the worst, and come to think of it, since the beginning of time there hasn't been a month of the year that a tornado has missed wrecking some part of Oklahoma City and maybe that's why the nickname "OK City" never really caught on. They're also pretty sure some guy somewhere has a basement full of dusty T-shirts emblazoned with the slogan, *It's OK in OK City.*

I pulled around the corner and headed east. Over the hood of the Kenworth, the sun was rising, fighting through the murky layer of sky. It was spooky, apocalyptic even.

That feeling stayed with me as I drove through the shitty part of town. I might be making quick assumptions, but I was also giving the whole town the benefit of the doubt by suggesting there was only *one* shitty area.

I slowed at an empty intersection almost coming to a full stop at the sign. It was definitely too early for crackheads and hookers but from the look of the group gathered on the street corner, it was primetime for baby gangbangers. Faced off in their baggy, low-riding jeans, bright white sneakers and oversized jackets, they might have been called the Crips and the Bloods or the Sharks and the B52s. I'm not up on gang culture. Whatever they called themselves, they had bicycles, not cars, not motorcycles. Shiny, chrome low-riding bicycles.

As I rolled past, the boys turned, two of them grinning, flashing gold and silver teeth. One grabbed his crotch and thrust his hips.

I thought, *Fucking losers.* I may have said the words out loud or they read my lips, because a few seconds later it was Newton's Law of Motion all over the place. The bottles, rocks and spray cans that were in motion from the sidewalk remained in motion until they met with my windshield. And because that motion law goes both ways, the fancy bicycle that *wasn't* in motion before I tapped it with my bumper, knocked it down and then ran over it, well, let's just say *that* won't be in motion anymore.

The biggest boy in the bunch stepped away from the others, tore at his jacket and hammered his chest like a modern Tarzan. He yelled something I couldn't hear over the screech of metal meeting pavement. I looked his way and gave him the steely-eyed *don't fuck with me* look which he returned with equal intensity though his had a bit more street-life badassness to it, something that made me look away. Skinny little fuckers worried me. I couldn't trust a man who didn't eat.

I kept rolling. Two more thumps and the mangled bike kicked out from under the trailer wheels, spat into the street.

His buddies in the same colors ran over to Bicycle Boy, yelling and waving their arms pointing in my direction as if he didn't know what had just happened. Some of them began to search the gutters, probably for something else to throw. One little bike-less kid tried chasing the truck as I sped up, but not before I saw Bicycle Boy take out a spray can and tag a message on the wall of the nearest house.

CHAPTER 6

I had to give that little gang banger credit. He'd kept up a good pace behind me for the first three blocks, but didn't have enough fight. Last thing I saw was the dude slumped over with his hands on his knees panting like an out of shape mall security guard chasing a shoplifter on a skateboard.

I gave him a little sendoff complete with a middle finger salute out my window, then un-muted the GPS and let the Aussie voice guide me to the warehouse.

The narrow roads might have been tough to navigate if they were busy, filled with east and westbound cars. As it was, I could drive practically down the middle of the street. I followed the right turn, left turn instructions until I reached the end of the road. The navigation system seemed as confused as I was—with its blinking screen and blue arrow pointing off into a vague green open space. I waited at the stop sign to see if it would clear, if it would autocorrect, if it would miraculously fix itself. As I looked through the windshield at a cloudy, stormy sky wondering if *that* was the problem, I knew it wasn't a weather issue, like the way you know smacking the side of the toaster never fixes the toaster.

After a few minutes, I flipped a mental coin, released the brake and pulled on the wheel, maneuvering fifty-three feet of trailer through a hard left turn.

The impact shook my seat before I understood what I'd heard was muted gunfire. *Bam, bam!*

"What the fuck?"

My first instinct was to hit the brakes, get out and kill someone. I took a breath and adjusted my gut reaction when a low-slung matte black car sped past then slammed on its brakes, fishtailing and sliding to a stop, blocking the road. Both blacked-out windows on the passenger side lowered, exposing two sets of dark hands and two handguns. Another car pulled in blocking my exit. As I watched in the side-view mirror, two shotgun barrels appeared. I'd never been great at math—it was the one thing that kept me from being perfect—but I could fucking count and two plus two equaled more firepower than I had. A glance over my shoulder showed Gator still out, noise-canceling headphones in place. Time for Plan B.

I raised my hands in surrender.

If they wanted our cargo they could have it. It never crossed my mind they might kill me. My biggest worry was that they'd unleash a shotgun on Sabrina's grill.

The driver exited the car arms swinging. Dressed in the same colors of the gang on the street corner, he must have been six-foot-three and about two-fifty. A bandana covered the lower half of his face, the hood of his sweatshirt was pulled low over his forehead. If he had eyes I couldn't see them. Sun glinted off the gun in his left hand and the knife in his right. He was either an ambidextrous bad guy or one who had a hard time making decisions.

I tried to yell without moving my mouth. It wasn't easy. "Gator! Gator, get up!" *Damn those headphones.*

The gun and knife-wielding guy was getting close. I stomped my boots, tried to rattle the keys dangling from the ignition with my knee, trying to turn off the engine. That always woke Gator.

The guy motioned me out of the truck, pointed to a space on the ground in front of him.

I nodded and slowly lowered my hands. Opening the door with one, I reached across and turned the key, silencing Sabrina's big engine, then climbed down and slammed the door shut, sending up a prayer that Gator would not only wake up fast, but wake up alert and grab one of the guns we stored in the oven. One of the armed guys from the car approached, gun-toting arm extended, hands bare and tattooed. Later, I'd learn they revealed not only his ethnicity, but also his jail time and gang hierarchy.

I figured I could take him, roll under the truck and come up fighting on the other side—was working this out in my head when Bicycle Boy appeared armed with his swagger and grin. Too badass to protect his identity.

So that was what this was about? I knew it wasn't hard to follow or find a big rig, but seriously, it was just a bicycle. These boys needed to chill.

As Bicycle Boy raised his fists, my brain went into survival mode, computing exit strategies, analyzing pros and cons, providing tactical support for a mission that would never happen. It told my body what to do. I exhaled, then relaxed to take the blow.

When I woke the cars were gone, the sun higher in the sky. The temperature must have risen thirty degrees and the wind appeared to have picked up. Those were the four things I observed laying on my side in the middle of the road. As I tried to stand, I also observed that it fucking hurts to get beat up. I got as far as my knees before the world went wonky. I took a few shallow breaths then tried again, making it to the side of the road. I grabbed the fence to steady myself, fighting off spikes of pain and nausea.

A thick vine wove in and out under the weathered sign for GeoWorld, Incorporated. Brown, twiggy and dead. I imagined it in the height of spring, green and alive, its tendrils reaching out, swaying in the wind, beckoning like zombie fingers.

I could see how maybe twenty or thirty years ago, this area had seemed full of potential, how the lawn and trees might have made it a little nicer coming to work. Maybe they even had company picnics in the shade of the oak trees, the boss taking time to mingle with his workers, make them feel appreciated. But now? The place was a disaster. Half the fencing was busted, wild wires poking out, whole sections missing, rusty shit everywhere.

How could I have thought this was where an expensive load of electronics was to be delivered? Why didn't I go right at the stop sign? And where was Gator?

I hobbled back to the truck.

"Gator?"

The gang bangers had done a job on the trailer. Graffiti covered the lower half, designs in red, black and yellow. It might have been pretty anywhere else.

"Gator!"

He was in the trailer, tied up and gagged, eyes duct taped shut, bandana shoved in his mouth. Behind him, three of the four pallets of electronics were still sealed, and it looked like only four boxes were missing from the fourth. A half-mangled bicycle pedal stood on top of the broken open pallet, like a soldier's flag in enemy territory. I dropped it in my jacket pocket, then gently peeled the tape from Gator's eyes. They looked grateful, and confused. He mumbled something and I toyed with the idea of leaving the gag in while I cut his hands and feet loose, but his eyes changed, telling me it was *not* a good idea. I removed the bandana waited for him to spit and spit again, then reached for my boot knife. Gone.

"What the fuck was that about?" Gator asked.

"Thieves," I said, moving behind him to work his hands loose, glad they hadn't used zip ties.

"Thieves?"

"Yep."

He craned his neck to see the missing cargo. "Not very good ones, were they?"

"You must have scared them off," I said releasing his hands, then moving around to work on his ankles.

He snorted, "Pretty hard to do when you're comatose."

I paused in my untying as he went on, "They stuck me with a needle, dragged me out of the truck. Jojo, this wasn't a cargo theft."

I concentrated on the rope, on his ankles, on keeping my hair covering my face. "So, what was it?"

"I don't know," Gator said, rubbing his wrists. "What did they say to you?"

"Oh, not much, after, "Get down here." After that it mostly sounded like *smack, jab, slap, punch, kick, punch* with maybe a little cursing thrown in for good measure."

Gator looked at me closer, reached out his hands to push the hair out of my face. "Jesus. I'm sorry, baby. Are you okay?"

I shook him off.

"Probably looks worse than it feels," I said, peering into the unsealed pallet of electronics, counting the missing merchandise. "How do you know they weren't after our load?"

"It doesn't fit," he said. "None of it. What did they take?"

"Four Xboxes. I think." I remembered my initial concern and slid down from the trailer, made my way to the front of the truck. The grill was intact, but the hood was a mess, trash strewn across it, a few small impact stars on the windshield from thrown bottles.

Gator let out a low whistle. "We need to report this."

I walked to the sleeper's back door, thinking of a way I could possibly explain the mess on the hood and windshield, the graffitied trailer, the bullet hole or holes? Luckily, Gator was also moving slow, in body and brain. Whatever they shot him up with must still be in his system. If he didn't ask, I wasn't going to offer. We kept ibuprofen and instant ice packs in the cabinet under the sink. I split the stash with Gator as he dialed the local cops. He knew better than I how to be respectful to people in authority, people who spoke in that *Don't fuck with the man* tone.

I started icing the places on my body that hurt the worst,

then realized we were a bit short on cold packs, so I stuck to my face and arms, things I'd need to use the most right now, and the body parts people would see.

The cops said they'd send a patrol car in less than twenty minutes. Either things were slow in OK City, or there was a donut shop close by.

I didn't tell Gator about the gang bangers on the corner, about the shit they threw or the bike I'd run over. I didn't say anything. Most of all, I did *not* tell him how Bicycle Boy had looked right at me, extended his arm and turned his finger gun sideways, then pulled the trigger as his lips mouthed, "Bang."

I managed to also leave out the part where he'd spray painted a message on the side of the house back in Shitty Town. It was just three things: our license plate, our rig number and the letters, DST.

What did it matter? He wasn't a threat. He was just some punk ass kid in Oklahoma City. He wasn't anything. Besides, we were leaving as soon as we were done with the cops and dropped this load.

CHAPTER 7

The Oklahoma City cops rolled up, looking every bit the picture of efficiency with the patrol car's interior-mounted laptop and wide-angle lens video camera on the dash. They stepped out in pressed uniforms, black shiny shoes and wraparound sunglasses, the mirrored kind.

They knew exactly where the right warehouse was and apologized for the missing street sign. One cop asked the questions while the other posed, thumbs hooked in his belt loop, chin angled just so, sun glinting off his badge. I'd been worried that dispatch would send a pair of good old boys with hick accents and beer bellies, their cheeks stuffed with chaw, but these were handsome young men who spoke clearly and filled out their uniforms beautifully.

I told my side of the story—a creative new story minus gunfire or gangbangers. A story that started with me getting lost and forgetting to lock the trailer and falling asleep, only to wake to find we'd been pranked by some kids with spray paint who helped themselves to four Xboxes. There were still a few foggy spots in the details—and seeing as I'd just had my brain smacked around, it was to be expected. Or so Hot Cop One said. I was thinking of asking him if their station sold cop calendars, and if his partner was Mr. December, because I had a thing for men in red velvet, when I heard Gator spin a flat out lie.

Hot Cop Two had wandered away from the pack like a curious puppy, and looked about as dangerous. He stared at the debris on the truck's hood, the damaged windshield, then back at us. "What happened here?" he asked.

Gator jumped in. "Oh, that? We ran into some trouble in Arizona last night with some kids on the overpass. You know how they are nowadays, up to no good. We'll hit the truck wash after this drop and take care of the windshield when we get home. It's not that bad."

The cop shook his head and mumbled something under his breath while his partner looked up from his notebook, squinting his eyes at the paint on the side of the trailer. Layers of paint that hid bullet holes. He glanced at Gator who suddenly was very interested in a clod of dirt under his boot. The cop shrugged and went back to work, tapping his pen against the paper, his lips forming the words he wrote. I raised a brow in Gator's direction and got the universal fingers to lip zip-it response. *All righty then.*

Gator and Cop One climbed into the trailer to discuss the missing X-boxes. Cop Two and I waited. I shot pictures with my phone and emailed them to myself beginning my own report. I even turned the phone around and shot my portrait, part evidence, part a memory of Oklahoma City. I even snuck in a shot of Hot Cop ass.

"You don't mind if I make a call to our carrier, do you?" I asked the cop.

"Be my guest," he said.

She answered on the second ring. "DeSalena Transport, this is Charlene."

"Hey, Charlene, It's Jojo. I'm in Oklahoma City, with…" I read his badge, "Officer Button." *As in cute as,* I thought. He might have been a mind reader the way he smiled back at me, pushed up his sunglasses and puffed out his chest.

I explained the situation to Charlene and assured her Gator and I were fine, we just wanted to deliver the merchandise and get back on the road.

"We'll be looking for a load to take us toward Louisiana. I'd like to make a stop in Bunkie to check in on Père and Pilar."

"Well, honey, I understand that. Of course, you know our

insurance will cover the missing merchandise, but you may have to answer to corporate. New regulations, you know."

My silence might have been all she needed to hear. When she spoke again she had a little tremble in her voice. I figured a part of her—the most nervous part—was remembering the time I pulled a gun on her. Actually, it was two guns, and one of them was hers.

She said, "We can, uh, discuss this further after you finish with the receiver, okay?"

"Yeah," I said. "Count on it." I ended the call, tucked the phone back in my pocket.

"Did you say, Bunkie? Good hunting there," the cop said, rocking back on his heels.

I waited for the *umm hmm* sound that usually followed a country statement of the obvious. Instead he changed the subject. "You sure you don't want to go the hospital and get that looked at?" Officer Button asked, tapping his own cheek.

I checked my reflection in his sunglasses. The cheek was puffy and my lips looked swollen, in a supermodel-I-meant-to-do-that way, but my eyes were clear and wide open.

"Nah," I said. "This is nothing compared to the time my chute didn't open."

By the time Gator slid off the back of the trailer and made his way over to us, I'd finished telling the officer about my sky-diving and base jumping experiences with Big Al, an ex-Marine boyfriend from Tuskegee.

I was pretty sure the wonder and awe on Officer Button's face as he left was the result of a man genuinely enjoying his time with me, hearing my stories. Perhaps, merely being in my presence. I had a new appreciation for hot cops.

As they pulled away, Gator laughed. "Were those the dumbest cops you ever met? I thought the cliché was dead, but seriously? Man!"

I didn't say anything, just got to work latching the trailer doors. The gangbangers had busted the locking mechanism and one of the vertical rods. We worked silently, jerry-rigging the doors in place using a combination of wire, rope and duct tape. It looked like something a toddler terrorist in training might have designed, but fuck it, it worked, and besides we only needed it to hold until we delivered what was left of this load. I didn't even want to think about washing the cab or restoring our trailer paintjob. I climbed into the driver's seat and cracked a bottle of water, downing it in five gulps.

Gator slid into the passenger seat, rubbing the spot on his neck where he'd been injected. He looked at me and sniffed the air. "Something smells in here."

I belched. "Like apples and sunshine?" I asked, referring to our ongoing fart joke. Gator was partial to the "Does anyone smell fresh lilacs?" comeback.

"No. That ain't it." He sniffed the air again. "More like *bullshit.*"

"Hmm. That's strange. Did you step in something out there?"

"Did you?" he asked.

"Nope, not me," I said.

Gator rubbed his neck again, tried to stare me down, but when I ignored him he just shook his head and clucked his tongue, then turned toward the window pulling a pouty little girl routine that I didn't think he had in him.

"Really?" I said. "Really Gator? Jesus."

I sighed as I released the brakes on the tractor and the trailer. I wasn't sure which hiss was louder. Tugging on the wheel I maneuvered the truck into the empty lot at the end of the street so I could turn around.

Gator's unasked question filled the two feet between us. *What kind of gangbanger/street thief carries a syringe of knock-out drugs in his pocket for impromptu half-assed burglaries?*

I said, "All right. Listen. I'll tell you all about it. But let's finish this job first, okay?"

He gave me the back of his head and I swore I could hear teeth grinding from across the cab.

51

* * *

The right warehouse was ten minutes away. It was taller, newer and nicer than the wrong warehouse and came complete with a supervisor named Mr. Ramirez at the dock.

He almost showed some compassion seeing my beat-up face and the dried blood on my jacket, but then he must have remembered his job. He had his own paperwork to file and some questions to ask. I answered most of them, and when he probed, I told him about the cars and the guns. It seemed like it wasn't the first time he'd heard the same story. He jerked a thumb at our messed-up trailer, the busted vertical bar and lock on the cargo door stating the obvious, "You're gonna have to do something about that before your next load. I might be able to help"

On his signal, two forklift drivers scooted in to unload the remaining cargo. Ramirez led us to his office in the warehouse, handed Gator a business card, said the guy was his cousin and he'd do right by us, could fix anything on wheels from skateboards to semis and had done of his share of welding.

"Can he fill bullet holes?" I asked.

"As long as they're not in people," he said.

We laughed and shared a smile, until Ramirez got serious again. "I wasn't going to say anything, seeing as you're not from here and just passing through, but what you told me? That sounds like the Somali Mafia. They *never* bothered our loads before." He waved his arm at the boxes and racks of electronics in the warehouse, the pallets being wrapped and said, "This isn't their line of expertise."

"What is?" Gator asked.

Ramirez hesitated, then lowered his voice. "Girls. You know for…"

He didn't have to finish. "Well, that's what I heard. Feds busted a bunch of them a few months back. Things got real quiet around here. It was nice. Now? I don't know. They must be back. Or maybe some friends of theirs."

"Ones I saw didn't look too friendly," I mumbled.

"What's that?" Gator asked.

"Nothing," I said.

Mr. Ramirez stared past us, looking at something beyond the truck and the warehouse lot and the chain link fence. I'd watched a pointer freeze like that once during a hunt. Three seconds later the largest black bear I'd ever seen stepped out of the woods right in our path.

"Is that all you need?" I asked, pointing to his clipboard and paperwork.

He blinked, then nodded. "Yeah. Sorry, I was just thinking I'd better warn my granddaughter, make sure she obeys curfew." He started to walk away.

I called after him, "How old is your granddaughter?"

"She's ten," he said. "She's just ten."

I strapped myself into the passenger chair still too wired to even think about sleeping. I put off calling Charlene back, instead clicked on the Qualcomm feed and started looking for a load in the area, one that might get us back toward home. I was missing Père and the plantation, and with the beating—literally— we'd just taken I was thinking a few days of downtime might be in the cards, maybe a few days of sunshine and blue sky.

I ran my finger down the list checking weights, loads, distances, payments, calculating in my head profit margins and possibilities of good weather.

Gator took over the number one seat, adjusted his driving settings, set the GPS to the address on the business card for Ramirez's cousin then pulled out of the lot quickly gaining speed as we approached the highway. I snuck a look at the stern set of his jaw, the vein throbbing in his temple.

A few minutes later he merged onto the highway heading south. He settled into the right-hand lane, checked his mirrors, then glanced over. "Why don't you wait on that," he said, tipping his chin in the direction of the Qualcomm.

"Why?" I asked.

"Why? Two words, Jojo. Somali. Mafia. That is *serious* shit. I need you to talk to me. Now."

I might have been able to finagle my way out of the conversation had we not been in the rig, had we not been rolling at fifty-five miles an hour down the open road, had he not looked at me with those eyes.

His words echoed in my head. *Serious shit.* "Okay," I said. "It's like this…"

I told him about the wrong turn, about the gang bangers on the corner, about how they'd thrown the trash, bottles and paint cans. I admitted to running over the bicycle and how the one guy chased the truck, how he must have figured out where I was going. I told him how they called me out and that they probably tagged the trailer and took the cargo just to fuck with me. I told him *almost* everything.

And then I made him tell me what he knew about the gang.

Gator was quiet. Not in the I'm-about-to-make-shit-up way, but more in the I-don't want-to-be-the-one-to-say-this way.

He started and stopped twice before he finally said, "Back there, when Ramirez said this gang is 'into girls?' He was only partly right. I did some independent work in Minneapolis a few years back. The information I handed over helped bust a ring of eight guys who called themselves The Somali Outlaws. They bragged they were associated with the Somali Mafia, but we could never prove anything."

"Does it matter? They both sound like trouble to me," I said.

"Yeah. But it's not what you'd normally think when you hear girls are involved."

"What do you mean?"

"I mean it's not just prostitution. It's not like these are twenty-three-year-old girls they helped put on the street, girls going to work each day paying off the pimp, then returning to their own place each night. A lot of these kids are runaways, or even worse, *throwaways*—that's a horrible term, I know. But *sex trafficking* is even worse.

"Gangs like the Somali Mafia grab the girls—and boys—when they're young, get them hooked on drugs, give them a place to stay. They get them thinking they need the group and their pimp. Soon enough, they don't know any other life. That becomes their family."

"Pretty fucked up family."

We looked at each other. No one had to say it. All families were fucked up.

I opened the browser on my phone and typed in *Somali Mafia*. I read about the Minneapolis arrests, about girls that were too afraid to testify. I read how the gang moved them across state lines in semis, took grade-school girls from playgrounds, conned lonely teenagers they met in chat rooms. They were in practically every state, using truck routes from California to Florida.

I clicked on a highlighted link. "Holy shit. They have a Facebook page?"

"I wouldn't doubt it," Gator said. "Real arrogant these guys, think nothing can touch them. The place they had in Minneapolis was a fortress. Armed guards, dogs, barbed wire, you name it. One of our guys went in undercover as a Miami "businessman," said the place was a real pleasure palace, filled with drugs, booze, girls of all ages—a lot of them virgins."

"*That's* a one-time sale," I said.

Gator ignored me and continued, "Once you're inside, as long as you have money, you can do anything you want, anytime you want with whomever you want."

"And when the money runs out?"

Gator smiled. "I'm sure you'd be politely asked to leave."

I scoffed. "Yeah right."

The GPS navigator interrupted our discussion with a kind suggestion that we might proceed down the proper road to the cousin's body shop, by turning left at the light. Gator had changed the voice to that of a sassy British chick. She sounded like the kind of girl I'd love to swap stories with over pints in a noisy pub. She didn't sound like the kind of girl who'd get messed up with the likes of the Somali Mafia.

I thought about what Gator's undercover pal had said about the pleasure palace, and I wondered what kind of people would go there. What were they looking for? The whole thing gave me a sick feeling.

"Gator, do you think they're doing the same thing in Oklahoma City, as in Minneapolis?"

"I don't know," Gator said, staring out the window. "But I sure as shit hope not."

Oklahoma City had undergone a recent multi-billion-dollar renaissance. People were migrating to the area for jobs and opportunities. Maybe that had something to do with the presence of the Somali Mafia. I imagined them moving around town in armored SUVs like dignitaries or movie stars with entourages and groupies. Not the kids on the street so much, not Bicycle Boy. I knew enough about bad guys and their hierarchy to understand those gutter dogs I'd run into earlier were far removed from the big man in the fortress. But I also knew a loyal dog would lay down his life for his master.

As Gator pulled into the lot for the body shop, I remembered what happened that day in the woods after the pointer froze and the bear began to charge.

The dog reacted in a split-second leaping at the growling beast going for his throat. Me? I'd calmly raised my rifle and dropped them both in one shot.

CHAPTER 8

We found the cousin's garage without problem. Warm, quiet and empty, we walked through calling *hello* and *he-ey*, the universal greeting.

The shop was neat and clean. Too neat and clean for a body shop. It even smelled good. I half expected a plump little housewife in a pressed apron to appear with a cake in one hand and a martini in the other. Maybe I was projecting.

An older Chrysler 300M painted a shimmering gold with big ass chrome rims was parked in the last bay, driver's side door ajar like someone was getting ready to leave but had to run inside for one more thing.

I looked at Gator who was looking at me. We were about to call out again when the back door of the Chrysler opened and a man stepped out. I reached for a gun I didn't have, before Gator grabbed my arm and shook his head.

"You must be the truck drivers," he said in a soft, lilting accent. In his tight black pants and white unbuttoned shirt, he glided our way, moving as if he was on wheels. His dark hair was pulled back in a slick ponytail, tight enough to smooth his forehead, his smile was tooth-capped bright.

"Forgive me," he said, half-bowing to me, then staring into my soul with the largest brown eyes I'd ever seen. "I had a long night and was catching a kitty nap."

"You mean a cat nap?" I asked, returning the stare, smiling involuntarily.

"Oh, *jes*. That is what I mean. Sometimes, I forget my English."

Gator stepped in, breaking the spell Mr. Sexy had on me.

"Let me guess. Tango, right?" he said, arms spread wide as they faced off. Bull and man, minus the cape and dancing heels.

Gator said something fast and low in Spanish—not my strong subject—and Mr. Sexy's eyebrows lifted. He said something back equally fast and with a question at the end. There were some more speedy words and hand gestures and then they were slapping each other's backs and grinning.

"Excuse me," I said. "But would someone care to fill me in?"

Gator put his arm around me as Mr. Sexy motioned for us to follow him. "We know the same tango instructor in Argentina. Esteban used to dance professionally before he came to America. Now he dances for love."

I stifled a giggle. "Wait. Gator, you can dance the tango?"

Gator smiled. "And you thought you knew everything about me."

Esteban opened the door at the back of the garage and I recognized what I'd been smelling.

"Café con leche?" he asked.

That was a language I understood. "I'd love some coffee, thank you."

For the next ten minutes we exchanged travel stories, drank our Argentinean coffee and finally got down to discussing the job we had for this tango-dancing body shop man.

"We need to get back on the road as soon as possible," I said.

"It's no problem. I am...very fast," Esteban said, staring into my eyes.

"I wouldn't brag about that, pal," Gator said, only partly joking.

I stood, before another confrontation began. "Why don't we go outside and you can see what we're talking about. You, uh, might want to put on a coat," I reminded Esteban, gesturing to his tan bare chest and rippled abs. "Or not."

Outside Esteban, in a parka, explained how he could weld the new vertical bar into place, repair the lock and clean the trailer sides, telling us it's better to clean, not paint over.

"*Jes*, they tagged you good," he said. "Do you know what says this?"

"I'm afraid to ask," Gator mumbled.

"It is like, you have made an enemy. A dangerous enemy. It is good you are leaving town."

Great.

Gator backed the trailer into the garage, disconnected it from Sabrina and left it with Esteban. We planned to get the truck washed and fill the tank, maybe go for a long walk at a local park.

As Gator drove I called Charlene and told her about our delay.

"The guy says he'll have it ready by tomorrow, next day the latest. Just wanted to let you know."

"What is going on out there?" Charlene said. "You're the third truck to call in with a problem."

"Full moon?" I suggested.

"I don't know," she said. "But I don't like it. Hopefully it's just the power of three—" She was interrupted by a loud buzzing sound. "Damn. Sorry, I gotta go."

I started to say, "Char—" but she'd already hung up.

Gator looked me. I shrugged.

"Good answer," he said.

Near the truck stop, we found parking at a local country store type of eatery. It wasn't my first choice but when you were driving a truck with an extended sleeper—even without a trailer—you ate where you could park.

We sat in the bar and watched TV, nursed some sodas and water with lemon. I gave the evil eye to a long line of beer tap handles and tried to not drool.

"You can have a beer," Gator said. "I'm driving and we're down for twenty-four."

I shook my head. "If I start, I might not want to stop."

He laughed. "That bad, huh?"

"No," I said. "That good."

The TV was tuned to the local news. Just a few minutes into the broadcast it became quite clear that not only wind ran rampant in Tornado Country.

A photo of a pretty, dark-haired girl with blue eyes and too much makeup was posted in the left-hand corner of the screen as words scrolled across about a recent crime—an seventeen-year-old missing girl had been found under a bridge overpass outside Oklahoma City. She'd been beaten, raped and then beaten again. She was in critical care, prognosis seemed grim. The pretty blonde newscaster winced as she read the report. I was betting she'd ask for an escort to her BMW when she left work tonight and would skip that solo run by the river in the morning.

The story ended with a table of statistics and a graph display showing the level and type of crime in their fair city, as compared to other cities. The last slide showed the income of convicted criminals against the income of blue collar workers, then white collar.

"What the hell?" I said.

"Guess it's true," Gator said. "Crime does pay."

"Not where I come from."

Gator raised his lemon water to mine, clicking glasses.

While Gator took the truck through the truck wash, I sat on a bench in the sun and watched the world go by. The day had warmed up considerably. Typical of the area, spring meant a big swing in temperature, as much as forty degrees from night to day. That could seriously fuck with a fashionista's wardrobe, I thought, forgetting for a moment where I was and what I was doing—until a fat man in a checkered shirt exited the convenience store hawking and spitting before climbing into a muddy Silverado.

OK City had its own feel, like many places do. It wasn't a

good feel or a happy feel. From the people who ran into the store for cigarettes or to use the restroom, even watching those who filled their cars at the pump, I got the impression that Oklahoma City was a halfway place—a sort of holding zone for people who knew of other places, better things. Maybe they thought at one time that those things might be here—then they opened their eyes.

The places we end up are not always what we hoped for. Like my image of Hollywood, fast, fancy, clean, streets paved in gold, littered with movie stars and famous folks who dared to dream. I had forgotten to imagine the ugly underneath: trash in the gutter, rats in the alley, rejected beauties, addicted monsters. It's never *all* pretty and polished and perfect. But you can't blame the surface. Without a base the top would fall. There is no bell if there is no steeple, and that steeple needs a building beneath it.

It was something to think about.

All my *lah-die-da* mulling went out the front door of my big ass brain when I saw a familiar girl cross the parking lot.

She was tugging on a knit cap trying to stuff her dark hair inside when someone yelled in a language I didn't recognize. The girl turned back, frightened, then slung her tan messenger bag across her chest, dropped the coat she was carrying and began to run—right toward me.

A black sedan careened through the lot swerving around slow moving rigs, crashing into a plastic trash barrel spewing its contents. The car screeched to a halt twenty feet away between me and the girl. A door opened, she screamed. Then she was gone, the smell of burning rubber in the air.

Shit!

I ran to the truck wash to find Gator.

He'd pulled the clean truck into the sun and was just starting the detailing when I blurted out what had happened.

"You're sure it was her?" he asked, pouring more chrome polish onto his cloth.

"Positive. It was Candy!"

"No shit. Wonder how she got here?"

"Yeah. So do I. But more than that, what the hell is she *doing* here?"

"Think about it, Jojo," Gator said, moving to the next wheel.

"I don't like where this is going," I said, following him.

"I'm sure her mother feels the same way."

"*If* she knows," I said. "I mean, what if she doesn't know?"

"Uh-uh," Gator said. "We are *not* doing this."

"Doing what?"

"You know what." He scrubbed a little too hard at a tiny speck on the wheel.

I squeezed my eyes shut, then snapped them open as the image found a match in my memory. I leaned over Gator's shoulder, my lips close to his ear. "Too late, lover. The car that took her? It was the same one that brought the boys who drugged you, the same boys who did *this* to me." I tapped my swollen cheek. He stopped polishing, but didn't turn around.

I said, "As you might have guessed, I don't like them. They *don't* get to win."

Gator finished shining the wheel, then stood slowly and turned to me, his slack face saying, *Yes, dear,* while his glittery eyes said, *This is one favor you will repay.*

"I know I'm going to end up regretting this." He reached in his back pocket for another cloth, tossed me the polish. "Help me with the other side while I think, then we'll go kick some ass."

I grabbed him and kissed him, mashing my swollen lips against his cold ones. "Oh, you sweet talking man."

CHAPTER 9

In theory, it was a nice idea, helping those in trouble. Nice ideas could even be fun, especially if they included an ass kicking.

Gator and I were on the same page with that one. Thing was, you kind of had to know the whereabouts of the bad guys if you were going to kick their ass, or asses, as it were. To further complicate things, we planned on stealing something they probably weren't willing to part with.

My father was right. I do love the smell of trouble in the morning, and the late afternoon, and also, sometimes right around dinnertime.

We finished with Sabrina, all the while talking through our options, then made our rounds at the truck stop looking for some answers by asking some cryptic questions about brown-haired girls and black cars while flashing twenties. We even hit up party row—the last row in the lot where the security lights were the dimmest and the most lot lizards could be found—but no one was talking. Guess if you'd been banging an under-aged girl in your work truck's bunk, right under the picture of your wife and kids, you probably wouldn't be so keen on sharing any particulars. Or maybe because Gator still smelled like cop to them.

We ended up back in the T-shirt and souvenir section of the truck stop store, trying to think of another approach.

"I could tell them she has some horrible disease," I suggested.

"What if they're the ones with the disease?" Gator said.

"True that," I said, with a sigh.

I thought about growing up in Louisiana, hunting with my

best friend, Ivory Joe and how I'd thought he knew instinctively where the raccoons would be, every time. Until one day he told me, "It's not like that, Jojo. We ain't no smarter than them. You just keep going back to the darkest, nastiest place and eventually you're going to find them."

"Hang on," I told Gator. "I'll be right back."

I headed to the ladies room, passing through the empty shower waiting area. The automated scent mister went off as I pushed open the door. As if the sweetness of berries could mask the scent of urine, shit and mold.

If I was a girl who'd been abducted by men, the only place I'd be sure to be alone, even for a minute, would be the restroom. This would be the place to make an attempt at escape—or make a connection.

I checked all four stalls—empty—and clueless. It wasn't as if I expected a note from Candy to be written neatly on the wall telling me who had her and where they were, but maybe, there was something. I used the toilet, washed my hands and stared at myself in the mirror. The rushing water helped me think, until cold water spurted from the faucet, splashing onto to the front of my pants. "Damnit!" I shook my hands, looking for paper towels.

No dispensers, but there were two high-powered air dryers on the wall by the door. As I dried my hands and my pants, watching my skin ripple under the jets, something caught my eye. A business card had been slipped under the edge of the restroom cleaning log mounted on the back of the door. One side said: *T.A.S.T. FORCE We can help!* Underneath, there was an easy to remember phone number and email address. The other side said: *Truckers Against Sex Traffickers. We have the force to set you free.* The message was repeated in several languages. Each time the word *free* was highlighted in bright yellow. I took a picture of the card with my phone and carefully replaced it, leaving the word *help* visible.

I found Gator by the snack row. "Nuts or pretzels?" he

asked, as I approached.

"Whichever one's dipped in chocolate," I said, brushing past him. "Hurry up. I'll meet you in the truck."

By the time Gator climbed in and stashed his goodies, I'd pulled up several pages on my laptop searching for information on *T.A.S.T. FORCE* and any known associations. Their website was professionally done, listed a slew of supporters and links to similar groups and relevant articles.

"Sorry," Gator said, glancing at the page I had open on my laptop. "There was a long line and a gabby cashier."

"I noticed that," I said. "She was about a 40DD kind of gabby, right?"

Gator had the decency to blush. He slid in beside me at the banquette. "What have you got there?"

"Saw this business card in the bathroom."

I tilted the laptop screen in his direction, scrolled through the *T.A.S.T. FORCE* website.

"Check it out."

The numbers were impressive. The group had helped more than two hundred and twenty-five children return home in the last six months. They now ran three halfway houses across the country for adults and families that had been trafficked and were fundraising to build more. They had been instrumental in passing laws which protected those forced into the sex trade from prostitution convictions—that was one of the largest reasons the girls didn't leave, or ask for help—the fear of getting busted themselves. Life in another kind of jail.

"Jesus, you think *this* is what happened to Candy?" Gator asked.

"You said yourself, she had no reason to be at that truck stop in California. And now, I see her again here—running from something, someone. What am I supposed to think?"

Gator looked at me and I could see the gears grinding away. "Jojo, this isn't your fight."

"Maybe not, but I'm it now."

Gator shook his head. "Correction. *We're* in it. What do you want to do?"

I leaned back, laced my fingers behind my head. "What do you know about coon hunting?"

Six hours later, we were sitting in Esteban's borrowed Chrysler back in the neighborhood where I'd had my introduction to the bottle throwing bad boys of the Somali Mafia.

"We could have bought two pairs of binoculars, you know?" Gator said, as I tapped his arm indicating it was my turn to search the faces of the boys on the street.

"Now that would be a waste of money. What's mine is yours, and vice versa," I said.

"Not sure I ever agreed to that," Gator mumbled.

I tweaked the focus on the field glasses and zoomed in on three boys in the shadow of a flickering streetlamp. They wore the same colors as our gang banger pals but looked older. I wondered if there was some kind of gangster rule: the kids take the morning crime shift and the older guys get the early evening. It gave a whole new meaning to *organized* crime.

"Wait," I said, poking Gator. "There he is!"

Bicycle Boy—minus his bike—approached the group, his baggy shirt billowing behind him. He wore gold sunglasses though it was dark, and a matching chunky necklace. The biggest guy slapped his back and they exchanged a series of complicated fist bumps, as the others peeled off. One jogged across the street, gone in seconds, the other hitched up his pants and sauntered off, cutting through the yard of a dilapidated blue house.

"Wish I could hear what they're saying," I said.

"Just watch the body language," Gator said. "Let me know if you see a weapon."

I tried to make sense of the bobbing and weaving that Bicycle Boy and the big man were doing, when headlights filled the rear window. I sunk down in the seat as a now familiar black sedan rolled past.

Gator said, "Is that the car from the truck stop?"

"Yes," I whispered.

The car pulled up beside the two men and the driver's side window opened a crack. The big man held up a hand. He finished up with Bicycle Boy, slapping him again on the back—hard enough to make him flinch, then pushed him in the direction of the blue house.

A few minutes later, two girls came out of the house, escorted by Bicycle Boy. They stumbled across the cracked sidewalk to the waiting car. Big Man opened the back door of the black sedan and helped them in, shoving each one a little harder, pinching the last one's butt through her short skirt making her yelp. My fingers tightened on the binoculars as Bicycle Boy slid in beside the girls and the Big Man got in the front.

"Did you get the license plate?" Gator asked as they pulled away.

"Too dark," I said with a sigh, lowering the binoculars, slumping in the seat.

"Strange," Gator said.

"What's that?" I asked.

"Was it just me, or did they look the same?"

"What do you mean?"

"The girls. Light skin, dark hair, same clothes—like a costume, or a uniform."

"I guess, but not school uniforms, right?" I pushed myself upright, searching Gator's face. "They're older than that. They've got to be."

He shook his head. "I don't know. I'm just thinking out loud. I mean, either one of them could have been Candy—"

"That wasn't her," I said. "I'd know."

"All right," he said, patting my arm, like I was his Granny upset about the quality of her creamed corn. "All I was saying was that they look similar, you know?"

"And all *I'm* saying is looking a certain way doesn't mean—wait a minute. Are you thinking what I'm thinking?"

Gator grinned. "Well, these aren't rocket scientists we're dealing with. If two dark-haired, light-skinned, uniform-wearing girls came out of that house..."

"There might be other girls in there, too," I said, reaching for the door handle.

CHAPTER 10

Clouds moved across the sky. The chill had returned, reminding me we were in Oklahoma City, a place that obeyed no laws of nature.

Crouching on a crumbled sidewalk in possibly the shittiest part of town, spying on gangsters, I was getting more pissed off by the minute. First dealing with those assholes, getting beat up as a result, then being put out of work because of the trailer repair, topped off by having to endure a crappy, mushy dinner. And now, being made to wait and watch and wait some more? It was too much for anyone, much less a Boudreaux.

Gator whispered, "Hey," then pointed, indicating the path of the clouds toward the full moon.

I adjusted my crouch, knees and thighs complaining louder than the voice in my head. Before the clouds could move to provide cover, I stood up, shook out my legs and traipsed across the street, in the light of the moon. That's right, I traipsed, the whole time muttering, *fuck this.*

Gator ran after me, catching up just as I crashed through the front door of the blue house shoulder first and ran in, gun arm locked, shouting, "Get down motherfuckers!"

In hindsight, it was a pretty stupid thing to do, and the motherfucker line? That didn't seem to help.

In my head, I'd figured the element of surprise would be enough. Well, that and the guns. I didn't figure on the door slamming into a very large, very black, and now very angry shirtless man, with a pretty badass gun of his own.

He grabbed my arm, twisted until I dropped my weapon,

then spun me around and bent me backward in a chokehold as Gator stepped through the doorway, a second too late.

Even in the dim light of a single hanging bulb, there was no mistaking my compromised position and the two approaching armed gangbangers. Everyone knows knives beat guns in close quarters.

Gator gently laid down his gun and raised his hands as they grabbed him.

Behind me, Mr. Beefy contracted his equally beefy arm, squeezing my throat. An odor came off him like ham and overcooked beans, or maybe it was just sweat, desperation and cheap cologne. He was three times my size and even if most of it was fat, he knew how to leverage his weight. The pressure on my neck was probably only a quarter of what the guy was capable of. When I relaxed my upper body and stopped struggling, his grip eased up. I locked in on Gator's face, sending him telepathic messages to stand down, be cool, to watch me, and please, please follow my lead.

"Can I say something?" I squeaked out. The pressure on my neck loosened even more.

The guys holding Gator, knives at the ready, glanced over their shoulders at me. One wore a T-shirt with a skull on it, the other's shirt bore an image of crossbones on a tombstone.

My captor readjusted his hold with a final jerk, popping me under the chin with his elbow, snapping my teeth together with a loud *thonk*. He slid his grip from throat to collarbone, grabbing my wrists behind my back in one of his massive hands, tugging hard until I grunted.

The guys with Gator chuckled. Crossbones snapped his knife shut and picked up Gator's gun. He looked at the Glock, stroked the shaft, then traced the air around Gator, moving the gun from head to heart to crotch and back again. The show was part threat and part stupid—the more loosely you held a gun, even if you thought you were in a controlling position—the more opportunity you gave someone to relieve you of said gun.

In the meantime, his buddy in the skull shirt stood there

smiling stupidly, angling his knife blade to catch the light from the ceiling bulb and throw it in my eyes. I knew that trick as well as I knew that knife.

He stared at me, squinting then said, "Hey, I know you. You the bitch that ran over Hollywood's bike."

It could have gone so much smoother, so much nicer, so much easier, if he'd just left the *bitch* out of it. I squirmed, and Beefy's grip tightened.

Crossbones let out a sound that was part pig call, part pubescent boy. His voice matched when he said, "You in deep shit, man. Both of you."

Gator grinned. "We're in deep shit? I don't think so. Why don't you tell us where Hollywood went and we'll let you get back to...whatever it is you were doing."

Skull Shirt said. "Even if I did know where he went, I wouldn't you, motherfucker."

"Fine, Gator said. "Just let her go and I'll stay here and wait for him. Have a little sit down, apologize for the misunderstanding, see what we can work out."

"Gator, don't—"

Mr. Beefy cut me off tugging me backwards, twisting my wrists, hard. I could feel him sweating on my back, feel him tiring against my straining. I gave him the false illusion that I was weakening also, dropping my shoulders, leaning against him.

Gator said, "What if I told you that I know your boy? That I know he's with two of your girls, right now?"

Crossbones piped up with his high voice, his foreign accent and properly worded speech. It was not what you'd expect to hear coming from a guy dressed like he was, standing in a house like this.

He said, "What is it that you know about these girls?"

"More than I'm telling you," Gator said. "I have business with Hollywood, not you. So, who was that in the black car? Where'd they go?"

Mr. Beefy finally smelled the coffee. He leaned in and

shouted next to my ear, "We ain't got to tell you that. We ain't got to tell you shit."

I quickly figured out who was the brains and who was brawn of this outfit. I said, "Don't be a pepper, Gator."

"What the fuck? You talking about?" Beefy said.

"Who's she calling a pepper?" Skull Shirt asked.

"Come on, you never heard that joke?" I said, forcing a laugh.

The boys, one on each side of Gator, stared, stone-faced.

"We do not like the jokes," Crossbones said.

"Yeah, but we like cutting people," Skull Shirt said, spinning his knife—*my* knife, the one they had stolen from me this morning—jabbing it into the cloying air.

"Wait," Beefy said. "I like jokes. Go on," he said, tipping his chin to me.

"Ok," I said, smiling, and catching Gator's eye. I twisted toward Beefy, forcing him to loosen his grip and asked, "What's a nosy pepper do?"

Beefy leaned in, his face crinkled up in thought.

Not wanting to cost him the loss of another brain cell, I put on my best Spanish accent and yelled as I broke his hold, "Gets *jalapeño business!*"

Esteban would have been proud of my smooth dancer-like moves, the way I stomped with my left foot, crushing Beefy's toes, met the forward motion of his pained face with the high, tight back swing of my skull, then spun into his huge body, regaining my arms and hands, only to slam my fist in his wide nose while raising my knee to deliver the final blow to his testicles—a dangling mass of nerve center and pride—his *business* calmly resting beneath baggy gym shorts.

It's true; the bigger they are, the harder they fall.

It is also true; the more pissed off they will be when they get back up again.

I didn't have to wait for Mr. Beefy to rise and take revenge. His moans and curses had drawn the attention of a wild-haired girl with a baseball bat. Instinct took over. I pulled out my best

Matrix-like moves, ducking and dodging, leaping as the bat swished empty air finally connecting with the swollen crotch of the rising Mr. Beefy.

As he went down for the second time, howling like a wild animal, the girl screamed and dropped the bat. "I'm sorry, Big Abdi! I'm sorry!" A skeletal girl crawled toward us, her pale nude body caught by the light of the bare bulb above our heads. She kneeled beside the man, stroking his back as he rocked and moaned, both hands on his genitals. Too little, too late.

While I'd been showing off, Gator had regained his Glock with a knuckle to the eye socket, elbow to the back of the neck move, then treated the other guy to The Gator Special: pointy knee to slack jaw, with a roundhouse follow through.

As I felt around on the floor for my Springfield XD-40, I heard a moan from the corner of the room. Using the flashlight on my phone I followed the sound, the beam of light panning the room, stopping on a nude, dark-haired girl curled into the fetal position on a mattress on the floor.

"Oh shit. Gator? Little help here?"

Gator stripped off his jacket, wrapped the girl in it and lifted her as easily as if she were a toddler. We stepped over the unconscious bodies and hurried to the car. Gator put her in the backseat beside me before he fired up the engine and U-turned us out of there.

I pushed her hair out of her face and raised her chin to the light. "Candy? You're going to be okay."

CHAPTER 11

Candy was still out of it thirty minutes later, as Gator wound us through the streets of Oklahoma City. We'd stopped at a strip mall where I picked up some clothes and a pair of sneakers. Gator made a point to not look as I dressed her. The plan was to head back to the motel we'd scouted earlier and hole up there until we heard from Esteban.

"There," I said, draping his coat over her shoulders and buckling her in.

"Is she okay?" Gator asked, catching my eye in the rearview mirror.

"Yeah, I think so."

Candy was even prettier asleep. I hear mothers say that about napping babies all the time. Usually it's because those same babies are red-faced squealing, horrible little devil spawn—not that I have anything against babies.

I saw something in the girl that touched me, in a way I didn't want to think about. In a way that I wasn't prepared to discuss with Gator, or anyone. Something tickled the edge of my consciousness, and suddenly it felt too warm in the Chrysler. I reached for the window button and leaned my head back on the seat, letting the cool breeze wash across my face and lift the hair off my neck. I needed a shower. I felt gross, probably smelled like the beany Mr. Beefy, his sweat now soaked into the back of my shirt.

"You okay?" Gator asked.

I nodded. "Just tired."

"Hey, I almost forgot," he said. "You might want this back."

He reached into his pocket, then handed me my knife.

"Thanks," I said, opening the blade to inspect it, soothed by its familiar heft, the heat of it in my palm. I closed the blade, slipped the knife in my boot.

A few minutes later, we pulled up to the motel, a garish brick structure with faded pink trim and bars on every window. Gator drove the Chrysler around back, tucked it between two cars that might have been abandoned—one with a broken windshield and dented door, the other rusty, its hood held down with bungee cords.

"Wait here," Gator said. "I'll get the room and check it out, then text you." He handed me the keys. "Don't forget to lock it."

He jogged around the side of the building and was gone. I had the sinking feeling I'd never see him again. Part of me thought that might be a lucky thing for him. This was all my fault. If I hadn't been so impetuous with the gangbangers, if I had just minded my own business, if only I wasn't so...me.

Before I could berate myself further, Candy stirred on the seat beside me, raising her head and moaning softly. Her eyes opened, lids flickering. "Where am I?"

"It's okay," I said.

She pulled at the sweatpants, rolled her head toward me. "Whose clothes are these? Who..."

"You're safe now." I reached toward her, meaning to pat her arm, but she batted me off, harder than necessary and stared me down.

"Who the fuck are you?"

"It's me, Jojo. From California? The truck stop? Remember?"

She drew back, pressing herself against the car door, lips drawn tight, eyeing me sideways. She was more like a wary dog being offered food than a recently rescued girl in a safe place. Her eyes, unfocused and glassy strayed to a point beyond me, their surface so dull they looked fake. If she hadn't moved, I might have thought I was staring at one of the stuffed animals in my cousin's taxidermy shop in Louisiana. Maybe a fox or a snake.

"Are you cold?" I asked when she shivered. She hesitated, scanning me and I saw the fox return, as she calculated an escape, something that might begin with me struggling out of my coat. I caught her hand as she inched it across the seat toward the Chrysler's door handle.

"I wouldn't do that if I were you," I said, attempting the right combination of threat and trustworthiness. It was a fine line.

Candy tried to worm her hand out of my grip, eyes on the door again. I pulled the Springfield from behind my back and held it so she could see it, my finger on the trigger. "Uh uh."

Still, she grappled, sliding her hand out of mine making one last attempt, and I jumped right over the fine line, saying, "Don't make me shoot you."

She took her eyes off the door handle and stopped struggling. I grabbed her tiny wrist, kept the gun on her, felt like I was the bad guy now.

"What do you want?" she asked.

What did I want? Good question. What was I going to say, *I want to help?* Sounded kind of stupid when you looked at the situation.

"Nice way to thank me for saving your life back there," I said.

The words must have made some sense in her muddled mind. She seemed to collect herself a bit, though I saw through the facade, right to the jittery leg and general itchy behavior of a junkie.

She slumped back against the seat. "Can you let go? You've got the gun. What the fuck am I going to do?"

She was right, and yet, I didn't trust her. I should have been the one asking her questions, not the other way around. Questions like: *What the hell were you doing with those men? Where are your parents? And why are you in Oklahoma, anyway?*

My phone buzzed in my pocket and I dropped her wrist,

waving my gun like a caution flag, letting her know just who was in control.

Gator's text told me which room he was in and how to find it. I stuffed the phone back in my pocket and reached across to open the car door.

"C'mon," I said. "My friend got us a room."

Candy hesitated. I don't know which word affected her more—friend or room—and I hated that my words put what looked like fear in her eyes. Why couldn't she understand that I wasn't her enemy?

"C'mon," I said, softer this time.

She let me guide her, firm hand on her elbow, didn't say a word.

Gator watched from the window, dropping the curtain back into place as we approached. He let us in, then locked the door behind us and pointed to the bathroom. "You're probably going to want to put her in there. But first, make it safe."

"What?" I said, wriggling out of my coat and dropping it in a chair. "Why?"

He tipped his chin in Candy's direction. I saw her for the first time through his eyes—unwashed, pale and rail thin, scratching at her arms, and then—bent over and retching.

I herded her into the windowless bathroom, clearing it of potentially dangerous things, while she puked a thin yellow stream into the chipped toilet.

"Get out," she moaned. "Leave me alone."

I backed out and closed the door behind me, setting the confiscated towel rod, ceramic soap dish and metal toilet paper holder on one of the double beds, then I went to Gator and collapsed in his arms, crying silent tears.

I hated being weak, hated worse to show it.

"It's okay," Gator whispered. "Even tough guys cry some-times."

I shook my head, punched his chest lightly. "What's wrong with me?" I stammered through the tears. "I've seen worse things than this happen to people I *loved*. *This* isn't what I do," I sniffled, raising my head. "This isn't Jojo Boudreaux."

"I know, baby." He stroked my hair and held me tighter. "It's okay."

I buried my face into his strong chest and squeezed my eyes shut. I let myself feel safe, just for a minute, and then an image flashed—a woman splayed on a wooden floor, her leg at an impossible angle, a pool of liquid by her head—I opened my eyes and the image disappeared.

I jerked away from Gator, wiping my nose, smoothing my hair, trying to collect myself, as I tamped the feelings down, storing them in a box that only I had the key for. I sat on the end of the bed and passed my gaze over the dingy room, looking anywhere else but into his eyes.

I patted my pockets looking for my phone, then got up to search my coat. Nothing. "Damn."

"What?"

"My phone. It must have fallen out in the backseat of the Chrysler. I'll get it later. Any word from Esteban?"

"Not since I last checked," Gator said. He took out his phone and slid his finger across the screen. "I'll try him again."

He stepped to the window, phone to his ear.

The moaning and retching in the bathroom had stopped. I wondered how long it took an addict to come down or detox, or whatever they had to do.

Gator said, "No answer. I'll send him a text."

As he worked his phone, I went to the bathroom door, laid my hand against it and listened to the rustling sounds and angry murmurs. I felt like a mother standing at the door to a toddler's room waiting for them to self-soothe.

"I think we should call someone," I said, turning back to Gator.

"Like who?" he asked, slipping his phone into his pocket.

"I don't know."

He scoffed. "Maybe in your vast repertoire you can come up

with an ex who's a doctor, or maybe a detox specialist?"

I might have just the perfect person, but from the snotty tone he was using I certainly wasn't going to admit it.

I said, "It's just that I was thinking she'd be safe in Bunkie. These Somali guys wouldn't go to Louisiana for her, right? And Père or Ivory Joe would know what to do, or at least know someone who could help."

From the look on Gator's face, once again I'd managed to find the wrong thing to say. I knew he was jealous of my friendship with Ivory Joe. No matter how much I tried to convince him, he was certain my childhood pal was still in love with me.

"I know what to do," Gator said." And so do you. We drop her off at a clinic, sign her in, then pick up our trailer and get the hell out of here. This isn't about us, Jojo. It never was."

"I'm not so sure about that," I mumbled.

"What did you say?"

"Nothing," I said, shaking my head. "You're right. We'll find a place that will take care of her while we're waiting for Esteban to finish the trailer."

He nodded. "Good. Now why don't I go find us something to eat, get some cold drinks? I saw a vending machine. It's not much but it'll get us by."

I smiled. He was such a good man. So much better a person than me.

I waited for Gator to leave, then checked on Candy, cracking open the bathroom door. She was on the floor, hair covering her face, arm as a pillow under her head. Her chest rose and fell in the rhythm of sleep. I counted to five, then closed the door, quietly as I could.

Sitting on the edge of the bed, I tried to not think about how hungry and tired I felt or how angry I was at myself, for everything. I tried to focus on good things, on the way Gator had kissed me before he left, on how the trailer would look fixed up, on the new jobs that were surely waiting for us. We'd be back on the road. And soon enough, I would be lying beside my man in our bedroom/office/kitchenette, his strong arms holding me, his warm breath against the back of my neck.

Jarred from my thoughts by a rattle at the door, I jumped to open it, figuring Gator's hands must be full.

"Hold on," I said. But before I could grab the handle, the door crashed open, flimsy chain lock dangling.

"Hello again."

It was Bicycle Boy, still wearing his gold sunglasses and behind him, my new pals Skull Shirt and Crossbones.

I held up my hands, and got out two words—"Hollywood. Wait."—before they grabbed me and jabbed a needle in my neck.

CHAPTER 12

I woke from a floating dream, the kind of dream that's more magical feeling, more mysterious place than a dream. You know who you are, where you are—pretty much—and you feel in control, knowing *everything*, you've even unlocked that part of your brain people say no one can reach. I tried to explain it to my father once over breakfast, how when I was in that dream state, it felt as if I could simply raise my arms, leap into the air and fly.

I told him, "When I'm in that place, anything feels possible, like I can read the minds of people passing me on a sidewalk. I can walk through the thickest walls, can know the future—exactly as it will occur."

He'd laughed at me, tousling my hair, telling me I sounded like the LSD advocates of the sixties, then shook his head and served me more eggs and bacon.

I'd read somewhere that humans only use twenty percent of their brain. When I was having those kinds of dreams, those *smart* dreams, I was positive that I was using a secret five percent too—and I wanted to tell the world. But, as soon as I corralled that idea—poof—the dream would change into something horrible. I'd freeze, an unknown weight on my chest pinning me to the ground. Unable to move or open my eyes, I'd start to feel as if I'd forgotten how to speak, how to walk, how to be human. I was transforming into an slug or a stone and somewhere under all that confusion, a hand was coming at me, and the breath behind the hand was sour and meaty, like a dog with decaying teeth, like a maggot-ridden corpse, like evil things I couldn't name.

I was stuck there now, in one of those nightmares, in one of those places and I wondered if I could make the bad thing go away if I used my bigger brain, if I changed my reality of the moment. So, I tried. I drew mental pictures of a lake and a copse of trees, a picnic blanket and a feast of beautiful food, of sunshine and butterflies, then I let go. I let the nightmare hand do what it wanted, because I no longer cared. I wasn't there.

When I woke again a few minutes, maybe a few hours later, my head felt thick and fuzzy. Every bone in my body ached, laced with a dull throbbing in the places underneath. I was on the floor, my back against the wall, one cheek on a scrap of carpet, the rest of me on cold, splintered wood. I tried to get enough saliva going so I could swallow, as my eyes adjusted to the dim interior. From the paneled walls, lumpy low ceiling, and remnants of built-in shelving, it might be the den in an old house. The only light in the room seeped from cracks in a blacked-out window. Another window was completely boarded up as if they expected a tornado on the inside. There were a few home-y touches—a small quilt across the back of a torn-up couch, an overturned metal bucket doubling as an end table— but none of it made me think that anyone really lived here or that anyone cared about the place.

I dated a guy once who decided the best way to protect himself against burglary was to make his house look like a shithole from the outside. He never mowed his lawn, left all sorts of crap on his porch, and hid his fine vehicles in a secret garage, accessed by a tunnel.

You'd never think behind that false front door there was a sleek modern house complete with indoor pool and swim up bar.

Sometimes though, it doesn't matter what you look like on the outside if you're ugly on the inside. Eventually, all that ugliness is going to leak out and spill over until every single bit of pretty you had stored up and tucked away is gone forever. Ugly trumps pretty every time.

For the moment, I was stuck in the ugly. I squeezed my eyes shut and ran a quick inventory; left foot, right foot, leg, leg, right hand, left hand, arm, arm. Despite the two beatings in twenty-four hours and whatever they'd injected me with, I appeared to be whole and functioning. I did a quick muscle tense and release exercise and focused on the most painful areas. My ribs felt bruised but not cracked, my neck hurt where the needle had gone in. My head throbbed—they must have dropped me. But it wasn't as bad as the concussion I'd experienced. My breasts ached—they must have...I didn't want to think about it. At least I was still wearing my jeans and underwear and they'd left me my boots. I snaked a hand down my leg, reaching my fingers into the boot shaft where I kept my knife. Gone. Of course.

I pushed myself up, tried to crawl to the cracked window, stopping twice to control the roiling in my stomach, the pounding between my ears. A shout and the sound of approaching footsteps forced me back to the carpet scrap, where I sprawled out limbs akimbo, hair over my face hiding my eyes.

The man who came through the door had changed his shirt since the last time I saw him. Maybe Gator's ass kicking had resulted in a little blood flow. I could only hope. No longer wearing his crossbones T-shirt, the guy was still recognizable as one of the gangbangers from the crack house. He hitched up his pants and glanced in my direction, then yelled down the hall in a strong accent, "She still out. Told you, Jabby, you give her too much."

The tone in the Somali reply from Jabby suggested he disagreed. Or didn't care. *Fuck you* in any language is still *fuck you.*

Peeking through the mask of hair, I watched Crossbones throw a single long middle finger in the direction of the man he called Jabby. He stepped into the room, mumbling, "Black Dog don't take no shit from fucking Jabby. He'll see."

Black Dog? And we refer to ourselves in the third person? Nice.

I closed my eyes as he approached, stilling my breath and heart, forcing my muscles to relax, when what they wanted to do was what they were trained to do—pounce. I wanted to knock this asshole back to Somalia, then run out the open door and beat the shit out of his pal, Jabby. As Black Dog lifted my limp arm, I tried to not think of what I wanted to do to these men, instead I tried to focus on playing dead, as I ran down the questions I wanted answers to: *Where the hell was I? Where was Gator? And what had happened to Candy?*

Satisfied that I was still out of it, Black Dog left me on my scrap of carpet. He nudged me once with the tip of his sneaker, before heading to the sofa across the room. I could only see his legs and feet as he plopped down on the squeaky cushions. A few seconds later, I heard the snick of a lighter followed by the skunky, sweet smell of high quality weed.

Black Dog was quite the smoker, taking long drags followed by coughing fits and then, giggles.

I had the brief idea that I could stand up and walk out. If he tried to stop me I'd convince him that I was a hallucination. The real girl was still lying on the floor waiting for him to drug her again.

I must have dozed off, because the light in the room was different when I opened my eyes for real and the hands on me this time didn't belong to Black Dog.

The guy was pulling on my arm, shaking me. Black Dog stood beside him, bright red headphones around his neck. Tinny music filtered out. He bobbed his head in time. "Where you got to take her, Jabby?"

I squinted at the second man. He was Skull Shirt, the guy who'd stolen my knife. Maybe twice now. He said, "I don't know. Another house I guess. Someone asking questions about her."

"Who? That man she with?"

"I don't know! Just do what Hollywood said to do. You want to know? You ask him."

"I'm not asking him," Black Dog said, backing up to the doorway. "She should go to the party. They would like her."

"That's not up to us. Besides, you know that's not how it works."

I sat up, batting away Jabby's hands, pushing my hair out of my face. My head felt too big for my neck and my back ached from sleeping on the floor. I stood, feeling like I was on a boat. "All right," I said, clearing my throat. "I think you guys made your point."

They grinned. Before they had a chance to turn my words into knife jokes, I continued, "You got Candy back, no harm, no foul. Now you let *me* go and we forget all about this. I'll leave town and you'll never see me again."

They looked at each other, then back at me and started laughing.

"No. No, no, no," Jabby said, shaking his head.

"What?" I asked. "Why not?"

"Because someone wants to see you. Come on. We're going for a ride."

He reached for my arm and I tugged it back. He reached again, and I stepped in and popped him in the face. The heel of my right hand making a splat sound as it connected with his nose.

Black Dog yelled "Hey!" as my left also connected though it fell short of the target—Jabby's throat—landing instead south of his collarbone.

"Fuck!" Jabby cried falling to his knees with his hands on his face, blood dripping through his fingers.

Black Dog stepped forward, then must have thought better of it, as he retreated to the doorway, pulling a gun, training it on me.

I raised my hands, but didn't stop moving, taking slow steps forward.

He shouted in Somali and a few seconds later, the beany beefy guy, Big Abdi, appeared. Black Dog said something to him and sent him off, then turned to me telling me to be still.

"You okay, Jabby?" he asked, as Jabby pulled himself upright, bracing himself on the couch, his hand leaving a bloody print.

Jabby looked my way and Black Dog warned him off, his Somalian words guttural and sharp.

Big Abdi returned with Hollywood. He tossed a wet cloth to Jabby who pressed it against his nose and moaned. Hollywood approached, looking older, less like a boy on the bicycle as he pulled a strap of tubing from his pocket.

Big Adbi grabbed me, pinning my arms behind my back as I twisted and yelled until Black Dog stepped in, his gun arm now steady.

Hollywood tsk-tsked and shook his head again, scolding me like a child. "You don't get it, do you? We will tame you. You'll see. They all break somewhere."

I fought them off the best I could, wriggling, kicking and squirming until Black Dog fired a shot into the floor between my legs, pitting the wood, spraying me with rot.

Hollywood tied off my arm with the tubing and pulled out a syringe. He leaned in, poking my vein and said, "In time, you will not remember how to fight. You will learn that girls who follow the rules get treated well."

"And the others?" I asked, my eyes beaming hate into his.

He whispered, "They get what they give. And sometimes, they find themselves under a bridge."

As the heroin kicked in, a girl appeared in the doorway smoking a cigarette. She was part real, part mirage. A snippet of music played—my ring tone for Gator. I searched the room expecting to see him, hoping beyond hope. The girl held up a phone, stared at the display, then slid her finger down the screen, dismissing the call. Her words floated to me on a haze of smoke, shimmering blue and green and yellow as my eyelids drooped.

"Say good-bye, Jojo Boudreaux. Enjoy the ride."

Candy.

CHAPTER 13

Over the next three or four days, I was moved multiple times. Once, I'm thinking they took me around the block and returned me to the same house, putting me in a new room. Each time I was moved I was bound, mouth taped shut, head hooded. I could still hear and smell. One time, the brightness of the day allowed me to see a bit more than they knew.

From the sounds of school buses, laughing children and loud southern men who disagreed about politics to the scent of a passing garbage truck, most of the houses—unlike the blue crack house—seemed to be in regular neighborhoods.

Unless we were in a vehicle, they kept me locked up and away from the others. I tried to keep track of time, but when they drugged or beat me, I never knew how long I'd been out. It could drive you crazy, wear on your sanity if you tried too hard to be right, if you thought you had to know everything, had to figure out the whys of faceless people. At some point, you have to keep your knowledge closer. Tell yourself, I have all my fingers and toes. I am dehydrated. I have no tears to shed. My right hand hurts far more than my left. I am still someone who matters. People are looking for me. I need to stay in shape. I need to stay strong. My name is Jojo Boudreaux.

Everything was skewed from the drugs. I couldn't trust my instincts. I was afraid my body was becoming used to the dosage they were giving me. At first it was just heroin, then they must have added other things to my food and water. I took in as little as I could and tried to act more wasted than I felt, thinking they would ease up on me, instead sharing the stash with the girls who were greedy for more, willing to do anything for a fix.

I heard the girls begging, offering sexual favors, making deals. I was glad I couldn't see. I wanted to smack them, ask them, *Where's your dignity?* Instead, I had to listen as Jabby and Black Dog ordered them around like dogs, telling them to strip, to dance for them, to kneel or bend over, to take what they were giving them and ask for more. When the men were done, they might give the girl a fix, her satisfied moans more real than theirs had been, or they might slap her, call her a dumb bitch and tell her to go see Big Adbi or Hollywood and one time they mentioned someone called Boss Man.

I wasn't sure where the other girls went in their heads when they got high, but for me, the drugs took me back. To Louisiana. To California. To days on the road with Gator in the Kenworth, the rumble of road beneath me, the shimmer of pavement ahead. To the plantation in Bunkie in the middle of a duck hunt, the sounds of fifty flapping wings, the smell of wet dog and bayou. I went down in those realistic dreams gladly to hide from the reality I couldn't change. The weak part of me that I had fought so hard to overcome after Boone's death was threatening to return, both in body and mind. Like Hollywood said, they were breaking me.

Jarred out of one of my drugged naps by shouting and gunfire, I wriggled upright, my back against a wall. More shots were fired, a woman screamed and I rolled over and over until I bumped into a couch. With my arms tied behind me, I pulled myself to my knees and dipped my head shaking it and shaking it until the hood slipped off. It was daylight in the curtained room, the door partially open, unattended. Somewhere a small voice said, *Come home, Shâ.*

The rope dug into my too thin wrists as I stretched and pulled. The responding tug at my feet told me I'd been hog-tied. A quick scan of the room yielded nothing helpful for my escape—no sharp edges or implements. I dropped to the floor, tucked myself into a ball and wriggled my arms down behind my legs, down the back of my calves, then under my feet. In front of me, shaking fingers worked at the rope and tape on my ankles, freeing one foot. More noise from the hall, someone ran past. I crawled to the doorway and peeked out. Nothing. I rubbed the rope against the splintery wood frame. *Come on. Come on.* Shouts came from the kitchen, men arguing. Another girl screamed, followed by a loud slap, then a thud.

Shit.

The rope began to unravel. I pulled, wrestling with the knots, alternating between lifting it toward my mouth to use my teeth, then back on the door jam, chafing my skin as I dragged my arms across the wood. Two more tries and the rope broke, freeing the connection from ankles to wrists. I stood fully upright for the first time in days, shook out my legs to get the blood going, then glanced down the hall in the direction of the kitchen, turned and hobbled away, muscles on fire, arms outstretched like a battering ram.

Another door in the hall was ajar, blue light from computer screens filtered out. I eased the door open. Three girls wearing headsets sat naked in front of large monitors. A timer ticked down the seconds on the top of each girl's screen. They danced and shimmied, offering body parts to their virtual clients as if they were negotiating at a produce stand.

In the corner beside a table of sex toys, a video camera on a tripod blinked green. One of the girls yawned loudly, then turned away from her screen to snort a line of coke on her desk. She rubbed a finger under her nose, readjusted her headset and turned back to the monitor saying, "What do you want me to do today, Bob?"

I closed the door and kept going. I made it as far as the back deck.

The hand that tugged at my leg was small and brown.

"Wha-at?" I hissed, almost tripping.

"Shhh. Get in here. Hurry." The hand raised a flap of the tarp draped over a patio table.

I scurried underneath getting a glimpse at her face before she dropped the plastic, putting us in darkness. I felt along the struts of the metal table until I found a sharp edge, then positioned my wrists over the point and sliced through the knot freeing my hands.

The girl watched silently as I tossed the frayed rope and rubbed my wrists. She offered me a section of the blanket she wore over her shoulders. I accepted and moved in closer. It felt warmer now than when Gator and I first arrived in Oklahoma City, but true spring must be weeks away.

The girl's fingers shook as she lifted the edge of the tarp and peered into the darkness.

I whispered, "What are you—"

"Shhh," she said, cutting me off. "They're just inside the door."

"Who?"

She dropped the tarp and turned to me, eyes blackened and teary, nose swollen with a tell-tale bump on the ridge, similar to the damage I'd done to Jabby.

"They hit you?" I asked, not really surprised, only that she had managed to get away, and then pleased that she didn't seem as wasted or desperate as the other girls.

She shrugged.

"You're going to be okay," I said, making my voice as soft as I could, trying to hide my real tone: that I-am-so-going-to-crush-the-guy-who-did-that-to-you tone.

"It's all right. First time I didn't make my trap. Guess I deserved it."

I doubted that. No one deserved to be smacked around, have their nose broken, or be locked outside on a cold night seeking safety under a picnic table in Oklahoma City.

Instead of the lecture, I asked, "Your *trap*? What's that?"

"What I got to bring in, to get my room at night."

"Like a quota?" I said, thinking Amway and Avon and traffic cops.

"Guess so," she said, in a faraway voice. "That makes it

sound so much more...."

"Legit?" I offered.

She scoffed. "Yeah."

She tapped at the tattoo on her neck, a curling vine shape spelling out her name, *Delight*. It might have looked pretty embroidered on a pillow, but the bold call letters for the gang that followed it cheapened the effect.

"You work in that room, on the computers?" I asked, lowering my voice to a whisper.

She hesitated, "Sometimes. On the street, too." She looked at me, closer now, more wary. But she kept her voice low. "Where they got you?"

I snuck another look through the tarp. Coast still clear. "The special room, you know."

She nodded, like maybe she did know.

I adjusted my crouch, tested the silence by asking, "So, uh, Delight, what are you doing out here?"

"Just taking a break. Waiting for Hollywood to chill out, you know?" She wiped her nose with the blanket, turned to face me. "So what are you doing out here, Trucker Lady?" she asked, brows raised, challenging.

I stared at her, wondering how much she knew. "I'm getting the hell out of here," I said. "And you should do the same."

"Leave?" She shook her head. "And go where? Trust me, I've been out there, and you know what? *Here* is not so bad."

She ran a finger under her eye, tapped her broken nose, then said, "It's better than where I was living. My mother took off and my stepfather treated me like a whore—only he forgot to pay me. Here, I got a nice place to stay, friends, someone who cares about me."

It took everything in me to not correct her, to shut up and not say anything about how they didn't care. That they were only using her, putting her at risk. Every time they shot her up, every time they put her on the street, her life was on the line—not theirs. This wasn't love. It was manipulation, control, power. She was just product with an expiration date.

Delight hung her head. "It's not perfect. I know that, but they're my family and this place, it's my home. I've been here over a year. And now it's all I know." She touched my arm. "You're still new," she said. "Wait a while and it'll sink in."

Wait? I shook my head. "No. You don't understand. They kidnapped me. I have a real family, a job, a place to go. People are looking for me right now."

She smiled. "Sure they are."

Listen," I said, handing her back the edge of the blanket and scooting to my knees. "I'm getting out of here and I want you to come with me. You can start over somewhere else. You don't have to do this."

She turned away, sniffling.

"You're not like the others," I said. "I can tell."

She scoffed, turning back to me. "I'm *not* like them. I'm not stupid, which is how I know you're not going anywhere. Boss Man has plans for you at the palace. Kidnapped or of your free will, you're *theirs* now and if they can make money off you, make you into a *dhillo*, then there is no way they're going to let you go."

Dhillo? Palace?

"What do you mean, let me?" I scoffed. "I'm not asking. Screw that. I'm out of here." I reached for the tarp. "Now are coming with me—"

The porch light flared yellow as the back door flew open. White high-heeled boots stomped toward us, a second later the tarp was ripped from my hand and pulled from the table. I scooted out, crouching in a martial arts stance ready to fight.

Candy sang, "Peek-a-Boo. I see you!" She giggled, almost tipping over on her heels, wasted. She took a long drag off her cigarette. I hadn't seen her in two nights, not since she'd stood in the doorway holding my phone.

She exhaled a long plume as behind her Jabby and Black Dog stepped into the light.

CHAPTER 14

The past few days taught me that the Somalis operated on two levels: attack or asleep. It might have been wearying for anyone else, but to me, it was simply reminiscent of boyfriend eight, a short-tempered, whisky-loving man who was better suited for the Wild West than twenty-first-century America. He certainly could handle a horse though, and what woman doesn't like a man in a saddle?

After pulling me and Delight off the back patio and shoving us headlong into the house, I sensed a change in the air around Jabby and Black Dog. It was more exasperation than their usual fury and I began to wonder how old these boys were, how they had come to be living in Oklahoma City and who was pulling their strings?

They brought us into the kitchen, sat us at a long table, then stood behind us.

"Give me your hands," Jabby said.

I scooted forward in the chair, bringing my hands behind me.

"No. Wrap your arms around the back."

I sighed, making a production of his demand. Delight watched me wide-eyed, biting back a smile.

Jabby pulled his knife and leaned over her, his voice low and mean. "What so funny bitch? I deal with you next. You might want to be thinking about that."

Delight's small smile vanished as the light in her eyes dimmed.

Black Dog stepped in with a roll of duct tape. As he bound my wrists, I scanned the room. No knife set on the counter, no hanging pot rack, no loose rugs, or glass vases or gas stovetop.

No obvious weapons except the one I carried with me—always.

"Is the Boss Man ready for me, yet?" I asked, tugging at my duct-taped wrists. I'd heard of the elusive Boss Man, but that was it, just his name and a reference to a place called The Palace. Now that Delight had brought him up again, it was worth a try.

Jabby grinned. "Boss Man? What you know about him, now?"

"Just what Hollywood told me," I said.

Jabby hesitated, then snuck a glance toward Black Dog who was busy ogling Delight, his steamy gaze everywhere but her face.

Jabby lowered his voice. "Well, Hollywood don't know everything. But maybe someone else do."

"Is that right? And who is that someone?" I asked.

He puffed out his chest, rocked back on his heels and grinned. "Some things you better off not knowing, Trucker Lady."

"Why don't you let me be the judge of that?"

Black Dog whistled under his breath and Jabby reached in and pinched me, grabbing an inch of flesh on the back of my upper arm and twisting. I tried to focus through the tears.

"No fucking judge here!" He said, twisting harder, leaning in, breath foul in my face. "No fucking judge."

"No marks, Jabby," Black Dog said, finally prying his eyes from Delight.

Jabby gave one last twist. "You talk too much Trucker Lady. You must learn to keep your mouth closed or I will make you."

He reached into his pocket, opened a small tin of pills.

Black Dog said, "Hey, remember what Hollywood said?"

"Shut up." He held the pill in front of my mouth. "Take it."

"Or else?" I asked.

"You don't want to find out."

The glitter in his eyes convinced me. I opened my mouth, swallowed. They stood over me until the drug took effect. The last thing I saw was Black Dog's gold-toothed grin as I slumped over.

I dreamt of Gator, of the last night we'd spent in Sabrina's sleeper. We'd put on an action film and turned up the volume until the truck windows rattled, the sounds of sirens and squealing tires almost too real. I'd made popcorn and changed into my pajamas, calling it my drive-in movie outfit.

"You're too young to know about drive-in movies," Gator said.

"Am not. Besides, they still have them some places."

"Really? Why would anyone go to a drive-in when you can have your own movie theater at home, with your own bathroom just steps away?"

"It's part of the experience," I said. "You can make your own hamburgers at home too, but millions of people go out for burgers every day."

"Millions? Sure about that?"

"You know what I mean," I said, punching him playfully.

"Hey," he said, tapping me back.

"Hey, yourself," I said, giving him a knuckled fist to the forearm.

"No. Hey *yourself*," he said, grabbing me by the waist and flipping me onto the bed. Before I could object, he scrambled on top and pinned me.

"Whoa," I laughed. "What is this? Is your secret life as a *luchadora* coming out?"

"Hah-ha. Funny." Gator leaned in to kiss me. I saw the fire in his eyes, and wriggled beneath him. He grinned. I strained my neck, reached his and gave him a nip. He pulled back and I escaped his grasp, but he regained his lead, using something he called the Tilt-a-Whirl. We tussled around a little, and I tried the move I knew from TV, the Turnbuckle Bulldog.

Gator countered with some fancy arm and hand winding

work, which had me on my stomach and feeling a little ticklish when he pressed his mouth near my ear saying, "I was pretty good in high school," he said. "Scouts came out and everything."

"Yeah," I said laughing. I lowered my voice and put on a Philly accent. "You *coulda* been a contender."

We laughed, collapsing into each other, feeding off the silliness, off the camaraderie, off the love.

I woke to the sound of urine splashing in a toilet, overshooting onto my arm. *What the fuck?* I sat up, smacking my head on the underside of the sink. My wrists were taped to the ceramic pedestal. I leaned into my hands, ran a finger over my cheek, feeling the imprint of the floor tiles, ridges where grout should be, before I recognized the shoes that belonged to the guy pissing beside me.

Hollywood said, "Good morning, Trucker Lady. Did you sleep well?"

I found a spot on the wall, bit down hard on the words threatening to escape. He shuffled his feet. The sound of his zipper preceded the flush of the toilet. His feet moved again and still I didn't acknowledge him. It was all part of our silent dance. He finally crouched in front of me, drew a knife, then quickly slashed the duct tape, nicking my arm in the process. He didn't help me up, but stepped back so I could rise on my own accord. I tried to look strong. I tried to look angry and mean, but I was weak and tired, soft, worn and wearied. I felt like a hand-me-down moccasin, the lost half of the pair.

"That way," he said, pushing me forward, his finger jabbing into my shoulder blade. "Nadifa needs to see you."

I'd heard the name Nadifa, along with some of the girl's names, or at least their aliases—like the ones you'd read on the credits of a porn movie—Starring Missy Delight and Maxi Pleasure! Some names could have been the Somalis idea of a joke, sounding as if they had combined a pet's name with a city—Fluffy Detroit,

Lady Paris and Heidi LA.

I wondered about this woman, Nadifa. The gang didn't speak of her in the same way as the other girls. From what I'd seen, most of these boys couldn't figure their way out of a paper bag. Sure, the girls they pimped were young and stupid—for the most part. Kept drugged up and needy, they'd probably quickly gone from being victims to willing accomplices. But it had to be more than drugs for some of them. Intimidation, suggestion, threatening the families, periods of isolation and abuse, followed by false tenderness, love, small kindnesses. Shit like that could break you too. We all had our weakness.

If there was some sort of mastermind behind their business, I certainly hadn't met him yet. Maybe that was the problem, maybe *he* was a *she*. Who else would know more about manipulation and mind control than a woman?

Another jab from Hollywood and I stopped short in front of a closed door. I looked back, trying to count the doors we'd passed, angry at myself for not being more diligent.

"Go on," he said.

"After you," I said, dipping my head.

His eyes clouded, then he shook his head. His hesitation was enough to pique my curiosity. I hadn't seen Hollywood back down from anyone, had never seen him show fear. Before I could say anything, he opened the door.

Big Abdi stood beside a long black desk, looking like a statue of a mountain. A seated woman stared into a laptop and without glancing up, raised one finger in our direction

Hollywood pushed me over the threshold, stepped back and closed the door. The carpet was thick, rich. The walls were painted red, matching curtains hung from shiny gold rods. What wasn't red or black in the room was gold. I wasn't sure what they were going for, Vatican chic, Renaissance meets Contemporary or perhaps, *The Business Office of a Whoremaster*.

The woman clicked a few keys, then made some complicated head and hand gestures as if she'd been on a video call.

"Come in, please," she said, closing the laptop and standing, smoothing out layers of draping fabric.

I stepped forward, taking baby steps like we were playing "Mother May I." Eyes on me, she tipped her head to Big Abdi, murmured something in their language and motioned to the door. He bowed and left the room, like an obedient puppy.

She was tall, rivaling my height inch for inch. It was hard to see what sort of body she had under all that blue fabric. I figured I could take her, but wished I knew what was behind those curtains. How high of a drop would it be if I crashed through a window? What might break my fall?

"Something amusing?" she asked.

"No," I said, shaking away the image of me using this woman's clothes as a parachute.

"Good."

She circled me, appraising, tabulating. When she reached for my wrists, her touch was cool, gentle. She raised my arms, asked me to turn, slowly, then she ran her hands over my head, fingers probing my skull, down my temples, to the back of my neck. I almost moaned in pleasure. It had been so long since I'd been touched with tenderness, since I had felt anything close to human kindness. I blinked myself back into the room and the situation, considering again, if I could take her down.

"Just relax, please," she said softly, as if she'd read my thoughts. "I'm almost done."

"What are you doing?" I asked. "What's this about? Who are you?"

She said nothing but stepped back to her desk, typed something into her phone, then smiled at me, her lips curling over perfectly straight white teeth, her glittery coal black eyes locked on mine. "So many questions. And none of them the right one."

The door opened behind me. I felt Big Abdi's presence before his hand clamped on my arm, before the needle went in.

CHAPTER 15

I was lying on a cot in the house that smelled like bacon, when Jabby brought me a sandwich and a bottle of water. He pulled the hood off my head, then the tape from my mouth.

"She says you are to eat. If you do not, she will feed you herself."

I ran my tongue over my teeth and looked up at him blinking. It was sunny, too bright. "Who?" I asked, looking around.

"Nadifa," he said, shoving the sandwich at me.

I reached for the bottle of water. "Why?"

"Why what?" Jabby asked. "Why will she feed you? Because you have not eaten much in days, and for this client, we cannot have you looking like this..." He ran his hand in vague circles, making me wonder what I looked like to him.

"What does it matter?" I scoffed. "You're going to kill me anyway."

"Is that what you think?" He laughed. "If we wanted to do that, it would be already done. But here you are."

Again, why? And who was this special client?

I drank the water, took a bite of the sandwich. Jabby checked his watch, then reached into his pocket.

"No," I said, dropping the sandwich and putting up my hands. "No more drugs. You said if I stopped fighting, there would be no more drugs."

"Relax," Jabby said. He produced a tube of antiseptic cream and a bandage. "Roll up your sleeve."

He's fixing me, I thought, making me look good for the *sale*, for their client. What was the point? I was already damaged goods. We were all damaged goods. I wasn't Jojo anymore. None of us were who we were born to be. They had taken that from us forever.

There were footsteps in the hall. Then her voice. Nadifa. I hadn't seen her since that day in her office. I didn't even know if we were in the same house, the one with the red room. I imagined her striding through the halls, her flowing garments like wings, her cruel eyes focused on something no one else could see, her hand on the door, opening it to men with brief-cases of money. Her red lips curled into a smile.

I was very close to putting all the pieces together. From the internet sex business to the private parties, auctions and hooker bartering. How some girls left the house and returned most days and others, like me, never got to leave. Every day I prayed that Gator would find me, that someone would talk, that my phone would be traced—the phone Candy had stolen from me and used in the motel to call the gang to rescue her.

I hadn't given up. I wouldn't be their slave, no matter how much they tried to break me. My ribs ached from the last beat-ing. Jabby and Black Dog each had a turn until Hollywood broke it up.

He'd handed me a wet towel, brought me ice, asking, "What is wrong with you? Maybe all you understand is violence? Is that your language? You need to stop thinking there is anything else for you. You are here and you are ours. We own you."

Stuck here inside the walls with a bunch of strangers, it wasn't what I knew but what I didn't know that would save me. I could only hope that as fucked up as I was, that as messy as my world had become that somewhere outside past this bed, that door, those assholes, somewhere out in the sunshine, Gator had his shit together and was doing everything possible to find me.

Once on a late-night drop, waiting for the receiver to show up, Gator and I watched a documentary about missing children and the people who search for them. One lady who wasn't able to have kids of her own, undertook each opportunity to find a child as her calling in life. Another searcher was a guy who thought he had special talents, not super hero talents, but more of a psychic nature, or as Gator called it, "Psycho nature."

I got it. Really, I did. In life, everyone was in it for themselves. On the outside, they might look like they were helping, using their talents for the greater good, wanting to help. But really, in the end, *they* had the story to tell, the experience to relive, the *look at me* moment. They were selfish bastards. And the kids they saved? They went back home to a place where people expected them to be the same kid they once were, to slip back into a world they may never have been comfortable in, in the first place. But now, abused, raped, addicted, belittled, adored, hated, renamed, they could never return to a past in which they were the little boy who played T-ball in the back yard, the sweet teen who liked to bake cookies and write poetry. The family, if it had survived at all, would never be "back to normal." Was there such a thing? No one would ever say it, but those stolen children were probably better off dead.

It didn't matter how much I tried to forget, the images came back. The first time, the fifth, or when they set me up in a room with a real bed, real curtains and carpeted floors. Candles lit that smelled like cinnamon. They had curled my hair into tightly wound ringlets that skimmed the tops of my breasts, barely covered by an itchy red teddy. There was no mirror, but I could feel the layers of makeup they'd applied, figured it was best to not know what I looked like. Easier to become Maxine that way.

The rap on the door wasn't to ask if it was okay to enter, it was to wake me up. I knew. They'd done it before.

The first guy came in, light filtered behind him leaving his face in shadows. Better that way. I always closed my eyes, didn't want to see faces, the shape of their mouth, the way pleasure changed their eyes. Didn't want those fucking nightmares, too.

He wore a belt. Unusual. Took his time unbuckling, unzipping.

"You want something extra?" I asked, tipping my head toward the "nightstand"—an upended orange paint bucket—where a plate held two toothpick-sized lines of heroin, a rolled-up single and an expired credit card.

He hesitated, clutching his pants. "How much?"

"Bump for five. Line for ten."

I wasn't supposed to sell the shit, just snort it and sometimes smoke it, but it was part of my plan to get the hell out of here, and to keep a least a little control. The other girls were doped up on the hour, most by choice. I'd learned to act like a fucking junkie and use the money the johns gave me to buy favors. Twenty more bucks and I'd get access to a phone. If the chick hiding it didn't OD before that.

Guy stepped toward the dope, reaching for the straw.

"Pay first," I said.

"Nah, I'm good. Omar knows me. I'll pay him."

I heard the accent in his voice, the way he trilled his Rs.

"*Esse*, this is a separate transaction. We keep it that way, *entiende?*" I said, pulling down the top of the silky nightie they made me wear, shaking out my hair, letting him get a good look at my tits.

"*Entiendo.*" He grinned, one gold tooth winking back at me.

I stuffed the ten under the mattress, found the lube bottle while he did his line, then turned around, kneeling on the bed before he could pull himself free from his boxers. Another thing I didn't want to see.

It was easier to face the wall, to offer my ass. To give them something fitting. It was a deal I'd made the first time they forced a man on me.

Afterward? He paid extra.

This one spit into his hand, stroked himself. I saw the shadow move. I hoped I'd used enough lube, hoped his cock wouldn't tear me any more than I already was from the last guy, and above all, hoped he'd be fast.

It was different each time. I wished it wasn't. I wished that I could just think a dick's a dick, or a lay's a lay. I certainly wasn't cataloguing the johns. I had a different approach. Forget everything. Immediately. I was no longer Jojo. I was the one they called Maxine and that girl had nothing, including memories.

No one loved her. No one was looking for her. She had no reason to be clean, or straight or free. She was a throwaway that no one would miss.

Gold Tooth sniffed, then sighed. I waited.

His hands were rough, worker's hands. They grabbed my hips, slapped my ass, gripped my shoulders and afterward, after he'd slumped over me with the heat of his fat stomach on my back, only then as his cock slid out, limp, soft, sticky, only then did he choose to reach around and tenderly graze my nipples with the back of his hand, as if he knew the calluses on his palm would hurt. As if he cared.

It was like this each time, a trivial form of thankfulness offered. A word, a sound, an action. I didn't dwell on it. I needed to hate them, pity them. I needed that anger to fuel my escape. I needed to refuse any tenderness so that my heart, like the precious parts of my body that I kept to myself, would never be touched by these animals.

CHAPTER 16

There were six of us with brown hair, some real, some wigs, but all long and straight, white blouses unbuttoned showing a peek of red, skin spray tanned to the same hue, skirts short enough to be lifted by a brisk Oklahoma City wind.

Behind the contacts that gave us light blue eyes, we were not the same girl at all. Some of us had loving parents, parents that spent three days a week in the church on kneelers, praying, begging, negotiating. Others had boyfriends, classmates, puppies or college scholarships waiting for our return. Some had no idea where they were born, who their father was or even their real birth date. I knew one thing. We were unique, special. But not to the Somalis.

They waited until the lunch hour, then drove us in a white van outfitted with extra rows, as if we were going on a field trip. Windows tinted too dark to be legal, music coming from the radio, nothing like I'd ever heard in any civilized place. Three men in front. Big Abdi driving, while Jabby sat in the middle, drunk and singing.

In the city, they dropped Omar with us. One of the meaner Somalis, he stood across the street watching, keeping us in line, gun bulging in the pocket of his thin coat, eyes piercing, tattooed cheekbone like a lightning bolt, or a scar. The van drove off with Candy, giving her a select spot two blocks south.

The girl they called Raquel was the second one picked up. The guy drove her down the street and pulled into an alley. We could still see the back end of his blue BMW.

Ginger went next in an SUV, with two boys wearing HBB

college sweatshirts. The one refusing to pay, saying he was just the driver. Omar didn't seem to like that much, but maybe there was a certain point where you had to trust that the fear and dependence you'd instilled in your girls was enough. Plus the fact they knew you had a gun, and a temper.

The wind was picking up. Part of me that remembered how being outside felt, knew this was the sort of gearing-up Mother Nature did before she jammed her fist inside you, wiggled her fingers and ripped open your walls. It was her brand of foreplay.

I pressed closer to Delight, trying to talk without moving my lips, playing up my fake high, eyes on our keeper. "Why does Candy get her own spot? What the hell, right? We all fucking look the same, so what's the deal?

Delight reached into the small purse hanging off her shoulder. They gave all of us one, place to keep our money, condoms, tissues. She fished out a bent stub of a cigarette, lit it with a pack of matches we weren't supposed to have, inhaled deeply, then answered me. "She's earned it. Don't worry. When she's busy, or if she don't like the guy, she'll send him down to us."

Her cigarette, or her voice had drawn the attention of Omar. He stepped into the street, headed for us.

I spoke fast. "I need you to borrow her phone. Just for me to make one call. I got money."

Delight started to pull away. I snagged her sleeve. "I won't tell. You know—"

A car skidded around the corner, tires squealing, bearing down on us, fishtailing, weaving, a blonde at the wheel. Omar jumped back onto the sidewalk, started yelling.

The car, an old maroon sedan with a rusted hood slammed to a stop, engine ticking and pinging, rocking as the blonde spilled from the driver's side, brown wig in her hand.

Fuck. It was Amanda. She'd snagged the first john within minutes of us getting dropped off. I'd almost forgotten she was gone, tried to remember the face of the guy, his build, age, anything.

Delight and I ran and caught her before she fell. Her face was too pale, eyes too wide.

"You okay? What happened?" I asked, scanning her for blood, broken bones.

She shook her head, pointed to the car with a trembling hand. "Not me. It's him. Shit. Shit. Shit. I think I fucking killed him."

Omar pushed past us, leaned into the car. The front seat was empty. Omar's gun peeked from his jacket pocket as he leaned over the seat to check the back. He moved faster than I thought he could, backing out of the car, ripping the back door open, pulling out a limp body. Guy must have been in his sixties—late sixties—gone bald on top, bit of a monk thing happening. His fly was undone, sad, shriveled penis flapping, dripping.

I forced myself to look away, eyes bouncing back to Omar with his hands full, that gun, a Walther maybe, pushing its way free.

All I had to do was step a little closer and grab it.

The old guy yowled, flipped his eyes open, started batting at Omar. Delight pointed at his dick, laughing, saying something in Portuguese.

Omar grabbed the guy's arms, glanced back at Amanda. "Hey, he pay you?"

Fucking Omar. All he cared about was the money.

"Yeah," She said, trying to put her wig back on. "I'm sorry. I didn't know what to do. He passed out or something. We was in the back and he—"

Omar stopped listening, started shaking the old man, yelling in his face, telling him he was lucky he wasn't dead, telling him he'd better not come around anymore, so intent on telling him that he didn't notice the slow-moving minivan with the woman and her phone.

I stepped into the road, willing the woman to react. *Come on, take a picture. Please. Call someone. Do something.*

I pushed my face into the light, as the other girls shrank back.

I did the one thing I could think to do and raised my hand in a salute gesture, but higher, tapping my forehead, then fisting my hand and pumping it in the air.

Omar looked at me. "What you doing? Get the fuck over there!"

He swatted at me, the back of his hand connecting with my bare, cold leg, leaving knuckle marks. I stood my ground, watching him. He had his hands full. The man with his penis sticking out of his pants, the woman in the minivan with the camera phone, me standing in the middle the road jerking my fisted hand up and down.

I took a step back, let Omar have one less choice to make. He reached in his coat pocket for the Walther, one hand still on the old man. The old man was blubbering, tears on his cheeks, saying, "Please. No."

Omar watched the minivan idling at the traffic light half a block away. He shoved the old man into the driver's seat, slammed the door.

"Get the fuck out of here and don't let me see you again!"

Omar grabbed my arm, dragged me over to the girls, then took out his phone and called someone, squinting at the rear of the minivan. The light turned green and the minivan sped away, the old man's sedan not far behind.

Omar said something into the phone in his singsong language. He used enough gestures and body language that I could tell he was worried and angry. Finally he nodded, tucking the gun deeper into his pocket, said something like, "Waa yahay," then hung up and turned to us.

"Fuck a shit. Too much noise here. We got to move."

I followed his eyes. Raquel was trotting back to us, shoving cash in her wristlet.

Omar roped her in, backed us up to the building we'd been standing in front of. We huddled together as the wind kicked up, tumbling a beer can in the gutter. The sound reminded me of cowboys with spurs in Westerns.

Omar flirted with Raquel, taking her money, stroking her cheek, thrusting his pelvis in her direction, as she described her john. We waited for the others to come back. Omar scanned the empty street, gave everyone a bump, something I couldn't avoid. I snorted it, ran my finger under my nose, pushing as much out as I could. I tried to stop looking at the Walther. I tried to stop remembering who I really was. Here. Now. I had to be Maxine if I wanted to survive.

As much as I'd tried to turn off my brain every second since they took me, I couldn't stop thinking. I'd go from plotting my escape, how I was going to put my stiletto heel through any Somali's eye, tear off his dick and stuff it down his throat—to figuring out a better way to run girls on the streets. How it could be so much safer and smarter and cleaner, and make more money. I was a problem solver at heart. A fixer. But it was dangerous to go down that path, believing there was a single piece of this fucked up life that was acceptable.

I pinched my leg, bringing myself back to the surface, shutting out everything but the girls. I was more determined than ever to get myself—and them—out of this.

The SUV with the Baptist college boys pulled up. Ginger tumbled out, giggling and smiling, blouse buttoned up wrong. She waved to the boys as they sped off, then joined the group.

Omar stuck his nose in Ginger's hair.

"What fuck is this? Smoking weed? You stupid cunt!" He slapped her, knocking her backward, bending her nose sideways.

Ginger yelped, crumpled to a heap, cupping her nose. Amanda dropped her purse, knelt to help her.

Delight looked at Omar. "You fucking broke her nose. How's she going to work, huh?"

"Yeah," I said. "Big Abdi is not going to be happy about that."

Omar looked at us, raised a hand, curled it into a fist, cocking it.

"Forget Abdi. What about Hollywood?" Candy asked.

She had sauntered her way back to us while we were busy watching the Omar Smackdown Show. Lipstick perfectly in place, not a wrinkle on her blouse, she held out a thick roll of cash.

"Here. I made my trap. Can I go home?"

Raquel stepped in, helping Ginger, moving her back a few steps. Omar's eyes slid from us to the wad of cash to Candy, then back.

He lowered his arm and reached for the money.

I thought about how easy it would be for us to take him. How that gun was right there, how I could race to the alley across the street, how it would lead to another, and another. How no one was watching, and if they were, they wouldn't give a shit about a dead pimp, or a runaway whore.

But the way Candy had said *home,* and the way the others had looked when she said it, told me I was on my own.

Omar counted Candy's money, added it to the mound in his pocket. "We wait for the van. Then you take that one and clean her up." He shot a curse at Ginger in his singsong talk, then spat on the sidewalk. "I'll be sure you get a special visitor later, just to remind you who makes the rules and who follows them."

No one said anything else until we were inside the van, Jabby in the driver's seat, hands tight on the wheel. He sang softly with the radio, stared at the darkening sky. The van rocked with the wind, trees bent sideways, the few people on the street were having trouble walking against it.

I leaned in toward Delight, pretending to adjust her blouse, whispered, "So, Candy and the phone, will you do it?"

Delight started to reply as Omar clicked off his phone call and spun around.

"You four," he said, pointing to me, Delight, Raquel and Amanda. "You got a private party."

"Not me," Delight said. "Big Abdi told me I have to do that no more."

"Not my problem. They need four. You're going."

"What about Candy? Can't she go instead of me?"

"Fuck you, bitch," Candy said. "He didn't pick me. He picked you." She smiled, showing the missing tooth on her left side. "You must be special." She laughed, poked Ginger in the side. "What you think, ho? Think she's special?"

Ginger didn't look up. The blood on the front of her blouse had spread across both breasts. I wondered how much blood a malnourished, emaciated, heroin addict could lose. Candy kept poking her, Ginger's head bobbing on her too long neck, Delight staring.

Jabby said something to Omar, pointing to the road in front of them, to the sky above it.

Delight met my eyes. I raised a brow, asking my question again. She blinked, then nodded once.

I shot her a quick smile as Jabby turned up the radio.

The storm was gaining in strength, being upgraded to tornado. It might be a day before it hit Oklahoma City, but it was out there forming. People were supposed to get inside, use their shelters, definitely get off the roads.

Omar said something to Jabby, then twisted the radio dial clicking it off.

CHAPTER 17

The van rolled up to the apartment complex where Jabby punched in a code that opened the gates, allowing him to drive through. Omar checked his phone, motioned toward the parking garage.

Jabby found a spot near the elevator and Omar came around to open the van door and let us out. "Let's go." He hustled us along, shoved us into a line. I glanced at Ginger slumped in the back.

"Have fun, girls," Candy said climbing into the front seat, waving like we were her fans.

Delight flipped her the bird and Amanda doubled it.

Omar corralled us into the elevator, hit the button for the fourth floor.

It was the last apartment in the hall. Music drifted out as the door opened. Omar went first.

A linebacker-sized dude with shaggy brown hair stood in the doorway. He put his hand on Omar's chest, holding him back. "Just the girls. That was the deal."

Omar leaned into the guy's hand, peered around him into the room. They exchanged a look, came to an agreement. Deciding factor might have been safety concerns, or the weight of the envelope Shaggy Hair held.

Amanda pressed past Omar. "Come on, girls. We ain't got all night."

Raquel followed, then Delight reaching for my hand, pulling me along. The apartment was brightly lit, curtains drawn back from sliding glass doors. It was clean, like hotel maid clean, furnished like a model home, down to matching throw pillows and drapes. The dining table was picture perfect, set with floral place-mats, china plates and silverware, dusty napkins blooming from dusty wine glasses.

Three men remained seated in the living room. Two were older, balding, visibly nervous, the other was muscled and young, checking his phone. I glanced over my shoulder to the doorway where Omar and Shaggy Hair were ironing out the details. It was fifteen steps away, the entry area too congested to make a clean escape even if I did have weapon—which I didn't. In the other direction, I could hit the sliding door to the balcony in twenty-five steps, but there was no way of knowing if the door was locked or had a security rod in the track. Even if I did make it to the balcony, there was the four-story drop to think about.

"You want a drink?" Balding Number One asked, pointing to the cooler beside the couch.

The guy had a whole kitchen, but filled a cooler for his beer? It wasn't like the place was that big, like you'd be inconvenienced to go the fridge for a refill.

I shook my head, stepped around the back of the couch, scanning for tell-tale gun bulges, running my hand over the shoulders of the two older guys, judging neck thickness, jugular proximity.

Amanda and Delight waited for Omar to leave, then grabbed beers, twisted off the caps and took long pulls.

Shaggy Hair came back in the room, made some sort of signal to the muscle guy who aimed a remote and the music got louder, much louder.

Raquel and the muscle guy left and went down the hall to a bedroom. I watched until the door shut behind them. Delight and Shaggy paired off, headed to another bedroom. Amanda and I looked at each other.

She finished her beer and began to dance.

Outside, the trees moved with her, bending and whipping, branches spread like her long brown hair. She turned her back to us and shook her hips, hands splayed on the glass of the sliding door. As the music sped up, so did her hips, until her miniskirt was a whirl of colors, her leg muscles rippling. She raised her arms, nudging the fabric of the blouse higher, exposing her smooth, brown skin. As the music slowed, the song ending, she turned around, one long hip roll, tongue tracing her lips, fingers on her shirt buttons, nipples erect, breasts straining. I didn't know if the dance had been for the men, or her, or me.

The one guy blurted out, "Are we going to have sex?"

The other one looked at him, shook his head, too vehemently. I smelled rat—or more specifically—pig.

The door to the back bedroom slammed open. Delight came barreling out, cursing, hand in the air, jutting her chin in the way she did right before she head-butted someone.

"Hey!" I yelled. "What's going on?"

"Apparently," Delight said, snugging down her skirt. "We are under arrest, bitches."

Muscle guy emerged from the back bedroom, badge on a chain, cuffs on Raquel.

She grinned. "Look at me, *chicas*. My man likes it nasty. Ooh, he's a bad boy, aren't you?" She laughed, made kissy faces.

I moved closer to the sliding door, Balding Guy Two close behind.

"Don't think about it," he said, grabbing my arm, twisting me around.

"I'm not," I said, lowering my voice. "Trust me, jail will be a step up from our current situation."

He spun me around, looked at me hard.

"What about..." I tipped my head to the apartment door.

His eyes never left mine when he said, "Collings? We good with the doorman?"

Shaggy guy answered, "Yep, got a text from downstairs. Somali in custody. Private ride leaving now. Two patrol cars on their way to take these *ladies* to processing."

"Processing?" Delight said, pulling up short, wrenching around. "Why you gonna bring us all the way out there? That place is a shit hole. We got to be in town. You know that's how we do it."

"Yeah. Why you gotta play like this?" Raquel asked.

The muscled cop grinned, tugged on Raquel. "Yeah, Collings. Why you gotta play like that?"

"Fuck you, Leroy. And just for that, miss, you're riding in the slow car." He pointed at Delight.

The older policeman with the bad breath pushed us through the hall. "All right, all right. Let's go."

We filed out, each with our own cop, their badge on display, our hands cuffed behind us.

The girls had gone quiet, as if there was some sort of unwritten directive on how to avoid prostitution prosecution. I definitely hadn't been issued the Hooker Manual. But I did read loud and clear the head shake and pursed lips from Delight, the warning look from Amanda.

They led us down to the parking garage, a dimly-lit concrete space that probably looked like a jail cell to these girls, but to me it was another opportunity to let someone know I was alive, being held against my will. I couldn't shake the feeling that Gator was nearby, looking for me.

Like a dog with a bone, Gator couldn't just drop something, simply walk away. I knew this from our disagreements. He always had to know the answer, the reason for something or it would be gnaw, gnaw, gnaw. Whether it was a question on a game show, the name of the artist who sang that song, or where we'd seen someone before, Gator could be wrong, but he couldn't be left wondering.

Sometimes I made shit up just to close the door for him. Just so the man would stop talking in his sleep.

Maybe that was what had made him such a good investigator. Or maybe that was what made him want to leave that career behind and stay on the road with me. I wondered what sort of monologue he was spewing night after night, berating himself for not being able to find me.

Rattling around in the back seat of the cop car, Delight

beside me, I shook my head to clear thoughts of Gator. I needed to focus.

There were a few possibilities. I could say nothing, get released, and take my chances making an escape from the Somali hidey hole—after they beat the shit out of me or drugged me again, or did whatever they thought they needed to do.

I could talk to the cops and tell them everything I knew. We could get word to Gator, arrange some sort of protective custody for me, for us while the case was worked, the Somali ring busted and the girls released, returned home. That one seemed a bit too hopeful, too cut and dry, so I had to add my own caveats—tell all, but to a righteous cop, have the case prosecuted by good lawyer, heard by an honorable judge, see the girls returned to happy homes. It was starting to sound like a fairy tale.

So, I decided my only choice was to play it by ear and stay open to options.

CHAPTER 18

Delight closed her eyes like she was taking a well-deserved nap, as if the back of a smelly police car was relaxing with its sealed, barred windows and hard plastic seats. Even if you got past that, there was the Plexiglas divider between you, a shotgun and two men who'd been bullied through high school but now strapped on a gun and badge every morning to serve and protect.

The cop driving, Officer Business told the cop in the passenger seat, Officer Whatever that he had to go by the station first. Whatever just shrugged as Business drove through another red light. There was no sign of the other cop car. I figured they were well on their way to the processing center wherever the hell that was.

I rehearsed in my head what I should tell them. It had to be enough that they believed me, that I was in danger, that I'd been kidnapped, forced into being this girl, Maxine. But how could I tell them that, and not the information that would get me busted too?

Part of me said they were the good guys. They'd help me, they'd listen and it would all work out. But another part of me, the cautious, streetwise part, whispered a reminder to never trust anyone.

I pushed that thought away as I leaned in toward the Plexiglas divider. "Hey, don't you need to know my real name, so you can—"

Delight smacked me from behind, her cuffed wrists scratching my arm leaving a long red line.

"What the fuck?"

I slid back into the seat my eyes lasering into hers.

"Shut up," she said.

"But I—"

She widened her eyes, shook her head tightly. "Just shut up."

I snuck a look to the cops, the driver caught my eye in the rearview mirror, licked his lips and winked like something in a bad porn movie—any porn movie.

Shit.

A few minutes later we pulled under a carport structure near a tall building. The wind that rushed into the open door as Officer Business stepped out was oddly cool, given the heat of the day.

He left the car running. Officer Whatever rolled down his window and got out his phone. He held it at arm's length, like he needed glasses, placed a video call to a chubby faced girl with pouty lips and a unibrow. I wished his home screen had a weather icon, or that he cared enough to check it.

I'd been watching the sky, the fast-moving clouds that were darker in the distance. I didn't know what tornado skies looked like, but something sure felt off.

"What do we do?" I whispered, elbowing Delight who rested against the hard plastic seat as if she was sunbathing in Monaco.

"Nothing. We just...wait. Besides, it won't be too bad," Delight said, not bothering to open her eyes.

"What won't be?" I asked.

"Jail."

"Jail? I thought we were going to some processing center where we'll get bailed out by Hollywood."

"Oh, he'll come for us eventually. Well, not him. The lawyer dude."

"What do you mean, eventually?"

"Kind of thinking we're not on his radar at the moment," she said with a yawn.

Fine by me. My mind went into escape mode.

By the time Officer Business returned, I'd played out a half dozen scenarios in my head, from kicking out the window, diving head first from the speeding patrol car—tuck and roll, tuck and roll, to feigning illness then making a run for it when they opened the handle-less rear door, even had an option of me leaping from a bridge at such a height no one would dare follow. There was the hopeful rescue, one in which a broad-chested cowboy in chaps rode in on a white horse, shotgun barrels blasting, tender fingers unlocking my cuffs, warm breath at my neck.

Eventually we arrived at the processing center, which looked like an ugly old jail to me, complete with security fencing, guard towers and barred windows. The outside lights were clicking on as the sun set, their mechanical buzz sounded like giant insects.

Officers Business and Whatever slapped a few backs, scratched their names on a clipboard, then left us in the care of two female guards, a frizzy redhead named Sloane and a chubby ponytailed troll called Waters.

They sounded as country as they looked. All Sloane was missing was a blade of straw dangling from her lip to complete the picture.

While Waters hunted and pecked on the computer, Sloane frisked us thoroughly, taking extra time between the thighs, running a stubby finger under our breasts telling us that we'd need to lose the bras because of the underwire. I didn't want to get into a discussion about there not being any underwire in our discount store undergarments and from Delight's posture, I made the right call.

"Wait a minute," Waters called from her perch behind the computer. "Check their hair."

Sloane patted my head roughly, poking her fingers at my hairline, behind my ears. The more she touched me, the more I wanted a shower.

The guard seemed a bit surprised when she tugged at Delight's hair and it moved. She pulled off the long brown wig revealing a head of tight black curls.

"Thought I recognized you," Sloane said. "Looky here, Waters, your girlfriend is back."

Waters came around the counter as Sloane pushed Delight forward. She stumbled, stopping just short of the troll deputy, revulsion on her face. I had never seen Delight as anything but strong, stubborn, determined. *What had they done to her?*

Waters smiled. She had most of her teeth, even if they were yellowed and chipped. She circled Delight, barely giving me a second look. Maybe I wasn't her type. Maybe she didn't know me well enough yet.

"Did you miss me?" she asked, hanging on the *Ss* serpent-like, as she leaned in. Her lips and Delight's cheek might have been positive and negative poles of magnets.

Waters backed off, her bravado dimmed. "That's okay," she said more to herself than anyone else. She planted her feet, one hand strayed to her firearm, the other to her crotch, stroking, patting.

Sloane tapped my arm, handed me a cloth bag. "Restroom's over there. Leave on your underwear only. Put on the jumpsuit and the bobos. Meet me right back here." She pointed to a tile square that looked like all the others.

"Wait. What do you mean? We aren't staying, right, Delight? I mean, we're supposed to get picked up."

"Not tonight sweetheart. See that clock? That clock says your ass is ours for at least fourteen hours."

"Fourteen hours?" I looked at Delight, watched her lips form a familiar word.

Shit.

"Just missed your friends," Sloane said, putting together another sack for Delight. "You're a seven, right?" She said looking at her feet, grabbing a pair of slip-on sneakers off the rack marked Women's Bobos.

"Well. I guess they were your friends. Dressed just like you.

Unless maybe that's what the competition does these days. You think that's it. Waters? They having dress-up contests down in Hookertown?"

"More like dress *off*," she said, giving her crotch a final pat.

"Go on now," Sloane said, pointing to the bathroom. "Be the last time you'll be anywhere private. Might want to, you know, do what you need to do."

I stared at her, then shifted my gaze to Delight, who nodded then tipped her chin toward the restroom. The door was heavy. It quickly clunked closed behind me, pinching off any light. Frantic, I ran my hands over the wall near the door. Two tries and I hit the switch.

The fluorescent light buzzing overhead didn't help to soften the hue of green someone had chosen for the walls and floor. Between the baby shit paint color, the scent of stale urine coming from the metal toilet and the unnamed brown smear on the wall over the chipped sink, I was pretty sure I wasn't going to be dawdling.

I opened the cloth bag and went through my stash. One threadbare sheet, a pair of plastic shower shoes, a hotel-sized bar of soap, a short-shafted toothbrush, one tiny tube of toothpaste and a plastic comb so flimsy it bent under my grip. I stripped to my underwear, used the toilet biting back tears, then washed up as best I could and stepped into the dark blue jumpsuit, snapping the front closed and tugging on the cloth sneakers.

I picked up the issued bag and my clothes, stared at the back of the locked door, the solid metal handle, then stepped out into the bright hall where Sloane was waiting, hand on her firearm.

Because there's only so much you can do in a five-by-five cinder block bathroom.

CHAPTER 19

Delight explained it to me later. How Raquel and Amber made the time cutoff. There were only two times of the day you could see a judge and get your bail set. By the time we'd arrived, thanks to the cops' impromptu office stop, we were fucked.

"Enjoy the slumber party, sweetheart," Waters had whispered to Delight before smacking her ass. "See you bright and early."

The girls were probably back at the house getting high, or working the computer room, or Omar, or all three. For the first time since they took me, I missed those assholes.

Delight and I sat on my assigned bunk sharing an itchy wool blanket, our hipbones sinking through the narrow plastic pad straight to the cold steel of the rack.

There were four bunkrooms upstairs, four below. Eight beds in each, no doors, no bars, each had a small window. There were too many buzzing, clicking overhead lights. One woman, her gray roots at least an inch grown out was sleeping with her back to us, her breath heavy, snuffling. Two other women read on their bunks. One moved her lips, forming words. Delight poked me, cautioned me not to stare.

Outside, the wind whistled and moaned. I felt like a girl in Kansas, and not just because of the storm. I was glad my mother was dead, that she'd never have to know me like this.

Below, in the large open area of the pod where tables and chairs were bolted to the floor, the television droned, cheery voices trying to sound serious as the tornado's path was redirected.

The lip reading girl said, "Last time there was a twister alert, we all got hung up an extra week, ain't that right, Bird?"

The other girl put down her book, rolled to her side and spoke in a high, trilling voice. "I was eight days over. And what did I get for it? Shit. Told those motherfuckers they should be applying that time to this here bullshit sentence. Gonna get my lawyer bitch on that tomorrow. Mother. Fuckers."

She'd earned her nickname with that voice, those long bony arms, that beaky nose. I wondered what they would call me if I was in long enough.

Lip reading girl looked at me. "Hope you don't got no pressing plans. Nowhere special to be. Might as well settle in for the long haul."

"No. You don't understand," I said. "We're only here over-night."

Lip reading girl laughed, showing tan teeth, one blackened. "Oh yeah, right. Just overnight."

The volume of the television increased. An announcement that all government buildings were closing, no school, no public transportation. Everyone should stay off the streets. This was an emergency.

A woman in the bunkroom next door yelled something in Spanish, someone below replied, followed by cheers and laughter. I went to the window and peered out. It was too dark to see anything. I walked to the rail above the open dining and gathering area where a television was mounted high on the wall. A short chubby girl in prison stripes stood on a thick Bible and used another book like an extension of her arm to press the channel button, stopping on a local news station.

The reporter stood outside somewhere, hair whipping her face, warning people of the severity of the situation, as if we were blind. Scrolling words across the bottom of the screen told people in three counties to evacuate, seek shelter, kiss their ass good bye. They cut away to a shelter with people running inside, then showed a close-up of a wailing siren and old foot-age of the last tornado's wrath—destroyed homes, toppled trees, mangled cars and everywhere crying people.

Delight joined me at the rail, her back to the TV as the chubby girl clicked through more channels.

"Don't let them get to you. Yeah, it might be longer than one night, I'm not going to lie to you, but we're safe here. I mean, look at this place."

Delight had a point. Thick-ass cinder block walls, reinforced windows. Built low to the ground, ugly and squat, this jail had been designed to contain bad people. I figured it would work in the reverse too, keeping the bad shit out.

"Stop! It's The Church Lady!" A group of inmates had gathered in front of the TV, pointing at a poorly shot video.

A woman's voice narrated the scene shot through a windshield with her shaky hand.

"As you can see," she said. "They're back. Even though our community ran them off last month, and the month before. We *still* have prostitutes and drug dealers just two blocks from our church, a blessed house of God. These heathens spreading their filth, less than four blocks to the nearest school, where innocent children pass by. If it was your child, would you want them to see this?"

The camera panned from the group of identically dressed girls on the sidewalk to the vehicle stopped in the street.

"This might be dangerous," the woman intoned, "But I need to be a witness, be strong in our Lord Jesus Christ, as we continue our quest to clean up Oklahoma City, make this town a place where our children are safe again."

I had to give her credit, she tried to keep up the narration, the ardent prayers, even as she filmed Omar smacking the old man around, that sad pecker flopping—partially blurred out. Omar pushing Amanda out of the way, yelling at us. The other girls cowering. Omar finally shoving the guy into the front seat.

It looked worse than I remembered. The guy looked sicker, the car shittier, and when the camera came back to the girls, it took me two tries to connect that the one who had stepped away from the group, the skinny, dirty broad standing in the road with her sunken eyes, slack lips, making hand signals...was me.

Most of the inmates had left their beds, their card games, their bunkrooms and were hanging over the rails or dancing around the TV chanting and singing, "Church Lady, Church Lady, We love you, Church Lady."

Bird stood beside me, squinting at the TV, looking from the images on the screen to me and back, an idea forming, solidifying as they ran the tail end of the video—the stop action slow motion part, where Church Lady had been filming just one thing—me.

She yelled, "Hey, ain't that you?"

I shook my head, scoffed, "Hell, no."

Bird looked closer, started to approach.

Delight put out her arm, stopping her. "She said it ain't her. It ain't her."

Some of the inmates were looking our way. More than I wanted.

Bird sucked her teeth, took a few steps back, arms swinging like broken wings. She turned toward the bunkroom. "Hey, Darby, what does this mean again?" Bird repeated the gestures I'd made for the woman in the minivan—visored hand to forehead, fisted hand pumping air. She laughed. "I did my four years, don't remember shit. Unless of course it has to do with a gun." Bird took a stance, Uzi arms.

Darby, the lip reader girl yelled down from her bunk. "Shut up, Bird. You never remember anything. Remind me to get a new partner when we get out of here. You'll end up shooting me in the ass."

"Wouldn't be the first time you had something shoot in your ass."

"Shut the fuck up," Darby said rolling over to face the wall.

Bird climbed up the bunk, started petting Darby's arm. "Come on, Darby. It was just a joke. Tell me what it means."

"Yeah, Maxine," Delight whispered. "What does it mean?"

I blew out the breath I'd been holding, then held her eyes with mine. "Search," I said. "Double time."

CHAPTER 20

I pretended to sleep. The humming, buzzing lights stayed on. It's never really nighttime in jail. Bird and Darby had socks over their eyes, makeshift eye masks. The old woman snored, worse than any man I'd ever slept with. Delight's shape above me in the bunk was as restless as mine. The bed felt too small, too hard. There was no pillow and the sheet was pilled and worn, the blanket, more like a throw. My feet touched the rails, my arms hung over the edge. No matter what position I tried, sleep wouldn't come.

Somewhere a girl sang, sweet and low, made-up words when the real ones failed her. I got up to peer out the window, seeing only dark beyond the dark with my hand to the cool glass. I imagined the way the wind might feel, knew that outside was much warmer than the cold air they pumped into Pod B. Maybe they thought the cold would put us in hibernation, slow us down, like we were snakes or bears.

I walked to the end of the row of bunkrooms, wad of toilet paper in hand, squatted over a steel bowl mounted to a concrete wall. There were no doors, no dark corners, nothing a guard or an inmate couldn't see.

Later, I would realize it was this semi-urgent bladder, that inability to sleep that saved my life.

The roaring train sound was as surreal as the shaking, bending concrete walls spewing pellets of cement, grout, caked layers of paint, pink, yellow, green, gray—decades of what psychologists claimed to be soothing hues. Rattling pipes, expanding and bursting added to the cacophony.

The floor beneath us collapsed. It was like ice cracking on a pond, reminding me of the first time I'd skated too early in the season, ended up soaked and scolded, but alive. Another train roar and the wall of the bathroom buckled, then fell. Wind now in my face, the raw smells of outside—dirt, decay, damp. Alarms wailed. A man's voice on a loudspeaker told us to stay in our bunks as the overhead lights sputtered, then blinked out.

Someone screamed, followed by hoots and cheers. I turned my face to the wind. I hadn't come this far in life to die in a fucking bathroom—in prison. Some of the concrete blocks in the wall had crumbled, one was split in half by a large pole, some sort of support structure that had speared the side of the building. I started working there, scraping my knuckles against the blocks, bending my nails backward trying to make a hole large enough to climb through, trying to remember how tall the building was on this side.

Downstairs, the women argued, screamed to open the door, let them out, someone please help. I glanced over my shoulder to the guard tower built into the opposite wall, the glass room where they watched us sleep, eat, pray, pee, shower. There were two uniformed men. One stared at me and shook his head, raised his gun to the bulletproof glass. The other pointed to the ceiling between us, where the crack had widened and turned to run.

Another gust of wind, another roar and the roof split in two. More blocks of wall fell, one bouncing off my shoulder, scraping my ear tearing away flesh.

Someone screamed in Spanish, "*Oh Dios mío, está muerta!*" Another glance at the tower showed an empty room, an abandoned post.

I pulled another block and three fell away. The hole was big enough. Maybe for two.

Delight. Shit.

I ran from the bathroom into a hall filled with debris. The sound was much louder out here. Mother Nature, supremely pissed off. Scooting as close to the railing as I dared, I scanned the area below. No sign of Delight's curls. No sign of a tall black woman. The inmates had broken into three groups. Some pressed call buttons, tried the phones and panic alarms, others were battering the main door with a piece of broken bunk bed, another group worked with a chair they'd pried loose from the floor, smashing it over and over into a windowed door that led to the exercise area, which in turn led outside. That was a smarter call. The main door led to a death trap. I remembered the long, winding maze we'd walked to get here.

I needed to tell them to escape up not down, to go into the storm, not away from it. But first, I needed to find Delight.

The nearest bunkroom was deserted, oddly pristine. Not a ceiling tile out of place. Messy beds and lined up shampoo bottles, the only sign it had ever been occupied.

The next room was a different story.

Take everything from a lived-in bunkroom, put it in a giant blender, then hit puree. That might begin to describe what I saw. But you'd have to add a few body parts and buckets of blood.

I hurried past the next room, dodging swinging fluorescent lights, climbing over broken ceiling tiles, thinking only about reaching the end of the hall, the room where I'd left her.

Through the thick cloud of dust, the room appeared empty, ceiling caved in on one side, metal support rods pushing through the walls, blocks bulging, electrical conduit exposed and sparking.

I yelled over the noise of the storm. "Delight? Are you here?"

She was huddled under the bunk, eyes squeezed shut, praying. She winced, pulling back when I reached for her.

"It's me. Come on. We have to get out of here."

"I can't."

"Yes, you can," I said, pulling her, fighting her, dragging her. Remembering how I'd said the same words to her under the tarp at the blue house before Candy found us. I wasn't going to fail again.

I had half of her out from under the bed when the wind

started to sound like someone had turned the vacuum on high. I glanced at the spreading crack in the ceiling, then grabbed an arm and a leg and yanked.

"Don't fucking do this, Delight. I'm trying to save your god-damn life."

She opened her eyes, tears staining her cheeks, white-knuckled grip on leg of the metal bed. "You don't have to."

"Yes. I do."

She looked at me like a scared little kid. Then let go.

We ran to the bathroom. Me pulling Delight, shielding her from flying debris. Her, yelling prayers and curses.

The women below gave up the door battering when they saw us and where we were headed. One yelled, "Up there! Look! There's a way out!"

We ran past the toilets and showers to the hole in the wall. The wind was stronger now, circular gusts whipping our way thick with dirt, grout, cement bits and pieces, some as large as my fist.

I heard the crack expanding, coming our way, splitting open the roof of Oklahoma City Correctional Facility Pod B. We had seconds before the entire ceiling caved in and trapped us all.

I started pawing at the new blocks that had fallen, Delight joined me, pushing some out the hole, others to the side, enlarging the space as best we could. I grabbed the big plastic trash barrel used for wet towels, shoved it through the opening.

I yelled, "Get in!"

"What?" Delight looked at me, shook her head, spraying white and gray dust everywhere. "No fucking way. I can't."

"You can and you will," I said, tugging her arm.

A group of women, one of them our bunkie Darby, came rushing around the corner as the glass guard room collapsed. There was a metallic ping and snap, the sound of exploding light fixtures, popping and crackling, the creaking of joists, followed by the clatter of supports, the *shoomp* sound of thick panels of glass falling thirty feet onto the women below, echoing.

Their screams muffled, pulled away by the storm, buried under layers and layers and layers.

I watched as the far end of the bathroom floor opened up beneath Darby stealing her feet, then legs, then—she was gone.

"Hurry!"

I shoved Delight into the barrel and jumped in, thrusting us through the hole, into the dark night.

Maybe I hadn't thought it through, the idea of riding in a trash barrel down the side of a half-demolished building in the passing eye of a tornado. But it was too late.

Delight cowered in the bottom of the barrel as we bumped and slid. I tried to keep us upright. We started two stories up and the first drop had been a big one, about eight feet to the ledge, then a jerky ride to the next shelf of debris. It was hard to see past that. There was a point where faith would have to suffice.

More rain now than wind. I could almost hear again. Voices of the women above trickled down. Two of them were at the mouth of the hole Delight and I had made. They hung half in, half out. Each step they made shook the pile we were on, like a huge Jenga set, ready to collapse.

"Hang on, Delight. We're almost there," I said, pushing off the ledge, angling the barrel to slide us down the crumbling concrete ridge, away from broken glass, jagged edges and black holes. We scraped and banged our way another four, then six feet, steadily picking up speed. I dragged my arms like useless brakes on a runaway train.

There may be a lot of good things to say about new buildings made of concrete, with improved internal flexible structures, reinforced walls, even the concrete itself is better. But this was an old, ill-maintained structure, one built before the codes of 1966, one that was expanded over time on a budget with substandard working conditions and untrained workers, (prison labor). A building that wasn't designed for beauty or efficiency with its labyrinth of halls, incompetent ductwork and obsolete electrical system. All this building was designed to do was keep people inside.

Whoever had thought erecting a squat concrete detention center in the middle of an open field in tornado alley was a good idea had never considered the way it would crack and twist. How ceilings would fall, walls collapse on themselves, metal rebar struts jabbing through the surface of exploded slabs like toothpicks in pound cake.

We hit the rebar at forty-five degrees, sliding fast enough to scrape the skin off my right arm. The impact threw me into the air, bouncing my head and shoulders into a slab three feet away. Delight screamed, kept screaming. Ears ringing, seeing in double vision, I willed myself to not puke as I crawled back to her over the slick concrete, rain mixing with my dripping blood.

The barrel shook, suspended inches off the ground. I looked inside.

"Maxine?" Delight said, "I'm stuck. Help me?"

I shook my head clear and looked again. The rusty rod of rebar impaled her body below the rib cage. Between the angle of the barrel on the precarious ledge and the way the rod extended, she looked like a shish kebab on the edge of a platter.

She stretched, reaching for me. The pain made her scream.

"Oh Jesus. Hold on," I said, thinking I could pull the barrel from the bar, could somehow remove the whole thing, could maybe even lift it up over my head and run away with her.

"Delight. Don't move, okay. You need to be still."

I made my way around the barrel, careful to not touch it, or shake it in any way. The rain was still coming down, slicking up the surface, making me blink. I pushed my hair out of my face, flattened myself at the base of the barrel where a river of red drained.

Shit.

I felt around where rubber met concrete, rubber mashed by metal, rubber bending, rubber barrel jammed in concrete debris. A new barrage of rocky chunks fell, rolling past me, one smashing my hand. Above me, an escaping inmate took too wide of a step and screamed, tumbling, her head bouncing, smacking and then, silent, her body angled all wrong.

The guard they called Chubbette had gotten smart. She was tied to something inside, rappelling her way down to a huddled group of inmates, grabbed one—a big blonde. She fought her off, slapping and pulling at Chubbette's clothes, tearing a pocket, loosening a shoe that bounced away, followed by a pink-cased cellphone.

Shots rang out. Another guard appeared, holding the rope and a gun. She waved the gun, fighting the wind, the pelting rain, all while managing the heft of Chubbette. One of the inmates threw a rock. The guard twisted, dodged, fired at nothing, as the big blonde lunged for Chubbette.

They made it a good ten feet. I could see the headline: *Inmate Uses Guard as Human Sled to Escape Wreckage.*

The guard at the top kept shooting, as her co-worker slid face down, bump, bang, crunch.

Delight called for me, her voice weaker. I crawled back up, looked in over the lip of the barrel, wishing I had a knife to cut away the rubber, a crowbar and a crane, a magic carpet, a weapon to kill.

I had nothing. It was just me and this storm and a whole bunch of frustration.

I had to stick my head all the way into the barrel to hear her.

"Maxine. You got to go. Leave me."

"I can't. You're hurt. There's a lot of…blood."

"I told you to go. Don't you ever listen to me?"

I held her hand, squeezed it until she squeezed back. "My name's not Maxine. It's Jojo."

"Jojo. That's nice." She squinted. "You never did look like no Maxine to me."

I smiled, unsure what to say, how to say it. Delight spared me.

"My name was Lara. Once."

She swallowed hard, eyes blinking. Pain washed over her face. "Something you should know. Candy is not just tricking. She's selling H on the street. To kids, moving it, too..." The words now wheezing from her chest. "Get those bastards. Help the girls..."

"I will. I promise."

Delight closed her eyes, squeezed my hand, weaker now. "There's something else. They're using truck stops. Candy—the two of them. They got a book, they got a sc—..."

"What, Delight? Lara?"

She was out. I checked her throat, got a pulse. Faint. But it was there.

My nursing was cut off by the *thonk* sound of a bullet hitting a rubber barrel. I backed out and slid down a few feet, using the barrel as cover. Something pink caught my eye. I scooted closer and worked it free. The not so brave guard stood twenty feet above me at the hole with one hand wrapped around an inmate's hair. She fired another shot, calling me a stupid motherfucker, telling me to stay put.

I hadn't been counting the bullets, but maybe the long-haired inmate had. She uncoiled, spun around and head-butted the guard.

I slid, bumped and leapt my way to the bottom, snagging a foot-long piece of rebar on the way. Running for the downed fence and the trees beyond, I checked the screen of the pink cellphone. Battery at two percent and draining.

CHAPTER 21

There should have been no way I could have picked the right path, fled in the right direction. I should be dead, or lost or horribly mangled, crushed under twenty feet of concrete. I should have been all of those things and here, I wasn't. I stopped trying to convince myself there wasn't a God, instead thanked Him and kept running.

The break of trees I'd thought was deep woods, the kind of shelter I was used to, had opened up to a grassy field. No one was chasing me—yet, but running into an open field, wearing jail clothes wasn't my preferred choice. The rain had slowed to a drizzle and the wind had died down so that I was no longer fighting to stay upright. The sky was eerily lit by moonlight and far away lightning crackled. I braced myself against a tree to catch my breath and took a closer look at the phone. The back was dented, one side chipped, the glass badly cracked, but there wasn't a password and Gator's number flew from my thumbs accompanied by a prayer.

No answer.

I started to leave a message when the phone began to chitter and blink like something was dying inside. I clicked *share my location,* encouraging the little red pin to appear and stay put. "Come on. Come on. Come on." The phone flashed once, then died. "Shit! Shit. Shit."

Plan two. I unsnapped and wiggled out of the top of the jumpsuit, gritting my teeth as the fabric scraped my raw bloody arms, then rolled and tucked it into the bottoms, stashing the phone and rebar, tightening the elastic waistband. From a distance, I'd look like a woman in a T-shirt and dark pants. A dirty, bloody, crazy woman out for an after-tornado stroll. But seriously, who would be rushing to a jail in the boonies? There were more pressing matters in the city and suburbs, more important people in danger. Like the inmates had said, they were the lowest priority.

Halfway across the field, I felt a shift in the air, a lifting. I turned in a slow circle. The sky where I'd come from was brightening, clouds dispersing. A songbird called out, another answered, then another. They began to chatter and squawk. I kept walking backwards, my eyes on the horizon, hoping to see the sun rise, hours early.

I didn't hear him until it was too late.

The dog attacked from behind, his jaws clamping down on a baggy pant leg. I spun around tearing the fabric as he let go to get a better grip. His first mistake.

We circled each other.

"Hey, now, come on, boy." I showed him my empty hands, didn't look him in the eye.

The dog growled, showed even more teeth.

He must have come from the buildings near the jail, a working dog trained to attack. I didn't have time to retrain him or negotiate. He would do what he was supposed to do, and I would do what I had to do. I reached into my jumpsuit for the rebar.

By the time I reached the road, scratched, bruised, bloodied and beaten, all I wanted was a warm, soft bed and a gallon of fresh cold water. Gripping the broken pink phone in one hand as if it were my lifeline, I must have been a sight. Ripped, bloodstained jail jumpsuit, ratty hair littered with leaves and twigs, tipped with mud, I stepped onto the road minus a shoe and a toenail.

But the tornado had also done its damage to the land. She

was littered with debris, from metal siding and roof shingles to branches, mailboxes even a rocking chair. I tried to climb onto an uprooted tree and fell backward, smacking my head, knocking myself out.

There are few sounds that always make me smile. My father's singing, a baby's giggle, my lover whispering my name, and the deep rumble of a Paccar MX-13 engine.

I must have been I opened my eyes, thinking I was dozing in the truck, safe and warm in Sabrina's sleeper, Gator at the wheel. It took me a minute to figure out I wasn't safe or warm, another to remember what the hell had happened and where I was. The throbbing headache didn't help.

But still, I knew that engine. Sabrina was nearby.

Holding a hand to my pounding head, I looked around for the pink cell phone. Nothing. Squinting into the bright, dry day, I tried to yell, tried to pull my shit together. No good. I was fading, seeing black, then stars. I feebly waved at headlights real or imagined in the distance, had to bite my lip to force myself to keep upright, be seen. Be found.

Thirty feet away, the familiar glint of the hood of a black truck. Twenty feet away, Gator, his mouth moving. The truck rocked to a stop as he flew from the driver's seat and ran. I fell into his arms.

"Jojo! Baby? It's okay. I'm here."

I let him hold me. Told myself this was okay. It was going to be fine. I let him cry in my hair. I let him love me. I didn't say a word.

He told me the phone's locator had worked. He was following the GPS to the pin when he saw me. He bragged about getting through road blocks with bogus FEMA credentials, flashing them to officials too stupid to realize there was no way FEMA would be on site so soon

"I'm sorry. I need to ..." I barely got the words out. My body was shutting down, doing for me what I wouldn't.

Gator shushed me, gave me a pill and water, more water,

something herbal he said would be good for me. He told me how he'd seen the video shot by the church lady. How he'd been eating at a truck stop cafe, and the news was on, and that the only reason he looked at the screen at all was because he heard guys commenting about how the hookers were dressed.

The reporter said they had an exclusive vigilante video shot by one of their locals, a woman they called The OK City Church Lady. They ran the clip, just a few seconds really, blurring out faces and some body parts, but when the minivan pulled away, the Church Lady captured one remaining girl, the one who raised her arm in the air and sent out a signal.

Gator had to do some convincing to get the waitress to rewind and pause the playback, thank God for DVR boxes, right? And then, the other drivers thought he was some sort of pedophile or freak or something and he had to explain how it was *me*, how he was sure it was me, the girlfriend who'd been kidnapped, how those hand signals meant he was supposed to search faster. And then the guys were slapping him on the back and offering to help and they did. Getting him the FEMA creds, sending him on the shortcut route and fueling up Sabrina.

"Those truckers today," he said, "helped more than all the people I hired, all the ads I ran, and all the flyers I put up. When he reached for my hand, I left him hold it, but I couldn't look at his face. Especially when he said, "So everything's going to be okay, Jojo. You see? Now it's all going to be okay. It's over now.

I patted his hand and tried to remember how it felt to be happy, attempted to pull that onto my face.

"Take us somewhere safe," I whispered. "But not too far away."

He nodded.

"Gator?"

"Yeah, baby?"

"You're wrong. It's not over. It's just begun."

CHAPTER 22

I let myself out the back of the sleeper while Gator shut down the rig. He'd found a small motel two towns south, far enough away from the tornado's swath of destruction that we'd have some semblance of peace. I wasn't sure about the anonymity, given the size of our ride parked out front.

We hoped there'd soon be a convoy of trucks on multiple highways making their way to OK City and beyond, where the real destruction was. Trucks filled with workers, supplies, materials, aid, and probably a bunch of politicians. The town would look like a parking lot at a trucking convention by afternoon. We'd blend right in.

I told Gator I didn't want a doctor or a hospital. "They have enough people to deal with, and besides, I'm pretty sure I'm now categorized as a fugitive."

"Unless they think you're dead," he said.

"Well, there's that." I said, nodding.

We stood four feet away from each other. It felt like forty.

He said, "Are you hungry? We can go get something to eat."

"Well, there is that whole fugitive thing."

"Oh, right. But I can make a few calls."

I knew he could and he would. I smiled and said, "Sure. After you get us some food. I'm starving."

"Of course." He started for the door. "You want anything special?"

I did. I wanted a time machine. I wanted a big-ass life eraser. I wanted the mother ship to return. I wanted...

"No. You pick. I'm going to take a bath, try to clean myself up."

"Do you need some help?" he asked, his face softening, as he ran his eyes over my scraped-up hands and arms, my scratched face and the dried blood that may or may not be mine.

I shook my head reaching for the duffle he'd brought. "No, I'm okay. Thanks for grabbing my stuff."

Gator nodded. "I tossed some bandages and shit in there, from the kit. You sure you'll be all right?"

We were both thinking about the last motel experience.

"No, I'm fine," I said. "Go on."

"Okay. Jojo, we'll talk when I get back, all right?"

I didn't answer, just waited for him to leave, then locked the door behind him and made my way to the bathroom, shuffling in the tattered Bobos, the jumpsuit hanging from my hips. I was grateful he'd given me some space. Gator was, at times, very perceptive.

I set the duffle on the counter, then tried to lock the flimsy bathroom door. It twisted, then snapped back with a rattle. I went back into the room and dragged the heavy desk chair across the carpet and into the bathroom. It wasn't much, but it made me feel better, that stupid chair jammed up against the door handle.

Hot water filled the tub as I stripped off the jail clothes, balling them up, shoving them into the wastebasket. I found some shower gel for bubbles and let those build as the steam rose fogging up the mirror. That made it easier for me to stand there brushing my teeth, patting my scraped face and arms with a washcloth, the white cloth first brown, then red, then pink. Finally, I lowered myself into the bath, wincing as the warm water touched my wounds.

The adrenaline that had fueled my jail escape added to the fear of dying in that shithole jail during a fucking tornado among people that neither knew nor loved me had vanished on the ride here. Tough, smart Jojo who'd survived all those days as a slave to human traffickers had also vanished. *Who the fuck was I now? Who could ever love this thing I'd become?*

Shame and disgust burned in me so brightly, it felt as though I was branding myself from the inside out, searing my skin, telling everyone what I had done, how I was the broken one now, how I was no longer worthy. How I truly was dead.

In retrospect, the bath idea was stupid. I couldn't really wash myself this way and as tired as I was I could easily slip under the water and drown. It might have been funny, if I could look at the situation from a distance, but I couldn't. I was too invested. All I could feel was self-pity.

In the end I made the best of it, leaving a ring of jail and tornado dirt in the tub and the stench of my self-pity on the shabby, scratchy motel towels.

Sitting on the edge of the bed in clean clothes, my wounds bandaged, wet hair dripping down my back, the desk chair returned to its spot, I waited warily for Gator, wishing I'd grabbed my gun from the truck.

He knocked twice, called my name. There was a crinkle of plastic bags, sound of shuffling feet. I checked the peephole. Just Gator, pinch of blue sky over his shoulder. I opened the door, then limped back to the bed.

"I wasn't sure what you wanted, so I got an assortment," he said, clearing the desk, setting out containers of eggs and bacon, grilled cheese sandwiches, hot coffee and cold lemonade, two donuts and something that looked like a steak sandwich, cheese dripping from the roll.

"Can I make you a plate?" he asked.

"Yeah. Thanks."

If he was waiting for more words, me to specify what or how much, he'd be waiting a while. I reached for my hairbrush, had to grip it with two hands, got it five inches through my tangled hair before the effort was too much. I let it hang there, not giving a shit what it looked like.

Gator turned at the sound of my sigh, the murmured cuss.

"Hold on," he said.

He set a plate of food on my lap, handed me a coffee, then sat beside me on the bed. When I had a few sips of the hot, strong brew in me, he asked in a voice I'd rarely heard him use, "Can I help you? Jojo. Will you *let* me help you?"

I took another sip, thinking of what he was asking, really asking. I looked at him, this beautiful man with love in his eyes. My pride would be the death of me.

Finally, I handed him the empty coffee cup and said, "You can start by getting this fucking brush out of my hair."

He sat behind me, tugging through the snarls and knots, being as gentle as he could, as I demolished eggs and bacon and went to work on a donut.

"What will they do?" I asked.

"Who?"

"The cops at the jail. When they don't find my body."

"Depends. Whichever way they go with it, you're secondary to the current situation."

He finished one section on the right side of my head, got up and moved to the other side to work on that rat's nest.

"Meaning?" I asked.

"We've got time."

I offered him a bite of the donut. He knew how much that took. It was huge for me.

"Thanks," he said, bending down to snatch it from my hand with his teeth.

I gasped, pulled back.

"What?" he said around the mouthful of donut. "I bite you?"

"No. It's not that. You just..."

He swallowed, licked his lips, dropped the chunk of hair he'd been working on.

"Scared you?"

I shrugged.

He took a deep breath, then cracked his neck, a resounding snap left and right. "I think we need to have that talk."

"Not now."

"Yeah. Now." He pushed himself off the bed so fast, he left me rocking in this wake. "What's going on, Jojo? I know you've been through the ringer, and I know how fucking stubborn you are. But something is off. I can feel it." He backed away, leaned on the dresser, his hands gripping the wood, knuckles white. "You said...you said they didn't hurt you."

I hesitated, then slowly shook my head, letting the hair fall in my face.

"Don't lie to me. What did they do?"

Gator smacked his hands on the dresser, began to pace. "Those assholes, those Somali motherfuckers. I'll kill them."

I turned my face to the wall, tried to find the anger that had served me so well in the past, but came up short. I could feel Gator looking at me. Could feel him judging me, pitying me.

He stopped pacing and came close enough I could see the tips of his shoe under my wall of hair.

"Jojo?" Gator said softly, reaching his hand to my shoulder, drawing it back before it connected. "Talk to me. Come on, babe. I want to help. But you've got to talk to me."

When I didn't answer or look at him he changed tactics. It was exactly what I would have done. The best way to get a fighter back in the fight is to piss the motherfucker off. But you had to know how. And no one knew me the way Gator Natoli did.

By the time he was done reading me the riot act, calling me names, breaking me down, then challenging me to get up, get mad and get in the hunt, my heart was about to burst.

I've always wanted to have someone love me enough to hate on me.

"Okay. Okay," I said, then scooted back on the bed, propped myself against the headboard and put a death grip on a very flimsy pillow. I glanced at Gator once, then found a spot on the bedspread that looked like a rabbit and started to talk in a voice I didn't recognize.

I told him about Candy, how she'd been the one to call from the motel and tell the Somalis where we were.

"I don't know what her deal is. She's not like the other girls. It's like she wants to be there, like she's one of them."

I told him about the girls that I'd been busted with, Amanda, Ginger, Raquel and Delight. The ones he'd seen on the video.

"There was a guy, too," he said.

"Yeah, Omar. He likes to use his fists." I took a breath and continued. "Remember the guys at the house?"

Gator nodded.

"They're always around. The two we met? That's Jabby and Black Dog. The fat one is Big Abdi. And our pal, The Bicycle Boy, AKA Hollywood? He's some kind of leader, or an assistant to the leader. Someone they call Boss Man. I don't know. There are others, they sort of look the same. I've never been that close to them."

"How many total, if you had to guess?"

"A dozen at least for them to be able to run multiple houses. And there's a woman, Nadifa."

"A woman in charge?"

I nodded, then shook my head. "I think so. I don't know, the days are pretty blurry."

Gator asked, "Would it help for me to ask questions to jog your memory, let you detach yourself, maybe see it from another...perspective?"

I thought about what he was asking. There was a line between remembering and admitting. Words unleashed in the air are harder to dismiss than images you can hide in your mind. Sometimes the words you unleash result in very wrong images in *other's* minds. I wasn't ready for that.

"I wish I had another perspective," I said, unable to say what I really felt, that I wish I had another past.

I shook my head and gave up the tough girl routine, leaning into Gator, letting myself cry, letting him soothe me. I kept hearing my father's voice in my head, remembering the way I'd hurt his feelings last year when I refused his help. I had been such a bitch when I was living in his house recuperating from the crash that killed my co-driver and boyfriend, Boone.

I didn't want to be that person. I didn't need to be. This was Gator. He and I had somehow—in all the ways we could have fucked it up—managed to find each other. We had something. And I wasn't going to let a fucking gang of Somali Mafia sex traffickers take that from us.

"It's okay," he said. "You can trust me. Jojo, you have to trust me."

He was right.

I told him *almost* everything I remembered. How they had moved me from house to house. How they kept me drugged. How each time I tried to escape and failed, I still never gave up hope that he was coming for me. He handed me tissues as I cried, sat beside me and pulled me gently onto his lap into his arms where I curled up as small as I could, my sobs eventually trailing off. When that moment morphed into minutes I might have dozed a bit, blaming it on his rocking, or on him being so warm, a portable human heater. When I opened my eyes I felt lighter inside, not quite hopeful or clean or pure, and certainly not godly or saint-like, but maybe a little less mired down by hate, anger and pity. And that was a good start.

Without raising my head from Gator's chest, I told him what I wanted to do. We needed to make sure Delight was okay, find the other girls and help them so they wouldn't go back to the Somalis.

When he didn't answer, I unfolded myself and crawled off his lap, started looking for my boots.

"And where do you want to start?" he asked.

"The processing center."

"Jojo, the last place you need to be showing your face right now is at the jail you just escaped from."

"I didn't *escape*. I left. I could have died there. It was self-preservation." I pulled on my socks and boots, and stood, started gathering my things.

Gator said, "I don't think they'll see it that way."

I started to object but he held up his hand. "No. Just. No. I'll find a way to check on the girls, find out about your friend. She's probably already been moved to a hospital."

I nodded, not because I thought he was right, but because his blue eyes were piercing. "Okay."

He pushed himself off the bed and went to the window, checked the parking lot then without turning around said, "When I was looking for you, I went everywhere that I could think of—the warehouse, the gangbanger street where you got lost, every truck stop in a sixty-mile radius. I asked, begged, pleaded for help. I even went back to the blue house where we found Candy. One of the guys there sent me on a wild goose chase that took me away for days. I thought I'd lost you forever. I went back to that damn house and I hurt him. Bad." He turned from the window, folded his arms and said, "I kept thinking that was where it started—"

"Technically," I said, "It started in the street by the warehouses when those little fucktards threw shit at our rig."

"Really?" Gator said. "You sure it wasn't when you ran over said *little fucktard's* bicycle?"

I shrugged. "Does it matter how it started? We're in it now and those girls need our help. Now, what are we going to do?"

"I think that depends on you," he said. "And your memory. Do you think you can find one of their houses?"

I hesitated, but when I finally answered, "Yes." I was more certain than I'd been in a long time.

CHAPTER 23

Still, I wouldn't go anywhere until Gator made the calls asking about bodies at the jail. I gave him the girls' street names again, their descriptions and as many names of the Somalis as I knew, in case any of them came around to claim their property. Gator understood how to get people to talk to him. Sometimes he had to pay, and sometimes he had to call in favors. However it worked, I was happy for the connections, and as far as I could tell, no one complicated his request with the need for specifics. They only wanted to know as little as they could get away with so that in the end they'd be telling the truth when answering. *I didn't ask* and *I don't know.*

There was a lesson in there somewhere.

I sent up a prayer for Delight, who I now knew as Lara, and the others, wishing I knew every saint and angel so I could multiple my efforts, boost my return.

Gator assured me we'd have news soon and pushed me toward phase two, even if I was mentally stuck back in the land of *I'm pissed off and still a little crazy in the head from being held as a slave whore. Sorry about that.* And I assured him that physically I was ready to kick some motherfucking ass.

We loaded up Sabrina with extra water and all the blankets, towels and linens from the room, one of the perks of paying in cash under a fake name.

I wasn't sure how bad the damage would be. All I knew about tornadoes was what I'd learned from disaster movies and news reels. Maybe looters were on the prowl, people playing Mad-Max for a few hours or days. Even if people had a security system at their house or business it was probably dead. Sorry pal. No one was coming, no chimes were ringing. There was no nice calm lady at a monitoring station to dispatch help. You were fucked.

I bet there were a slew of people regretting not purchasing that generator when Sears had a big sale three years ago. They'd be hearing the wife and her *I told you so's* for a long, long time. And hey, those weird-ass hoarders and zombie apocalyptic freaks? They didn't seem so stupid now. Lots of folks in OK City probably wished they'd been nicer to crazy old Uncle Billy who was currently holed up underground with a year's supply of ramen, canned fruit and spring water.

I tried to hold onto the present, tried to reel in my thoughts as we passed news vans with satellite dishes and pickup trucks loaded down with bottled water and firewood.

"Check the GPS," Gator said

"We're good. Two more blocks, then take a left."

Guided by the sounds and smells I had described to Gator— sirens and a sweet, sugary scent in the air, he'd referred to online maps and satellites and come up with two possibilities. The first one didn't pan out, but this address looked good. We passed the local fire station. Sirens? Bingo. A half mile later, the neon sign for Sally's Donuts: Hot and Fresh Baked Daily sealed the deal.

Even if I had not been blindfolded when they transported me, I/m not sure I would have recognized the street. Half of the houses were missing. The road itself was buckled and twisted, potholes connecting into massive maws threatening to swallow this part of OK City.

I wondered how many survivors would later wish their town *had* slipped into that hole, or been sucked into a whirling funnel, then spewed out over a fifteen-mile radius, so splintered and scattered that no one would ever be able to put it all together again—like a horribly exaggerated Humpty Dumpty story.

But this one didn't have kings. There would be churches and charities, reporters and news anchors looking for a twist on the age-old story of bad Mother Nature. Something to the tune of, Look here: broken stuff, misplaced dreams and a slew of deep-pocketed politicians with personal attachments to construction firms waiting in the wings.

There would, of course, be postings on YouTube, Vine, Twitter and Tumblr, heartfelt Facebook statuses and lots of volunteers coming to town. Some would help the old and the infirm, others would focus on the kids and the animals and many would focus on the buildings and the debris, stuff that was tangible, billable, profitable.

Maybe it was just the way I saw the world, and not the way it was at all. I hoped there would be rebuilding and insurance payouts and that, of course, all the families who'd lost loved ones would know closure, and there would be new, better homes for the dogs. Always, the dogs.

Gator carefully maneuvered our rig through the debris-laden streets. We'd thought about leaving the trailer back at the motel, but secondary storm damage made us think twice. Besides if we had to run or fight, I wanted as much of an upper hand as possible.

"Which one?" Gator asked, rolling slowing by cookie-cutter houses. "You said there was never street noise, but sometimes you could hear cars."

"Yeah. But not arriving as much as leaving. Does that make sense?"

"It does," Gator said, as we entered a cul-de-sac. "They'd accelerate leaving, but just coast in."

It felt just the opposite in my head when I thought the people visiting the houses I'd been in, but it wasn't worth the argument, or pulling up those angry feelings. Not now. I matched up the houses with the satellite image I'd saved on my tablet.

"That one," I said, pointing to the house on the left. Its front was mostly intact. Up close the brick steps and iron railing felt like a false front propped up for a school play, where stairs lead nowhere and behind the fake door is just empty stage, black curtains and cobwebs.

"Go on," Gator said, stepping aside.

My hand shook as I gently pushed on the door. It swung open, creaking. Where the tattered couch and scarred table used to be, there was a hole slowly filling with water, a broken pipe chugged and drained. The ceiling was on the floor. The entire second story was gone and the back of the house and most of both sides were missing. For a second, I thought about how many times I'd cursed the Somalis, how I'd wished they'd die, be wiped from the earth and sent directly to Hell.

Gator pushed his head in. "Any bodies?"

"Get right to the point, why don't you?"

Gator shrugged, then jumped through the doorway onto a pile of debris that shifted underfoot. He balanced himself with arms akimbo.

"Careful," I said.

He looked back at me, grinning. "Always. Come on. Let's see if they left anything good behind."

"Like a clue as to where the fuck they are?" I mumbled, stepping into the house.

Gator picked up ceiling tiles, tossed them aside, then righted overturned furniture, as I tried to see the house whole again, see the layout in my mind. I remembered the night I'd tried to escape, running down the hall to the back porch.

"The room they held me in was back there," I said, pointing to the northeast corner. I worked my way around a chunk of crumpled metal that might have been a furnace or an oven, heard Gator behind me.

"There was a hall that led to a computer room," I said. "I'll bet all their houses have one. Gotta make that internet porn money, you know, draw in the johns."

Gator made a sound in his throat like he swallowed something that didn't agree with him When I turned around, he was staring at me working his jaw without words.

"Gator?"

He shook his head and pushed past me, plowing his way through the house, kicking hard at stuff that didn't need to be kicked.

"Back here?" he said.

I nodded.

He moved chunks of drywall and siding, tossing aside anything structural, along with some stuff from outside—branches, plants, even a red mailbox. We found broken keyboards, a printer and three monitors. No hard drives, no towers, no laptops. Eventually, Gator pulled up a fistful of cables and wires. We followed them to a dead end, a solid concrete wall.

He said, "They must have run the cables underground, stealing electricity and internet from somewhere else, in effect making themselves untraceable."

I scoffed. "They didn't seem that smart."

"Maybe not the people you were face to face with. Whoever's behind all this has been at it for a while, and from what we learned searching for you, they're pretty well established, with money and connections. It's going to hurt when we take them down."

"You sound so sure."

"I am. We will take them down, Jojo."

"Not that. The *it's going to hurt* part." I turned my back, pretended to be interested in the pile of crap on the floor. I couldn't bear to have him see the doubt on my face. As I toed some of the debris a pad of paper caught my eye.

Fishing it out, I brushed off layers of dust to reveal pencil swirls and trees, some tiny tattoo-looking flowers. Someone was a doodler. I imagined the girls working here, headsets and monitors, the blue glow and hum of the room, webcams capturing seconds of fake sexy that became meaningful moments to horny strangers.

I flipped the pages of the pad to more scribbles, bubbles and drawings. On one page there were the names, Tom, Bob, Max and more words written lighter, what might be a time and an address, something else, could be a date, with the letters FF. It looked as if someone had tried to erase it, or maybe she wasn't writing because she needed the information, just writing what she heard. In the way most people that try out a pen in the office store write the name of the color of the ink in the pen.

"What do you think of this?" I showed the pad to Gator.

He dropped the pieces of desk he was holding and stepped closer, reached for the pad.

I waited for him to flip through the pages, then showed him the faint writing.

He tapped the date. "That's today." He ran a finger under the address. "You know this place? Ever hear it mentioned?"

I shook my head, took a slow look around the decimated house, then held my breath, stilling my heart. It was a hunting trick I'd learned from my best friend, Ivory Joe. We'd grown up tracking every sort of animal from woods to fields and bayous.

It was part of my culture, how my family was raised. Here, in the shadows of big buildings, in a crowded, poverty stricken city I was far from my roots, far from the clean, pure country-side of Bunkie, but I could shut off that part of my brain and still think like a hunter.

I heard Ivory Joe in my head, telling me to look closely, gather clues, get in the head of the prey, do what they would do, go where they would go.

"There's a thing about tracking prey—"

Gator interrupted. "Are we? Tracking prey? I thought we were tracking people, not animals."

"They are animals." I fought the shiver that ran through my body, the disgust that filled me.

Gator tucked the pad into his pocket. "Where do we start?"

"We seek them out in their own territory," I said, stomping through the destruction.

"And then?" Gator asked.

"We attack with impunity."

CHAPTER 24

In the rig, strapped into our expensive custom seats, sipping our bottled water, watching our high-tech global positioning system aim us in the right direction as our cellular phones/mini-computers charged up, I spoke to Gator about Louisiana, about hunting as a kid with my father and cousins. About growing up knowing the heft of a proper knife, with my ring finger bearing calluses from a bow, taking pleasure in the sweet ache of a shoulder after a day with a shotgun. But it wasn't just the implements of the hunt that I loved, it was also the tricks of the game. It tested all your senses, took your will and made it bigger, stronger. If you honored the hunt, you never stopped learning, never stopped challenging yourself. Sure, some of it was instinct, being able to feel subtle changes from the land to the sky, predicting what an animal would do, when and where, how they would react, how you could win.

"You ever hear of persistence hunting?" I asked.

Gator shook his head. "Is that like a stubborn redneck with a shotgun?"

I sighed. "No. They've been doing it for two million years."

"I'd say that's persistent."

In the Kalahari Desert, Bushmen run down game in the heat of the day, force their path away from any shade while keeping the pace fast enough that the animal can't pant to cool himself. It might start with a group of three or four men who separate a Kudu bull from his herd, then use the weight of his antlers against him. Chase him, yelling and swinging a rope overhead to distract and annoy him."

"Yeah, that would be annoying," Gator mumbled.

"I saw a film once where the first guy, the one with the spear who was chosen to go in for the final kill, lost track of the bull. His buddies were far behind, and it was up to him to find the path the animal might have taken."

"Good luck with that," Gator scoffed.

"Yeah, but that was thing. He just stood there under a bush and did this weird thing where he *became* the Kudu. Just for a few seconds, but it was enough for him to figure out which path to follow."

"Was he right?"

"He was. When he caught up to him, the bull was barely alive, dying from heat exhaustion. The hunter didn't even need his spear."

I rolled up the window, adjusted myself in the seat so I faced Gator. "But he used it anyway, as a ceremonial gesture. Then he rubbed dirt into the hide, giving thanks to the gods for providing the meal, for allowing him the victory."

I thought about the moment when a hunter sees his kill succumb, how there's a mixture of pleasure and remorse.

I closed my eyes and recited, "'When you kill a beast, say to him in your heart: By the same power that slays you, I too am slain, and I too shall be consumed. For the law that delivers you into my hand shall deliver me into a mightier hand.'"

Gator nodded his head. "Nice. Who said that?"

"Khalil Gibran. See? You aren't the only one who can pull a quote out of his ass."

He laughed and the sound of it lightened my heart. I couldn't help but smile back.

When we'd gotten into the truck after checking out the house, Gator wanted to go straight to the address on the notepad I'd found, but I had an idea that maybe my memory could be jogged to recall something the drugs had blocked.

"Let's make a circuit, keep the route under five miles." I cracked open my window and took a pre-emptive sniff. It felt good to be doing something productive, like I was almost myself again, even if it was mostly on the outside and a bit of a put on.

As he drove, I told Gator more about the days they'd moved us. Sometimes it was in a car, sometimes in the cold, hollow-sounding van. I'd pretend to be more out of it than I was so I could concentrate on clues, anything to keep my mind sharp. I counted blocks and turns, tried to focus on street noises, and smells, hyper-aware of any little difference.

I didn't always get the chance to play my spy game—not when they cranked up the radio, or kept talking bullshit in their singsong language—not when they picked a new girl who was crying or junked-up real bad and moaning.

Gator kept his eyes on the road, as crap appeared out of nowhere—not like the movie scenes where tornados blow shit all over the place, spear-chucking cows and doors—no, that part was over. This was more like an errant bucket blowing into our path, a chimney where a mailbox should be, and on one street, people too busy thinking about survival to watch where the hell they were going. Which was sort of ironic, all things considered.

"Anything?" Gator asked, scanning the street.

"No." I shook my head. "Nothing feels familiar. But that doesn't mean I wasn't here. Sorry."

"Don't worry about it. We can't get down all the streets, and some of them are totally destroyed. The other Somali houses might be too. What do you want to do now?"

I held up the scrap of paper with the address. "I guess we should go here."

Twenty minutes later, we pulled up to a painted brick build-ing in the middle of a gentrified city block. It was sandwiched between a bank and hipster cafe offering wheatgrass smoothies. "Closed" signs hung on both doors. There wasn't any indica-tion a tornado had struck anywhere near here from the look of the street with the perfectly parked shiny cars, neatly trimmed topiaries in planters, mint scooters locked to railings. The only thing missing was people.

"Hmm."

Gator looked at me. "What does that mean?"

"Nothing. It's just it's not what I expected. For the Somali Mafia, I mean."

Gator laughed. "What were you expecting? A camel service center? A neon sign: GIRLS GIRLS GIRLS?"

I felt stupid. "No," I said. "Of course not. Let's find a place to park and go check it out."

We went around the block and Gator nudged the rig up to the curb behind a delivery van, taking up the whole "No Parking" zone.

"I'll put the hazards on," he said, catching the look on my face. "It'll be fine."

This state of emergency thing had its own rules.

We unbuckled and headed for the sleeper, where Gator put out some ideas as we pulled our guns out of the oven hiding place, pocketed some extra ammo and prepared ourselves the best we could. For Gator that was doing twenty pushups and a quick series of stretches, for me it was a taking long pee, then posing for a selfie with my Kimber. We left out the back door, locking it behind us.

Before we made the corner, Gator grabbed my elbow, more shirt than skin.

"Jojo, you're okay with this, the way we discussed, right?"

"What? Yeah. This is the right call, we go in there, get these fuckers to tell us where they stashed the girls and leave the rest up to the cops. Trust me, I don't want any part of that."

Gator looked at me sideways, his eyebrows saying, *Oh yeah, I bet you don't,* while his mouth said, "I'm only asking because I know you agreed to it back there, but I also know you like changing your mind."

I tugged my arm away, gave him the stink eye. "Jesus! Yes. I told you six fucking times I'm not changing my mind. I got it, okay. That's the plan. Now, let's go."

"I just need to know because well, we're going in there armed and—"

"And you think they won't be?"

"I don't know what to think, and you shouldn't either. We don't even know what this place is."

"Well, we're about to find out. Come on."

There wasn't a name on the building or on the first three glass-fronted doors we passed. It smelled and looked clean enough in the hall, like somebody cared to vacuum, or at least hire someone with a good supply of lavender cleanser.

At the last door, we hit pay dirt. Stick-on numbers matched the address we'd found in the ruins of the blue house and bold letters announced the company name, Hidden Treasures. There was a list of open days and hours, a website address and the tag line, "We list it, sell it and ship it. Your trash is someone else's treasure."

"Huh," Gator said.

I stopped him before he scratched his head or sucked his teeth and added an "Ay-uh."

I said, "It's one of those places for people who want to do the auction or online selling thing, but they don't want to do the work. They're just lazy, or maybe the shipping part's a hassle."

"Have you done that?" Gator asked.

"Me? No. Why would I need to do that? Come on."

I put my hand on my gun inside my jacket, then pushed the door open slowly. It was a simple layout, one open room with two desks, stacks of boxes against one wall, bag of Styrofoam peanuts under the windowsill. I pushed the door open wider. A stout woman in a floral top and matching head scarf had her back to us, singing quietly, swaying. She was bent over a trash-can, trying to dump it into a large bag. She'd almost transferred all the trash, when she saw us in the doorway and startled. She dropped the bag and the bin, shredded paper going everywhere, as she raised her hands and cried, "*Ay Dios Mio!*"

I looked at Gator who gave me the go ahead nod and I withdrew my hand from under my jacket and raised both, miming her. "It's okay," I said, slowly approaching. "Sorry we scared you."

There weren't any other doors or closets, no place to hide a bunch of junkies or a ring of sex traffickers. There was just this woman and her cleaning supplies. I was beginning to think we had the wrong place.

The woman continued to babble in Spanish, backing away from me like I was contagious. I finally noticed the cord running from her belt to her head. I motioned to her ears.

Remove your headphones must be a universally understood hand motion. As soon as she did, Gator told her in Spanish that we were there to see someone about listing some furniture.

I moved toward the desk he'd been standing by as he spoke to the woman, calming her, asking her about the business while he helped her collect the spilled trash.

I caught a few words, something about deliveries, *dinero,* and *caramelo.* She did a lot of nodding and Gator seemed pleased with her answers, I understood that much of the conversation. I was still learning the language, so I let Gator take point and would ask him to fill me in later. By the time I was backing toward the door, the cleaning woman was blushing and giggling, tucking Gator's number and a few twenties into her cleavage.

I hoped he had something worthwhile from *Señora* Clean, because the few papers and bits of mail I'd been able to get a look at on the desk didn't tell me much. And the scrolling wallpaper pictures on the computer monitor might have been generic stock photos from some travel site.

I waited until we were on the sidewalk, then asked, "Was that all necessary?"

"What?"

"Oh, come on. You, the flirting, the suddenly perfect Spanish accent? I'm surprised you didn't slip the money into her bra yourself."

I started to walk away, heading for the truck.

Gator laughed, then ran to catch up.

"Jojo? Wait. Are you jealous? Wow. I'm flattered."

I picked up the pace, reaching the truck, then remembered he had the keys.

"Listen," he said, touching my arm. "That was nothing, I mean, come on, she had beautiful eyes, but—"

I tugged my arm out of his grasp, held my hand out for the keys.

He knew when he was beat. He sighed, handed them over. I unlocked the door, climbed in and took my sweet time unlocking his side.

I didn't know what had gotten into me. I was jealous and it felt horrible, like shrinking from the inside, worse than the hardest gut punch I'd ever taken.

Gator climbed into the passenger seat, tried to read the look on my face.

"Sorry," I said, before he had to chance to open his big mouth. "That was stupid. I know what you did back there was necessary. I don't know why I reacted like that. I never should have gotten you involved in this mess. I—"

"I'm happy to be involved, Jojo. This is *our* mess. We're in this together. And maybe I like this new Jojo. The softer side of you. It's...sweet."

I threw the first thing I laid my hands on—a half-empty bottle of water. It careened off his head and landed on the dash as I said, "I am *not* sweet. And don't you forget it!"

Gator smiled. "By the way, I think I know where to find your pal, Candy."

I grumbled for a bit, then finally gave in. "Oh yeah, where?"

"Well, we've got to find a truck first."

"A truck, huh? Well imagine that. What kind of truck?"

"Well, Roma said—"

"Roma?"

"The cleaning lady. She said Candy pays her every other Friday and sometimes she sees other girls coming in. They come in empty handed, but leave with boxes and envelopes, which is strange enough, but sometimes she'll see a tractor trailer parked out front, stays overnight each time. Which I think is weird, because of city block regulations."

Before I could ask how Gator knew about city block regulations, he gave me a description of the rig, told me to ask around.

"Use that social media for good," he said, putting off modern technology with a brush of his hand.

I typed the information into a group Facebook message, then onto our Twitter feed, asking anyone with knowledge of the rig to contact me immediately. I waited for the ping telling me the posts had gone through, then closed down the phone, but before I set it back in the dashboard holder I remembered one more place that might be helpful.

I keyed the same information about the truck and the area into the message boards of the T.A.S.T. Force website, the sex trafficking rescue group whose card I'd found tucked in the corner of the truck stop bathroom mirror.

CHAPTER 25

While we waited for someone to ID the rig, we drove. I told Gator how much I'd missed driving. I didn't tell him why I needed to feel the steering wheel, cold and solid under my hands, the slight shifting of the seat as I leaned into a turn, the solid and ready response of the T-800 pulling us along. I needed the reassurance that my world as I once knew it, still existed. A few miles down the road, heading away from the path of the tornado, my shoulders dropped, the annoying cramp in my lower back relaxed a little more.

I hit the radio buttons until I found a local news channel, then listened for reports of missing prisoners, or a body count at the jail, but the reporters seemed more focused on collecting tornado displaced animals and clearing roads for emergency vehicles. There were updates on some other local news stories, and they continued to ask people to stay off roads in the affected areas, to sit tight and wait if they needed help. I knew how well a message like that would go over with me.

Gator's phone rang from the sleeper unit.

"Isn't that your phone?" I asked as he unbuckled and hurried to the back.

"Why don't you have it on you?" I called after him. I stopped myself before I reamed him out for stupid shit like not having his phone on twenty-four-seven, for not being there when I needed him, not—I squeezed my eyes and concentrated on the road. It wasn't Gator's fault. He wasn't the bad guy. He didn't kidnap me or make me a sex slave. He didn't force himself on me, or—

Gator slid back into the passenger seat, saying into the phone, "Hang on, Mac. Say that again. I've got Jojo on speaker."

Gator clicked up the volume on the phone, held it so I could hear the man's voice.

"Hey, man, sorry. I couldn't get close enough to ID your girl. Cops all over that jail, and no one taking a dime. If you want, I can go back later, let you know?"

"What did you see?" I asked.

It took him a second to respond. I imagined him trying to get the details right, sort out what was irrelevant. This was someone Gator had handpicked; he'd be good at his job.

"Emergency vehicles on site, ten guards moving prisoners into vans, coroner was there, some press. I had eyes on eight body bags. No one fitting your description. If she's a runner, she'd better be good. They had dogs all over the grounds."

I shook my head. "She was badly injured, no way she ran. At least not alone."

Gator held the phone to his mouth. "Thanks, Mac. Let's spread out the search to local hospitals, see if you get a hit there."

"Got it."

The phone went dead. Gator ended the call and slipped the phone in his pocket, patting it, looking at me, reading my mind. "It was just this once. I needed that charger. Every other time. It's right here. Promise."

I turned back to the road, thinking. The mention of hospitals had given me an idea.

"Sometimes, Gator, you have to go back to the beginning to get the answers you need," I said checking the empty road, then swinging wide and U-turning Sabrina in a move that rattled the dishes in the cupboard and made Gator buckle up.

I found a parking spot in a hotel construction zone three blocks from Oklahoma City General Hospital. It was business as usual on this side of town. Shops were open, with A-framed sidewalk signs offering tunic sales, deli sandwiches, coffee specials. The area was bustling with lunchtime traffic, people on the street seemingly oblivious to the recent tornado. Or maybe since it happened so often they were immune to Mother Nature's temper tantrums.

Gator paced me as I hurried down the sidewalk following the big blue "H" signs.

"So," Gator said. "Did you hear from your friend? Is that why we're here?"

"No. It was something I heard on the radio about the girl they'd found raped and beaten under the bridge underpass. Remember her?"

I could tell he did, the way his face went taut, his fingers unconsciously curling into fists. I told him how the reporter had said she was lucky to be alive, saying if those two college kids hadn't missed their ride and tried to walk home, she wouldn't have been found for days. He'd described the girl, tall, slim, with long brunette hair, clear blue eyes. He'd said the cops were calling her Girl X to protect her identity, but her mother had been interviewed, and as happy as she was to get her daughter back she'd let a few details slip, like the fact that though she'd enjoyed the water view from the hospital room, she was looking forward to the day her daughter, a competitive swimmer, could get back into it and on with her life.

I pointed to the sign for the hospital, and under it a sign announcing the entrance for the lakeside walking trail.

A quick scan of the building layout showed that the only lake view rooms would be on the southwest side, probably upper floors. In the lobby, I scanned the directory and found the name of an urologist with office space that fit the bill. Gator used his charm on the young desk volunteer and we were on the floor in less than four minutes, having decided to take the stairs. Gator struggled to open the door, balancing his complimentary donut on top of his complimentary coffee—all from Miss Helpful.

"Here, geez," I said, reaching past him and pushing open the door. I resisted the urge to let it slam shut on him.

"Sure you don't want some?" he asked, offering both coffee and donut.

I shook my head.

"Left or right?" he asked, downing the donut in two bites, washing it down with a few slugs from the paper cup.

I blinked. "You tell me, Einstein."

Just then a girl laughed, followed by the deep guffaw of a man. "That way," Gator said, taking off to the left.

I followed slowly, reading the names on the doors, peeking inside a few. By the time I'd caught up to Gator he had his arm around a uniformed cop, their backs to me. The empty chair propped against the wall next to the door labeled U-21 might as well have been a red flag.

Gator used his free arm to snake around and pull his cell phone out. I retraced my steps and slipped into the first empty room I saw. A second later my phone buzzed.

I had to smile. "So, you finally listened to me, huh?" I mumbled, remarking how a stubborn, technologically frightened man had figured out how to talk text. "Good for you."

But, bad for me. I had to find another way in to see Girl X, because that guard wasn't going anywhere.

It took three tries to find an unlocked room, four to find one with a spare set of scrubs. They weren't pristine and they weren't my size, but they would do. Finding a spare hospital badge might be a little more difficult.

Turns out, it wasn't. A little bump and snatch from the white-haired nurse in the elevator, a stolen lunch tray off a cart outside the wing, and there I was, standing in front of Gina Sharp's hospital room. Gator did his bit to distract the guard long enough for me to slip by, just another faceless nurse.

I backed into the room like I'd seen on countless soap operas and TV shows over the years, wished I'd thought of snagging some white shoes, but figured no one was looking at my feet.

A woman, who had to be the girl's mother—same profile, same slight build—stood at the end of the bed, barely looking up as I came in. I set the tray by the sink and went straight to the computer, glad the screen was frozen on the patient's name and status. I clicked the mouse pretending to be checking charts, meds, something, anything.

"Mrs. Sharp, would you like to take a break?"

She looked at me, and I saw that she'd been on her phone, updating a Facebook page, the tell-tale blue screen blinking off as she stammered, "What? I'm sorry. Take a break?"

"Sure. Go get a cup of coffee, stretch your legs. I'll feed your daughter lunch, keep her company until you get back."

"Well, I—"

The girl looked up from the magazine she'd been pretending to read. "Go Mom. Please, go. I'll be fine."

The mom made a big show of leaving, kissing her daughter, tucking in the covers, hovering, patting. It was painful for me to watch and I wasn't the one in the bed.

Eventually she grabbed her purse, smoothed her hair, then stared, as if she'd finally noticed me.

"Do I know you?" Mrs. Sharp asked, craning her neck to see my ID badge.

I put on my most annoying voice, added that little sunshine-y lilt that was designed to make people all over the world uncomfortable and smiled the widest my mouth could go. I was pretty sure I looked like a snake about to swallow a baby deer.

"Hi-ya I'm Nurse Nancy. I'm in training. First day in this wing. Glad to meet you. I'd love to talk to you about your feelings and how we can help little missy over here know just how much you love and care for her and how important it is to know Jesus Christ our Lord and Savior. Isn't that right, Mrs. Sharp? Can I call you Judy?"

The woman practically ran out of the room.

I turned to the gawking teen in the bed and winked.

"Don't worry. That's just a thing I do, kidding around, you know."

I stepped closer to the bed. She looked like any young girl, fresh faced, except for the healing bruises and cuts of course, but I knew I would never see the worst of her injuries. No one would. That was her private burden.

"How are you feeling, Gina? I heard you were going home soon. You're probably excited."

The girl looked away, eyes at half-mast. I wondered if her system was still drugged up from the Somalis, if they had done the same things to her that they had done to me.

I said, "It's going to be okay. You have to believe that."

"Don't," she said. "If I hear one more person call me lucky, or tell me I am blessed or some kind of shit like that I'm going to scream. You can't say it's going to be okay. You have no idea what—"

"But I do. I escaped them too."

Her head snapped back, eyes wide, hands clenching the blanket. "What?"

"Omar, Hollywood, Big Adbi, Jabby, Black Dog, Nadifa, Candy. I was there too."

"Wait. Who are you?" Her scared eyes darted to the door as she pushed herself upright in the bed. "What do you want?"

I rushed to get the words out before she freaked, before she screamed for the guard.

"My name's Jojo Boudreaux. It's a long story. Too long for now. All you need to know is I'm on your side, Gina, and I need your help to rescue the other girls. We need to stop the Somali Mafia before they hurt anyone else. We need to shut them down for good."

I could see her weighing my words, evaluating me, not trusting anyone, especially herself, knowing that her last judgment call had not been a wise one. Going against the Somalis had led her here, to a life where she may never be safe again. She was the half-dead girl found under a bridge. But more than that, she was living testimony to monsters in our midst. I reached for her hand, saying nothing, willing her to understand what this was—an opportunity. Gina Sharp had fought for herself at least once.

I needed her to do it again, this time, for the other girls.

Maybe she saw we had something in common, somehow saw our twisted character, that piece of us the Somalis had fucked over and would remain forever bent no matter how many Hail Marys we said. I believed in Heaven and Hell and I knew in my heart of hearts that my soul was headed north, and not because I deserved it, or understood a gnat's ass of the eternal "why." It was just the way it was and I was damn thankful.

Whatever Gina Sharp had done, she could never deserve the way it would change her forever, leaving her with a permanent hesitation in speech and action. It might one day cost her a job, a marriage, a kid. You could survive a thing, but you would never be the same. Nothing was ever the same when the hand of the clock ticked around.

She finally had to courage to meet my eyes and saw something there that made her nod. When she spoke, her voice was just above a whisper, as if by saying the words out loud she might give them too much power, too much truth.

CHAPTER 26

We were holed up in another little motel, trying to stay out of the way of tornado clean-up crews, building inspectors and street-corner preachers. Why did the mighty hand of Mother Nature bring out the Bible thumpers? Every avalanche, flash flood, tsunami, hurricane and superstorm of the last two thousand years had been charted and studied. Not one of them had brought back Jesus. I was beginning to think their efforts of salvation might be put to better use building an ark, or at the very least, studying climate change.

Gator had picked up Chinese food for dinner. Across the room, the television droned. Road closings scrolled across the bottom of the screen as a reporter spoke of clean-up efforts and told folks where they could go for a hot meal if they were homeless. I wondered how many homeless people were sitting around watching TV.

Gator handed me a take-out container and a fork, knowing how I felt about eating with wooden sticks.

"Thanks," I said, reaching for another beer.

The beer was our treat, knowing we wouldn't be driving any time soon and had no business to attend to. Gator had updated Charlene only to tell her I was fine and she could stop worrying, but not to tell anyone, as they were still working out some details. He had his cop and government buddies working on clearing my name and was talking to an attorney about me coming in to discuss a deal. The more we could gather on the Somali Mafia, the stronger my end of the bargaining table.

I'd been telling him about Gina, how she'd been their prisoner for a week, a runaway who'd changed her mind and just wanted to go home. But it wasn't that easy. That last night on the streets, she tried to run. Omar and Hollywood caught her. She had a knife, tried to kill herself when they found her. They beat the shit out of her, but in the end the deepest cuts were her own.

"She's going to be okay," I said, finishing my beer. "I mean, as soon as she gets out of there and gets her mom off her back."

Gator rolled his head. "Sure. That ought to be easy."

"Anyway, I asked her if she knew about Candy and Hollywood running heroin. She said everyone did—except Nadifa and this man who only came to the house once. They called him Mufasa."

"What?" Gator asked.

"Mufasa. You know, like in *The Lion King*."

"*The Lion King*?"

"Oh come on, Gator. The animated movie with the lion and the wombat? Wait. I think it was a wild boar. Yeah, a pig."

He snorted. "Sure it wasn't a honey badger?" he asked.

"Right. Like a honey badger would hang out with a lion. "

"Why not? They're both badasses, right?"

We might have gone on discussing wild animals and the virtues of animated heroes, or might have finished our Chinese and beers and begun hatching plans in our twisted little minds.

I said, "What Gina told me about this Mufasa guy makes me think he's also the Boss Man. She mentioned the palace place, said they took certain girls there, called them *auction girls*."

Gator stopped chewing. We looked at each other, neither one of us wanting to say what we were thinking, neither one of us ready to admit how ugly this was.

"I know," I said. "We said we were going to turn this over to the cops once we knew what was going on, or at least more. But Gator, they may not be able to help. I mean, not like we can."

He swallowed and reached for his beer. After a long slug he pointed the bottle at me and said, "You mean because we aren't the law and aren't bound by rules and regulations?"

"I didn't say that." I poked around in my rice container, no longer hungry.

Gator set his food aside and lifted my chin with his thumb. "Well maybe *I'm* saying that. Jojo? Come on. Let's get those motherfuckers."

I smiled as my heart went pitter-patter.

"Okay," I said. "But first we have to find them."

"Right. Let's start with the palace Gina told you about. Where do you suppose that is?"

"Knowing these guys...wait a minute." I reached for my laptop, activated the browser, then typed, "Palace, Oklahoma."

"Is it a town?" he asked, leaning over my shoulder.

"No. Hang on." I tried some other combinations, opening predictive search pages. "Wait. Here." I scrolled down. "It's an event venue, a place where people throw large parties, host weddings, wedding receptions."

I clicked on some photos of elaborately decorated rooms and gardens, just like a palace.

"Look at this. A miniature version of the room at Versailles," I said, enlarging the mirrored room, a blonde bride and her court reflected over and over again in all their shiny happiness.

"Check it out," Gator said, pointing to the red arrow on the page. "It's been closed for months, undergoing renovations."

There was a tag at the bottom of the website apologizing for the change, telling people they would reopen under new management.

"Where is this place?" Gator asked, clicking the directions icon.

The pop-up map detailed driving instructions to a town west of Oklahoma City, called El Reno.

"Well, I know where we're going," I said snapping the laptop shut and reaching for my jacket.

Gator pulled me back. "Not so fast. We may need reinforcements."

I laughed, punched his arm. But, from the look on his face, he wasn't kidding. He even went so far as to add the head-tilt and brow-raise.

"Seriously?" I said.

He stared at me.

"Okay. Okay. Geez."

It was my idea to call Ivory Joe. Gator agreed. We could work together. We'd done it before, and I trusted Ivory Joe with my life.

It was Ivory Joe's idea to call Mickey B.

"Really?" I said, staring at the phone in my hand. "I thought you two, you know."

"What?" Ivory Joe asked, his voice booming through the speaker.

"Hey, the last time I saw you guys together you weren't exactly pals."

"Yeah, well, we've moved on since Shannon and Bunkie. We've got an agreement."

"An agreement, huh?"

"Yeah, Jojo. An agreement. We work together sometimes. That's all you need to know. We'll see you soon."

I wasn't going to tell him I was worried that he was hanging out with a guy who courted trouble, a so-called *special agent* for an agency that can't be named, because I'd been in touch with Mickey B, too. A girl could do worse than to have a man like that in her pocket.

Waiting for the guys to arrive in OK City, I read up on human trafficking, the monsters making millions acting as modern day slave holders. Before I became thoroughly depressed about humanity, my phone started blowing up. Twitter direct messages, replies to my Facebook posts and at least four texts, with more loading. Our description of the rig was working.

"I think we've got him," I said, scrolling through the messages. "He's been parked at The Fuel Fox since this morning. A driver a few stalls over dropped a pin and sent this photo."

"Let me see." Gator held his hand out. He pinched and pulled, enlarging a trailer painted with flames. "Roma said *fire*, but she must have meant flames."

"Flames? "Shit," I said, staring at the big red atrocity. "I know that rig. It's the Flamethrower. And, unfortunately, I also know the driver."

"Of course you do," Gator said, grabbing his jacket and scooping up the keys to Sabrina. "Wait, don't tell me. You used to date him."

"No!" I said, closing the motel door, hurrying after him. "Not him. Of course not."

Gator glanced back at me, not slowing a bit.

"It was his brother, or cousin."

"Great," Gator said, climbing into the rig.

"Hey, it was only a fling. I barely remember the guy," I said, buckling in. Gator's door slammed on the other side of the truck, louder than normal.

My mind quickly went to all those other guys, the ones *Maxine* had been forced to spend time with. I took a deep breath and concentrated on giving Gator directions. Left turns. Right turns. Yield. Merge. I kept my mind in a place where things made sense.

CHAPTER 27

At the Fuel Fox, Gator drove past the red rig and pulled into an open stall, parked Sabrina, unbuckled his belt and reached for the door handle. "Okay. Let's go."

"Slow down," I said, grabbing his sleeve. "What are you doing?"

"I'm going to have a chat with Mr. Flamethrower."

"Is that right? And what are you going to say? That you think he's in cahoots with the Somali Mafia and he'd better stop it, right now? Because if that's your plan, you'd better not forget to wag your finger and stamp your foot."

Gator met my eyes, saw through my ridiculous petulant toddler routine and ignored me just the same, jerking his arm away.

I hurried after him as he bulldozed toward the truck. We approached from the front, worked our way around. She was a beauty. Mack's iconic bulldog held court on the gleaming red hood, hunkered over a custom chrome grill and matching twenty-four-inch Texas square bumper, the whole thing was almost too shiny for my eyes. She was a truck lover's paradise with brilliant little details from flame-shaped hood strips and latches to delicately curved fenders and intakes—more flames—all the way up to a set of tall, fat chrome stacks, finished off by an amazing fiery 3D paint job. It was hard to believe this was a working rig.

I pulled myself up onto the running board to check the cab. No sign of the driver. The engine wasn't even idling. He'd either been here for a while or planned to be. I hopped down to catch up with Gator who stood listening to something by the trailer. He held a finger to his lips, then motioned underneath. I followed, running my hand over the shiny steel rear doors of the refrigerated trailer. The reefer appeared brand new, and empty— no padlocks or plastic ties on the door handles, no hum of a generator running. There was just the sound of music coming from the other side of the trailer.

Between the rear wheels and the side locker behind the belly tanks, the driver had strung a blue nylon hammock, a blanket hung off one side, the weighted-down center swaying a mere inch above the oil-stained pavement of the truck stop lot. A small Bluetooth speaker was propped on the legs of the man in the hammock. Someone with a fondness for nineties' pop.

As we drew closer we heard something else, a whimpering, followed by a sharp yip and cry. The asshole in the hammock was throwing stones at a skinny, dirty mutt hiding under the neighboring truck.

"Hey!" I yelled, scaring both the hammock swinger and the dog. "What the hell are you doing?" A bushy brown head popped out of the hammock, unfurling himself from the blanket. Before he could reply, I lit into him educating him on the finer art of humanity. At least that's what I told myself later.

Gator stepped between my judgmental pointing finger and the shitbag in the hammock, who was now halfway out of it and rising to his full height.

The bushy brown hair topped a handsome face, bit slack in the jaw for my tastes, but the rest of him rounded out nicely. Not too tall, definitely not too short and well-proportioned in the chest to thigh area. He was muscular, with a probable body fat of nine, maybe ten percent, bit hard to tell with the baggy jacket, but I had a feeling about what would be underneath— tan, taut skin, rippled muscles, and a few scars. I prided myself on knowing such things. I also knew, all that pretty on the outside was probably hiding something ugly inside.

"It ain't what you think," he said, pushing the hair from his eyes, turning off the speaker. "That dog is mean. Took a piece of my pants yesterday." He tugged at a tear in his pants dangerously close to his crotch. "Besides, that meat over there's gone bad."

I squatted beside the trailer, squinting to see past the hammock and under the neighboring truck. A burger wrapper flapped in the breeze, sections of meat and bun squashed, ketchup looking like dried blood. The dog was gone.

"Forget about that," Gator said, getting us back on track. "What were you doing over at Hidden Treasures?"

"Where?"

"Come on. Don't bullshit me. The shipping place over on Seventh?"

"Don't know what you're talking about," he said, but his posture and his eyes said different.

I stood, put a hand on Gator's puffed up chest and looked at the handsome hammock hanger, gave him one of my supermodel smiles, the one that made me look super nice.

"You don't remember me, do you?"

Handsome squinted his eyes. Maybe vanity stopped him from wearing glasses. He started to shake his head, then broke out in a grin. "Montana. The girl with the iron stomach." He ran his eyes down me like he was erasing every article of my clothing. "Tommy was right, you did fill out."

I felt Gator bristle.

"Guess I did," I said. "Also got that black belt. Two actually."

Handsome deflated a bit, stuffed his hands in his pockets.

I said, "And how is your..."

"Brother?" he finished.

"Yeah, brother. He still driving?" I held my ground, solid stance, confident shoulders, firm jaw. I'd changed more than this guy could imagine since the last time I'd seen him or his brother.

"No. He's doing the whole ball and chain thing now, got a few kids." He looked at Gator, back to me, blasted me with a smile and said, "Would you believe that Tommy the badass is a stay at home daddy?"

The image of the man I knew Tommy to be and the image conjured by the phrase *stay at home daddy* were so incongruous I had to laugh. "You're kidding," I said. "Don't tell me, he cooks and cleans too."

Handsome laughed. "He's a regular Marty Stewart. Oh yeah, not only that. Tommy Badass is the president of the PTA. Jojo, he drives a fucking minivan!"

We both lost it at that. Between our guffaws, I tried to tell Gator about Tommy, how he killed a wolf with his bare hands, how he fought off a gang of bikers, how he was a drinking, partying, hardworking trucking legend. The guy *always* got the load delivered. Once even latched a chain to his bumper and pulled his broken rig to its destination. I left off the part about me and Tommy, the Jimador and hot sauce bet, the fifteen-hour poker game and tie-breaking chainsaw challenge. After all, every girl needs a few secrets.

Handsome kept riffing on Tommy's new life, saying, "Skyped him last week, caught him sewing some kind of tutu for his kid's dance recital, and it wasn't his daughter. Can you imagine that? My brother with a needle and thread? He knows all the Disney princesses. Told me which ones he'd bone. I mean, is he kidding me? He doesn't even drink anymore. Says it makes him a bad role model or something."

It felt good to laugh, to finally really smile. I shook my head saying, "So you don't see much of him, huh?"

That set us off on another laughing fit.

When I finally collected myself enough to speak, I caught the look on Gator's face. No one likes feeling left out.

"Sorry," I said, wiping the laughter tears from my eyes. "You kinda had to be there. Back then, I mean."

"That's for sure," Handsome said, still chuckling.

He extended a hand to Gator. "Tim Ferguson. Nice to meet you."

"Gator Natoli. I'm Jojo's partner." Before Ferguson could comment on that tidbit, Gator tipped his head in my direction. "We drive for DST, were hoping you could help us out."

"Well, sure, anything I can do for a fellow driver." Handsome looked at me.

I looked at Gator, then back at Ferguson, suddenly unsure what we were doing there. "So, um. Like my partner asked earlier, what were you doing parked on Seventh overnight? Lady told us she's seen you there a few times."

Ferguson opened his mouth, then snapped it shut.

"Listen, we're not here to bust your stones for parking downtown overnight, or anything else. I mean *anything* else," Gator said. "We're just looking for some people we've got unfinished business with."

Ferguson folded his arms and rolled his impressive head on his thick neck, then sighed. "What's this really about?"

"You tell me," I said.

He shook his head. "There's nothing to tell. I meet a girl there when I'm in town."

"What's her name?"

"I don't know, she never told me. I never asked."

I raised a brow.

"What? Maybe I don't want to know. It's not like I'm going to friend her on Facebook or anything."

Gator said, "Let me guess. She's tall and slim, a brunette with blue eyes."

"That's right. You know her?"

"Yeah," I said. "We know her."

Before I could ask about his meetings with Candy, someone shouted, followed by a yelp—the sound of an injured dog. I squatted, scanning the open space under a row of trailers, searching for the source and caught a glimpse of white. The mangy dog from earlier hobbled past, two trucks away, dragging his back leg, something in his mouth.

"Be right back," I said, barely hearing Gator call after me as I cut down the row, jogging between trailers, heading toward the green space, in the general direction the dog had gone.

At the edge of the parking lot, a large garbage can was tipped over, its lid long forgotten. Assorted fast food bags and plastic containers were strewn across a scruffy dirt and grass area that led to woods. I righted the can, glanced inside at the trash and filth, putrid with flies and maggots. Gagging, I stepped away, took a few shallow breaths and scanned the area for the dog. If he was hurt he might be aggressive, might take me for an enemy. I didn't want that.

"Here, dog, come here boy," I called, crossing the open area, approaching the woods. I called again, alternating with a few "Here, girls," just in case.

Nothing.

I closed my eyes and blocked out the rumbling engines behind me, the whoosh of air brakes, the clank and scrape of loads being refastened, the hooting and hollering of drivers greeting each other, the PA system calling out shower numbers and open fuel lanes.

Instead, I tuned into the sound of wind rustling leaves on the hardwoods, blowing through the evergreen, like a drummer's wire brush on a well-worn skin. A bird called somewhere deeper in the wood and something skittered and hopped in the brush. There. A whimpering. I opened my eyes and stepped through the high grass toward the sound.

"Where are you, pup? It's okay. I'm not going to hurt you."

As if he understood, the dog whined again and picked his head up.

"It's okay. Easy now," I said, making my way to him. He lay on his side on a patch of tamped down sedge, pokey blades rising around him like a fence.

It took me a few tries, but I finally got near enough to diagnose his gender and injury. With a soft voice and a treat—

the remains of a forgotten protein bar in my pocket—he allowed me to touch him.

"Good boy," I said, scratching his ears, running my hand down his spine. He licked my hand as it passed over his back end, as if to tell me that was where it hurt. I could feel the fleas and ticks under his thin coat. He had sores on his feet and head. The back leg he'd been dragging hung at an odd angle. There was no blood or bone visible.

"Well, now. You aren't going to like what I'm about to do, but trust me, it has to be done."

Our eyes met and I swear he blinked and nodded. I made it as quick as I could, one knee on his shoulder to hold him down and then a swift twist, tug and pop to reposition the ball of the femoral head back into the socket. I looked around for something to tie up the leg. At home on the plantation when one of the hunting dogs dislocated a hip, Père used an ace bandage and wrapped the leg up tight against the dog's side to keep weight off the hip, give it time to heal and stay in place, but if I did that to this guy, I wasn't sure he'd survive with only three legs.

"Well, only one thing to do then. Come on, boy."

I scooped him up, careful of the bad leg. He licked my neck, draped his head over my shoulder. I tried to not think about the fleas and ticks as I made my way back to the parking lot.

Gator stood by the trash can, arms folded, shaking his head. "I let you out of my sight for one minute and you're already playing hero. What am I going to do with you, Jojo?"

As I walked past him, he called, "Wait. What are you going to do with *that*?"

It took him a few seconds to remember the old Jojo—the girl who wanted to save all the dogs—the girl who made up her mind and nothing could change it. But when he did, he ran ahead and had the door to the sleeper open, warm shower running and when I asked, he found a cloth we could use as a splint. A little more coaching and Gator came up with tea tree oil and instant white rice.

While I was bathing and flea-combing, plucking ticks and feeding the pup, Gator watched. He opened his mouth a few times, as if he finally figured out what he should say, but then closed it and made a small sound that might have been a swallowed argument. His face said *We can't keep him, this is nuts,* but his mouth said, "Shouldn't we take him to the vet? Make sure he's all right?"

"He's all right," I said, laying him on the towels and T-shirt bed we'd made in the shower. "The hip and leg will be fine and with some proper nutrition, his coat will fill in, pads will heal up. He's going to be a pretty boy."

"He's already smelling better at least," Gator said, handing me a bottle of water.

Nursing the pup gave my brain the downtime it needed. This whole time, Gator and I had been talking about finding the gang members, about shutting them down, getting retribution for the trafficked girls. We were looking at facts that pointed to the Somalis and their movements, their connections. We had never looked at the situation from another angle. I'd been running the early days through my mind, like rewinding a taped show, skipping the commercials, stopping when something got interesting. I kept coming back to Candy. The girl jumping in front of our truck in California.

That was where it started. Delight said that Candy and Hollywood were using truck stops. Gina mentioned a schedule. Ferguson said he saw the brunette when he was in town. The dots were beginning to connect.

"What did Ferguson say when I left?"

"Not much. Why?"

I drained the water bottle, crushed it and looked around, as if finding the recycles bag was the most important thing on my mind.

Gator sighed. "Okay. Out with it."

Stowing the plastic bottle, my eyes kept returning to the oven AKA secret weapons stash. "What do you mean?" I asked.

Gator slid into the banquette. "Jojo, I know how that mind of yours works. Come on. Let me help."

I hesitated a beat, knew he was right. As much as I wanted to end what *I* had started, I knew I couldn't do it alone. I'd been trying so hard to play a game, keep up this *old life facade*, that I was physically and emotionally drained. Part of me wanted to scream and hit something, but I knew that it wouldn't help. Maybe all those self-help people were right. I needed time and space to heal. And I'd get it. I would. Eventually.

I sat across from Gator, told about the drug angle. How it would be easy to hook up with a driver who had a regularly scheduled route, as most did. How maybe Tim Ferguson The Flamethrower driver was innocent. He could be in it just for the sex, and Candy was stashing her illegal cargo without him knowing. If he was meeting unnamed women at or through truck stops, they could be passing on the drugs without him knowing.

Gator was following along. "So, Candy leaves a—"

"A backpack or messenger bag of heroin," I said, remembering the schoolgirl outfit, the book bag.

"Right. She's hides it in his rig where he won't find it, and somewhere along his regular route, another girl picks it up."

"Maybe she sends back money?" I said.

"It could work. Especially if the driver has no knowledge and nothing to gain."

CHAPTER 28

I thought about that fancy paint job on the Flamethrower, how all those drivers had hit me up with a photo or a time and place where they'd seen the unmistakable rig. Would anyone be so stupid to move heroin like that? Would Tim Ferguson?

You couldn't point a finger and say without doubt who the bad guys were these days. Recently, the line of upstanding citizen and drug dealer had blurred considerably.

My father taught me to listen to my heart, to my body, to the subtle twitches beneath my skin. To always trust those instincts—one's animal nature. His lessons began on early morning duck hunts and continued with days spent fishing the banks of the bayou finding honey holes rich with fish, following creeks from a trickle to a pond, watching fat deer sleeping in the meadow, one ear alert for danger, a fawn nestled snugly with her mother.

Those instincts were easy to follow when I was outdoors, but after being cooped up in the city for so long, after being held captive, after…everything, I was afraid I'd lost the ability, afraid that natural, easy, trusting feeling would never come back.

"Let's go back and have another chat with Ferguson," Gator said.

"Chat? Forget that. I want to get inside The Flamethrower," I said. "If he already met up with Candy, she might have left something behind."

I ran my fingers through my hair. Ignored the heart palpitations and sweaty palms, I started to get up, but Gator put a hand on my arm. "What are you doing?"

"I'm going back there."

"Not alone you aren't."

"Gator, I can do this. He's going to be more willing to let me in if—"

"If what? What the hell are you thinking?"

I pulled my arm away and went to the oven, reached into the false bottom, took out my Kimber and turned to him. "I'm thinking that Ferguson will be more willing to talk to someone he knows and possibly trusts. That's all. What the hell are you thinking?"

"I'm thinking you should have learned your lesson by now. You're not going alone and you're not going armed."

" Or what? What are you going to do, Gator?" I lined up the Kimber with his right knee.

"What are you going to do, Jojo? Shoot me?"

We may have stayed that way for a few seconds or several minutes. Enough of a stand-off that it began to feel ridiculous. Who had I become?

"How about a compromise?" he said.

I tipped my head and he kept talking.

"You go alone. But, take one of the burner phones I picked up and wear these." He reached for a padded envelope sticking out of our mail sorter.

I put my gun on the counter and caught the package he tossed. What slid out looked like a cheap pair of earrings. "Your timing for gift giving could use some work," I said.

"Put them on. I lost you once. That's not happening again."

I turned the silver studs over, weighed them in my hand. "Are these—"

"Yes. Put them on. Or I will."

"I'm not a dog. You don't have to track me."

The look on Gator's face was one I knew all too well. This wasn't a negotiation.

"Fine," I said, slipping the earrings on, inserting the backs. I may have imagined the slight tingle when he activated the app on his phone.

I shoved the burner phone in my front pocket after confirming that the battery was fully charged, location services were activated and being received on Gator's phone.

The Flamethrower hadn't moved, but her engine was idling and the hammock was gone.

"Tim?" I banged on the passenger door. Country music blared through tinny speakers.

I climbed on the step, tried the door. Locked. Peered in the window and called again, as I scanned the cab—cell phone with a cracked face being charged, empty bottle of water on a torn seat, fast food bag on the floorboard of the passenger side, some sort of medal or necklace hanging from the dash.

Ferguson had been sinking his money into the latest and greatest for the outside of his rig, and neglecting his interior and his security. I was inside The Flamethrower in twenty-three seconds. I counted.

I sent a text to Gator: *Inside. No sign of Ferguson.* Took a few pictures of the interior as I searched the sleeper. There wasn't much to search. Unlike our unit, Ferguson only had forty-two inches of living space.

I went back to the cab and scrolled through his phone, duplicating his contacts and recent trips. I took a chance on a very sexy text to someone called "OKC Girl" being Candy and sent her a message: *need to see you FF#23 ASAP.*

The burner phone buzzed in my pocket. *You good? Find anything?*

Before I could reply, a wet-headed guy with a towel around his neck appeared in the driver's side-view mirror. I scrambled over the passenger seat, opened the door as quietly as I could and slipped out. On the other side of the cab, Ferguson inserted his key and opened the door. The cab shook as he hauled himself up. I pressed the passenger door closed and scooted under the neighboring trailer, out of his mirror view. I duck-walked under two rigs, and made my way to the front of the row, planning on approaching The Flamethrower as if I had just arrived.

What I didn't plan on was running into Candy.

She was in her school girl outfit and platforms, hanging on the passenger side of a deep green Mack, talking to the driver through the open window. License plate on the dirty, dented trailer said Michigan and the side of the truck boasted *Johnson and Sons, Detroit*. It could have been real or it could have been bullshit. The trailer itself bore no identity. They could be hauling cheap booze, expensive electronics or child safety seats. There was no way to tell.

I leaned against the trailer catching my breath, settling my brain. As much as I wanted to beat the shit out of Candy, I wanted to rescue those girls more and shut down the Somalis for good.

"Make sure you've got those trucks ready when I call," she said.

The voice from inside the cab yelled something which seemed to piss Candy off. She said something that was lost in the sound of his brakes releasing. Candy barely made it down the steps when the rig began to roll.

I grabbed her from behind, using the clunky shoes to my benefit, placing my right foot on her right heel, my left knee behind her left knee. When her arms flung out for balance, I grabbed one, bent the elbow and mashed it between the two of us as I swooped my arm around and clamped down on her throat. She squirmed and twisted as I dragged her to the back of the row, behind an orange trailer. Her scream was cut off as I hissed, "Don't," accentuating my words by a not so gentle poke in the ribs with the only thing I'd convinced Gator to let me take—a steak knife.

We wrestled some more and she managed to get in a painful

shot with her free hand—a three-fingered torso jab—one of my signature moves, though not as effective from her angle as it was when used in a shot to the kidneys. I'd never seen Candy like this.

Readjusting my grip, I yanked her jaw, pressing the tip of the knife a little deeper until she grunted.

"Easy," I whispered into her ear, though I could have yelled and no one would have heard over the sound of idling engines. "I'm here to make you a deal."

She relaxed a bit, tried to speak behind my hand, saying something that sounded like, *Don't hurt me,* but might have been, *I'm sorry.*

I twisted her face so she could see me. "You answer all my questions, tell me what I need to know, I'll let you go. No harm, no foul. You fuck with me? Well, then, no promises. Do you understand?"

It took her a second to process the limited options offered. When she nodded, I let up on the knife pressure and shoved her into the trailer with a gratifying thud.

I pulled the belt from my jeans as I stepped forward to catch her on the rebound. It might have been a record for hog-tying, if cowboys got to work with skinny girls, leather belts and the latch on a side box of an idling tractor trailer.

Candy tugged and squirmed, then rose to her full height and composed herself. Her recovery was impressive.

"I was hoping you'd figure it out," she said. 'From the day I picked you, I knew you were the right one."

I tried to look badass and wise, but all I could think was: *What the fuck was she talking about?*

"It hasn't been easy you know, pretending to be one of them, watching the shit they do to the girls. Undercover gigs suck ass."

She turned to me, and the way the dimming light hit her face, she suddenly looked older. I was reminded of twenty-five-year-old actresses playing high school teens on television. I still wasn't sold on this undercover cop thing.

"Kudos on the jail thing. You're kind of a legend now. Oh—" She held her breath, squinched up her face, like she thought I was going to hit her. "Delight didn't make it, by the way." The words *by the way* fell on me like a punch to the gut.

I crossed my arms, leaned on the adjacent trailer. "What about the others?"

"They're okay. Back with the gang, as it were."

"About that," I said. "Why don't you give me the short version?"

She stretched, wincing as her back cracked. "You mind if I sit?" she said. "Fucking stupid shoes."

"Not yet," I said, as I tightened the grip on the knife behind my leg. "What about those answers?"

She sighed, then spoke quickly, precisely, not like she was reciting something she'd learned, but like she'd been trained to give facts without emotion, without hesitation. I assumed that same sort of training meant she was equally able to lie—without emotion, without hesitation.

She told me she was working with a special task force. They'd been trying to infiltrate the Somali Mafia for years. They knew how they found the girls, how they lured them in, where the drop off and pick-ups were, from truck stops across the south. They were still working on the Palace and the auctions. She seemed surprised that I knew about it. Maybe a little impressed. She said she'd been trained in the vice unit, so the whole hooker thing wasn't hard for her. She shrugged, went on to say they'd been close to busting the group wide open, until the tornado hit. Now, there were complications.

I wanted to ask about the heroin and Hollywood. And there was that thing she'd said to the driver about having trucks ready, but I figured I'd have time for all those questions, in a safer place, a quieter place with Gator, Mickey and Ivory Joe backing me up.

Candy cocked her head as if she'd just realized something. "Hey, maybe you can help," she said in a way that made me feel like it had been my idea all along. "Listen, I'm sorry about...well, you know, everything that happened to you. I want what you want."

"Oh yeah? What's that?"

"To take these fuckers down. To save the girls. To end trafficking."

I was beginning to believe her. I wanted to believe her.

"Come on. Cut me loose. Let's work together."

There were of course, reservations. I wasn't one hundred percent yet, and there was still that tiny part of me that didn't trust anyone—that part had grown ten times stronger since my abduction by the same people I was thinking of voluntarily returning to—yeah, that part was feeling a bit tingly. Then I thought about the stray that let me fix its leg. About how it only took one leap of faith to get shit back on track, and for all those girls the Somali Mafia had fucked with, maybe this one step I was taking would be that break for them. I owed them at least that much.

"Hold that thought," I said, starting to walk away.

"Hey!" Candy called. "Aren't you forgetting something? She tugged at her bound hands.

I walked as slowly and calmly as I could to the front of the truck, then slipped around to the other side and called Gator.

He didn't like it. None of it.

"We have the upper hand now," I said. "There's two of us and she's on the inside."

"If she's telling the truth," Gator said, always the pessimist.

"Listen, between the trackers and the phone, you'll be with me. Plus, you've got Mickey and Ivory Joe.

He made some more noises about not liking the plan, and then his breathing changed, like he was running.

I hurried back to the orange trailer where I left Candy. Reaching behind her, one hand on her waist, one on the belt around her wrists, I said, "If I help you, we're doing this my way, got it?"

She tipped her head and agreed. As if she had a choice.

CHAPTER 29

Minutes later we were in the back seat of an all too familiar sedan. It had almost been as easy as calling an Uber.

Omar drove, with a cloaked and veiled woman in the passenger seat. *Nadifa?* She never looked up from her phone.

Candy and I worked well together. We'd come up a story that Candy had found me hooking on the lot and convinced me to come back with her, luring me with drugs. I'd pretend to be fucked up and out of it. She'd reached into a small hip bag, handed me her kit: a compact, razor blade, baggie of white powder and a straw, then brushed her hair into a ponytail and added more make-up.

"You only have to do enough so, you know, your eyes..."

I knew she was right. All the acting in the world wouldn't affect my pupils.

I snorted a small line off her compact mirror, left a little in the lining of my nose, and tried to fight the euphoria, but lost.

In the backseat of the car, staring at the glossy black hair of Nadifa, I played the drugged-out whore, a role I'd come to think of as a protective coat of armor. Forget the prostitute with a heart of gold scenario. This was wasted tough ass bitch, or maybe a girl playing turtle.

Candy spoke to Omar in a put-on sexy voice—much different from the one she'd been using with me. She leaned over the seat as he drove, telling him where to go, as if he'd never been there, correcting him as if he'd never driven.

I waited for the backhand that never came.

A few miles from the truck stop, Candy said her phone was

dead, asked if she could use his. "You know, to tell Hollywood the news." She tipped her head in my direction, grinning.

When Omar hesitated, she leaned into the seat back, giving him a perfect cleavage shot, ran her fingers across his shoulders, tickling the hair on the back of his neck, all the while pretending to not see his eyes locked on her chest. He handed her his phone, wordlessly, robotically, while Nadifa busied herself on her own phone, the screen glowing with scribbles and swirls, a language I couldn't read. She seemed indifferent to anything Candy was saying or doing.

I got the feeling the two of them weren't exactly pals.

As we drove, I slipped the steak knife out of my pocket and stashed it in the seat back. I hated giving up the only weapon I had, but there was no way they'd miss it if they patted me down, and I had a feeling that was one thing they wouldn't forget to do. Though *pat down* was a kind way of looking at it. My phone was tucked in my sock, as far down into my boot as I could get it. Candy told me to turn it off, said if they couldn't hear it, they wouldn't find it.

She typed something into Omar's phone, hit send, then quickly deleted the message. I watched her scroll through his texts and emails, check his call list, screenshot a few pages and send them to another number. All the while she kept up the inane banter, jumping from celebrity gossip to stupid animal videos she'd seen on someone's Instagram feed to the shitty weather and how much she missed the west coast.

I didn't know whether I should be more concerned with her phone antics, or where we were going. I tried to maintain the zoned-out charade by staring out the window through slitted eyes, while counting every street, memorizing every turn, mentally repeating the keyboard pattern Candy's thumb had made.

When the car slowed near a gated neighborhood I couldn't stop thinking how it reminded me of the first place we'd dropped Candy in California, a lifetime ago.

But here she was, looking as young and pretty as always.

Playing her part to perfection.

Nadifa looked up from her phone. "Five-one-seven-two," she said in her clipped speech, pointing at the keypad near the gate. Omar pulled up, powered his window down and stretched a long, ropy, black arm out the window. Sun glinted off the large gold watch on his wrist.

Within seconds the gates began to open and we rolled through. The houses weren't exactly cookie cutter, but the community was planned and stringently maintained. It was the sort of place empty-nesters lived, or young couples just starting out. I imagined Sunday afternoons at the pool where someone's grandchildren would mingle with the new neighborhood babies.

Omar left the window down, a warm breeze drifting back, bringing with it the smells of someone's cooking. It was spicy, ethnic, curry maybe. I looked at the houses as if one would have an obvious sign announcing the occupants.

I may have nodded off a bit because the next thing I knew I was being dragged down a hallway by Candy.

Somewhere a woman and man fought, loud, angry voices in Somalian, the singsong sounds fighting each other, like the people. I started to laugh. Candy poked me, whispered. "Shut up."

That only made me laugh harder, collapsing on the floor.

"What is the fuck?"

Feet approached. Shiny black loafers. I followed the feet to the legs to the rodeo belt buckle to the broad chest to the dangling gold chains to the gritted white teeth in the dark face of Hollywood.

He said again, "What is the fuck?"

I was reduced to giggles. *What the hell had Candy given me? This wasn't the same stuff the Somalis were giving us.*

Candy sidled up to him, pressing her breasts into his arm, running a finger down his chest. "Never mind. I told you I'd find her, didn't I? Now what did you want to talk to me about?"

Hollywood's anger dissipated under Candy's touch. He called over his shoulder, telling one of the boys to take care of me, or something. All I knew was my legs were rubber and they had to carry me.

We passed a room on the right that looked like a living room without any proper furniture, went down the hall past two other rooms—one with the door propped open, a smell of hot electronics drifting out. I wondered if everything had a distinct smell, like the musty taint of frustration, or the medicinal bitterness of revenge. What did I smell like? Failure? Desperation? I shook my head to clear it, felt the feeling begin to return to my legs, fought to hold it together.

They dropped me on a bed in a room with a window. Only one window, but it wasn't shuttered or boarded or barred or nailed shut. From the outside, this house probably looked like all the other cookie cutter houses, just as normal, silent and empty by day, filled with family and friends at night.

It was a great way to hide evil. In plain view.

The bed was soft enough to make me think of sleep, but as soon as I heard the men leave, I forced myself to sit up, slapping my face, pinching my thighs, then doing jumping jacks and pushups to get my blood flowing, hoping to move the drug out of my system. If only I had a gallon of water.

The yelling moved from the house to the yard. I went to the window and peered around the frame. A man in baggy pants and an oversized white T-shirt yanked the arm of a struggling girl, pulling her toward a van. *Black Dog.* The girl was crying, kicking, twisting her body to plead with someone who stood in the shadow of the house below my window.

"Please, don't let him take me back there," she cried. "Please? I'll do anything. I'll be good. I promise. Just not The Palace. Not again."

I couldn't hear the reply, but as they stepped from the shadows I recognized Nadifa. She was still wearing the Somali guntiino. She motioned and said something to Black Dog, the words muffled by the thick blue veil were short, clipped, certain. Inches of gold bangles on her arms accentuated the order, their tinkling sound carried all the way to my room, to my memory of another place and another time.

The girl took advantage of the distraction and made a run for it, slipping away from Black Dog. She ran into the street, crossing to a neighboring house, rattling the front door calling for help.

The street was deserted, most of the driveways were empty. This was the sort of suburban middle class neighborhood you'd find duplicated ten times over in a zip code. The kind of neighborhood where folks left at seven in the morning and returned at seven at night.

Black Dog sauntered across the street as the girl frantically tried to get in the house. Trapped on the porch she had little choice but to run. She made it as far as the mailbox. I could see her clearly. Pretty Latina girl with long brown hair and large eyes. She was like the rest of us, except for one thing. She was strong and feisty. She wasn't drugged or agreeable or tired, so tired all the time.

She put the mailbox between her and Black Dog, swung herself around the decorative metal post. Black Dog grabbed a handful of hair. She pulled back growling, ramming him into the mailbox, knocking it over. He fell, stunned, part over and part under the downed post. It would have been comical, big tough bad guy taken down by a girl and a mailbox. If only he hadn't reached into his waistband as he rose, hadn't drawn his weapon.

The gunshot echoed in the empty street.

Omar and Jabby ran outside yelling. Nadifa fell back into the shadows.

I sank to the floor, hands clamped over my mouth, willing away the image of the girl, running, stumbling, screaming, and then—her body jerking, frozen for a moment then collapsing.—

Voices downstairs quickly became voices in the hall. Fast-moving footsteps approached my room. I flung myself onto the bed, curled into a ball, my hair over my face, feigning sleep, I willed my heart to slow its frenetic patter.

The door creaked open. A deep voice said, "Told you. She's out of it."

I snuck a look through one half-lidded eye. It was Big Abdi.

A woman's voice said, "How can that be? Move."

The familiar floral scent reached me before she did.

Nadifa told Big Abdi, "Leave us."

The door shut, footsteps receded.

"It's okay. You can open your eyes. It's just us," she said, sitting on the corner of the bed.

Her hand was warm, gentle, brushing the hair away, revealing my face, seeking my eyes with the only exposed part of her—her large dark eyes.

She released the face veil, detaching a clip near her cheek, then pulled the fabric over her head. The guntiino was a bolt of intricately wrapped and tied cloth. Indigo blue was a good color for her, accentuating her burnished brown skin, her high cheekbones and full lips.

Gold rings on her fingers shined as if she'd polished them recently, or maybe she was one of those women who removed her jewelry every night, set it in a crystal bowl by the sink, never once worried it might be tipped over, the gold falling down the drain, entangling itself in greasy gobs of soap and hair, making something shiny and pretty into something dirty and disgusting.

Wasn't that what Nadifa and these men did to the girls they stole? These young women who started as perfect pieces of gold, shining with potential until their lives were stolen from them, until they were thrown away by parents, given up on by teachers, employers, elders. Until they became something society deemed disgusting.

Nadifa hummed softly as she stroked my hair, her bracelets jangling, a melody for her unsung song. I barely felt the stab of the needle in my arm.

She sat beside me on the mattress, her weight lowering one side of the bed, rolling me toward her, my hip bones bumping into her, part soft fabric, part soft padding of her hips. She smelled like outside, like sunshine and earth, like flowers and grass. It might have been her soap. I imagined a hand-hewn bar infused with jasmine, rose petals, buds of hibiscus, sprigs of lavender. Or she might have come to me through a meadow. The meadows of Oklahoma? Before I could erase that image, replace it with something more sensible, she reached for me, ran her hand over my hair and shoulder and arm, trailing her fingers down to mine. She whispered soft words, like a mother soothing her baby to sleep. I was afraid to open my eyes, afraid that she wasn't real, afraid there would be no one there and I'd be alone again. Alone and forgotten.

Nadifa said something, her breath warm on my neck, then arms scooped me up and carried me. The arms were gentle, not like before. The hands were light, not grabbing, not pinching or poking. I tried to open my eyes, to thank her for the small kindness, for the peace. And to thank the hands, the person behind them, those gentle hands that felt like feathers, but something was nagging at me. Something else I should be saying. Something I should be doing. If only this warm, soft place wasn't so deep, so inviting.

CHAPTER 30

I came around to the sound of music, the sort of pounding beat that made you dance, that you felt in your pores, as if your body knew what your brain couldn't understand. It was too loud for the neighborhood we'd been in. I thought for a second that I was wearing headphones, maybe the reason I could hear the music so well was because it was inside me. I tried to focus on that one repeating sound, telling myself to wake up, come to the surface, emerge.

My legs were cold, something dragged across my thighs. I concentrated on waking every sense, tensing and releasing my muscles, taking deep breaths. The swivel chair beneath me felt like plush leather, the sort I imagined finding in a man's library, the kind you'd sink into when smoking a cigar and sipping whisky.

I opened my eyes, blinked the room into focus. Nine other chairs, four to my right, five to my left, lookalike girls in each one—long brown hair, red silk robe, Lucite heels. Our wrists were strapped down. A corresponding number in the line-up was painted on the floor in front of us. We faced the glass wall of a dark room where the glow from computer screens illuminated two rows of chairs, men in each.

I pretended to stretch my neck, saw two guards at the door. Omar and Big Abdi. The ceiling was open rafters with long pendant lights mounted over each girl.

A monotone voice came from a speaker, "Remove the restraints. We are ready to begin."

Omar and Big Abdi unstrapped our wrists, then moved to

back to their position at the door.

The speaker voice said, "Three."

As the light over the girl flickered on, she stood. Her silk robe fell away like a whisper.

"Turn around."

The more I stared at the glass wall, the more I could make out the images behind the glass. The computer guys wore headsets or spoke into phones, others held up fingers, or fanned cash, some with odd colorful printing.

There was a disturbance behind the glass, hands and arms raised, two men rising from their seats, another ripping off the headset, gesturing wildly.

When someone stepped from the back of the room they appeared to settle down.

The speaker clicked on, the same robotic voice. "We will move things along more rapidly this evening. Let us begin. Please stand, drop your robe and turn slowly."

When no one moved, Omar said, "That's you. All of you. Get up!"

Number one untied her robe and let it fall onto the chair, then slowly turned, as the rest of us followed suit.

"Face the back of the room," the voice said.

I used the chair for balance, jamming my shins against it, trying to remain upright in the slippery shoes, pinching the tops of my thighs to wake me up, keep me from drifting.

The voice again. "Bend over."

The girl beside me leaned forward, palms on the chair. "Whatcha waiting for?" she whispered to me through her curtain of hair.

"Ginger?" I asked. Her nose looked perfect. I would have thought the hit she took from Omar would have left her with a crooked shnozz or at the very least a tell-tale bump.

"Yeah. Shhh. Listen, the quicker you do it, the quicker they decide and we can go. C'mon."

I glanced down the line. The girls were all complying. Some

less steady than others, their asses swaying, wigs sliding askew.

A few seconds later, the speaker crackled. The voice smooth and sure said, "One, seven, eight, nine and ten, please stay standing."

Omar stepped forward, touching the shoulder of each girl whose number was called. One of them smiled. I wanted to tell her she wasn't a winner.

But what did I know? Maybe the guy behind the glass was a good person. Maybe he was here because he was shy and didn't like dating, Maybe, he would shower my lookalike hooker friend with gifts and money and maybe I would wake up tomorrow from this dream and laugh about the whole thing, or maybe, just maybe, I could attack Omar and Big Abdi, access the glass room and kill every fucking one of them.

Big Abdi told the lucky five to get dressed and follow him. Number ten looked toward Ginger, eyes wide, frightened. Ginger shook her head tightly, lifted her chin. The girl got it. A quick nod and she bit her trembling lip, pulled back her shoulders, then wrapped the robe tighter and walked out.

"Now what?" I asked Ginger.

"You'll see," she said, reaching for her robe.

A light went on in the glass room as if someone had opened a door. The men were shaking hands, patting backs, one adjusted the crotch of his pants, spending too much time cupping his balls. I tried to memorize every face, something about each one of those sons of bitches. I wanted to make sure that when I took them down, I got the right douchebag.

I called to Omar, "Hey, can I use the bathroom? I really gotta go."

"You can hold it," he said.

"I don't think so," I said. "I've been holding it."

Ginger said, "What's your problem, Omar? Let her use the fucking toilet. Unless you gotta ask someone first?"

He seemed to think it over, the two ideas, me using the bathroom, and him having to ask someone if it was okay, meaning him admitting he couldn't do his job.

"All right, come on," he said, "Hurry up."

He unlocked the door and held it open for me. "The rest of you stay here."

The hallway was empty, dingy wall-to-wall carpet masking our footsteps. Every other overhead lamp was out forcing us to walk in a light, dark, light, dark pattern. I glanced back at Omar, saw the glint of the gun in his waistband, caught him yawning. I pretended to be sluggish, confused, letting the robe slip open, exposing my breasts and ass with each step. I sung under my breath, bumped against the walls, feeling for switches, looking for doors, security cameras or monitors. I fake tripped on the heels, cursed and kicking them off, leaving them behind.

Omar grabbed my elbow. "Come on. We don't have all day."

At the end of the hall he opened the door to a single toilet restroom, ushered me inside then took his place in the doorway. "Make it fast," he said, crossing his arms.

"You mind?" I asked, motioning for him to turn around.

He shook his head and grinned.

I stepped closer, pointing wildly, waving my arms. "You're a real pig, you know that? A real fucking pig. What would your mother think, huh?"

I poked him in the chest. He loomed a foot over me, twice my width. All I needed was to get his hands away from the gun. One more poke and he reacted—grabbing my shoulders, trying to push me back.

I pulled down on his right elbow, as I pushed in hard on the side of his clavicle with my index and middle finger, hooked around the bone and pulled. Omar winced, fell to his knees, howling. I guided his fall into the door, broke his arm against my thigh, then struck hard and high behind his ear with the heel of my hand knocking him out.

"And *that* is how Wing Chun takes down a pig," I said as I stole his gun and the set of keys on his belt loop.

I raced back to the room of girls, unlocked the door and slipped inside, glad to see the glass room dark again. Ginger had swiveled her chair around to face the door. Before she said anything, I put a finger to my lips, then mouthed, "Let's go."

Ginger motioned to the others to swivel their chairs too. They took off their wigs and hung the hair off the chair back. From the glass room, it might look like they were slumped in the chairs. It wasn't a great ruse, but if it bought us time, it was worth it.

Ginger gathered the girls, pushed them into the hall.

"How well do you know this place?" I asked her as I closed the door behind us.

"I know where the exit is and that's all we need right now."

"Good, "I said, nodding. "Get them out of here and as far away as you can." I took off one of the earrings. "Keep this. It'll help them find you."

"Who?"

I told her about Gator, Ivory Joe and Mickey. "They'll take care of you."

"What about you?" Ginger asked.

"I've got some unfinished business. Don't worry about me."

The girls huddled a few feet away, looking like nervous mice. Ginger jerked her thumb in their direction. "I'd better go. Wait. Thank you," she said, hugging me, whispering, "Whatever you've got to do? Do it for Delight."

I nodded, hugged her back, then watched them hurry away.

Gripping Omar's gun and wishing I was wearing more than a silk robe, I tried to make my way to the entrance of the glass room. The building was a maze of corridor and dead ends. It didn't help that I was distracted by the swishing fabric against my skin and that I was chilled from the cold floor under my bare feet.

The third door I tried opened. It was a storeroom of sorts—racks of cleaning products and paper towels, boxes of decorations, tablecloths and a bin of lost and found items. I dug through some kids' clothes, hats and mittens and found a baggy shirt, a pair of sweatpants and some ugly plastic clogs. It wasn't my first choice, but getting covered up helped me focus and that was the important thing.

I slipped out of the room and closed the door behind me. Angry voices carried down the hall. I pressed my back against the wall and moved toward the noise, gun first. Around the second corner, I hit pay dirt. The glass room. I crept closer, trying to see without being seen.

Inside, a man with a Southern twang spoke. "Tornado? That wasn't nothing. I've taken shits that did more damage. And hung around a lot longer too." The man laughed, an annoying donkey sound. No one joined in.

A chair scraped the floor as another voice spoke, softer, feminine. "As I was saying, I'm sorry we weren't able to do more business tonight. There have been a few setbacks that I'm working on and expect to have full operations up and running shortly."

The door opened slightly. The speaker was partly visible, hand on the doorknob, sleeve pushed up revealing several inches of gold bracelets.

"Full operations? Well I should hope so," Donkey Laugh said.

Nadifa's grip on the door tightened. "Excuse me one moment," she said, before stepping from the room. I flattened myself against the wall, hiding in the shadows as she typed on her phone, the ting and whoosh registering her sent text. She slipped the phone back into the folds of her dress, gathered herself, then went back into the room saying something in Somalian, pointing and shaking her head, I took the opportunity to approach, slinking down the hall, positioning myself behind the half-opened door. Peeking between the frame and the door's edge I could see the back of a man's head, part of Nadifa's leg and facing them both, Candy and Black Dog.

Donkey Laugh was saying, "I don't think you heard what I said."

Candy took a step forward then stopped abruptly and raised her hands. "Listen, Mr., uh, Mufasa. Let's be reasonable. Put the gun away. You know we've had issues before, and we always come through, don't we?"

She lowered her hands, saying "We did okay tonight with the girls, the others we'll move on. We'll do better next week. I've got the trucks lined up and took care of the T.A.S.T. Force thing, like I said I would. So, we're good, right?"

Mufasa tapped his gun against his thigh, debating.

The indecisiveness must have been too much for Black Dog. He lunged off the glass wall, arms flapping like a rapper on stage. I expected him to grab his crotch, or toss a mic any second.

"Oh we good. Ain't that right, Mufasa?" he said, leaning in, getting into the guy's face. "We sure are good. From how I see, you got no problems."

"Maybe that's not how I see it," Mufasa said, raising his Glock, snugging his finger up to the trigger, taking aim.

"Dog," Candy said. "You don't—"

Black Dog mean-mugged her. His face looked just as it had before he shot the girl in the street. He stared at Mufasa, cocked his head, smiling. "Why we need you, again? You saw them. We have a sheik. We have politicos. We have men with billions. You and your trucks, your cowboys, are how do you say, small nuts?"

Mufasa wrapped his other hand around the gun. A gold lion thumb ring glinted, diamonds for eyes. He scoffed. "You mean, small peanuts?"

"I mean what I say." Black Dog leaned in, pushing his forehead into the barrel of the Glock. His eyes widened as he whispered, "I am the Black Dog."

Mufasa hesitated, then tried to pull his gun back, but Black Dog grabbed his wrist, pressed the barrel harder onto his glistening black skin.

Mufasa tried to laugh. "Hey. You're crazy. You need to lay

off the product, son. Making you mad in the head."

Candy stepped in, but Nadifa cut her off, saying something to Black Dog. She waited for him to let go of the Glock's barrel. When he did, a perfect circle was impressed on the skin between his eyes.

Nadifa looked at the man in the chair, saying slowly, "A madman does not lack wisdom."

Mufasa said, "And what in the Sam Hill does that mean?"

"It is a Somali proverb. A lesson."

"Only proverbs I know are in the Bible," Mufasa said, dropping the Glock back to his lap, shining the barrel on his pants. "And I know you whore-selling dope-dealing camel jockeys ain't reading no goddamn Bible."

He looked at Candy, licked his lips. "Now you, you might be able to recite some proverbs. Unless your mouth was full." He laughed at his own joke, tried to explain, complete with hand motions, his tongue poking out his cheek. Black Dog clenched his fists.

"Shut the fuck up," Candy said.

"What? Are you a sensitive junkie whore?" He leaned forward, dangling the gun, then lowered his voice, mocking. "Did I hurt your feelings? Wah. Wah. Wah."

"I said, shut the fuck up."

"Wah. Wah. Wah."

Candy reached into her waistband, spun around drawing a small .38, pulling the trigger.

The back of Mufasa's head exploded, spraying the rear wall of the room with brains and blood, his Glock falling to the floor, his body following with a thud. I gasped, covering my mouth with my hand and slipping back into the shadows, ears ringing.

Candy said, "I told you to shut up, you stupid motherfucker."

I peeked back into the room. Candy holstered her gun, then stooped to pick up the Glock. Behind her, Black Dog furiously wriggled a finger in his ear. "That was loud."

Nadifa leaned against the wall, arms crossed, staring at the dead body, when she suddenly looked through the glass to the other room.

"Curious."

"What?" Black Dog asked, tugging his ears.

"Look," Nadifa said, as Candy joined her at the glass wall. "Like Dog said, that was loud, but they didn't move or scream or anything."

Candy banged on the glass. "Hey! Turn your chairs around."

It didn't take them long to figure it out.

She said, "They're gone," then, "Shit!" Exactly what I was thinking.

Nadifa yelled, "Dog, Get Omar and Big Abdi. Hurry!"

Hurry was also in my plan. I backed away, making a run for it, just as the three of them barreled out of the room. I slid right of my plastic shoes and fell face first with a splat, Omar's gun clattering and sliding out of my reach.

"What the hell?" Candy squinted in my direction as I got to my feet, scrambling.

"Get her!" Candy yelled. "Don't shoot. We need her."

I ran back the way I'd come, at least I hoped I was. With each turn, I prayed I was moving in the right direction, the way Ginger had gone with the girls.

I slid around another corner, slapping sounds of shoes growing closer as I spied a steel door, unlit exit sign above.

I slammed the bar with my hip. No alarm sounded as the door opened then bounced back. I took a few gulps of fresh, cold air. Maybe not that fresh as I was beside a dumpster, but it was outside without bars or doors or locks or assholes. Before I could ruminate any more on the beauty of freedom, I heard shouts.

Too close to give me enough time to gain cover. I also didn't want to lead them anywhere near the girls. Ginger would have headed toward the main road, hoping to catch a ride or at least use it to navigate back to OK City. In my head, Gator and the boys would be here any minute.

I ran behind the building. Three tractor trailers were backed up to the loading dock. Under the orange glow of the security lights they all looked gray-green, until I got closer and saw the telltale flames on the side of the shiniest rig. Flamethrower.

I raced to the rear, worked the lever on the trailer doors and climbed in, closing but not locking the heavy door. The inside of the reefer was dark. I was counting on an empty or at least mostly empty trailer and wasn't disappointed. Quietly, I made my way to the front of the trailer as my eyes adjusted to the dark. Creeping along barefooted with one hand in front of my face and the other waving the air around my shins, I felt the load lock before I bumped into it.

It wouldn't be installed this far back from the front of the trailer unless it was being used to hold something in place. I hoped whatever it was would be large enough to hide behind. Gator and I had used this same sort of retaining system a bunch of times in the last year, especially when separating shipments. It made things much easier upon delivery, and I never worried about a shifting load.

Even though I was in an insulated refrigeration trailer, I could hear Candy and Black Dog shouting, the Somalian shouts of Nadifa.

I ran my hands over the sides of the cargo. It was a single three-by-three cardboard box. Not big enough to hide behind and the way it was jammed up against the wall of the trailer, there was no way I was going to get in there anyway.

I worked my way down the trailer wall to the back doors, dragging my hand along the metal side. Just as it slid over a light switch the trailer door flung open and a long black arm grabbed my leg and yanked.

CHAPTER 31

There is a time when all ideas turn to shit. Maybe the idea was worthy at the start, or maybe it was shit all along, you just never saw it.

That's what I was thinking as I came around, the pain behind my eyes like a knife. Another was more of a dull throb on my tailbone where I'd hit the ground hard, courtesy of the yanking arm of the Somali Mafia.

I replayed the scene: Black Dog and Candy pinning me down, kneeling on my arms, straddling my chest, telling me I was a pain in their ass, shaking me, asking about the girls. "Where are they? Who helped you?" The questioning stopping only when Big Abdi appeared with news about Omar.

Omar. Shit. The sound his head had made against the hollow floor had been the sound of a watermelon dropped from a roof onto concrete.

I said nothing. Bit my tongue. Candy looked at me with a combination of disappointment and pride. She sighed then held my head between her knees as Black Dog jabbed a needle in my neck.

"See you on the flipside," she whispered in my ear.

Here I was, on the flipside, gagged and bound, leaning against a box in a quickly cooling reefer unit that was rolling. I did another body scan—wrists and ankles zip-tied in front of me, with little feeling in the fingers and toes. The gag wasn't too tight; I'd be able to drag it out of my mouth, but first I curled up tighter, feeling the warmth build. If I just had a tiny nap I was sure I could wake up refreshed and strong. I'd be able to bust out of here in no time.

I rested my head on my arms. Eyelids fluttered, then my breath grew deep. In the cold, it was hard to make things work—brain, fingers, legs, mouth. It was easier to lay down and sleep, to let go of things you thought you were supposed to do and do instead, absolutely nothing. I felt like the junkies the Somalis had made, how they stole their lives, took their heart, their drive and their will. How they deceived these girls, how they made them their slaves.

It sickened me and moved me, raising a fire in my veins. I wasn't sure how long I'd been in the reefer, but from the size of this trailer, I knew I didn't have long. When Gator and I had worked a beef route in Texas, our reefer could take the load to minus twenty degrees in less than thirty minutes. I clenched my fists, then slowly, painfully raised my bound hands to my mouth and began to work at the gag, trying to coordinate numb fingers and chattering teeth.

As I worked the gag, I began a distinctive breathing pattern taught to me by an ex-boyfriend, a yoga teacher. As I inhaled deeply through my nose, the Ujjayi breath made a hollow, whispery sound. I contracted my diaphragm and exhaled just as deeply through my nose, exhaling the sound of an ocean. By the third round, I could feel my fingers and was able to loosen my jaw enough to pull the gag over my lip and chin. I blew warm air on my hands, and began to move my arms and legs, heating up my core, stilling the shivering to a manageable shake.

I rose to my knees, noticing that the air was warmer as I rose. So, they weren't planning on freezing me, just chilling me out. Literally.

I found the cardboard box I'd tried to hide behind before, braced myself against it, pulling my knees to my chest, warming my feet in my hands. I pulled the sweatpants over my heels and readied myself to stand.

Since I'd been out cold when they zip-tied me, they'd been able to do a good job ratcheting down the locks. I liked to think I was just as strong, maybe stronger as I'd been when performing the break-out trick five years ago on a dare, but I'd recently been drugged, beaten, half-frozen to death and I couldn't remember my last meal. Needless to say, this would not be a comparable challenge. Especially with my ankles bound.

I tried working on that first, pulling at the plastic strap, sawing it against the box. Hit or miss. More miss than hit. It was too dark to see what I was doing. I remembered the light switch by the back door.

Talking myself into standing up, I balanced as best I could on my tippy toes, trying to keep the breath of internal heat going. I got two steps before tripping over my own feet, and the load lock. I went down hard, smacking my glass chin on the cold metal floor, my teeth clamping down catching my lip, as I knocked myself out.

I woke thinking I'd been dreaming. That this whole thing from the very first day on the street with the gang and the bicycle boy and the thrown bottles was just a dream. There was something else—the smell of bacon and sweet, maple syrup. But I wasn't in a diner. I was in a yellow kitchen with flowered wallpaper. A stream of rose gold light came through a window over a sink overflowing with dirty dishes. On the floor, a broken plate and a woman weeping. She looked up at a man in a doorway and begged him to stay, her words changing languages until I couldn't understand her at all.

In the dream, I watched from above, hovering like a ghost or an angel. Then, I was a little girl holding a rag doll calling, "Maman? Maman?" But the woman didn't look at me, she went to the man, her makeup running down her face, lipstick smeared, she kissed him, clung to him, then reached into his coat—

My eyes snapped open. I licked my cut lip, swallowed hard. The blood and the memory fueled me. I pushed myself to my hands and knees and crawled to the back of the trailer, trying to not think of the final image: the beautiful woman with the gun in her mouth.

I hit the back door with my head, used it to guide me as I stood, then felt around with my zip-tied wrists for the light switch I'd found before, hoping whoever was driving the rig hadn't disabled it. I needed one fucking break.

On the third pass, I found it.

One flick and I was squinting painfully. As my eyes adjusted, I scanned the trailer's interior. The cardboard box in the corner was held in place by an aluminum-load lock running horizontally about eight inches high across the width of the trailer. I strained against the ties, my fingers and feet growing numb. If only I had a box cutter or a knife, any sharp object, but the rest of the trailer was empty, except for a large unsecured wooden crate by the rear doors.

There was one thing my cold, slow moving brain remembered. Thanks to that weekend with Eddie, the tactical instructor and the things he'd wanted to do with zip ties.

"Oh yes, I remember," I whispered to myself as I balanced against the trailer wall, preparing.

Raising my hands in front of me, I took a deep breath, visualized the motion, the final result, then twisted my wrists so the zip tie was over my wrist bones, raised my hands over my head and chicken-winged my arms down and out with a loud *huhhh* sound. It hurt like hell, and the plastic held.

"Come on. Dammit."

I steeled myself for the pain, adjusted my footing and really leaned into the chicken-wing motion this time, breaking the plastic with a big snap, and yielding minimal damage to my skin. Maybe numb hands can't feel pain, or they feel so much pain they can't differentiate between the pain of the cold and the pressure of plastic strips digging into flesh.

I shook and worked my fingers to get the blood circulating, then took a better look at the zip-ties on my ankles. They were tight and interlocked, but with my hands free, I could use the end of one as a shim, essentially picking the lock by reverse inserting into the feed. I pulled my knees in close, found the locks and shimmed first the right then the left, widening the ties enough to slip them off my feet. Pulling the gag from my neck, I tore it in half and made fabric sock-shoes. It wasn't much, but it kept my bare feet off the cold metal floor.

I punched and jabbed, did some jumping jacks, anything to warm up. The whole time I stared at the crate, wanting and not wanting to know what was inside.

The truck slowed, gears downshifting, brakes setting. The radio. Someone's voice. I hurried up front, stepping carefully over the load lock.

It sounded like Big Abdi. The way he paused between words, his monotone English.

"Hold on. Hold on."

The radio volume lowered.

"Okay."

"Can you hear us now?" Candy's voice came through the trailer wall punching me in the chest. I fell back onto the cardboard box. It took me a second to realize she was on the other end of a speakerphone call, not in the cab.

"Yes," Big Abdi said.

Another voice spoke. "Abdi, Waxaan u baahanahay in aad is ogow Eey."

"Ok. Hollywood. I do the Whitney, like you do to the girl in Detroit. War-rm tub, right, Candy?" Big Abdi laughed.

There was a second of silence.

"I don't know what you're talking about," Candy said. "Do you know what he's talking about?"

Hollywood said, "No. I think he mentions the young lady who went home to her father, after saying goodbye to our friend who is on a trip."

"Yes, of course that's what he meant, didn't you, Abdi?"

"What? What is this you say?"

Candy and Hollywood burst out laughing.

Candy said, "Relax, we're just fucking with you. Yeah, take care of our problem, then wait for us at the truck stop. We have to go to the hospital. That girl's being released and we need to get to her before she talks."

"What about Trucker Lady? What if she talked to someone?"

"Leave her in there. We'll take care of it in Michigan. Far as she knows I'm DEA and one of the good guys."

It was Big Abdi's turn to laugh. "You? Now that is a good joke." He laughed even harder.

The brakes released, gears shifted. The trailer shuddered then bumped along picking up speed. Someone honked their horn. Abdi cursed back at them, something in Somalian.

Candy came back on the line. "Listen. We gotta go."

"All right. All right." The phone clicked off. Abdi turned up the music, some pop song about shaking things up.

There had to be a way out. I scanned the walls, ceiling, floor, for a weak spot. Nothing. I squatted beside the box held in place by the load lock. There wasn't an invoice or a barcode or any sort of label. I didn't know what I expected, a box full of electric metal cutting tools? A satellite phone? A machine gun? My brain was freezing up.

I sat on the mystery box, leaned against the trailer wall and thought about the stories I'd heard from Canadian hunters about those people in winter, lost, disoriented, who strip down to their birthday suit before they die, how your mind fucks with you one last time before hypothermia kills you—and how some people don't die butt-naked, but get saved—and have to spend the rest of their lives discounting stories of the size of their dick, due to the cold.

Tapping my head against the wall, lightly, then harder, hearing a resounding echo-y thonk, I had to smile. The irony of killing a trucker by sealing her in a refrigerated trailer, possibly one she'd used herself to haul meat to a grocery store. Really? Was that the way I was going to go? Were all those psychics wrong? Where was my soft bed, gentle sleep, easy passing after a long, long, long life?

Fuck this. I had guardian angels. They would know what to do if I just got up and started moving. I had faith in them, in the idea of them. It was all I had. That and the thought: *Gather information.*

Looking around, it appeared that would be a simple request. Two boxes and me.

"All right then," I murmured, no stranger to talking to myself.

I found the discarded zip-ties and used the poky end of one to lift the tape on the mystery box. Pulling back the flaps I found a cheap Styrofoam cooler, pulled off the lid, moved aside a bag of ice and found three baggies of odd looking fish. It wasn't nearly enough to fill the cooler. I lifted one of the fish baggies and saw the real cargo. Heroin. A cooler full of tiny blue baggies of heroin, separated in fifty-baggie increments—bricks.

Sealed the box, I went on to the crate. It wasn't even secured. No nails, no plastic straps, not even a strip of tape. Shitty packing, or rush order, maybe.

Pulling up the lid, I expected to see more Styrofoam or fish or little blue baggies.

"Jesus!"

I jumped back, shielding myself with the lid. Slowly lowering it, I peeked over at the contents of the crate. One dead Mufasa, complete with shiny gold lion ring. I pulled it off his finger and slid it onto my thumb, then replaced the lid as best I could, then used my sleeves to wipe any places I'd touched.

At the front of the trailer, trying to hold the creepy factor at bay, I sat on the box of fish and heroin—a seat that suddenly didn't seem so bad.

The radio from the cab was loud, annoying rap music. My thoughts were jumbled, my brain fuzzy, panic rising. It was time to rely on muscle memory, on instinct, not fear. I ran down the *what I know* list, my swinging foot tapping the load lock.

Bump. Bump. Bump.

That was it. The load lock. I slid off the box and found the locking lever. It was an older model, the kind you could still take apart. I released the tension and pulled it away from the walls, then pulled out the pins and broke the length down into three sections, I brought these to the back of the trailer and ran my hand over the small rectangular vent door in the lower part of the left side door. I was almost certain we weren't headed to a dock where a receiver was going to kindly open the vent door and insert his temperature probe. Instead, I was going to have to MacGyver my way out of here.

I rigged up a lever, jamming one load lock between the trailer wall and the big-ass crate, then made a "T" with another bar and jacked the shit out of the vent door until it started to give. A few hammer-like whacks, and it popped open with one jagged metal edge. The air outside was much warmer than the instant winter I was in. I wished I could fit my whole body through that tiny door, slide right out and run far, far away. I crouched in front of the door, trying to see out into the dark night. Car headlights, highway median, a field beyond. We could be anywhere.

The opening was just large enough for my hand and forearm to fit through. I mashed my face against the cold metal door and stretched. It took two tries, my fingers fumbling, teeth chattering, trailer bouncing and swaying, until I found the flip safety. The resounding clang as it released was all the encouragement I needed to go for the door lever. Leaning all my weight against the trailer door I hoped to open suddenly seemed like a bad idea, especially if I fell out when the door flew open as we were speeding down the highway. No, that wouldn't work at all.

And yet, I kept at it, trusting in my vision: me, kicking Big Abdi's ass. Me, getting away.

Five straining minutes later, I went to Plan B. Grabbing one of the load lock pieces, I fed it through the vent door, holding it as tightly as possible, while wrenching my wrist back and up, seeing in my mind's eye the handle of the trailer door, blindly batting at where it should be, willing the bastard to connect, to make that handle swing enough to release the door.

One the fourth pass I connected. Too hard. I dropped the load lock, watched it bounce in the road behind us. The car behind the trailer swerved into the other lane, honking.

"Serves you right for tailgating. And gee, I don't imagine you've called the police to tell them someone is someone is trying to break *out* of a trailer? Yep, now I'm talking to myself. I've got to get out of here."

I hung both hands out the vent door, warming my fingers, willing blood flow into my cramped legs and frozen feet. The truck slowed and I heard street sounds. I looked out the vent door. We were entering a town, hopefully large enough to warrant a stoplight or two. This was my chance.

"Okay, Jojo. Reach, connect, release."

I repeated the mantra as I grabbed the second load lock piece and fed it through the vent door.

The sound of metal striking metal was louder now without the highway sounds to mask it. I grunted and lunged, swiping up and away. Once, twice, three times.

"Uhhh!"

My fingers slipped on the aluminum bar, my legs gave out beneath me. I fell to my knees, then tried one more time, snugging up my grip on the bar using it as an extension of my arm. There. A solid connection. I pushed. The door released with a sucking sound. I pulled the bar back into the vent door, braced myself and shoved the door open with my feet.

Red brick buildings glowed orange in the light of energy smart street lamps. A dozen cars were parked at the curb. Maybe people lived above the closed shops or maybe we were approaching a bar or a row of restaurants. My stomach growled at the thought of food.

Holding on as the rig slowed, gears shifting down, the hiss of brakes setting, I counted to five, then jumped out of the trailer, ran to the side and yanked off the emergency air line.

Big Abdi would figure out his brakes were locked and come out to investigate. The thought of a corpse falling out of the back of the trailer made me think I ought to latch the back doors. As I did, a car slowly approached, stoner boy at the wheel, rock music blaring. I waved him through. He waved back. I shook my head, held up the load lock bar I was brandishing like a baseball bat and shot him an evil look mouthing, "Get the fuck out of here." This he understood.

He peeled out, cutting around the broken-down rig and a crazy broad with a metal pipe.

The driver's door squeaked open, steps creaking as Abdi climbed down.

When he leaned in to check the air line, I jumped him, swinging the load lock and playing Whack-a-Mole on his fat head. I'll give him props, he gave it a fight. Sure, he was bigger than me, but he still went down. Metal versus head. Skull loses every time.

Stepping over him, I was glad he'd fallen mostly out of the path of the wheels. I reconnected the air line and ran to the cab, pulling up the seat so my bare feet could reach the pedals. Checking the street signs and compass on the dash, I grabbed hold of the wheel. When the light turned green, I was ready to roll.

CHAPTER 32

I shouldn't have known Oklahoma City as well as I did. I never should have spent this much time in a place I didn't love. I grew more and more angry as I thought about it. Life was precious. Life was short. This wasn't where I was supposed to be. Not in this town, not in this state, not running alone, not wanted by the cops, not driving a stolen tractor trailer loaded with Somali Mafia's heroin and definitely nowhere near a dead body in a packing crate.

I continued to talk myself up a tree as I made my way across town, ticking off the ways I'd fucked everything up, and how I was letting so many people down. Gator was going to be pissed that I gave one of the earrings to Ginger. He was probably going to lecture me on trusting people—how he was right about Candy all along. Mostly, I was sure that he would never forgive me if I got myself killed. Between my jerky driving in the stop-and-go traffic, my blurry eyesight and throbbing dehydrated brain, I wasn't any good for anybody. If there had been a ditch on the side of the road, I might have parked and jumped down to wallow in it. I was that pitiful.

The truck drifted to the right as I lay my head on the steering wheel. Front tires bumped over the lane marker. Cars zipped past, swerving out of my way. Just before I blacked out, a voice in my ear made me sit up. It was so loud I almost turned around to see who was standing behind me. The voice said, *We don't quit. Remember who you are.*

I opened my eyes. "I'm a Boudreaux," I said, gripping the steering wheel, shaking my head to clear it. Perè's words from my youth repeated in my head: *A Boudreaux never gives up. A Boudreaux never quits. A Boudreaux never loses sight of what's important.*

I eased off the gas and guided the truck back into the lane, just as something vibrated under my ass. I felt around. Jammed in the back of the seat was a beautiful thing. Big Abdi's cell phone notifying him he had not reached his daily fitness requirement. I braced my forearms on the steering wheel and sent up a special prayer. "Please, don't have a password."

He didn't.

"Hello? Who's this?"

"Gator, it's me. Listen. You were right, Candy was lying. She's one of them. She killed Mufasa. They're moving girls from The Palace to Michigan. You need to get —"

"Jojo! Where are you? Are you okay?"

"I'm okay. I'm driving The Flamethrower, heading to the motel."

"The Flamethrower? Is Ferguson with you?"

"No. Big Abdi was driving. He had a little accident."

"A little accident?"

"Yeah, you might want to send the cops to First and Elm. And the rest to The Palace."

"They've been there. A few hours now, when we finally got your signal."

"So Ginger, and the girls? They're okay?"

"Yes, you did good. Ivory Joe is with them at the police station. Where have you been?"

"I'll tell you when I see you. I'm just a few miles away."

"You don't have to talk," Gator said, his voice soft. "But please, don't hang up."

Pulling into the No Tell Motel, the parking lot was nearly empty. Sabrina's shiny front end peeked out from the far side of the building and parked in front of our room was a kickass lime green

1968 Charger R/T with the plates: MICKEYB.

It didn't get much better than that. I felt my second wind coming on as I opened the door and climbed down.

Gator scooped me up and squeezed me. My feet dangled as he swung me like Papa Bear.

"I. Can't. Breathe." I managed to grunt.

"Sorry," he said, gently setting me down, then scooping me up and carrying me when he saw my bare feet.

In the room, I was instantly swept up again by a thickly bearded Mickey, his formerly platinum white hair now dark brown, sun bleached at the ends to match the beard.

"Hey. Hey," I said wriggling and twisting, trying to avoid inhaling the hairiness.

Mickey boomed, "Jojo! Dammit, you had us worried. You're okay?"

"Yes, yes. Could you put me down?"

As he did, there was a bark, followed by a distinctive whine. I'd almost forgotten the dog.

Gator opened the bathroom door. The white streak that dashed out was a cleaner, happier version of the mutt I'd rescued from the truck stop. I scratched his head and let him lick my face while I complimented him on his soft coat and bright eyes. He seemed to listen as I spoke, his tail never missing a beat.

"Been calling him Oscar," Gator said.

"You know because he was living out of a trash can," Mickey added.

"Oscar. I like it," I said, feeling their eyes on me, wondering what they saw: dirty bare feet, borrowed ill-fitting clothes, scratches, bruises and dried blood from the zip-ties, smeared make-up and wild hair. I picked up the dog, buried my face in his fur.

Gator grabbed a blanket, wrapped it around me and led me to the edge of the bed. "Ginger told us what you did at that place. How you saved them. How did you get away? How did you find The Flamethrower?"

I told them everything I could remember, from the faces of the bidders in the dark room to everything leading up to Candy shooting Mufasa, the racist, lion-ring wearing, rich country boy with a trucking company, and a penchant for sex trafficking. I told them how I ran and they caught me, put me in the reefer, how I heard them talking in the rig and how I broke out.

They took turns telling me how they spoke to the cops on my behalf and made a deal, told them I was on a special mission. How they followed the earring tracker that eventually led to Ginger and the girls.

"We lost the signal when you were inside The Palace. Must be something they run during the auctions to block the server, protect the anonymity of the buyers," Mickey said. "I'll have to share that with the locals. Let them know what they're up against."

"One pretty detective in particular, right Mick?" Gator said.

Mickey grinned, passing off his dalliance with a cocked head and a wink. "Lauren, I mean, Detective Summers, put us in touch with T.A.S.T. Force. Good people, spoke to a local guy named Dino."

Gator said. "Like you know, Jojo. T.A.S.T has been chasing the Somalis for years. Those creeps are just out of reach. Connecting them to the heroin could be the key."

"I should talk to this Dino guy," I said. "I heard Candy say she'd 'taken care of the T.A.S.T Force thing.' I don't know what she meant, but I know we've got to take these assholes down."

Gator nodded. "I'll set it up. But first," he said, taking the sleeping dog from my lap, "You'd better call your father. You know how he gets when he doesn't hear from you."

"Okay, while I do that, can you get my bag from the rig? I need something to wear."

He pointed to the bathroom. "It's all in there. I knew you'd be back."

* * *

In the bathroom, I called my father, assuring him I was safe and well—without giving any details. I told him I'd come to Bunkie so he could see for himself.

"Tell Pilar I send my love," I said.

Père murmured something in French that I recognized from my youth. It was an entreaty from the Saint Suaire, a Cajun prayer book. He ended his plea with, "*Dieu nous en fasse la grace. Ainsi-soit-il.*" May God grant us this grace. Amen.

I cleaned up the best I could, tucked my hair under a ball cap and emerged from the bathroom wearing my regular outfit: jeans, boots and T-shirt. Mickey was on the floor doing a complicated series of sit-ups and twists, while Gator paced, tapping his thighs with his thumbs.

They both stopped what they were doing when I said, "Something I may have neglected to mention, guys." I cleared my throat. "You know that bright red rig out there?"

They nodded.

"There's a dead body and a shipment of heroin in the trailer."

"Who's the body?" Gator asked.

"The guy Candy shot. This is his." I pulled the lion head ring off my thumb and tossed it to him. He turned it over a few times, his face clouding over before he passed it to Mickey.

I waited, as if someone was going to say a magic word and have all the puzzle pieces fall into place. The trouble is, you can't fill in a puzzle without a frame.

Gator joined me at the motel room window. A few seconds later, Mickey stood beside us, his hand on my shoulder. We stared across the parking lot at the rig I'd stolen: a bright shiny red truck lined with chrome and lights and a matching custom trailer sporting a wall of flames.

"Well," Mickey said. "I'd say this place is pretty much blown."

"We could bring it to Esteban," I said. "Ask him to—"

"What? Make it disappear?" Gator said.

"Well, kind of. I mean with the right paint job and accessories..."

"I like where you're going," Mickey said, one hand stroking his beard.

I reached out, pulled his hand away. "Don't. Just don't."

We hid the rig in the back and got a few hours of sleep. In the morning, we split up, Mickey in the Flamethrower with directions to Esteban's body shop, and me and Gator in Sabrina, our trailer now hauling a crated corpse and a specialty seafood/heroin shipment. We had plans for both.

Gator had recognized markings on the crate similar to the markings on the lion-head ring, connected them to a trucking company called SHIPit, Inc. We figured that must be Mufasa's business and that was a good place to start.

On the drive to SHIPit, I thought about something Mickey told me that night in Bunkie, after all the shit went down last year. Sure he'd had a few too many beers—Ivory Joe said it was a bunch of bullshit, just a story a guy tells a girl to get in her pants, but I don't know. There was too much pain in Mickey's eyes when he spoke, and some of the parts of the story didn't exactly make me want to lift my skirt, if you know what I mean. It wasn't like he was talking about rescuing a puppy at a shelter or saving a baby drowning in a pool, or even bringing his Granny to church on Sunday every week until the day she died—in his arms—while he sang every verse of Kumbaya.

No, the story Mickey told me was about clandestine men in back rooms, planning and working together to overcome evil. Not in a superhero way, or a military-political way, just regular folks who used ordinary means to expose and rectify. He'd never said how he knew those guys, but I could tell it mattered, righting wrongs, doing justice—it was his religion. It moved him.

I wanted to believe that could still move me, that I could still be a good guy and overcome evil, be someone on the right side of the law, making and keeping the rules. But in my heart, I knew I'd commit murder at the very least, if I was given a chance to get close to any of the Somalis again. I'd be all too happy to play judge with my XD-40 and a six-bullet jury.

CHAPTER 33

"Hit me with it again," I said, leaning out of the passenger seat to mute the GPS's turn-by-turn instructions.

"Is that your way of saying you don't like my plan?" Gator asked.

"No. My way of saying I don't like your plan would be me saying, 'I don't like your plan.' This is my way of reminding myself what the fuck we're doing driving a trailer of dead guy and heroin into the same company dead guy probably owns, or is that owned?"

"Owned. And we're just driving it onto the lot. No one opens the trailer."

"Uh huh. So, what's our reason for being there?"

"We're just stopping in to say hello."

"Really?"

"I don't know. I didn't get that far. Okay, what if we're trying to organize a truck driver charity fund raiser?"

"For what charity? Truckers with big balls and pea-sized brains?"

Gator looked hurt. Then he grinned. "You think I have big balls, huh?"

By the time we pulled onto the SHIPit, Inc. lot, we had a plan that started with this warehouse and ended with meeting Dino and the T.A.S.T Force people.

Gator said, "We'll go in, hat in hand, ask for information about leasing, say we're unhappy with our current company and have heard good things about SHIPit." He tried out an Okie twang, adding a bunch of *aw shucks* and *golly gees.*

Planning on sticking to my own voice and accent, I simply added an extra layer of lip-gloss, changed into a tighter fitting shirt and shook out my hair.

Gator whistled his approval when I buckled back into the passenger seat, pressing my lips together.

I gave him the finger, saying, "Way my luck's going, they'll have a woman running the show over there."

"So?"

"So, she isn't going to—"

Gator's grin widened, a brow arched.

"Seriously?" I pretended to be offended, smacking his arm. "Just drive."

The gate was unmanned and the bays looked deserted. One of the doors wasn't even pulled all the way down.

We circled the building and counted four cars, and two trucks, most of which looked like they'd been parked a while. One of the trucks, a dirty white Volvo with a tall condo sleeper had a cracked windshield and at least two flat tires on its trailer. An older Mack day cab hauling a black trailer with worn and scraped letters on the side was pulled in close to the building, Gator said, "What do you want to do now?"

I pointed to the bay with the open roll up door. "I think someone's inviting us in."

We tucked our guns into our waistbands and left Sabrina idling twenty feet out, angled for a quick getaway.

A quick search with the flashlight yielded the all clear. Gator rolled under the gate, then motioned me in. It took a few seconds for our eyes to adjust to the dim interior. The warehouse didn't appear well-maintained, definitely not up to OSHA standards with its exposed wires and holes in the roof.

I tipped my head in the direction of an office, indicated I was going to check that out and pointed with a circling finger for Gator to check the stock racks. We met back less than a minute later, both shaking our heads.

"What the hell?" I whispered. "Place is deserted."

We lowered our weapons and looked around. A whirring sound grew louder.

"What's that?" Gator asked.

We followed the sound to what looked like a refrigerated trailer without wheels. Someone had hooked up a generator to it. Apparently, the electric bill had been paid.

Reaching for the door handle, I started to pull. "It's stuck," I said, tugging harder.

"Here. Let me," Gator said, tucking away his gun.

I stepped back, raised my gun and took a stance, ready for anything except—*what if this thing's rigged to blow?*

The door came open with a wrenching noise, ice crystals fell from the face of the metal door. The icy blast in my face was welcome, then chilling.

Gator noticed my hesitancy. "Stay here," he said, drawing his weapon.

As he stepped inside, I took a position with my back to the open freezer and my weapon held high. I counted to fifteen before I heard Gator curse.

"You okay?" I called.

"I am. She's not."

The short, chubby blonde might have been cute as young girl. She might have even been someone's *darlin'*, but here, she was just cold and dead and a little blue.

I walked through stacked crates marked *Seafood* and stamped with the lion head symbol to reach her hanging body. A glint of gold poking from her pocket caught my eye. I tugged, setting the body swinging as it released the treasure.

"Gator, look." I rubbed my fingers over the metal, scraping frost off a detective's badge.

"Guess we know where Candy got the undercover cop idea from," Gator said.

"You don't think she did this, do you?" I asked.

The swinging body made a creaking noise and the room suddenly felt too small and unbearably cold. I wrapped my arms around myself.

Gator pulled me close warming me instantly. "Come on, let's get out of here."

We retraced our steps to the office to poke around. As I rifled messy desk drawers and an overflowing inbox of receipts and past due notices, Gator tried to gain access to the computer, a sleek iMac.

"Nothing here," I said, closing the last drawer. "Unless you want to donate shoes to Africa." I held up a brown bag. There was a crude sketch of a barefoot boy above the words: Give old soles a new life.

"No thanks," Gator said, banging away at the keyboard, taping and sliding the wireless mouse. "I don't believe in reincarnation."

From where I sat I could see the computer plug dangling off the side of the credenza.

"You might want to try plugging it in first," I said, pointing.

A few seconds later, the screen came to life. I rolled my chair next to Gator, watched as he opened minimized windows and scrolled through emails, dispatches and manifests, none of them recent.

"See if they had GPS tracking on their trucks," I said.

"Hang on. I'm not exactly up an Apple guy," he said, rolling the cursor over the tiny icons. He clicked on a grainy frozen image, enlarging it.

The forward arrow in the center of the screen covered up most of the picture until the video started to play.

The overhead lights were sharp and unforgiving. The camera panned a row of naked women, slowing and zooming in on someone's command.

I held my breath as the camera moved from the fourth girl to the fifth.

Gator tensed beside me, fingers hovering over the mouse.

"Jojo, you never said anything about—"

"That's right. I didn't." I reached across and hit the escape button, wishing that was all it took in real life. "Can we get out of here?"

"Yeah, sure," Gator said, unplugging the computer and tucking it under his arm.

"What are you doing?"

"Taking it with us."

Walking to the truck, I tried to erase the memories crowding my brain. *Focus. Be in the moment. Fix what you can.* I thought about the disabled trailer we'd seen parked around back. I was half turned to Gator saying, "Hey, do you think—" when the first shot was fired.

The bullet whizzed past my head, plinked up a patch of pavement and bounced away. Before I'd registered that the shot was meant for me, Gator throw the computer and yelled, "Get down!"

He pushed me toward the truck, shielding me with his body, as bullets careened off the iMac. We huddled behind a tire on the backside of the trailer, drawing our weapons at the same time. We didn't need words. Hand motions were universal. *Go that way. Find the asshole. Shoot to kill. Get the fuck out of there.* Maybe there wasn't a universal hand motion for the last one. Maybe no one needed it.

My first shot was low, chipping off a big chunk of wood at the roofline. But it would do as I intended, force the shooter to duck and switch positions allowing Gator time to cross the open lot. It appeared there was only one gunman, but we had to assume there were more, here or on the way.

I concentrated on the guy on the roof. Maybe he was a lousy shot or he wasn't shooting to kill, which was lucky for us as he had the element of surprise and the advantage of sight.

I fired another shot when the guy popped up six feet to the left, rifle barrel first, followed by a head of bushy black hair. His yelp was a good indication I'd hit more than wood that time.

Still no sign of Gator. I was expecting to hear a firefight or see him stand victorious on the roof and wave me in. Now I was wondering if he needed help.

I fired a barrage of bullets in the direction of the shooter, then ran for the warehouse and the half-open dock door. I searched for Gator, then a blood trail. Sadly, I didn't find the first. Gladly, I didn't find the second.

There were stairs to the roof, going straight up then turning at the top. I could see daylight from above, a door swinging open smacking the concrete wall. I ran up the metal steps crouched, whisper yelling, "Gator! Gator!"

As I stepped onto the final landing, we smashed into each other.

"Go!" he yelled, pushing me back. The look on his face said this was not the time to ask questions. I went. Fast. The first blast took out a three-foot chunk of concrete and ripped through the iron railing. My ears rang.

"What the fuck!" I stumbled forward. Gator caught me, braced me against the concrete wall, stairs shaking beneath us. They weren't going to hold. He leaned over the railing, straddling it with one leg.

"What are you—"

Another blast from above cut me off.

Gator grabbed my hand and yelled, "Jump!"

We landed on a pile of cardboard boxes, flattened and ready for recycling. A quick body scan assured me everything was working and the adrenaline boost had me running for the exit right behind Gator as we catapulted ourselves toward Sabrina.

Seconds later we were speeding out of the lot, careening down the road toward the fence line and the open gate when I remembered our cargo.

I smacked the dash. "Gator, stop!"

"What? Why?"

"Trust me," I said. "Do it. Now!"

He let off the gas and stomped the brakes. The back end

shuttered and slid, a wiggle turning to a skid, trailer rocking then settling as we came to a not so graceful stop.

Gator looked at me. "This better be good."

As much as I could imagine a rocket launcher aimed in our direction, I also understood speed and velocity and target positioning. "I have an idea," I said smiling. "It's okay." I checked the side mirrors again. "No one's coming."

The corpse was heavier and stiffer than I'd figured. Sweaty and panting by the time the deed was done, we climbed back into the truck and aimed the rig toward OK City.

A mile down the road Gator was still going on about something. It might have been about the shooter on the roof or the dead broad in the freezer or the more recent dead guy. I wasn't listening. I was trying to remember something, something that had happened that I thought might make everything fall magically into place like the final turn of the tumblers on a complicated lock. Click. Boom. Done. But it wouldn't come to me. I only saw yellow walls, a muzzle flash and a swinging door slapping shut.

"Aren't you going to say anything?" Gator asked.

I took a deep breath and gave up on the memory. I shot my eyes in his direction. "About what?"

"Jesus, Jojo. About that—" He jerked his thumb behind us. "About anything."

When I didn't speak, he sighed. "What's wrong with you?"

I couldn't look at him. "Where do you want me to start?"

We drove in silence, me unable to tell him what I was thinking. The memory issues weren't the only thing bugging me. I was starting to feel like I'd lost myself, the person I used to be. I was the planner, the organized one, the person you could count on. I was strong and independent. Wasn't I?

Look at me now, without a fucking clue, too proud to admit I needed him, that I wanted him to be the one who helped me. I was pathetic. I wiped a tear from my eye, then snuck a peek at Gator, glad he had his eyes on the road and not me. Even more grateful for the buzzing phone.

"Shit."

"What?" Gator asked, raising his foot from the accelerator.

"Don't slow down. Get to the hospital. It's Gina."

"Is she okay?" he asked.

I scrolled through the message. "She spoke to the press, told them she's going to testify against the Somali Mafia. It's all over social media."

Gator steered toward an opening in traffic and used the train horn to encourage cars to let us over. After a barrage of angry honking and a few illegal moves, he managed to get us headed in the direction of the hospital. "Why would she—"

"I don't know," I said. "But we've got to stop her. Before they do."

"We?" Gator said.

I didn't answer. I was too busy texting Ivory Joe and Mickey B.

CHAPTER 34

I checked the time, then dialed a number on one of the burner phones as Gator headed for the off-ramp, following the hospital signs.

"Here," I said clicking on the speaker and handing him the phone.

When the call connected, Gator put on an affected feminine, slightly British accent, gave the address to SHIPit, screamed loudly and for longer than probably necessary then threw the phone out the window over the hood crushing it with at least six tires and thirty thousand pounds.

I shook my head. "What the hell was that?"

"What?"

"I thought you'd ask for the detective you and Mickey were talking about, or even Officer Button and maybe, you know, explain what had happened and that we..."

"Nah. That was good," he said gesturing to the phone, the strange conversation, the scream. "They'll get it. Besides you don't really want to be involved, do you?"

My involvement with anything Oklahoma City hadn't really worked out the best for me, so, I had to agree with him there.

I said, "I didn't know you could—"

"What? Do accents?"

"No. Scream like a girl."

"There are so many things you have yet to learn about me, Jojo Boudreaux," Gator said.

The light at the intersection was red with traffic at least ten cars deep on each side. Gator left the predictable car length open in front of us so any asshole in a hurry could slip in and think he was smart for getting in front of the slow truck.

Signs peppered the intersection from road names to going out of business sales, some guy who'd buy your house for $$$ and a warning about a slippery area under a bridge.

The faintest sound went off in my head. Like the ding of an egg timer telling you the muffins were ready.

"Hey."

"Hey, what?" Gator asked.

"Remember that thing about the bridge?"

"What bridge?"

"The first girl, wasn't she—

"Found under a bridge? Yeah."

"And then Gina was, too."

"Yeah?" Gator said, accelerating through the intersection.

"Hollywood said something to me. He said that girls who didn't behave, didn't follow the rules, found themselves under a bridge."

Gator looked at me, waiting.

"I kept thinking. It's something about the bridge and the trucks. I can't—"

"No. *They* can't." Gator said.

"What do you mean?"

"To go over a bridge, you have to be a certain weight, right?"

I nodded.

"Well, to drive under a bridge, you have to be a certain—"

"Height!" We said together.

"Remember that white rig at the warehouse with the flat tires?"

I thought about the trailer, then the tractor pulling it. I said, "The Volvo with the tall condo sleeper?"

"Yeah. Looked like it took a bridge strike."

"Could be. What are you thinking?"

"I'm thinking we need to check on the height of the over-passes the girls were left under. Be easy to eliminate some trucks that way."

I ran the images of the rigs in the back lot of the truck stop through my memory. I could see Candy climbing out of them, the Freightliner, the Peterbilt, the green Mack. They all had short stacks, regular sleepers, low trailers. They were all trucks that could run the same route.

I sent the same info to Mickey and Ivory Joe, then started checking maps and roads from OK City to El Reno, confirming the heights of the underpasses where the girls had been found. We didn't know what we were looking for, just hoped something would click.

The scene at the hospital was a media lover's dream. By dinnertime, there would be a multitude of stories each with their own twist—told from the perspective of genuine TV and radio reporters to the independents—people providing juicy news updates to their audiences via blogs, video channels and social media. There was no way to stop anyone from voicing a version of the event. The station-appointed reporters would have to answer to a higher authority, but the others were their own editor, supervisor and conscience.

From the sidewalk to the drop off lane to the lobby and the fire exits, the place was teaming with the curious.

We found Ivory Joe near the bank of elevators. I recognized him right away, even from the back—there are some things a girl never forgets.

"There he is!" I called to Gator over the noisy reporters then hurried to greet Ivory Joe. He picked me up and swung me around practically knocking out three bystanders.

"*Coooh*! Look at you, *beb*."

I laughed as he hugged me tightly babbling Cajun endearments.

"You gave me a scare, Jojo." He set me down, tipped up my chin and locked eyes. "You okay, really okay?"

I hesitated. "Yes."

He opened his mouth to say something else when Gator approached.

"We'd better get a move on," Gator said motioning toward the entrance where the reporters were gathering around the new arrival—an important-looking man and his entourage.

Ivory Joe reached in his pocket. "Here, put this on," he said, handing me a hospital ID tag. He motioned to the one on his own shirt. "Flip it over." I did, hiding the fact that I wasn't Ellen Moss, a plump black woman in her fifties.

"Got you one too," Ivory Joe said, handing off another laminated tag to Gator.

The photo on the front could have passed for Lyle Lovett.

"Really?" Gator said.

Ivory Joe grinned. "It'll be fine. Good to see you too," he called over his shoulder as he used his badge to open the service elevator then ushered us inside. It was a quick ride up, with just enough time for Ivory Joe to fill us in on Gina's change of heart.

"Her mother convinced her it would be good therapy."

"And I thought I didn't like the woman before," I said shaking my head.

The elevator opened onto an empty hallway, loud voices coming from the left. Ivory Joe pulled me aside. "You talked to Mickey, right?" I nodded.

"What's this?" Gator asked.

Ivory Joe's pocket buzzed. He read the text. "Detective Summers is ready for us."

I turned to Gator. "Mickey set it up. She's running a distraction. It will give me a chance to talk to Gina before she makes a big mistake."

Gator touched my arm, stopping me. "You may only have this one chance."

I held his eyes in mine and nodded. "Then I better make it count."

* * *

233

Gina looked stronger than when I last saw her. Though her cheeks were still gaunt and her skin held a greenish pallor, due to hospital lights or hospital food I wasn't sure. But she was sitting up, dressed in a T-shirt and leggings. Most of her bruises had faded and she'd taken some care with her hair and makeup.

I tried to see her as her mother had, a young girl who loved to swim, who was quiet and perfect. Innocent. But the shell had been broken.

She only seemed a little surprised to see me again. "I'm sorry. It wasn't my idea," she said, as I sat beside her. "My mother says it's the right thing to do. I think she likes the attention." She closed her eyes and shook her head. "I feel like a coward, for not wanting to talk about it. But what if I go through all of that…" She waved her hand indicating the TV vans outside, the reporters and crowds. "And nothing happens to them, nothing changes?"

She opened her eyes, blue, shining and filled with tears. I reached for her hand.

"What am I supposed to do?" she asked, her face pinched, scared. "I can't unrape myself. I can't go backwards. And the dreams." She winced. "I'll never be the girl I was or who I thought I was supposed to be. I don't know who that person is anymore."

Her words could have been mine.

"Gina, I —"

She squeezed my hand, cutting me off. "I want to be as strong as you. I wish I was—not for my mother—but for the girls." She bowed her head. "I can't do this. I don't want to talk about what they made me do. I don't—"

I squeezed her hand back. "You don't have to. That's why I'm here. I'm going to help you."

"What do you mean? They know where I am now. There's no place to hide."

The door to her room cracked open, a shadow alerting me. I reached for the knife in my boot as Gina, unaware, dropped my hand, wiped her eyes and stared past me toward the window. "I just want to disappear."

Before I could throw the knife, the shadow revealed itself—Gator. He slipped into the room closing the door behind him. "Disappear? Good idea. Let's go."

Gina looked from him to me and back again.

I slipped the knife in my boot and reached for her hand. "Trust me."

The door to an adjoining room opened letting in Ivory Joe, Gina's mother and a young nurse.

Her mother must have had a Come to Jesus revelation or a nice long talk with Ivory Joe who could be very convincing.

"It's okay," her mother said, hugging Gina. "They have a safe place and a way to get you there. You need to go. I love you."

The last thing I saw before we ran was the nurse putting on Gina's hooded jacket and a pair of sunglasses.

We slowed our pace on the stairs not wanting to draw any attention. We didn't need to worry as the only people we saw were a few nurses whispering on their phones, appeasing angry lovers or soothing upset children and on one floor, two orderlies sneaking a smoke.

"This is the tricky part," Ivory Joe said standing at the last door, the one that opened into the parking lot. The red bar across the door warned of a fire exit alarm.

"Do you have a car?" I asked Ivory Joe, telling him that we'd left Sabrina over by the park behind a Winnebago.

"No. Hang on." He pulled out his phone and sent a text. "Okay, give it a minute."

We huddled by the door until Ivory Joe's phone pinged. The screen said *now*.

We pushed through the door. The alarm was quiet compared the roar of megaphoned petitioners, yelling police officers and people chanting, "Over here! Gina! Over here!"

But they there were all facing the other way. We'd exited on the west end of the rectangular building, while at the north entrance, a pretty blond detective escorted Gina's mom and fake Gina, protecting them from the reporters and crushing crowd. Cell phones were raised on poles to grab the shot that would sell. People stood on cars to gain vantage. Every window of the hospital was full of faces. Someone even sent up a video drone.

"Go slow, be cool," Gator said as we walked toward the parking lot, taking a circuitous route back to the truck.

Gina saw them first. Her scream blended into the squeal of tires as the low-slung black sedan whipped through the row of cars heading straight for us. Some of the crowd turned from the Fake Gina spectacle, pointing in our direction.

I shoved Gina behind me. Ivory Joe and Gator formed the first line of protection in front of me. The car slowed. Hollywood was in the passenger seat, his window gliding open as two fingers of his empty hand made a gun gesture, his lips saying, "Bang."

The window rose and they drove off.

Ivory Joe looked at me. "Friend of yours?"

I shook my head, turned my attention to Gina. "Are you okay?"

She nodded, her eyes wild, lips quivering.

"Good. Come on."

CHAPTER 35

We drove back to the truck stop and pulled Sabrina into a tight slot on party row, parking between a patriotic rig adorned with a flag waving over purple mountains and a brand new hologrammed Peterbilt with an overdose of neon lights. The truck was better suited for a dance floor, but she was pretty and if that's what the owner was going for, they'd nailed it.

I was worrying a ridge into my lower lip with my thumbnail when Gator said, "She's going to be fine. That was a good thing you did. They'll take care of her and the dog. Ivory Joe will be back before you know it."

He was right. It had only taken a five-minute phone call to Père and Pilar. They didn't need the details, just where to meet Ivory Joe and the girl's name. Throwing Oscar in for the trip was an easy sell. Père had never met a canine that didn't love him. I couldn't think of a better place for Gina or Oscar right now than the plantation in Bunkie.

Before I could dwell on it any longer, my phone buzzed and dinged as a text came in.

I said, "It's Mickey. He says Esteban's almost done with the Flamethrower and wants to know where to meet us."

"Have him come here, and tell him about SHIPit—"

"That's not such an easy thing to text. I mean I'm pretty sure there aren't emojis for dead cop in freezer or shooter on the roof."

Gator smiled, as he rose from the driver seat, stretching. "You'll figure it out."

After I sent the text, I joined Gator in the kitchenette where

237

he was reloading our guns and breaking into the ammo stash.

We were quiet as we made our way through the lot to the truck stop and its diner-style restaurant. I'd let Gator think I was all in for his plan to talk to the T.A.S.T. Force guy, but I wasn't sure I could trust anyone these days, especially a strange man. I was reserving judgment until I met the guy, trying hard to be an optimist—an optimist with a really sharp knife in her boot.

The waitress that handed us menus looked like she'd stepped out of a fifties' shampoo commercial. I had never understood calling someone's hair *bouncy* until now. She had almost mastered the art of eyeliner, but honestly, at her age, her time would have been better spent learning how to properly floss.

Gator seemed soothed by her presence, even ordering pie, which I thought was a bit much, given the circumstances. When she left, I told him so.

"What do you mean?" he asked.

"Pie? Fucking pie?"

"I like pie."

Dino didn't need to be introduced. As soon as he opened the door, he was greeted by name by every waitress and one short order cook. He took time to speak to each person, had hugs for all the women and a salute for the cook. He was a big guy who moved slow and sure, like someone recovering from an injury, like someone worried it could happen again. Gator waved him over, and we both stood to greet him, as if he was trucker royalty.

"Thanks for coming," I said.

Dino nodded. He had the sort of hangdog face that could be misconstrued as mean or harsh, or worse, stupid. The mutton-chops didn't help. But when he smiled, it all changed.

The waitress returned to the table with coffee and pie for Dino. His slice considerably larger than Gator's, and probably free.

"Well now," he said. "Where should we start?"

It didn't take us long to catch Dino up on where we stood with the Somalis, or at least where we thought we stood and how we'd arrived there. Gator did most of the talking, with me interjecting specifics, from the number of Somalis in the houses to the set-up in the computer rooms and how they move the girls. I left out my own story, focusing instead on the who, what, when and where. I told him I'd heard Candy telling the guy in the green Mack to have the trucks ready when she called. How we figured out the trucks they were using were attached to SHIPit. I left off our visit to the warehouse and any mention of heroin, Mufasa, or the auctions at The Palace. I didn't want to put this old man or his group in any more danger than they already were.

"Something else Candy said." I hesitated, waited for Dino to raise his eyes to mine. "She said they'd 'taken care of that T.A.S.T. problem.' What does that mean to you?"

Dino sipped his coffee, set it down gently. "Could be a number of things. We run a sort of neighborhood watch in truck stop lots and highway rest stops. Most of our volunteers are good people with good hearts who genuinely want to help." He held my eyes, then looked at Gator. "Unfortunately, *most* is not all, and we all know money can sway a person from their duty."

Gator leaned in. "Are you suggesting—"

Dino held up a hand. "No. I'm not suggesting anything. I— we can't prove anything. I'm simply stating a fact." He looked at me, his eyes more sad, if that was possible. "Thank you for letting me know."

I stole a swipe of Gator's pie before asking Dino, "So, how did you get involved with T.A.S.T.?"

He ran his hands down his face, fingers disappearing into overgrown muttonchops, meeting under his chin. "It's not easy to talk about. I noticed how you didn't."

I tipped my head, went back for more pie.

"I'm sorry for your experience, for what you had to go through," he said, looking at me the way a priest eyes a guilty parishioner.

"I'm fine," I said.

He shook his head. "You might not be yet," he said. "But you will be."

I knew he meant well and I figured he was a kind person, maybe even one who was invested in this as much as we were, but the last thing I wanted was the pity of a stranger. As much as he might have cared it still felt like pity. Until he said, "My daughter ran away when she was thirteen. My wife and I looked for her for three years. The marriage didn't last but I never gave up the search. Until the day I got the call I was dreading. She was dead on the street at sixteen. Overdosed."

He looked away, tears welling in his eyes.

"It's okay," I said. "You don't have to..."

He swallowed hard, wiped his eyes then turned back. "No. I do. It's good for me to go back there, to feel that again. It keeps things straight." He tapped his head with one finger. "Up here."

I knew what he meant. Anger can fuel a hell of a lot of good if it's aimed in the right direction.

"I told myself at first that she was just a kid, didn't know what she was doing. But the more I work the streets, or the truck stops, the more kids I help, I see their side. They grow up fast on their own. You have to, or you won't last. We helped a girl last month, got her away from her pimp, cleaned her up, found her a job at a grocery store. Last night? I saw her working the corner. She told me she made more in two hours on the street than she made in a week punching the clock. What was I going to tell her?"

I knew how that could seem to these girls, to come from nothing and see all that money. If they stuck around long enough they might start thinking about how that same money passed right through their hands to the pimp. There could be a desire to slip a few bills into a pocket or a shoe. Some might even dream of starting their own business, going to college, buying a plane ticket to a place far, far away. Some might want it to feed a drug habit or appease a mean boyfriend. Money could do a lot of things.

"You see," Dino said, "I finally realized there are choices. There are always choices. I can't keep blaming myself or anyone for my daughter or any of the girls. They need to take responsibility for the choices they made, up until there weren't any more."

"But even then, the choice is to survive, isn't it?" I said.

Dino continued turning his coffee mug in his hands. He stared past us to the fuel pumps and the busy truck stop. Finally, he nodded and turned his gaze to me. "Yes. The choice is to survive. T.A.S.T. Force is making a difference. We've doubled in size in the last three years."

He told us how in the beginning when he was looking for his daughter, he connected with truckers all over the country, went to all the conventions, set up booths, spoke on trucker radio broadcasts, printed up flyers and stickers, and generally made a pest of himself.

"My wife said I was a natural," he said with shrug. "Amy—my daughter—would have said the same thing."

I reached over and laid my hand over his. He took a deep breath, then squared his shoulders and continued.

"I got an anonymous tip saying Amy been seen at a Florida hotel that was a hot spot for sex traffickers. The man that left me the message said a woman was in charge and that all the girls were marked with the same tattoo."

"A woman?" Gator asked.

Dino nodded. "We now know quite a few rings are run by women. It's not unusual. They tend to be trusted more, looked upon as motherly figures."

"Until...Jesus." Gator said.

Dino nodded. "Yeah. They get these kids hooked on heroin or something or just scared to death and that maternal thing goes out the window. The girls become their property. Nothing more than income producers."

Modern day slavery. I could relate to it first-hand. I slipped my hand back to my side of the table.

Dino caught my eye, held the gaze longer than necessary. He

didn't blink when I asked, "What do you know about a woman named Nadifa?"

"Nadi? Is she here?" He looked surprised.

I nodded.

He sighed, then shook his head, leaning back in the banquette. "Didn't think she'd come back. Things must be bad in up north." He reached for his phone, typing as he spoke. "There's been talk about a group that calls themselves Lady Outlaws. We thought they were new to OK City, but if Nadi is involved, it's just old players with a new name. They run a back page crew, pulling in Johns from online ads, work the computer and phone. Sometimes, they'll have a rotating street crew, make it hard to find the same girls on the same corners. We've heard that they're trying to get into the auction scene. They have access to advanced technology and possibly have political connections. Put them in jail and they bounce out faster than a rubber ball against cement."

"I wasn't thinking about a jail cell," I said.

Dino glanced around, then leaned in. "I'm going to pretend I didn't hear that."

"Well good," I whispered. "Because later, you're going to want to pretend you never met me."

Before Dino could say anything, his phone buzzed. His eyes darted over the screen. As he read the texts coming in, he shook his head mumbling, "This isn't good. This isn't good."

Gator leaned in. "What is it?"

Behind Dino, the door opened and two large men walked in with a young woman between them. I looked at her hard, trying to see the things any of the signs that the T.A.S.T. flyers said we should be looking for in an entrapped woman. My stare only drew the woman closer to the bigger of the two men, only encouraged her to raise a finger in my direction. I looked away, noticed we had become a popular table. Maybe the window seat overlooking the fuel pumps was a hot spot, maybe we'd overstayed our welcome, whatever it was, Gator felt it too.

Dino was still on his phone when Gator threw a few bills on the table. "Let's go to the rig, we can talk there."

We cut our way through the busy parking lot, trucks backing up, pulling out, the hissing of trailer brakes co-mingling with the sound of laughter and country music. It was too noisy to talk without yelling. But I heard the sharp whistle and knew exactly who it belonged to.

Mickey was leaning against the bug-splattered grill of our dusty Kenworth. "Sabrina's seen better days," he said, scooping me into a hug.

"Haven't we all?" I said, when I finally broke free. My voice sounding as tired as I felt.

Mickey and Dino shook hands and exchanged a few words as Gator unlocked the sleeper door. We filed in, taking seats at the kitchenette like we'd done this a thousand times before.

Dino spoke first. "That call was from a driver who runs a day route to El Reno and back, takes the West Bridge underpass twice a day."

He looked at me. I gave him nothing.

"He said they found a body."

Now he had my attention. "Body? As in dead?"

He nodded.

"You get any details?"

"Just that it's a girl. I mean, it was." He froze, seeing my face. "Let me read you what Gus said." He scrolled to the text and read, "Body reported at West Bridge underpass. Young girl, long brown hair, short, slim, Somali Mafia tattoo, Latina—"

"Latina? Is he sure?"

"Yeah. He'd know. Gus married one."

I exhaled and sunk bank into the banquette. "It could be the girl Black Dog shot in the neighborhood." I hung my head. "I didn't know her, but I saw it."

When I raised my head, three sets of eyes were on me. Dino's phone dinged again. He glanced down and read the incoming text. "Goddammit."

"Don't tell me," Mickey said. "Another body?"

"Gator put out his hand for the phone, read the message, then looked at me. "It's your pal, Ferguson. Gunshot to the back of the head. Found him in a park."

"Now we know how Abdi got the truck," I said. "And for the record, he wasn't my pal."

"For the record," Gator said, "They'll be looking for the Flamethrower next, and anyone connected with him or his rig. We weren't exactly tiptoeing around the truck stop when we met with him."

"Lots of eyes and ears here," Dino said. "And when it's a fellow driver..."

"We watch out for our own," I said. "Even if it means turning in our own."

It would be easy enough to find Sabrina, and us. If someone wanted to. A single phone call by authorities to our dispatcher would access our location tracker. Or—at least fifty truckers could simply look out the window of fifty semis at the Fuel Fox in OK City.

"We need to get out of here," Mickey said.

"Wait a minute," Dino said, taking back his phone. "Did they say what park?" He re-read the text, then opened a map on his phone. In a few seconds, we were looking at a satellite image of a bunch of trees and a small pond.

"Here's the park," he said. "And look what's right next door." Dino pulled the satellite image to the right then zoomed in until we had a bird's eye view of the roofs of what looked like a hundred tractor trailers.

"Shit," I said.

"Shit," Gator echoed.

Mickey didn't say a word, just kept scratching his cheek, the sound of man nails against beard scruff.

CHAPTER 36

Mickey gave me the idea. I didn't tell him, because I didn't think he needed the credit. If his ego got any bigger he'd have to hire more disciples.

It was the one word he said mixed in with a bunch of others, but it was the one I heard the loudest, *decoy.*

That word allowed me to look at our situation differently. Us versus them was a simple idea if you left out societal rules and sticky regulations. I started to think like a hunter, reducing the world around me to signs and systems, to expectations in a controlled environment. It was exactly what we needed to catch our Somalis, and take down Nadifa.

When I was thirteen, my father gave me his old Browning shotgun. "You'll grow into it," he said, handing me the long-barreled gun. It was heavier than I expected, the steel cold and oiled, the wood stock and butt worn smooth. He'd carried it to my room like a baby, cradled against his chest. In some ways it was. The gun had been in our family for as long as I could remember.

I thanked him and assured him I'd take care of it, as I swung the shotgun toward the window of my room and hoisted the butt to my shoulder, finding the perfect spot to rest its weight.

"All right then," Père said, as he turned and left.

The next morning at breakfast, he handed me a big red book, pages furled and swollen, like someone had dropped it in the bath or the bayou.

"You know what this weekend is?" he asked.

"Open season," I said.

He pulled a call from his pocket and trumpeted a perfect imitation of an eager goose. "That's right." He walked away, calling over his shoulder, "You've got three days, Shâ."

I studied the pages of *The Louisiana Duck Hunter's Almanac* every free minute I had, and woke up two mornings straight with the imprint of the spine on my cheek. I was going to make my daddy proud.

On the morning of the third day, he woke me before sunrise and led me out to his truck loaded with thirty large plastic geese frozen in various positions. The dogs were in the back seat, excited, panting and itching to work.

I got my first goose that day, but more importantly I learned something about the similarities of human nature and animal instincts. And that was definitely more satisfying in the long run than a freezer full of fowl.

I couldn't help myself. I did that thing people hate. I started talking mid-thought, as if everyone around the kitchenette had also been with me in my head, reliving my youth and the successful goose decoy set up with Père all those years ago. "I think we should start by opening up the killing hole."

Dino's mouth dropped open. Gator's temple vein began to throb and across the table. Mickey grinned. He put a hand on Dino's arm. "Easy, pal. She's just talking in hunting lingo."

"Decoy spreads, specifically," I said.

"Oh," Dino said. But he looked a little less sure of us than he'd been back when we were buying him pie.

Mickey started in with the broad strokes then let me expand on the subject, illustrating the particulars of search, seek, destroy. It was the little things that I excelled at.

"You see Dino, waterfowl are not so different from people."

Dino nodded as if I was actually making sense. I liked him

more for it.

"In this case, we're going to play duck, duck, goose with the Somalis, and draw them in with the classic J-hook." I went on to describe the way decoys worked in patterns to make migrating geese feel at ease to land or at least come in close enough to make an educated decision, without ever calling attention to the waiting hunters, their blinds or the salivating dogs on choke chains.

"They're thinking: land or fly. Eat or go hungry. A good hunter will set the stage, tweak reality for a minute or two so the scene is perfectly set."

"And that's the trap," Gator said with a smile.

Dino's furrowed brow suggested he wasn't following my symbolism. A second later he said, "I don't know shit about hunting geese but what these Johns want is a good time with little to no complications. Easy in. Easy out."

Gator dropped into a full Texas drawl saying, "I'm not here for a long time. I'm here for a good time."

"Trust me," I said. "Geese think the same way. They look for where the other birds are, figure they can swoop in, feed and get out before any...complications arise."

"But how are we—"

"Watch," I said grabbing a piece of paper and starting to draw.

We had the plan mostly figured out before the coffee filled the carafe. Like my hypothetical goose hunters, we needed some additional help but it wouldn't be a string of plastic geese or a truck full of Labrador retrievers.

Mickey used his network to score some local enforcement aid, while Gator and Dino worked the phones using Qualcomm leads and sweet-talking the dispatchers to gather a list of drivers within thirty miles of OK City. I, on the other hand, took the high road, catfishing female drivers on Facebook and Twitter to get them to play hooker decoy for us.

Dino hit pay dirt thirty minutes later with a driver named Twisty who was sitting in a busy truck stop off I-35. He confirmed seeing the black sedan with four, maybe five girls.

"Describe them."

"I can do better than that. Let me show you," Twisty said and forwarded a cell phone snapshot of three girls with long, brown hair wearing plaid skirts and white blouses.

"Those outfits are better than a gang tattoo," Gator said tapping on the text message.

I leaned in. "And that picture is worth—"

"A thousand whores."

"Isn't it...words?" I said, sliding my fingers across the phone's screen and enlarging the image, pointing it to the dark green Mack truck in the background. "But, maybe not in this case. I know that truck."

Gator glanced at the image. "Are you sure? This is a busy truck stop with three major highways intersecting at their front door. I know of at least four Macks painted that color."

The look on my face must have said I wasn't buying what he was selling.

Gator took the phone. "Tell you what. Let's ask Charlene for a favor."

As our dispatcher, Charlene wasn't only our eyes and ears for business, she was also the eyes and ears of thousands of drivers across the nation. Folks knew her. She'd been around—and I meant that in the kindest way.

Gator enlarged the lettering on the side of the truck, screen shot it and sent it to Charlene's personal cell phone with a short note asking her if this rig was supposed to be anywhere near the photographed location.

"And find out where else *Johnson & Sons* has been," I added.

Gator finished texting then tipped his chin toward Mickey who was leaning against the back door, arms crossed, looking like a redwood. "Until we hear back from her, why don't you and Dino go check it out? These guys don't know you."

Mickey's face said, *Why me?* but he was already following Dino to the door. "Speaking of recognizing trucks? You two better change your ride. Find a place to stash Sabrina."

"Right," Gator said.

Mickey stepped through the door. At the last second, he turned back saying, "Hey. Even if they did know me? They wouldn't know *me*," then closed the door.

Gator stared after him, then looked at me. "Is he for real?"

I nodded slowly. "As real as a two-headed cow at a state fair."

Though I hadn't seen Mickey arrive, I certainly knew when he left. The Charger's 426 Hemi was unmistakable, especially with Mickey at the wheel. Revving, roaring, squealing and skidding out of the lot, I was pretty sure he'd skipped second gear—on purpose.

"Show off," Gator said.

I smiled despite the pang of jealousy. If things had been different...if there was a parallel universe where all the shitty things became really, really awesome things if we just thought about them hard enough or placed enough wishes on butterfly wings...if *that* place existed, then I'd be the one behind the wheel screeching down the street away from all of this.

My mind wandered back to the problems in front of us, where do we hide our well-known rig? And, I tapped the phone in my hand, what were the Somalis doing at the Flying T truck stop? I looked at the picture again, recognizing girls number seven, eight and one. Why were the auction girls on party row in OK City? They should have been in the trucks enroute to the out of state and out of the country buyers.

I slipped my phone in the charger, and buckled in as Gator joined me in the cab.

"Where are we going?" he asked.

"To hide a rig in plain sight. Call Esteban, tell him we need the Flamethrower."

CHAPTER 37

A decent waterfowl hunter knows there are at least nine variables to consider when setting up decoys. Most are related to the science of the task, like water type and levels, weather and seasonality, visibility and wind conditions. But a great hunter understands there is also an art to playing the spread, something unquantifiable—the perfect combination of instinct, finesse and patience. Today, I would need all three.

We'd moved Sabrina down the street to the Country Kitchen, where we filled our holsters and grabbed our bug-out bags. Tucked behind the brick building between two RVs, bathing in the stench of fried food and composting trash bins, I was trying to hold my nausea at bay when Esteban drove up in the newly painted Flamethrower, ex-Flamethrower, I should say. The rig was now a deep blue black with accenting silver and glittering white stripes. The old flames had become shooting stars flaring up and out over the name: Starship.

"She is beautiful," I said, as he parked and climbed down.

"Beautiful? She is fantastic!" He grabbed me by the waist and twirled me, lifting my feet off the ground, staring at me so long that I wasn't sure if he was talking about the rig or me.

"Who's that?" Gator asked pointing to the hot pink pickup truck that had followed Esteban.

"That's my ride home. You see, I don't mind helping you my friends, but I am a lover, not a fighter. I wish you the best." He blew a kiss and cha-cha'ed off to the pickup where a buxom blonde, no younger than seventy-five sat behind the wheel.

Before Gator or I could close our gaping mouths, my phone

rang. It was Mickey.

"What's up?" I asked.

"It's good we got here when we did. They were going to move the girls, so we started Plan A without you."

"Plan A?"

"Yeah, the one where we replace the real hooker with the fake hooker."

"I don't think that was Plan A," I said.

"It is now." Mickey said.

"Don't worry," Dino called from the background. "It's going fine."

Don't worry. Two words I hated to hear.

"We're getting in the Flamethrower—I mean, Starship. We'll be right there," I said. "And Mick? Don't do anything stupid."

"Too late."

The Flying T truck stop located at the intersection of three of the busiest trucking routes in the Midwest had certainly seen better days. Most of the pumps bore signs warning of leakages or outages, the building itself was graffitied to an inch of its life and the pavement leading in was cracked and potholed. It was the ghetto of truck stops. Anyone who thought this was a fine place to hang out should definitely have their head examined. We drove the Starship through the parking lot following Mickey's directions.

Gator was still trying to convince me to not over react. "Maybe Dino saw something that wasn't safe. We've got to trust that he knows what he's doing. Hey, look at it this way, your decoy idea worked."

I couldn't argue with that. The two girls that greeted us as Gator pulled the Starship in next to Mickey's Charger looked happy and, more importantly, safe.

"Where are the others?" I asked.

"You're welcome," Mickey said, crossing his arms and leaning against his car.

"What's up?" I asked.

He shook his head telling me it was nothing, but his body suggested otherwise. I tipped my chin at Gator who took the hint.

"Dino, let's get the girls into the truck before someone spots them. They'll be safe there."

I turned to Mickey. "What's your problem?"

He ignored me.

"Mick." I stepped in closer, then closer still until I could feel the heat of him. Finally, he turned to me.

"You lied to me."

"What are you talking about?"

He met my eyes. "You said you were fine, that no one hurt you."

I waited, holding his gaze until he broke me. I stepped back, shook my head. Tears clouded my vision but I refused to let them fall, refused to appear weak. "What the fuck did you want me to say? That they got the best of me? That I couldn't beat them? That I...that Jojo Boudreaux failed? Fuck that. Fuck them!"

"That's right. Get mad."

I stared at him. *Was he mocking me?*

"You'll be better out there mad. Safer. Smarter."

I scoffed. "Smarter? Jesus. I—you don't know. You just...don't know what I—"

"I don't have to."

He caught my arm as I turned away and reeled me back in. He pulled me to his massive chest and held me. Every part of me felt safe and secure. I let him hug me and after a few seconds I hugged him back, until the hug became more clinging than hugging, then I pulled back, but not before I wiped my tears and snot on his sleeve.

In the shadow of the Starship, I felt small, but a little stronger, definitely more sure of what I had to do.

Gator leaned out the window. "We need to go," he said.

"What do you mean?"

"Me and you, now."

"Gator, what—"

Gator opened the passenger door, climbed down and pulled me away from Mickey.

"Mick, Dino needs your help. Go on in. We'll be back."

"What the shit?" I said, watching Mickey climb into the Starship as I raced to keep up with Gator.

"Two of the drivers we asked to be decoys are missing. Dino just got a call. He has a hunch they're inside the truck stop. He didn't want to freak out the girls and—"

"Or me? Because you're kinda freaking me out here. We should go back, get Mickey."

"No," Gator said. "We can handle this. Me and you. You need this."

I need this?

My brain started doing that busy, busy thing it does, plus I was panting, unable to catch my breath. By the time we were at the side of the main truck stop building I had to force myself to slow down. I took a deep breath and put on a plastic smile before I turned the corner and walked to the entrance in full view of the security cameras.

Inside the store, we pretended to browse the shelves as we got our bearings. Gator chatted up the cashier. Stupid little conversation about her grandkids, her dog, whatever kept her eyes off the security cameras.

I headed to the back of the building toward the shower rooms and toilets, skimmed the waiting list for the women's section. All the names had been crossed off, the last shower time was more than forty minutes past.

I looked in the bathroom and the quiet room, then circled back. The only place left to check was the one place two women shouldn't be—the men's area.

I stepped across the hall, hand on the small of my back, fingertips resting on my Kimber.

One very embarrassed cross-dressing man and two empty

shower rooms later, I hit pay dirt. The drivers had been duct-taped and zip-tied, but the room's automated lock had timed out, so getting in was easy. Releasing two squirming women from sticky bonds was another thing.

In hindsight, I should have left the gags on.

The black girl tugged down her wig and started in on me. "Where you been? You're Jojo right? Tell Dino he can go fuck himself. Need my help, he says. What the hell kind of help is this? Two assholes tie us to this bench in a stinky men's shower room. Me with this crybaby. I should be out there where the action is. Should be teaching those Somalis a lesson, be getting those girls back home."

The other woman, petite and blonde, moved from mumbling and whining to full out crying. I was beginning to think the Somalis had left them behind because they were more trouble than they were worth.

The mouthy black woman said, "Oh, here she go again. You got more motherfucking tears? We ought to send you to California. Fix the damn drought."

"It's okay," I said, pulling off the last of the tape, then extending a hand to the tiny blonde. "The girls are fine. They *will* be fine."

"Praise the Lord," the blonde said through her tears. "That's good news." She wiped her face with the back of her hand, looked around as if expecting someone. "Wait. They will be? You don't have the girls? Where's Brenda? We've still got a load to drop."

"Brenda?" I stared at my shoes, then at the tough black girl rising to her full six-foot height, her name badge *Bam Bam* clearly visible as she stretched. "Yeah, what she said."

I swallowed hard. "You still want to be where the action is?"

Bam Bam and the blonde, Suzie, took off with Dino in their sleeper. We had them headed northeast on Route 44 towards

Tulsa. They would meet up with Sludge, a driver hauling a flatbed of copper wire spools. He knew Suzie and Brenda and would be able to spot their moving van.

Bam Bam hadn't been happy to leave her rig in the lot, but once she realized there was no certainty the rigs wouldn't be damaged, perhaps irreparably, she conceded to ride with Suzie, but only if she was driving.

Suzie, upset about her co-driver being mistaken for a hooker and now on her way to God knows where was too scared to say no, so she'd strapped into the passenger seat spouting prayers as Bam Bam drove off grinding the gears, the rig shuddering beneath them.

Gator put his arm around me. We were leaning against the newly painted Starship. "Don't worry, she'll get the hang of it before they hit the highway."

I hoped he was right. We were going to need all the help we could get.

By the time the T.A.S.T. Force's black van pulled up, the two auction girls were fully sober and beginning to regret the decision to split from the Somalis.

Dino helped them into the truck and waved as they drove away.

"Good luck," I said, partly to the girls and mostly to the driver and his wife who had agreed to bring the girls to a safe house and stay with them.

I joined Gator and Mickey in the cramped sleeper of the Starship. There was barely had enough room for one large man, verses two. I'd brought sandwiches back from the truck stop that I put on paper plates, paired with energy drinks and fruit. I tuned in a classical music station and passed out the food. I was placing my bets on the long-held knowledge that food—or music soothed the savage beast. Sometimes, you've got to hedge your bets.

"Dino might have given me a good idea."

"Why don't you let us be the judge of that?" Gator said.

I wanted to smack his arm, tell him to be nice, but instead I said, "What's that, Mickey?"

Mickey gestured with his half-eaten apple. "He was talking about the other gangs moving in and the competition." He took a bite, and spoke around a mouthful of apple. "Now, we know about the heroin that Hollywood and Candy are moving, and that Nadifa wants to break into the auctions, right?"

I made an encouraging noise and nodded.

He continued. "There's a saying, 'It takes a gang to beat a gang.' Or something like that."

Without looking up from my phone where I was texting Johnny B. Goode, a driver with a wiggle wagon who we needed to follow Bam Bam and Suzie, I said, "I think the saying is, it takes a village to raise a child, but—"

"Nah, that's not it," Mickey said. "What I'm saying is that we should let the Somalis know—or at least believe that there's another gang who wants their product."

I stopped texting. "And by product you mean, *girls*?"

He nodded, not looking happy about it.

"How do you propose we do that?"

"We set up Nadifa and the Lady Outlaws."

Mickey walked us through his idea. I had to admit, it had some merit. What better way to take down a gang than with another gang? In my head, it was like West Side Story, only the accents were different, and there was much more fabric involved.

CHAPTER 38

There's a camaraderie among drivers that rarely extends to the outside world. Some days when you feel all alone behind the wheel driving through the night you have to connect with something and in most cases it's your higher power, but for some it can be an outreach of sorts, a *cause*. I couldn't think of a better cause than taking down drug dealers and slimy sex traffickers.

I was pacing in the shadow of the Starship when Mickey's phone rang. Leaning against his Charger, watching me pace—he said watching me helped him think, too—he answered with a "Hey," then clicked off a few minutes later saying, "Okay. Stay on it. Yes. I'll tell her."

"What?" I asked, figuring I was the *her* he was referring to.

"That was Detective Summers. Her team ran down the lead at Hidden Treasures. The cleaning lady finally broke down and showed them a hidden storeroom where they found enough heroin to keep a stadium full of junkies high for a week."

"Really?" I said.

"Nah. Well, I don't know. That second part was all me. Anyway, they can connect the heroin to SHIPit and Candy and your pal Hollywood, but that's where the trail goes cold."

"Maybe we should—"

A woman's scream pierced the air. Mickey yelled, "Get down!" then pushed me behind the Charger. He was crouching and scuttling toward the orange truck to our left before I'd even registered the potential danger. Maybe my ordeal really had killed some instinctual part of me. I couldn't worry about it right now, but I knew it needed fixing and soon before it got me killed.

Gator came running, Glock in hand.

"Are you okay?" he yelled.

I nodded.

"Get in the truck."

"No. I—"

"Jojo, Get in the truck, Now!" He pushed me toward the rig. The girl screamed louder. "I can't lose you again. Go!"

There was no sense arguing with him. I ran to the far side of the Starship, pretended to climb in, opening and slamming the door. I counted to five then crouched under the trailer. Crawling and scooting, I worked my way back to where I'd left Mickey and Gator.

They were ten yards away, drawing down as a big Somali pushed one of the auction girls into a dirty, unmarked trailer.

I backed up and circled around. Gator was yelling, telling the guy to get on his knees. The guy hollered something in his singsong language, then another voice chimed in. *Hollywood.*

I crawled under their idling rig. The noise masking my movements, any sound I might make. But that also meant I couldn't hear them. Positioning myself behind a tire, I had a clear view of Gator and Mickey, and two pairs of Somali white sneakers, one considerably larger than the other. Gator had his weapon raised, finger snugged up to the trigger.

He said, "Show me your hands."

Hollywood said, "Hey, now. Is that how you do, Cowboy?"

"Yeah. That's how I do. Tell your pal to step away from the trailer, get on his knees."

"You tell him. You're the one with the gun."

"On your knees!"

The big Somali's feet shuffled.

"On your knees!" Gator repeated.

"Oh for fuck's sake," Mickey said, adjusting his aim and firing one bullet into the big man's right patella, dropping him to the ground, yelping and writhing.

Mickey said, "There. You happy? He's on his knees, well,

knee."

My ears were ringing, but Hollywood's feet had barely moved. The big Somali was on my level now, groaning and rolling around, hands clasped over a bloody shredded knee.

"What is next, Cowboy?"

"Where are the other girls? The drivers?"

"I don't know."

"Who are you meeting?"

"I don't know."

Mickey's said, "Apparently, he doesn't know dick. Let's take him with us, see if I can jog his memory."

I craned my neck. Gator was holstering his gun, saying something to Mickey, who nodded.

Gator approached Hollywood, zip ties in his hand.

Hollywood laughed. "Just like that? You think this thing is the right thing? You don't know what you do. You don't know who this is. They will come for you. Fuck the shit out of you, like they did to your woman." He laughed, long and hard.

My fingers turned white on the Kimber's grip. I slid forward another two feet just as Gator knocked Hollywood to the ground. His face was turned to me, eyes wild as Gator kneeled on his back, pinned his arms and started to zip tie his wrists.

"This is how we do. Asshole."

"You don't know what you're into." Hollywood's eyes found mine. He grinned. "You don't know. They will kill you."

"Shut the fuck up," Gator said, struggling with the plastic tie. "Or I'll have to gag you. With your dick."

Above me in the trailer, feet shuffled, followed by the clomping of heels on metal and the undeniable banshee-like yell of a wronged whore. I could make out some of the words, interspersed with yelps of Hollywood trying to dodge her blows.

But when the other girls jumped from the trailer and joined in, it was a clusterfuck with Hollywood attempting to duck and cover as the blows rained down. Screams of "You son of a bitch!" and "Motherfucker!"

Gator got nailed by the flailing arms, a long scratch down his cheek was starting to bleed. I glanced toward Mickey, saw him lower his weapon, tuck it away as he approached.

"Hey, come on now," Mickey said. He pulled the smaller of the three girls off Hollywood and strong armed her away. The others lost their steam when Hollywood, now on the ground in a fetal position stopped struggling.

Gator wiped a hand across his bloody cheek and stepped in to grab Hollywood as Mickey hauled the girls away.

I crawled out from under the trailer, brushing off my jeans saying, "Well, that was fun."

Gator spun around, loosening his grip on Hollywood. "What the hell, Jojo? Where have you—"

It was only a second, maybe two but it was enough. Hollywood snatched Gator's Glock from his waistband, pointed it at Gator's heart.

"No!" I yelled.

Hollywood faced me, grinning, then pulled the trigger.

CHAPTER 39

It's okay. It's okay, I told myself. He's not dead. Gator was fast. He ducked or twisted out of the way. But if he did get hit, Mickey's out there. He would have heard the shot and run back to help. There's no way he'd let Gator die. There is no way God would fuck with me that bad. Not after everything I've been through. Not after all the deals and bargains I made with Him. Right?

You are fine. You are fine. The mantra wasn't working.

"Fuck." That felt better.

"What's your problem, Trucker Lady?" Hollywood asked, shoving his face in close to mine, stealing my air. "Not having a good day?"

"No. I'm not having a good day. I'm actually not having a good month or a good year for that matter. Do you really fucking care? Because this..." I spread my arms wide, raised my voice. "This is all because of you. You're the reason for all this shit."

Hollywood laughed.

"Don't laugh at me. You think this is funny? It's not." I stepped in, pushing Hollywood back. It was time to be the hunter, not the prey. If a man who has nothing to lose is dangerous, then a woman with nothing to lose is unbeatable.

"I am so sick and tired of being bullied by you. I'm sick of your friends, of—all of this." I gestured madly, my arms wind milling like my brain. He'd closed us into the trailer, the only light from the Lucite ceiling above. I felt trapped, claustrophobic, manic.

I lost it. "Hollywood? What the fuck kind of name is that?

You're no star. You're just a scrawny little fuck from some third world country coming over here playing the big man, ruining the lives of little girls, taking away their childhood. You're pathetic." I was close enough now to spit in his face. He wasn't laughing anymore. His hand holding the gun was inches away.

"What now tough guy? You want to kill me. Is that your solution?"

He adjusted his grip on the gun, stepped back. His body and his eyes told me everything I needed to know. This little boy was just a little boy, after all.

"Come on. Do what you want with me. I don't care. It means nothing. *You* mean nothing. What do I have left, huh? Haven't you taken everything already?"

His gun hand drooped as if a weight had been placed on his shoulder. I pressed on. "What's the matter? It's not so exciting if I'm not afraid? You can't get it up? Is that it?"

Something grew inside me, giving me the sense that this wasn't the way it was going to end. I had a new thought and this one said: survive. It said fight. It said…lunge.

We went down together, rolling and clanging around in the trailer. He was wiry and fast, but I was mad and fearless. He got in a few punches, nothing hard enough to stop me. He wasn't a fighter. He was a scrapper.

I'd managed to kick the gun out of his hand, hadn't managed to get to it, but made sure I knew exactly where it was and kept circling Hollywood, keeping him as far away from that side of the trailer as I could. In the second I took my eye off him, he dove to the side, swept me off my feet and hauled me up, pushing me against the cold metal wall of the trailer, his forearm at my throat, his other hand splayed against my abdomen and moving south.

"Now who's the big guy, Trucker Lady? Now who wants to tell stories?"

His breath was rank, bitter. Like something had died inside him. Maybe something had crawled into his mouth and buried itself in his gums or under his tongue so every time he spoke the thing woke and moved.

He looked around, then back at me. The gun was in a shadowy corner. I didn't move my eyes from his face. Before I could decide my next move, someone rattled the trailer doors, then yanked on them.

Hollywood threw me to the side, scrambled for the gun. I hit my head on the way down, cut open my forehead. He was back on me in a flash, and this time, he had the gun.

The rattling became banging and yanking on the trailer doors. The pole Hollywood had used to lock them inside was moving.

"Hey! Jojo! You okay in there?"

Mickey.

"She's fine," Hollywood said. "Go away now if you want her to live."

"I can't do that," Mickey called pulling harder on the doors, smacking them with something, forcing the door open another inch.

"He has a gun!" I yelled, as Hollywood swung the weapon toward the doors.

Mickey sounded farther away when he yelled, "It's over. Hollywood. Or should I say, *Fatah Ahmed Hashi*?

The name threw him. I saw the glint fade in his eyes.

"They took your brothers into custody. The Palace has been shut down, as well as the houses. The girls are with T.A.S.T. Force, they're cooperating with the police. It's over."

Hollywood stepped back, two steps, three, his gun hand lowered as the weight of Mickey's words hit home. I could take him. Even if he got off a shot it wouldn't kill me. Nothing could kill me. Even the devil didn't want me.

"We've got it all," Mickey said. "The guns, the money, the drugs and the suppliers. If you give yourself up now, if you agree to come in peacefully, there may some leniency for you. But you've got to let Jojo go. No harm can come to her."

At the mention of my name Hollywood turned to me as if

he'd forgotten I was there. I held my hands out to the side, palms open, like a martyr.

Mickey had stopped pulling on the door. From my side of the trailer I could tell the opening was now large enough for his purposes.

"Hey!" I locked eyes with Hollywood on the other side of the trailer, willing him to look at me, not at the muzzle of the rifle Mickey was feeding through the opening. "Whatever you think you are doing, whatever you think you need to do. Think again. Not everyone gets a second chance. A chance to erase a wrong, to face someone they hurt and ask for forgiveness. We have a saying in Bunkie. 'Truth is like rain. It don't care who it falls on.' He's giving you a chance to face the truth."

Hollywood leaned against the trailer wall and began to raise the Glock, crazy eyes wide, stupid grin. "In Somalia, we too have a saying, 'A brave man dies once, a coward, a thousand times.'"

He turned the gun on himself, two hands shoving the muzzle into the space between his eyebrows, and closed his eyes.

"No! Don't!" I yelled.

The hollow point 9mm bullet entered his brain at more than one thousand feet per second busting through his skull, destroying connective tissue and fibrous membranes before entering his cerebrospinal fluid and exiting the back of his cranium at a slightly slower rate, taking with it blood, hair, bone and gray matter.

Hollywood's arms dropped. His eyes dulled as his legs gave out and he slumped to the floor, his life smearing the wall in a three-foot trail.

My ears rang and pulsed, the high-pitched whine of my insides echoing back in the air of the small space. My breath caught in my throat as I tried to scream. I scrambled to the trailer doors, slid out the pole and shoved the doors open wide.

Falling into Mickey's arms, it wasn't his name I called before I passed out.

"Gator? Gator!"

CHAPTER 40

A wiry little man in white twisted something around my arm, then squeezed.

"Ow."

"Sorry, ma'am. Just need to get your blood pressure. The way you...dropped, we need to be sure everything's okay."

Squinting at him, head pounding, I noticed the life cross symbol over his heart and let him live. I ran a hand down my face, looked at it, sticky with blood. "Is that...?"

"Not yours," he said, reaching for a wide gauze pad, handing it to me apologetically.

I dabbed at my face, checked the cloth, then scrubbed as hard as I could with one shaking hand. He said something about dehydration and shock, then came at me with a needle. I couldn't help it. My first reaction was to kick him in the balls.

"Lady, listen. I'm trying to help you," he groaned, clutching his groin, trying to stand.

"Sorry. It's...habit?"

Mickey jogged over, patted the guy on the back and continued my apology. His was more heartfelt as he'd been on the receiving end a time or two.

I stood with a bit of effort and retrieved the fallen syringe. "What is it?"

The paramedic's reply came in bursts as he got his breath back. "I was just trying to help. You wouldn't take the IV, said your head hurt. I—"

Mickey said, "Maybe you should—" that was as far as he got before I uncapped the syringe and jabbed myself in the leg.

He was right. I did feel better. I grabbed a bottle of water out of the hand of a passing cop and hurried over to the ambulance. Gator lay on the stretcher, shirt torn open, wires everywhere, oxygen mask on his face, machines beeping and flashing. The paramedic, a stout brunette spoke without turning around.

"You ready? We need to move him."

"Give me a minute," I said, climbing up.

She turned. "You're not Steve."

"Observant, aren't we? Steve's over there nursing his balls."

She looked past me to her colleague pale and sweaty, leaning on Mickey.

"Yeah. It was an accident. Sorta." I shrugged. "Anyway. Can I have a minute here?" I motioned to Gator. Her face was as blank as a wall. "I won't be kicking him in the nuts, if that's what you're worried about. He's my...boyfriend."

That must have been the magic word, because she nodded and stood. "Okay. Three minutes then we have to go." She tapped her watch.

"Thanks," I said, switching places with her. "Hey. He's going to be okay, right?"

She stepped off the back of the ambulance facing me. "He's stable. But he needs surgery. And soon."

I looked down at Gator. He was so flat, so empty.

"Three minutes," she called, before she stepped away.

I laid my hands on his arm. "Gator?" I whispered, my mouth inches from his face.

His eyes fluttered then opened, taking a few seconds to focus. "Jo—"

"It's okay. Don't talk." His hair was damp, his scalp clammy under my touch as I brushed it off his forehead. "You're going to be fine. They're going to take you to the hospital and fix you up." I searched his eyes, looking for fear or anger but there was none.

"I'm sorry," I said. "It's all my fault. You wouldn't be hurt if it wasn't for me. I swear, I'm no good. I'm like a shit magnet.

Just drag me around the farm and I'll pick up all the manure a cow can make. Put me in the trenches where tilapia breed and they'll be hungry when I crawl out. Throw me into the sewer and—"

He tugged on his oxygen mask, pulling it away from his mouth, gritted his teeth and growled, "All right. Enough. Stop it. Just stop it." He winched and paused. "It's not all about you. Maybe just this once, it isn't about you, Jojo. Maybe it's—"

Lights flashed, an alarm went off, as Gator's arm dropped to his side, oxygen mask dangling from his limp fingers.

"Move!" The paramedic pushed me aside, yelled something to her partner and then I was on the ground and they were gone, speeding out of the lot toward the hospital.

Maybe it's...what?

I stumbled in circles, the euphoria from the shot fading quickly, leaving me numb.

"Miss Boudreaux?"

The cop grabbed my elbow. "Maybe you should sit down." He gestured to the patrol car.

"I'm okay," I said, pulling my arm out of his grasp. I wanted nothing to do with the caged back of a car.

He grabbed again. Not so kindly. "Let me restate that. I need you to come with me."

As the cop dragged me away, I looked for Mickey. "Hey!" I yelled over my shoulder spotting him head to head in a group of men. "Mick! Over here!"

He excused himself from the group and jogged over. "Officer! Hold up. What's going on?"

"This is none of your concern, sir. I'm going to ask you to step back." He pulled me with him away from the patrol car and the people. I glanced at his sidearm, not police issue. There was something wrong about the uniform, too.

"And I'm going to ask you to get your hands off her," Mickey said.

The cop kept walking, his grip tighter, dragging me.

"Now! Let her go." Whether it was the tone of Mickey's voice, the sound of the round being chambered, or the scampering of people in the background, one yelling, "Gun!" Mickey got his result. The cop stopped walking and turned around with me tucked up beside him. I was getting fucking tired of being played like a pawn. The cop shifted his weight and I read his move and countered before he figured it out himself. Right heel stomp, left elbow to his rib cage, following up with a palm to chin and stole his weapon before he collapsed in a panting heap.

Mickey was on him in a second, closely followed by the real cops, including Detective Lauren Summers.

"We've got this," she said, as her men moved in.

"What the hell was that about?" I asked.

"That's McKenzie. His partner was the woman you found in the freezer at SHIPit. We've been looking for him since the investigation started. Heard he left town after we pulled his badge. Guy never was very stable. Why don't you…" Her voice trailed off at the sight of my face. I wasn't going anywhere until I had some answers.

Summers told her partner she'd be right back, then walked with me and Mickey. We stopped at a ratchety picnic table someone had braced up against a fence blocking off a small patch of grass. It reminded me of the parking lot that I'd found Oscar in and that reminded me of possibilities. At least Oscar was far away from all this. His old life hopefully just a foggy, doggy memory now that he was at the plantation.

"Cops got here pretty fast," I said, jerking my thumb in the direction of the flashing patrol cars and bevy of cops milling about.

"Yeah," Mickey said. "My guys were on the road, handling the Somalis and the trucks, bringing back the girls. I needed the manpower, so I called in the cops, well, Summers, anyway." They shared a glance, one that said he was doing more than calling her.

"What happened?" I asked, hating that I'd missed out on the

action. "Is everyone okay?"

"Depends on who *everyone* is to you," he said, arching his brow.

It didn't take him long to tell the story, and the version he told me was pretty much the same as the one he gave for his statement. Pretty much. There was a tiny, little piece about purposely blowing up a moving van hauling a barbeque stocked with two propane tanks that *may* have been omitted.

Turned out the drivers working with Hollywood had been so confident in their escape that the surprise attack had been just that.

After we got an update that Gator was in stable condition, with a good prognosis, I was able to focus as Mickey and Detective Summers filled me in on what T.A.S.T. Force and the drivers had been up to.

I had to ask twice for the details of the take down. "Wait. They blew up a moving van?"

"Technically," Mickey said, "they only blew a hole in a moving van."

I shook my head as he went on. It seemed the grill the family was transporting had not one but two propane tanks. It had been Suzie's idea to turn the tanks into missiles, blowing through the steel sides of the trailer across two lanes of traffic and into the trailer hauling the auction girls. The hole they made was large enough for the girls to escape.

"You should hear Dino tell the story," he said. "They had a few hairy moments there."

"It's on YouTube," Detective Summers added.

"Yeah, I'll have to check that out in my spare time."

Mickey continued, "Driver out of Texas had an empty hay hauler and was able to snug it up close enough to the girls to drop a ramp and get them out of the blown-out trailer. Pretty ingenious, actually. Reminded me of an extraction we did in

Afghanistan." Mickey got a faraway look in his eyes.

"Anyway," I said, bringing him back to the present. "Everyone's okay and the Somalis have been neutralized, right?"

"Yes," Summers said. "The info the girls gave us was invaluable. Thanks to them and T.A.S.T. Force, we took down one of the largest trafficking groups in the United States."

I thought about the way the drivers had come together, how the girls were safe and if I dared to say it, justice would be served. It was disconcerting, this whole nice little wrap up. I couldn't help thinking we were just waiting for the other shoe to drop. Then I remembered a small detail.

I asked, "What about Candy? And Nadifa?"

"We've got a team on it," Summers said, exchanging a look with Mickey. She stood, brushing off her pants, avoiding my eye.

"What aren't you telling me?" I asked.

"Nothing," Summers said. "Listen, I'd better get back."

"Tell her," Mickey said.

Summers shook her head." Mick, I don't think that a good idea."

"She deserves to know."

"I'm right here," I said.

Summers looked at me and finally said, "Candy may be holed up with the rest of the Lady Outlaws."

"The rest? What are you saying?"

"We have reason to believe that Candy has been working with the group all along, and that Nadifa has been leading their attempt to integrate heroin into the trafficking business."

I scoffed. "You're kidding."

"I wish I was. Look, I—"

"I know, "I said. "You've got to get back. But, Summers. I want to know the minute you find them. You owe me that."

Summers hesitated, then nodded before she turned and jogged off.

CHAPTER 41

After some convincing, I'd taken Mickey's advice. He was right, there was no sense going to the hospital right now. Gator wouldn't be out of surgery for hours and whatever had been in the syringe I'd jabbed myself with had long worn off. I ached all over, all I wanted to do was sleep. The three steps up to Sabrina's back door had never felt so steep.

I kicked off my boots and fell onto the bed.

I heard a voice from far away, the same one that had whispered to me when I was high and alone in the Somali houses. The same one that came to me when the nameless men visited me in the dark, telling me I wasn't alone, I wasn't forgotten. I mattered.

And now, it came again. But this time the whispery, soothing voice sang my name, my Christian name...Josephina. The name my mother gave me in remembrance of her mother, Granny Jo. A woman I had never known. She died in a car accident soon after my mother's passing. *All the women in my life seem to leave me. Will all the men in my life die because of me?*

Père may have told me the details of Granny Jo's passing, or someone else had. It was a shadowy area of my memory. The only thing I remembered about her was that she collected salt and pepper shakers, had shelves and curio cabinets filled with all sizes and shapes. She used to let me hold one pair each time I visited.

"Just one," she would say. "And remember them, so that the next time, you choose differently."

Her eyes watched me as I looked at the hundreds of choices,

not wanting to disappoint and not knowing why.

It was after one of these visits that Père had to go away, and Maman and I were left alone.

I thought about that time as I forced myself to relax, laying corpse-like on the small pull-down bed, concentrating on my breathing, slow and deep. Images began to flood the space behind my eyes, running a movie I never bought a ticket to see.

The stranger in the hat filled the doorway. He wore a hat, a long coat and had very shiny shoes. It was a detail I'd never seen before. I willed myself to see more, beyond the place where the dream always ended, beyond the image of the woman on the floor, the discarded doll with its one winking eye.

"You're fine. You're fine. You're fine," I told myself, the mantra one with the breath. I let the images come as I sunk into the dream deeper and deeper.

This time the little girl stepped forward when the screen door opened, then slammed shut. The rattle and squeak was a noise that always alerted the mother when the girl wanted to escape into the garden. But this time it was a noise that said they were alone. This time, she wasn't leaving and neither was Maman.

The little girl reached for her mother, the woman quiet now in a ball on the floor, something hard and shiny in her hand, red and sticky. The girl knelt beside her. "Maman." She tried to lift a limp arm, looking for a cuddle, for a hug. The girl pushed hair from Maman's face, the strands leaving patterns across her cheeks as it swept across blood from her chest and neck. The little girl curled herself up next to the woman, pushed her thumb in her mouth and began to hum the familiar lullaby. *Galine, Galine, Galine, Galo. Galine, Galine, Galine, Galo.* Soon she was asleep—the little girl in the dream and the girl in the bed. Jojo past and present.

"Hey, you okay?"

I opened my eyes to someone jostling my shoulder. The pillow was damp with tears, my eyes sticky and swollen, my nose stuffy.

I ran my hands over my face and sat up blinking. "What is it?" I focused on the figure in front of me. "Ivory Joe? What are you doing here?"

He smiled. "Good to see you too."

"Sorry, it's just...wait. Is Gator okay?"

"Yeah. Far as I know. Mickey said he's still in surgery. He gave me a key, told me to check on you. So, here I am. Checking on you. Glad I did. By the looks of it, you were having a bit of a tussle with the sandman."

I smoothed the rumpled covers and readjusted my twisted shirt. "I'm okay. Really."

Our eyes locked and for a second, I was back in Bunkie. We were kids again, running around the woods, setting traps, chasing dogs, climbing the big cypress trees and telling stories, talking about the lives we wanted, what we would do, where we would travel, the things we wanted to see.

"Guess I'm just worried about Gator."

"He'll be okay. You two will be fine."

"I'm not so sure about that," I said under my breath.

"What's wrong?" Ivory Joe asked, sinking onto the bed beside me.

"It's nothing. You're right. It's going to be fine."

"Hey," Ivory Joe said, lifting my chin with his fingers. "This is me. Your Ivory Joe. Talk to me."

It took me a full minute before I said, "Gator doesn't understand. He thinks I'm too fragile. That I'll break. He won't touch me. I mean *really* touch me."

"Be patient, Jojo."

"I have been."

"You? Don't make me laugh."

"It's not that, Ivory Joe. It's more of me not knowing how to talk to him about it. Any of it." I sighed and fell back on my elbows, closing my eyes.

"You can't avoid him forever. That is, if you want him to stick around," he said.

I ran my hands over my face.

"Well, do you?" he asked.

"Want him to stick around?" I said. "I don't know. I'm tired and confused and..."

Ivory Joe leaned in, cradled my face in his hands. So softly. He ran his thumbs across my jawline as his eyes pierced mine. His lips were soft and sure, a memory that came complete with music and scent and a pathetic tactile sense of belonging. I was home. Here with my best friend. He knew all the good and bad parts of me. I leaned in meeting him halfway.

Pulling back from the kiss, he whispered, "Do you know how long I've been waiting to do that?"

The sadness in his eyes reflected the ache in my heart. I knew that tiny freckle on his nose, that white scar on his forehead, the way his day-old stubble would feel against my cheek. He was a part of my past. One of the best parts and I wanted nothing more than to go back there right now, embracing a comfort only the arms of someone I knew and trusted could give me. I didn't stop to think, simply fell into the moment and shut out the world.

Ivory Joe started to speak but I closed off his words, sealed his mouth with mine. A second later his shoulders relaxed and I felt him give in. We moved together, the urgency rising as I met each of his kisses, each of his inquiring thrusts of this tongue with mine. He slipped a hand under my T-shirt his fingers strong and warm on my back, his large hands circling my rib cage, his thumb finding my nipple. I moaned. We pulled our clothes off and pressed flesh against flesh, every part of me alive for the first time since the abduction. Ivory Joe murmured in my ear, his breath on my neck sending shivers down my spine. I wanted him more than anything. I needed him. I hooked my legs around his back and pulled him into me, arching my back to meet him, kissing him deeper, tangling my fingers in his hair as he thrust himself inside me. We cried out together, but didn't stop. Ivory Joe circled my waist, snugged me to him and rolled over taking me with him. This time I set the pace, slower, softer. I trailed kisses from throat to navel and back. My nails dragged lines down his inner thighs, firing up nerves, making him shudder. His moans pushed me further, until he begged me to stop, begged to be inside me again.

As the light rode in on dust motes, the setting sun falling behind idling big rigs, Ivory Joe ran a finger down my spine stopping at each scar, naming the places I'd got them and how. When he stopped at my forearm, the strange zigzag mark, he said, "I know you don't like to talk about this one. I'm sorry for that day, Jojo." He lifted my limp arm, kissed the scar and it all flooded back.

It had been Ivory Joe who sat with me that day I found my mother dead in the kitchen, my arm bleeding where I'd cut myself on her knife. It had been Ivory Joe who held my hand when the policeman asked all the questions, it was him who calmed me for years when I couldn't sleep. He was the one who collected me each time I ran away from home, each time I broke down. How did I forget all those moments? What was wrong with me that I'd blocked it all out?

Père should have told me the truth about my mother. She abandoned me. I was no different than these girls we'd saved. Those throwaway girls no one wanted. I had been that same sort of girl once, making promises to be good, but I must have broken the promise, because my mother left me.

She didn't love me enough to stay. She was the reason I had to make walls around my heart. She was the reason I found solace in wilderness, the reason I trusted nature, not man. The reason I was never happy enough, never good enough. I was not worthy. Not of love, not of happiness.

I remembered what I told Hollywood, that he had a chance

275

to right wrongs, to ask for forgiveness, but he had chosen another way out. Like Maman. Like me. What is more difficult? Giving up or trying again?

Truth is like rain. It don't care who it falls on. I was standing in a downpour. Waters rising around me.

The buzz and ting of an incoming text shook me out of my reverie. I found the phone under the pillow and glanced at the screen.

"I've got to go," I said, pulling myself free of Ivory Joe, reaching for my jeans and shirt, tugging on the clothes while I searched for my boots.

"What? Wait. Jojo—"

I finished dressing, pulled my hair back into a knotted pony-tail and reached into the oven for my holstered gun and ammo.

"Where are you going?" he asked.

"You don't want to know."

He scooted to the edge of the bed. "I'm going with you."

"No. There's something I need to do. Something I need to finish."

I shoved an armload of clothes at him. "Take these to Gator. I'll meet you at the hospital in a few hours."

"Jojo, you can't."

"I can," I said, pushing him back, my hand small on his chest. "I can."

CHAPTER 42

I made one stop before meeting Detective Summers at the station.

"Thank you," I said, as she led me from the back door down a dim hallway.

"You've got ten minutes, maybe less before the Feds get here," she said, stopping before we were aligned with the security cameras. "They're down there in room two. Hurry."

I pulled my hood up and walked purposely around the corner into the busier halls of the Oklahoma City Police Department. No one noticed me. They all had their eyes on their phones. I found the room and slipped in locking the door behind me.

"I gotta pee," Candy said, not looking up from her seat at the table.

"Too bad," I said, dropping my hood and facing the shackled Lady Outlaws.

Nadifa looked surprised to see me.

Candy smiled. "Well. Long time no see, Jojo."

"Did you miss me, Candy?" I asked, scooting up a chair. "Never mind. There's no time for small talk. I just wanted to be the one to tell you whatever deal you thought you had isn't going to fly. Not anymore."

"What did you do?" Nadifa asked.

"Something that can be undone, if you give me the information I need."

"And we're supposed to trust you?" Candy scoffed.

I leaned back in the chair. "I don't see what choice you have. The Feds are on their way. If the heroin I planted in your house, along with Hollywood's confession and the data on Omar's phone aren't enough to convince them, I'm sure the Somalis in Minneapolis would be very interested to hear from me."

"You wouldn't," Nadifa said. "They will kill us."

"Maybe," I said. "Or maybe they will get you hooked on heroin and turn you out on the street."

Candy and Nadifa exchanged a look. Finally, Nadifa spoke. "What do you want to know?"

The car was waiting when I stepped out of the alley. I slid into the back seat and gave the Uber driver the hospital address. As he drove I wrote an email detailing the interview I'd just had with Nadifa and Candy, attaching the recording I'd made on my phone: their list of The Palace auction clients. The names of police officials, businessman, judges, politicians and celebrities were just the start. I also had passwords to access the entire Somali Mafia databank which I sent to Mickey. And Mufasa's real name.

Before he'd come to Oklahoma City, before he opened his trucking company, Arthur Strauss been a mechanic in Missouri. He'd had a thing for the dark, almond-eyed girls of the Midwest. One of which had been his wife and later, his own daughter, Rebecca.

It had taken the state almost three years to build their case against him, another to make it stick, but the things he had done to them both couldn't be undone. The wife committed suicide, tried to take her daughter with her, but the bullet missed and instead, locked the girl in catatonia forever. A state in which she was alone with her memories, her thoughts and her every fear. Arthur was told that his daughter was dead, that she didn't the gunshot. Meanwhile, the case was thrown out on a technicality and Arthur didn't serve a day behind bars.

Nadifa said Mufasa found the men he dealt with through the dark web on the kinds of sites that bred evil, a place where the buying and selling of a human was everyday business. Mufasa

LINDA SANDS

was known for his specialty, the almond-eyed brunette, the ingénue. Before the auctions, he used trucking routes to move the girls, keeping them rotated so that they didn't get comfortable and clients never got bored. His connection with the Somali Mafia created a need for more girls, and the occasional boy. Auctioned goods, as they were called, were sold or rented, sent to the client with a "watcher." According to Nadifa, it was one way to assure the girl would come back alive. There were no other assurances. Many times, the man who bought the girl would invite a few friends over to celebrate his purchase, feed his ego.

It made me sick. I knew there was nothing to be done about the past, but I was determined to change the future. For everyone.

I re-read the email, then clicked the send button.

CHAPTER 43

Gator couldn't drive with his leg in a cast but that didn't stop him from yelling directions and criticisms from the bed in the sleeper unit.

I'd tried flipping him the bird, turning up the radio and dosing him with Sleepytime tea, but the most effective thing so far had been the laptop and the TV. The man had no limit to the amount of news reports he could read and comment on regarding what was now being called The Somali Sting. The exposure of an assembly of high ranking government officials, congressmen, attorneys, local businessman and a housewife from Tulsa who wanted an anniversary gift for her husband, all served to fuel the fires of reporters and ramp up social media posts, some of which called us heroes—a term I was not at all comfortable with.

Gator had been telling me since he woke in the hospital that we could make a difference, and that he had an idea, but it was a surprise. The weeks of his rehabilitation from the shooting were peppered with secret meetings and phone calls, visits from lawyers and briefcase-carrying men.

By the time we arrived in Bunkie, six weeks later, Gator's plan was in effect, with a fully recovered Gina Sharp at the helm.

"You look fantastic," I said, hugging the once frail girl. "How are you?"

"I'm good. Getting better all the time. Thanks to you," Gina said. "I owe you my life."

"Not me. *You* made the choice to survive. To make a difference. A lot of people will be thanking you. Wait and see."

She shook her head, but there was a glint in her eye that hadn't been there the day we pulled her out of the hospital. I grabbed her hand, led her over to the rocking chairs on the porch.

"Tell me what you've been up to. Gator has been very secretive. I want to know everything."

"Well, Gator introduced me to Dino and then, Bam Bam, Suzie and Brenda."

"Really?"

"Really. They're great."

Her smile this time was genuine and infectious.

"My mom's even helping. We have one rig—Starship, the refurbished Flamethrower—and a few small donations. But this week, we were given an entire building and two more trucks. Three more female drivers signed on as trainers and our list grows every day for the truck driving school. I think this could work. We're calling it, Girls And Their Rigs. GATR for short."

"Of course," I said, laughing.

Gina went on to explain how GATR would help the trafficking victims and any other women wanting a new opportunity. Some would become drivers and others could find work in any of the multiple facets of the trucking industry. Their school would help them get real jobs with a future, and increase the number of women in a male-dominant field.

She was interrupted when Gator pushed through the screen door, let it slap shut behind him. He had his iPad in one hand, a beer in the other.

"Listen to this," he said, pressing the play button. A reporter's deep voice announced the station call letters then said, "Truck drivers across the nation are being honored by the president tonight as new information comes to light regarding the recent sex trafficking arrests. Thanks to the efforts of truck drivers working with T.A.S.T. Force, more than fifty-two members of the Somali Mafia and Lady Outlaws gangs have been indicted..."

Gator slapped the cover shut on the iPad and raised his beer. "I'll drink to that."

With all the press, people had begun looking at drivers and the trucking industry a bit differently. It would be a long climb for truckers to change the public's presumptions and character assassinations of the past. And as in most industries, bad apples will surface first and make their presence known. But, with the new funding for T.A.S.T. Force and the political backing, they would be able to help more people than ever before. Laws were in the works to protect the victims of trafficking while seeking tougher penalties for traffickers.

In OK City, local developers joined forces to revitalize the rundown neighborhoods that used to draw drug dealers and addicts, prostitutes and johns. They bulldozed tornado ravaged houses and put up subsidized housing that would be both safe and economical. A few local country western singers put their names on the project and added a basketball court and a health clinic. It seemed like everyone was ready to move on.

CHAPTER 44

Gator and I rented a house in Texas on the Gulf Coast, way out in the middle of nowhere on a broad expanse of beach. It wasn't prime season and I had the feeling even if it was this part of the coast wouldn't be overtaken by teenagers or families towing coolers. It was more of a birding, hiking, kayaking beach. A place where ordinary people came to escape an ordinary life.

I still struggled with the ordinary part. I tried. I was trying, but something just wasn't clicking, like there was something stuck in a gear, making it slip before it took hold. All I could think was, *I should be happier.*

The third night at the beach house, I slipped into bed naked and scootched up to Gator, pressing myself against his back, whispering in his ear to wake him, to let him know I was ready.

"Don't say anything," I told him. "Just let me love you."

I kissed him slowly, tenderly, then harder, urgent as slid my body over his, skin against skin, feeling my body respond, heat rising as our molecules collided. I closed my eyes, losing myself, knowing at once the difference between having sex and making love.

I opened my eyes, only to find Gator's locked on mine. Neither one of use blinked as our breath quickened, he pressed his hard cock against my hip, lifted me spread legged. I clasped my thighs around his waist, angling my hips to give him the room he would need to enter me, giving him permission, wanting him, needing him. We rocked together like that, with each thrust he claimed me. Each time I rose up to meet him I gave in. I pulled him closer, burrowing into his flesh, pressing my breasts against

283

his chest, grinding my pelvis against his as if I would melt into him, as if we could stay like this forever.

He whispered, "I love you baby. God, I love you," thrusting a final time before he groaned, coming inside me. I let go, the rush flowing from my toes to my temples as I cried out, jamming my heels into his back, riding the orgasm until the last wave left me spent, then collapsing under him, burrowing my face into the pillow.

Gator sighed above me, kissing my cheek, my neck, resting his lips on the crest of breast just above my beating heart, then slowly rolling off and nestling himself beside me.

"I love you," he said.

"Um hmm," I murmured.

"No. Jojo. Open your eyes. Look at me."

I did, one eye then the other.

"Do you see me? I. Love. You."

I blinked away the tears pooling in my eyes. I saw him. Broken and bleeding. I saw him shot by Hollywood, falling to the ground. I saw him worried for me when I was missing. I saw him, his face strained and lined, his bright eyes weary, tired. I saw him now scarred and troubled. I closed my eyes, and I didn't see him. In the dark, I saw Ivory Joe. I saw the way I would hurt Gator.

I knew what he wanted me to say. And I knew the way to form the words but not how to make them convincing—to him or me. I wasn't who he thought I was. I was a liar, a cheater. I was sick, tainted. The things I'd done, the things I could never tell him. What sort of life would he have with me, with all those secrets I wasn't willing to share? He'd almost been killed at least twice because of me. How could I know it wouldn't happen again?

Morning sun bathed the room. There were no curtains, no shades, no shutters, no locks. The view from the bed was exactly the same as it had been six days ago. For a trucker, that in itself was unusual enough, but the fact that the view was an endlessly blue ocean with tips of waves rising, cresting, adding pops of creamy white to the perfect landscape only added to the dream-like sensation.

My heart caught in my throat, believing for a few frightening seconds that none of this was real, that I was there—back there—with them, and any minute the door would open and Nadifa with her jangling bracelets would let a man in.

A gull cried, swooped into the surf and scooped up a fish, then flew away, silver scales shining, a tail dangling from his mouth.

You are safe. You are safe. You are safe. Maybe if I said it enough I'd believe it.

I closed my eyes, the sounds of sea and shore replaced by the last memory of my mother, her soft sobs, the deep voice of the man, the pattering of my little girl feet as I ran to her. What did I think I could do? Why wasn't I afraid? How did I get to be so brave?

The moon had been bright, pushing its light into the kitchen past the cracked glass of the open window, past the dandelions in the juice glass on the sill, past the stack of dirty dishes in the sink, past even the stained dishrag, all the way to the scarred wooden floor and the slumped body of my mother.

Her long, dark hair covered her face, her back and shoulders rose with her weeping. The man in the doorway looked back, just once, then stepped out into the night.

The image changes. It's brighter, different. In the kitchen the mother reaches for the girl. There is no knife, no blood. The mother says, "You're safe now. You know where you belong. I never did. That was my problem, Shâ. I never knew where I belonged, never understood who I was. This is what I wish for you, *ma petite*, I wish you to always know your heart."

The mother's arms wrap around her child as she kisses the girl's head. "Maman will always love you and watch over you. I am with you always." She sings, "*Galline, galline, galline, galo...*" and the little girl falls asleep, her head on her mother's breast.

Gator's shrill whistle woke me the second time me. He whistled again, calling for Oscar. I climbed out of the bed, padded across the cool tile floor to the kitchen. From the window over the sink I could see him down on the beach, waving a stick, trying to get the attention of our healthy, happy dog. A dog who was now chasing terns and sandpipers on four strong legs.

Gator had left a plate of sliced fruit and a full pot of coffee on the counter next to the laptop. I nibbled at the fruit and filled my mug, then woke the computer. There were a few new emails, one from Charlene. It had been weeks since we'd spoken. Gator told her we needed some time off. I didn't argue. For once.

I opened the email. Charlene had a high security run for us from The Carolinas to Indianapolis. It was good money. Really good money. The kind of money that could pad a retirement fund. One little click to reply. That was all it would take.

I scrolled up to the tabbed pages. Gator had been following the Somali Sting cases. There was a new article, a human-interest piece written by a student in Somalia whose Twitter posts had gone viral when he tweeted comments and photo-graph of a citizen accused of prostitution being publicly stoned to death. I scanned the story, my throat clenching as I read the name, Nadifa Ali Ahmad.

A side bar linked to the current case in the United States, and below that was an updated story about The Palace auctions and the family life of the man behind it all: Arthur Strauss.

I refilled my mug and opened the page.

Twenty minutes later, I stepped through the sliding glass doors to the deck. The heat of the sun pushed the chill from my bones, warming my cold, cruel thoughts. On the beach, Oscar jumped and played in the surf, biting at the white caps, pawing at shells being drawn back into the wash. A pelican flew overhead, its gullet full, wide strong wings cutting the air, pushing his way home.

As the sea pulled back, clearing the shoreline, reclaiming its treasures, Gator bent to the sand with a stick. A moment later he straightened, tossing the stick for Oscar and waving to me.

It took me a moment with the glare of the sun, the leaping dog, the bare-chested man staring through me, but the words were there. No matter how much I squinted, I saw the same writing in the sand: *Will you marry me?*

CHAPTER 45

The day I arrived the crocuses bloomed. They may have been blooming all along, bright purple petals slowly opening as if captured in time-lapsed footage. Perhaps there was a tiny unfurling each second of each minute of each day that went un-noticed until the final stages. The stage of the end, really. How could all of that work to make the flower most noticeable, the scent sweetest, the open bloom brightest, to expose that delicate yellow stigmata like an umbrella cluster over the pistils, how could all of that beauty be the beginning of death? The crocus would never be as brilliant as it was at this moment. Tomor-row, no in ten minutes, it would begin to die, the amount of sun and air and rain and even the insects that might visit, would lessen every day. They were no longer needed. Instead of attend-ing a dying flower in the end of its bloom, they would go else-where. They would choose something else.

There was no use for something that was used up, tainted, dying on the inside.

I found the delivery entrance, took the stairs and went up to the girl's floor. I didn't know what to expect, not whether she'd be alone or awake, but I knew I had to be there. I had to see her and I had to let her know she wasn't alone. She had never been alone.

The room was dim, blinds angled so that the only light was that from below. Large machines beeped and whirred at the side of the elevated bed, green lights and red diodes gave off a Christmas glow. The private room was well equipped, yet stark.

Rebecca Strauss appeared to be asleep. Propped up and

tucked in, her face was expressionless, lids at half-mast. One arm was braced in front of her, a stylus strapped to her finger. I walked closer to the bed and she stirred. Her finger tapped once, waking the touchpad.

"Who are you?" The computerized voice spoke, breaking the silence.

"My name's Jojo Boudreaux. I read about you, about what happened. I would have come sooner, but—"

"You thought I was dead."

Rebecca moved the stylus again, tapping and scrolling, selecting words and phrases for the computerized word to speak. "Did my father send you?"

"No. He's—he's dead."

The girl didn't move.

"I saw him die. A woman shot him."

She raised the stylus, as if she was erasing the words she'd written. Her eyelids fluttered as a computerized voice said "Thank you. Thank you," followed by applause. She looped it three or four times, the sounds echoed in the stark room.

I said, "It's okay. You're safe. There's nothing to be afraid of anymore."

She typed, "I'm not afraid. You have to be alive to feel fear."

I looked past her at the wires leading from her to the machines pumping and whirring, at the stacks of charts and files, the rows of medicines, creams and vials.

I moved closer, wanting to comfort her.

"You want to help?" she typed.

"Yes, of course. What can I do?"

There was no hesitation. Rebecca Strauss tapped one phrase. "Help me die."

As I drove away from the Blairsville Hospice, headed toward the NASCAR garage in North Carolina, I checked my phone: five missed calls, ten urgent text messages.

I imagined the sun setting in Texas, the tide coming in, erasing the writing on the shore. For the first time in months, I felt a stab of fear, not for what I had done, but for what my future held. I thought about what Rebecca had said, that you have to be alive to feel fear. Maybe she was right. Maybe I was finally coming alive again.

Sabrina's power window regulator hissed as I laid my thumb on the button. I threw my phone out into the night and turned up the radio. There were a lot of sad songs to be sung on a fourteen-hour drive.

ACKNOWLEDGMENTS

Thank you to the drivers who allowed me to interview them for this story, especially the awesome Steve LaFleur, who helped answer all my driving and industry-related questions. Any errors are my own. Big thanks to Eric and Lance at Down & Out Books for believing in Jojo and allowing me to hang out with all the cool kids in the house, even if I do drink their good bourbon. And of course, the best is saved for last—my family. Without your support, no part of this strange life I live would be possible. I am a very, very lucky woman.

Georgia Author of the Year Linda Sands is the multiple award-winning author of five books in four genres. Always on the hunt for unique characters, fabulous settings and compelling story-lines, Linda divides her time between the suburbs of Atlanta, the beaches of The Emerald Coast and a secret place in the Blue Ridge Mountains.

In the Cargo Series, Linda introduces tenacious trucker Jojo Boudreaux and a cast of characters whose adventures are directly influenced by the stories of real truckers Linda has interviewed, and possibly pieces of her own life.

If pressed or bribed by bourbon, Linda will admit that Jojo is definitely more bad ass.

lindasands.com/

BOOKS

On the following pages are a few
more great titles from the
Down & Out Books publishing family.

For a complete list of books and to
sign up for our newsletter,
go to DownAndOutBooks.com.

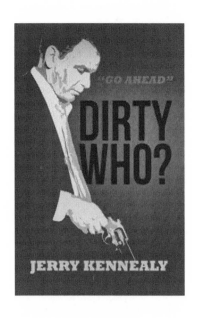

Dirty Who?
A Johnny O'Rorke Novel
Jerry Kennealy

Down & Out Books
July 2018
978-1-946502-64-3

San Francisco Police Inspector Johnny O'Rorke, assisted by Cosmo the Wonder Dog, a Lakeland terrier, get tangled up in the search for a sadistic serial killer and along the way brush up against the likes of Frank Sinatra, LSD guru Timothy O'Leary, a porno movie star by the name of Pierre LaTongue and get involved in a deadly game of Irish Roulette.

Jerry Kennealy was the recipient of the 2017 Life Achievement Award by the Private Eye Writers of America.

Tushhog
A Scotland Ross Novel
Jeffery Hess

Down & Out Books
May 2018
978-1-946502-60-5

It's 1981 in Fort Myers, Florida, where Scotland Ross squares off with a redneck clan, a Cuban gang, a connected crew from New York, and one friend who does him wrong.

Crimes of violence, drugs, and theft pale in comparison to the failure of self-restraint.

Tushhog is a story of compulsion, the types of people who take what isn't theirs, and the repercussions that follow.

I'm Not Happy Till You're Not Happy
Crime Stories by Ryan Sayles

All Due Respect, an imprint of
Down & Out Books
978-1-948235-19-8

From a bank robbery gone horribly wrong to a shipwrecked man with a serious anger problem to a lonely teenage Peeping Tom, Ryan Sayles's second collection of stories steam rolls along.

Need a transvestite beating up her drug dealer? Got it. What about a guy trying to stuff a dead hooker into his trunk? Got it also. Need a Richard Dean Buckner story? Got two of 'em.

Come on in and join the mayhem.

Fast Bang Booze
Lawrence Maddox

Shotgun Honey, an imprint of
Down & Out Books
March 2018
978-1-946502-54-4

After seeing Frank deliver an impressive ass kicking in a bar fight, Russian mobster Popov hires him to be his driver. What Popov doesn't know is that when Frank is sober, he's inhumanly fast, deadly, and mute; when Frank is on the sauce, he's a useless twenty-something wiseass.

Double-crossed in a drug deal gone bad, Frank and Popov have one night to recover their stolen cash or get wiped off the map. Frank's special abilities put him in the spotlight, and he struggles to keep it all together…

Made in the USA
Columbia, SC
27 March 2018